Kylie stripped off her ruined pantyhose, expecting to find the marble floor cold underfoot. Instead, the smooth stone seemed to have absorbed her body heat and felt warm under her bare feet. She tossed her bra and panties onto the growing pile of clothes on the floor. Leaning over, she adjusted the temperature of the water flowing into the tub.

"Kylie?" The knock on the door had her scrambling for a towel.

"Yes?" She poked her head out the door, holding the towel together at her chest with one hand.

"I thought you might want some clean clothes to wear after you're done." David held out a pile of garments.

"Oh, I don't know. I'm becoming rather fond of this towel."

David laughed. "The color suits you, but you might get tired of holding it up after a while. Although, come to think of it, that could work to my advantage." He raised his eyebrows suggestively.

Reaching out for the pile of clothes, she smiled, enjoying this flirtation. David's eyes sparkled with good humor as he teased her, and Kylie thought this was as close to heaven as she might ever get.

More...

ST. MARTIN'S PAPERBACKS TITLES BY
BEVERLY BRANDT

True North

Record Time

Record
Time

BEVERLY BRANDT

St. Martin's Paperbacks

RECORD TIME

Copyright © 2002 by Beverly Brandt.

ISBN: 0-312-98184-8

Printed in the United States of America

St. Martin's Paperbacks edition / October 2002

St. Martin's Paperbacks are published by St. Martin's Press, 175 Fifth Avenue, New York, NY 10010.

10 9 8 7 6 5 4 3 2 1

To Wes,
For always being my #1 fan.

ACKNOWLEDGMENTS

My thanks to Laron Glover—you are the Goddess of critique partners, and I can't thank you enough for the insights you've offered me over the years. I am a better writer because of you.

I'd also like to thank my agent, Deidre Knight: a woman of courage, honor, and wisdom. Thank you for answering all my questions, for always knowing the right thing to do, and for honoring your commitments even under the most trying circumstances.

To Kim Cardascia, my editor, thank you for all you do. Being a new author is a strange and exciting thing, and I appreciate your enthusiasm and encouragement. I couldn't ask for a better team than the one I have at St. Martin's!

I'd also like to thank my writing buddies who took the time to read this story and give me their feedback: Lori Grube, Libby Muelhaupt, and Wendy Linstad. I know how much effort a good critique takes, and I thank you for giving me so much of your time.

Record
Time

CHAPTER 1

She was trapped.

He had her cornered between the ten-foot-high potted silk fig tree—which looked surprisingly real, she noticed, glancing to her left for a means of escape—and the wall to her right. The only way out was through him and, considering he was at least six inches taller and sixty pounds heavier than she, that wasn't much of an option.

Defeated, Kylie Rogers pasted an interested look on her face and prepared to spend the evening listening to Bradley Nelson pour out his version of "My Life as an Up-and-Coming Country Music Star." She supposed this was her curse for having a sister who was a famous singer. Every rock, country, jazz, or rap music star–wanna-be who couldn't get an audience with Robyn Rogers latched on to Kylie instead.

". . . and when I was ten, my dad took me on vacation to Nashville. That's when I knew what my destiny was," Bradley expounded with all the sincerity of a televangelist.

Kylie felt her left foot beginning to cramp and wiggled her toes, silently cursing the inventor of high-heeled shoes. Taking a sip of wine, she watched a drop of condensation roll down the stem and drip onto the hardwood floor. Someone had opened the French doors to the cool night air, but the room inside was warm from the crush of bodies. Kylie wondered what the neighbors thought of the loud music blasting through the stillness of their exclusive Seattle suburb as she waited patiently for her chance to escape.

". . . at twelve, I got my big break—the church talent contest," Bradley droned on.

Tuning out his monologue, Kylie studied the man in front of her. Bradley Nelson could be considered handsome, with his tall, lanky frame, sandy brown hair, and dark eyes. Tonight, he was wearing the standard all-black uniform of the country music crowd: black jeans with a button-down shirt, a belt with a silver belt buckle shaped like the state of Texas, and a fascinating pair of snakeskin cowboy boots. Kylie was beginning to think those cowboy boots were, unfortunately, the most interesting thing about Bradley Nelson. She should have known she'd spend the entire evening at music mogul David Gamble's lakeside home fending off her sister's castoffs. If she hadn't had her own reason for attending the party, she would have begged off. As it was, she wasn't accomplishing much, trapped here in the corner by Bradley Nelson as she searched the crowd for Robyn's telltale platinum blond head.

"I got a letter from Willie Nelson when I was thirteen and, shucks, that's when I really knew that music was my calling," Bradley drawled, interrupting her perusal of the crowd.

Kylie slid a glance at her watch. Mickey's big hand was on the nine and his little hand was on the twelve. She figured that at this rate, Bradley wouldn't get past puberty till long after midnight. Desperate measures would need to be taken. Surreptitiously, she slid her arm behind her back and watered the fake fig tree with her Chardonnay.

"Boy, I sure could use a drink. Would you mind getting me another while I freshen up?" Widening her eyes innocently, Kylie held out her empty wineglass.

"Uh, sure." Bradley glanced over his shoulder at the huge crowd at the bar. "I'll be right back," he promised.

"Great." Kylie smiled, waiting until his back was turned to make her move. Her short blue skirt swirled around her legs as she bolted from her prison in the corner.

"I knew we should have taken separate cars," she muttered, once again searching the loud throng of people for her sister. Robyn loved these overcrowded, raucous parties where she was usually at the center of attention. Kylie herself didn't mind them as long as she had a reason to be there. She'd thought tonight's party would give her a chance to meet some new people, maybe even talk to David Gamble about donating some money to her pet charity, the EmCee Foundation. Unfortunately, the elusive Mr. Gamble had disappeared shortly after she and Robyn arrived, just as she was being cornered by Bradley Nelson.

So, rather than spending the evening trying to solicit donations for a worthy cause, she was stuck listening to yet another aspiring musician's life story. It was her curse for being born into a family of entertainers, she supposed, but at times it got to be a bit tiring.

Taking her melancholy mood down a deserted hallway, Kylie searched out the peace of a powder room. Trailing her fingers along the dark patterned wallpaper, she thought about the home's owner. Even before she'd moved to Seattle two months ago, she'd known about David Gamble, founder and president of Gamble Records. He was one of *Fortune* magazine's top-forty under forty; one of the nation's young, wealthy bachelors who had started his climb to success with a small, independent record company that he'd built into a multibillion-dollar empire by leveraging the power of the Internet.

According to one of the articles she'd read, Gamble.com had been one of the first successful e-tailers. They'd started off as nothing more than an Internet record store, allowing Gamble Records to become their own distributor rather than having to rely on the national chains, who took so much of a small record label's profits. Their success would have probably ended there, making David and his employees moderately wealthy, but, in a move cited as nothing short of prophetic, he had pushed technology even further.

In a television interview Kylie had seen recently, David Gamble had asked, "Why should consumers have to wait four days, or even one day, for music to be delivered to their homes when the technology exists for them to download it right off the Internet today? And why should you have to buy an entire CD if all you want are two or three of your favorite songs? Just think," he'd said, looking into the camera with his intense, midnight-blue eyes, "no longer will you be at the mercy of record company executives forcing you to buy music you don't want. This technology is good for consumers, and it's also good for the artists, who will receive a larger cut of the profits for the songs they record."

Of course, it had also been good for David Gamble, Kylie thought as she pushed open the door to a cavernous bathroom. He'd become an overnight billionaire with an Internet site that was now a household name.

There was no doubt in her mind that he could afford this mansion in one of the best neighborhoods in Washington State, but Kylie shuddered as she looked around the oversize room. It was done in stark contrasts: all black except for the glaring white fixtures. The floor was tiled in black marble and the walls were papered with some kind of textured material. Kylie rubbed a hand across the surface and decided it felt like bamboo. Unable to stop herself, she peered around a glass block wall into the shower area. As she had suspected, it was spotlessly clean—not even a half-used bar of soap to mar the pristine perfection of the place. She resisted the urge to open the cupboard under the sink, feeling she'd already pushed the line between innocent curiosity and outright snooping too far.

"It's so impersonal," she said, looking around the room again, trying to imagine David Gamble here. She had yet to meet him in person, but had seen him in interviews so often, she had no trouble conjuring up his image. Unfortunately, her active imagination conjured him stepping out of the shower, droplets of warm water falling from his naked, tanned body onto the cold marble as he reached for a towel. All at once, the room didn't appear quite so impersonal, and the temperature seemed to have increased a few degrees.

Kylie glanced in the mirror above the sink. Almost involuntarily, she raised a hand, touching her cheek. Instead of feeling the smoothness of her own skin under her fingertips, she imagined that she could feel the roughness of David's beard just before he shaved, the crisp stubble gently abrading as her fingers moved toward his firm chin. As her fingers reached the end of her own, softer chin, she dropped her hand and laughed guiltily.

Robyn was right. She needed to get out more if just being in David Gamble's bathroom was enough to set her pulse racing.

Kylie exhaled a deep breath and pulled a bright red lipstick out of the tiny purse draped across her shoulder. She smoothed a fresh line of color across her lips and ran her tongue across her teeth to make sure none of her lipstick had ended up there. Shaking off the last of her images of the elusive Mr. Gamble, Kylie flipped her head upside down, fluffing her shoulder-length brown hair. Feeling her skirt ride up in the back, she moved her hands to the bottom of the gauzy blue material only to find that she was about two inches from showing off more than she ever wanted revealed in public.

"Note to self: Never do that outside of closed doors," she said with a smile into the empty room.

Flipping her head back up, she figured she'd given Bradley enough time to get tired of waiting for her. Blowing an errant curl out of her eyes, she opened the door and headed down the darkened hall, the clicking of her high heels silenced by the richly colored rug running down the center of the hardwood floor.

"I'll just find Robyn and tell her I'm ready to go," Kylie

murmured, inching closer to the high-ceilinged, cream-and-brown-toned living room and peering cautiously inside. She spotted her sister across the room, holding court with two of Gamble Records' top artists and several of the city's most popular deejays. Although she hadn't thought it possible, the immense living room seemed more crammed with partygoers than when she'd left. Smoke hovered over the room like a rain cloud. The music had been turned up to a tooth-rattling level and people raised their voices to be heard over the din. By all counts, Gamble Records could chalk this party up as a huge success.

Leaning against the wall, Kylie wondered where David was. She had spotted him briefly when they'd arrived two hours ago, but he'd disappeared with a beautiful brunette before she could extricate herself from the corner with Bradley Nelson. Kylie wondered if he were having a party of a more intimate nature with Lisanne O'Neill, Gamble Records' newest star and, it was rumored, David Gamble's most recent conquest.

"Lucky girl." Kylie sighed, gazing over the crowd for a glimpse of her host's dark hair and dazzling blue eyes. Chatting up their handsome host would sure beat hiding out in the hallway, hoping to escape further conversation with Bradley.

A flash of movement out of the corner of her eye caught her attention. It was Bradley, and he hadn't yet latched on to some other poor unsuspecting victim. Kylie looked from Bradley to her sister. She couldn't get Robyn's attention without attracting Bradley's, too. He turned toward the hallway just as Kylie stepped back into the shadows.

Kylie did what any desperate woman would do in the situation—she ran, weight balanced on her tiptoes to silence the tread of her heels on the hardwood floor as she hugged the wall. The closest means of escape was a closed door on the left side of the hallway. She opened the door just enough to slip through, quietly pushing it shut behind her.

Standing behind the closed door, Kylie listened to the heavy tread of Bradley's cowboy boots as he walked past the room and down the hall to the bathroom. Looking around, she realized she was in an office. It was small in comparison to the other rooms she had seen in the house. From the moonlight shining in from a large, high window opposite the door, Kylie could see the built-in bookshelves that flanked the wall to her right. One bookshelf was almost completely filled with a complicated sound system.

Just the sort of thing one would expect to find in the office of the president of a record company, Kylie thought with some amusement.

The other bookshelf was filled to overflowing with books. It wasn't light enough to read the titles but Kylie figured, considering the occupant of the house, they were probably books about how to run a more efficient business, with a biography or two thrown in just for fun. Her own bookshelves were stocked with all her favorite romances and mysteries. She'd be hard-pressed to find a nonfiction book among the bunch.

The only furniture in the room was a comfy-looking overstuffed leather chair and ottoman in the corner to her right, a massive desk facing a wall of black-and-white pictures, and a swivel chair behind the desk that was turned toward the window. On top of the desk were some neat piles of paper, a pen and pencil set, and an antique Tiffany lamp with stained-glass flowers on the shade.

"Kylie?" The loud whisper jolted her out of her observation of the room.

Bradley was still out in the hall. Kylie contemplated giving herself up, but the idea of two more hours stuck listening to yet another musician's boring life story helped make her hasty decision.

She'd have to go out the window. Right outside that window was her car, and freedom. She could hunker down in the backseat and wait until Robyn finally decided she was partied out. Bradley would never think to look for her out there.

Resolutely, Kylie marched over to the large ottoman in the corner and dragged it across the carpeted floor. Pulling off her shoes, she hopped up onto the burgundy leather, opened the window, and pushed out the screen.

The air was chilly, even for an early autumn night in Seattle. The wind raised tiny goose bumps on her arms as she peered out the window to the ground below. It was farther down than she had hoped. On top of that, she would have to clear the row of bushes surrounding the front of the house like a moat.

"Here goes nothing," she whispered, tossing her shoes out the window and positioning both hands on the ledge for leverage. She flung her right leg over the sill. Teetering halfway between in and out, Kylie grimaced as the cold metal of the windowsill made contact with her warm inner thigh.

From his seat in the swivel chair behind his desk, David Gamble watched as one of the woman's shapely legs disappeared out the window. Her skirt settled itself high up on her remaining thigh. The filmy, almost transparent material caressed her stocking-clad skin and David felt his body respond instinctively. He took a deep, controlling breath, searching his mental Rolodex for the identity of his midnight intruder. He was very good with names and faces, and he was sure he would have remembered if they'd been introduced. It was obvious that the woman was trying to escape, but he wasn't going to let her go without knowing who she was and what in the world she was doing leaving through his office window.

"May I help you with something?" he asked politely.

Startled, the woman jerked her head in the direction of his voice.

The sudden movement threw her off balance. Before she could steady herself, she lost her hold on the windowsill.

Her left leg flew up in the air and she tumbled out the window into the shrubbery below.

David stared at the place where the woman had been just a moment ago, surprised at this sudden turn of events. Having women tumble out of his house was not a usual Saturday night occurrence.

Stepping up onto the ottoman, David rested his folded arms on the windowsill. There was a rustling from the box-woods below.

"Are you all right?" he asked.

Before she could answer, he heard a tentative knock on the door behind him as it opened.

"Excuse me, Mr. Gamble. Have you seen a woman with brown hair, about so tall?" a man wearing a black cowboy hat asked, holding his hand up around chest-level.

David paused. In the bushes, the woman with brown hair, about so tall, vigorously shook her head. He shrugged. If she didn't want the cowboy to find her, he had no problem playing along.

"No, I haven't seen anyone," David answered, leaning nonchalantly against the wall as if he often stood on the furniture to get a better view of the shrubbery. The cowboy was obviously not the suspicious type because he seemed to accept David's answer as he closed the door behind him.

"That was close." David heard the woman's relieved comment from the bushes.

He looked out over the sill. "May I ask why you chose to leap out the window rather than use the front door?"

"It's a rather long story," the woman replied, trying in vain to extricate herself from the greenery.

David hoisted himself up onto the windowsill. His jump to the ground was much better executed than hers. He cleared the shrubs by at least a foot. "Here, let me help."

Grabbing the woman gently under her armpits, he hauled her out of the bushes. His stomach muscles clenched as he felt the warmth of her fingers through his shirtsleeve. As she straightened, the fresh scent of her hair filled his nostrils. David felt a silky curl brush against his arm. Unable to resist, he reached out a hand to touch its softness.

She looked up at him questioningly. The corners of her brown, almond-shaped eyes crinkled with amusement when he showed her the twig he'd plucked from her hair. It was as good an excuse as any for touching her, he supposed.

"Thank you. I wouldn't be surprised to find birds nesting in there after this." She grinned infectiously, shaking her head to dislodge anything else that might be caught.

The woman bent over and stuck an arm in the bushes. David watched as her filmy skirt crawled up the back of her legs. The urge to reach out and trace his fingers up the path the skirt had exposed was so strong that he shoved his hands into the pockets of his jeans to resist the temptation. She straightened, one navy shoe in her hand, and the hem of her skirt shifted back to its original position. David felt a conflicting mixture of relief and disappointment.

"Lost one." She held it up for his inspection, as if he might need verification that she was one shoe short of a full pair. Holding onto his arm for balance, she picked up her right foot, dusted off the bottom of her stocking, slipped her foot into the shoe, and then did the same with the left one.

She smiled at him, and David stood still, feeling like a tongue-tied teenager rather than the self-confident, successful businessman he was supposed to be. It wasn't that she was beautiful. She was hardly the type of woman who would stop traffic, but there was something about her brandy-colored eyes, or maybe it was her bright smile, or her unruly hair . . . Hell, he didn't know what it was that had him gaping at her like an idiot as the silence between them lengthened.

She obviously sensed the awkwardness between them as well. "Thanks for a great party. The, uh, the wine was great. And your home is very, um . . . well, the view is great, too."

Nodding her head as if to reinforce her politely delivered lines, she turned and started walking toward the line of cars in the driveway. The gravel crunched under her feet and David felt himself being pulled inexorably along behind her.

He caught up with her. "So, why don't you like my house?"

She blinked up at him, apparently surprised that he'd caught her slip. "It's a nice house."

"But you don't like it."

She shrugged, giving him a small smile. "I don't have to live here."

David let the matter drop. She obviously didn't want to say anything impolite about his house, but if the truth were told, he wasn't all that fond of the place himself. He'd bought it a year ago, furniture and all, and hadn't changed anything except his office and bedroom. He spent so much time at work that it hadn't mattered that the furnishings weren't exactly to his liking. Besides, everything was in excellent condition and he hated to buy new things if there wasn't a good reason. He'd learned early in life that it didn't pay to be frivolous with one's money. So he'd kept the bland furniture and the stark, almost shocking décor that had apparently suited the taste of the house's previous occupant.

"You still haven't told me why you were so desperate to escape the party," he said as they continued their walk down the drive.

"Bradley Nelson," she answered, as if that explained everything.

"What about him?"

"He was trying to tell me his life story."

Either she wasn't making sense or he'd lost all of his heretofore formidable mental capacity. David wasn't sure which one of the two he'd put his money on. "And?" he encouraged.

"Not the *Reader's Digest* condensed version. I mean the whole thing from conception forward."

"He was boring you so you jumped out the window to escape him?" David asked incredulously.

"That about sums it up."

"Why didn't you just tell him to get lost?"

The woman stopped abruptly and turned to face him. "But that would have been rude," she said, her eyes opened wide with astonishment. "I didn't want to hurt his feelings."

"I see." David paused, not really understanding at all. It seemed that she had gone to an awful lot of trouble just to avoid hurting the cowboy's feelings.

David studied the night sky in the comfortable silence surrounding them. The trees bordering his driveway showed up black against the inky sky, and the white moon peeked in and out among the branches moving with a slight breeze. The woman had stopped near an antique cherry red Mustang with a gleaming white leather interior. He presumed this was her car, since she leaned against it with her back against the driver's-side door. His perusal of her stopped abruptly at the third finger of her left hand. A large, obviously expensive diamond ring glittered mockingly in the moonlight. David felt his jaw clench.

"You're married," he said, without meaning to voice his observation.

The woman followed his gaze to the ring on her left hand. "Oh, no. Left-handed," she answered cryptically.

"Pardon me?"

"I'm left-handed. It feels awkward wearing rings on my right hand." David watched as her brown eyes warmed to the color of finely aged brandy. "My dad gave this to me years ago."

"Hmm." The last thing David wanted to talk about was family, so instead he fished in his breast pocket for a pack of cigarettes and offered one to the woman.

"No, thanks. I don't smoke."

"I quit years ago myself, but I keep a pack around just in case."

"Just in case what? You get arrested and need to

exchange smokes for a spoon to dig your way out of jail?"

The unaccustomed noise of David's laughter sounded rusty, even to his own ears. He continued the bantering, surprised to find that he was actually enjoying himself. "Even worse. I keep them on hand in case one of our highly temperamental artists has nicotine withdrawal. You haven't seen chaos until you've seen a nineteen-year-old singer holding up a studio full of musicians because she hasn't had a cigarette in five minutes."

"Yes, I could see where that might get dicey. There are lots of sharp implements in a recording studio, aren't there?"

"Yeah, sometimes we have to hand out Kevlar vests with the cigarettes. By the way, I don't think we've been properly introduced." He held a hand out to her. "I'm David Gamble."

He enveloped her small hand in his and looked at her expectantly.

Kylie stared down at their intertwined hands, wishing this moment would never end. It had been so pleasant talking to him, and she couldn't help but wonder how his attitude would change once he knew she was Robyn's sister. They were so different, she and her sister. Robyn was petite, beautiful, blond, and above all, incredibly talented. Compared to her sister, Kylie was so . . . well, so average. She knew her own limitations, and, for the most part, she was happy with her lot in life. But now, staring into the eyes of the most attractive man she'd ever met, even knowing that she'd probably never see him again after tonight, she couldn't bear to watch the inevitable mental comparison she always saw whenever she told someone her name.

David shifted his weight, pebbles crunching under the soles of his shoes, and Kylie realized that she still hadn't given him her name. His hand, warm and firm, continued to hold hers.

"I'm Kylie McGillicuddy. Pleased to meet you," she blurted.

"Nice to meet you, Kylie McGillicuddy."

Her name rolled off David's tongue, sending a tickle of awareness down her spine. His voice sounded huskier than it had moments before. Kylie raised her eyes to his and fell into their deep blue depths. He increased the pressure on her hand, and Kylie didn't fight the urge to lean into him. She knew he was going to kiss her, and she knew that she wanted him to; wanted it more than anything in her entire life.

She shivered from the cold and a hint of anticipation. David leaned closer, the heat from his body wrapping around her like a cloak. Kylie froze with her other hand on the door handle, her fingers suddenly nerveless at the intense look in his eyes. She felt hypnotized by his presence, like a mouse caught under the spell of a cobra waiting to strike. Her mouth went suddenly dry and her heart began to race. She wondered if the mouse felt this same sense of dread and anticipation as it waited for the snake to make its move, and licked her newly parched lips.

David placed one large, warm hand under her chin and her lips parted on a soft sigh as his mouth met hers. She pressed closer and his hands moved to her hair, embedding themselves in the unruly mass of silken curls.

It was heaven. His tongue teased hers; and it felt so right to be here, being held in David's arms as the cool late-September air caressed her skin. Kylie put her arms around David's waist, crushing her blouse as she pulled him closer. She felt his strength, in the solid arms he wrapped around her, in the tautness of the muscles of his thighs pressed against her. For a brief, intoxicating moment, Kylie felt protected, cherished, and, even better, desired.

Pressing her against the car door, David ground out her name as his mouth moved to the sensitive hollow under her ear. She leaned back against the cold car, her body heating the metal where she touched. Never before had she wanted a man like this. Right here, right now. If she'd been physically capable of moving away from him long enough, they'd both be lying naked in the backseat of her Mustang. As it was, David had her pressed so tightly against the car that she could barely move. Her skin had gone from chilly to feeling as if someone had set her on fire. She felt David's hands through the material of her shirt, cool now on her hot skin.

Having completed an assault on the delicate skin of her neck, David reached again for Kylie's mouth. The tastes and smells of her muddled in his mind, leaving only vague impressions of sweet wine, spicy perfume, and the earthy scent of boxwoods. He wondered what she would look like, naked here in the moonlight, as he reached for the top button of her shirt. His progress was slowed as he felt Kylie's hands running down the length of his back. Involuntarily, his hips pressed against hers and a wave of desire shot through him.

At that moment, David knew he was in danger of losing control like some uninitiated teenager. He was not going to make love in the backseat of a car, especially with so many people around who could easily discover them. He was not about to become the subject of some tabloid story. He could just imagine the title some sleazy reporter would pound out: "Local Billionaire Buck Naked in Backseat."

It would be his worst nightmare, his private life exposed for everyone to see and ridicule.

Intending to cool her down slowly, he reached down to stop Kylie's wandering hands. And instead of deepening the kiss further, he gently pulled away from her heated body.

"Kylie, stop." His breathing was ragged against her mouth.

It took a moment for Kylie's brain to register that David was retreating. The cool air between their bodies hit her like a spray of cold water. She heard a woman's voice in the distance calling David's name, and all at once she was mortified. His girlfriend was calling; he had to go. She was such a fool. Of course he'd been willing to take what she was so obviously offering. Kylie closed her eyes, feeling a heat of a different kind creep into her face. Pushing herself away from him, she yanked open the car door and hurriedly slid into the driver's seat.

David held the door open when she would have slammed it shut in his face.

"Wait a minute," he pleaded, cursing Lisanne's bad timing and his own hesitation for not jumping into the car with Kylie and driving away to someplace where they could continue this in private.

Ignoring him, she shoved the key in the ignition, pulled the door out of his grip, started the car, and drove down the long driveway, not bothering to look back.

David stood, unmoving, watching until he saw her turn onto the paved road. Disregarding Lisanne's summons, he absently raked his hand through his hair. Fingers of cold night air slipped through his shirt, chilling the places Kylie had touched. His fingers strayed to the pack of cigarettes in his pocket and he fought back the urge to slide one out of the pack. His answer to Kylie's question about why he kept them around was not quite truthful. He did not keep cigarettes around to appease the artists he worked with. He kept them to prove to himself that he could control his impulses. It was something he had become quite good at, actually, he thought, giving the pack one last reassuring squeeze before dropping his hand to his side.

David lifted his gaze to the moon. A thick, dark cloud had wrapped itself around the bright crescent. He turned and walked back to the party, his eyes hard and empty.

CHAPTER 2

Rubbing her cheek against the soft pillow beneath her head, Kylie sighed with pleasure. Still half asleep, she allowed herself to remember the kiss. The glorious, exciting kiss from David Gamble. Her lips still felt warm from his touch. If she reached out her hand, she was certain she'd touch hair-roughened skin. Her fingertips tingled with the sensation. Groaning, she rolled over onto her back and reached out a hand to test her theory.

She felt something all right, but it wasn't what she'd been dreaming about. Her eyes popped open wide as a large black-and-white cat hopped up onto her stomach and proceeded to make himself comfortable. She smiled sadly, the illusion dissipating in the air like a million tiny particles of hope.

"You're not David Gamble, but I guess you'll have to do, Mr. Chips." She stroked the cat's furry white neck as he turned around three times, making sure to step on all her tender parts at least once before lying down on her chest. "I don't know what came over me."

The cat regarded her silently, his yellow-green eyes watching her knowingly as he began to purr.

"Stop looking at me like that. I would have to be dead to not be attracted to David. You know I don't just leap on every attractive male who makes a pass at me. Just because I was brought up in Hollywood, where people change lovers as often as movie roles, does not mean that I'm that way, too."

She kissed the downy fur on the cat's neck just below his ear. Annoyed at the overly affectionate gesture, he swished his tail and hopped onto the floor as if to say there was only so much attention a cat could endure, after all. Kylie slid out of bed, pushed her feet into a pair of fuzzy pink slippers, and padded down the stairs to the kitchen, Mr. Chips following closely behind.

"He must be laughing himself silly by now, thinking what an easy mark I am."

She continued her one-sided conversation as she ladled a scoopful of cat food into a bright red bowl. Kylie set the bowl on the floor and the kibbles rolled around in the ceramic dish. The cat's nose immediately disappeared as he devoured his crunchy breakfast.

She scratched his ear and placed a bowl of fresh water next to the food on the floor. "At least we were interrupted before I could humiliate myself completely. What was I thinking anyway, that a man like David Gamble would choose me over the gorgeous Lisanne O'Neill? I must have lost my mind."

The only answer she got was the continued munching of cat food. Kylie turned away, almost wishing the cat could have answered her.

The jarring ring of the telephone startled her out of her glum monologue. She looked to the battery charger for her cordless phone. Of course, it was empty. She waited a few seconds for it to ring again so she could try to locate the darn thing. Following the sound, she scooted on pink, fuzzy feet out of the kitchen and through the dining room. She found the receiver on the fifth ring on the living room floor under the couch.

"Hello," she answered, out of breath, just before the answering machine would have kicked in.

"Good morning, honey. How are you this morning?"

Kylie winced. Elizabeth Rogers's cheery voice was a bit much to take before eight o'clock in the morning.

"Hi, Mom. I'm fine." Kylie pushed herself up from the cold hardwood floor, taking the cordless phone with her on her journey back to the kitchen. She stopped at the thermostat in the hallway, pushing the little red pin up above seventy-five degrees. She was chilly, wearing only the plaid boxer shorts and cropped Mickey Mouse T-shirt that were her usual bedtime attire.

"That's nice, dear. How's your little job hunt going?"

Kylie gritted her teeth. She knew her mother meant well, but Kylie never thought of her search for a suitable career as a "little job hunt," more like a "little way to pay the bills." But, of course, as Elizabeth was fond of pointing out, Kylie always had her trust fund to fall back on if the whole career thing didn't work out. Kylie didn't have the heart to tell her Mom that, with the exception of the money she'd used to buy her house, she'd anonymously given all her trust fund disbursements to the EmCee Foundation. That was a little secret Kylie wanted kept just between her and her father, who understood why it was important to her to have some higher purpose in her life. Managing the funds for the EmCee Foundation gave her more happiness than anything else ever had, more so because almost no one knew that she was involved in the charity. Unfortunately, she had underestimated the amount of time it would take her to find a job in Seattle, and the meager funds in her savings account were dipping dangerously low. Her "little job hunt" was becoming more and more critical every day.

"I have six interviews lined up next week, Mom."

"That's nice, dear. I'm sure you'll find something soon. Why, I'll just bet you're the best CPA that town has seen in a long time."

Suddenly desperate for some caffeine, Kylie managed to cradle the phone between a scrunched shoulder and her ear as she began measuring coffee grounds into her Mr. Coffee. She was on the third scoop when she realized she'd forgotten to use a filter. Rolling her eyes heavenward at her own forgetfulness, she rinsed out the machine and began the process all over again.

"I appreciate your confidence in me, but I keep telling you I'm not a CPA. I couldn't pass the exam, remember?"

"Oh, pooh, I'll just bet you could pass it if you took it again."

Kylie grimaced into the phone and pushed the button to start the coffee brewing. She'd failed the exams miserably right after college, then had taken an incredibly expensive prep course and tried again, only to get even lower scores the second time around. She was not planning to try again. She'd gone into those tests knowing the material cold. Unfortunately, the pressure of the ticking clock and the stern watchfulness of the test's proctors tripped her up every time. Something about the whole thing just smacked of stage fright, and she wasn't about to put herself through that humiliation again.

"Say, how's Dad's picture coming along?" she asked, changing the subject. It was no use trying to talk to her mother about her career. For some reason, even in light of the mounting evidence to the contrary, Elizabeth Rogers continued to believe that her untalented middle child was destined for greatness.

"It's just awful, honey." Her mother launched into her usual diatribe of typical Hollywood cost overruns, overconfident actors, bad sets, and incompetent stagehands. Kylie knew that Elizabeth Rogers would soon be reminiscing about the days when she and George Rogers had ruled the stage. But, as much as her mother seemingly loathed the way things were now, her father loved them. He loved the technology, the props, the huge budgets, the blockbuster hits. Kylie thought her parents were a good match, the new with the old, devoted to each other in an industry that neither rewarded nor encouraged long-lasting relationships.

She stared out the kitchen window into her tiny backyard as she sipped a cup of strong, black coffee, listening to her mother's monologue. A few of the rosebushes she'd planted along the fence right after she'd moved in were still in bloom, and she hoped they wouldn't stop flowering for at least another month. It was nice to see some color still holding on this late in the year.

"Kylie, did you hear me?"

The question brought her back to the conversation. She set her cup down on the white tile countertop and shifted the phone to her other ear.

"Sorry, Mom. You asked if I'd seen Robyn lately?"

"Yes. I tried to call her last night, but she must have been out."

"We both went to a party at David Gamble's house. I, uh, I had to leave early, but I called Robyn on her cell phone to see if she could get another ride home. I'm sure she should be home now."

"I would certainly hope so." Her mother sounded shocked to think that her youngest child might not be snuggled safe and sound in her bed at eight A.M. on a Sunday morning. "Why did you leave early? Weren't you having fun, dear?"

Kylie smiled at the concern in her mother's voice. She had no intention of telling her mom how her night had really ended or what had almost transpired in David Gamble's driveway. There were some things a mother just didn't need to know. "I wanted to get to bed early, Mom. I have a lot of things to do this week besides going on all those interviews."

"You're such a good girl. I'll just bet you'll be running one of those companies soon," her mother said proudly, making Kylie's eyes water as she said good-bye and placed the phone in its proper place of rest. There were times in her life when she wished her parents would just accept her for what she was rather than holding on to the hope that she possessed some undiscovered talent.

"This is one of those times," Kylie muttered dispiritedly. The rubber soles of her favorite slippers slapped the hardwood floor as she trudged back up the stairs with her coffee and her cat to take a shower.

As a child, she had run the gauntlet of artistic, athletic, and intellectual events as her parents searched in vain for her hidden genius.

At gymnastics lessons when she was six, she continually fell off the balance beam. The instructor worried that perhaps she might be suffering from vertigo. After thousands of dollars of tests, the doctor told her worried parents there was nothing physically wrong with her—she was just clumsy.

In ballet class at seven, she had a hard time telling left from right. After months of watching Kylie crash into the other dancers, the *danseuse* begged her mother to try the tap dancing class down the hall—anything to get Kylie away from her graceful little ballerinas.

At a writing retreat at eight, she had trouble distinguishing an adverb from an adjective. Her older brother, Daniel, also attended the week-long retreat. His entry won first prize in his age category, then took best of show.

Nine was the worst, though, Kylie remembered with a shudder as she tested the temperature of the shower with a tentative hand. Stepping under the warm water, she recalled the horror of standing on a stage in front of all of those staring eyes as if it had happened yesterday. She could feel them all looking at her as she tried to conjure up the lines she had so carefully memorized. Someone backstage waved a cue card just inside her line of vision, but she wouldn't have understood the words any less if they had been written in Gaelic. In any event, there was no way she could have forced a sentence past her chattering teeth. She stood there, rooted in place, unmoving even after the director mercifully closed the curtain so her understudy could step in.

"Just a touch of stage fright," her father had said.

Her parents always took her failures with such equanimity that Kylie didn't have the heart to tell them what she already knew at the tender age of nine. She was ordinary. Average. There was no other word for it, and there was no way she could change it. No matter how hard she tried, no matter how many hours she practiced, she was never going to be great at anything.

But that didn't mean that she wasn't good at a lot of small things. Like being a loyal, caring friend and enjoying giving her time and money to help out a worthy cause. Like being able to appreciate people for what was in their hearts, not in their bank accounts. These were the things about herself that she was proud of, things she wouldn't trade for all the talent in the world.

Stepping out of the shower, Kylie squinted at her reflection in the steamy mirror. She was at peace with the woman who gazed back at her.

The mirror quickly fogged up again and Kylie vowed for probably the hundredth time that she was going to remodel this tiny bathroom. With just an aging fan for circulation, it was impossible to air the room out after she'd taken a shower unless she opened the door and let some cold air in. She wiped off a circular area of the mirror so she could see to put on her makeup. A little mousse in her hair, a few minutes with the blow-dryer and she'd be finished.

She washed off the sticky residue from the mousse and dried her hands, then paused to pet Mr. Chips, who had taken up his usual morning spot on the bathroom counter.

"Sometimes I think you're more dog than cat."

He turned his yellowish gaze on her and meowed in protest at the insult.

"Don't the other cats tell you that you're not allowed to like me? You're not supposed to follow me around either," she admonished. "In fact, to be a proper cat, you are required to ignore my presence entirely, except at mealtimes."

His eyes narrowed in feline ecstasy as she scratched the downy fur below his left ear.

"Don't worry, I won't give away any of your secrets."

She picked up the blow-dryer and Mr. Chips leaped off the counter on cue, escaping to a quieter spot where he could catch up on his sleep in peace.

"I'm sorry, David. I've been through the entire guest list three times, and there's no Kylie McGillicuddy there."

David narrowed his eyes, pressing his cell phone to his ear. "Someone must have invited her as a guest."

"Would you like me to start calling the invitees to find out who brought her?" His assistant's voice held more than a tinge of curiosity, but David knew Deborah wouldn't ask why he was so interested in this particular guest. She'd been his assistant for three years—two years longer than anyone else had managed to last—in large part because she did as he asked without any prying questions.

"No, don't do that." He could just imagine the type of publicity *that* would arouse. David glanced down at his gold watch, sparkling in the brisk California sun. His appointment was in fifteen minutes. He pressed the button on the dashboard of his rental car to raise the convertible top and looked at the mirrored gray windows of the high-rise across the street. "She had been trying to get away from someone. A guy with cowboy boots and a black hat," David offered, frowning at his unusual memory lapse. Kylie had mentioned the young man's name, but he couldn't remember it now, had been too focused on her to pay any attention to the other man.

"Was it Bradley Nelson?"

"Yes, that's it," David answered, noting the amusement in his assistant's voice as he stepped out of the car and into the pale sunshine filtering through the Los Angeles smog. Pressing a button on the keychain to lock the doors and engage the alarm system, David kept the phone pressed to his ear as he walked down a flight of stairs in the parking garage to the sidewalk below.

"I'll give Bradley a call and see if he knows anything."

"Thank you, Deborah. Is there anything else before I go into the meeting?"

David sensed his assistant's hesitation before she responded. "Lisanne O'Neill has called twice today. She said she's been leaving you messages since Monday."

"Hmm," David responded noncommittally. His rumored relationship with the glamorous singer was nothing more than that—a rumor, no doubt started by her manager or publicist to get some free publicity for their client. There was no doubt in his mind that Lisanne would like their relationship to be more than a rumor, however. She'd made that plenty clear over the past few weeks with her constant phone calls and tendency to stick to his side like Milk Duds on dentures whenever possible.

"I told her you're out of town and are scheduled to be back in the office tomorrow," Deborah said.

"I'll take care of her tomorrow, then." Apparently it wasn't enough that he hadn't encouraged Lisanne. He'd have to come right out and tell her he wasn't interested. Ever since he'd become successful, women from all walks of life had freely offered him their affection. He supposed he couldn't blame them for looking up the ladder and seeing him as the easy way to skip a few rungs on their way to the top, but he couldn't help but wonder where they'd all be if Gamble Records' stock suddenly plummeted earthward. David shuddered involuntarily at the thought. He hoped he'd never have to find out.

He ended his call as the crosswalk light turned to "walk" and started across the street, his mind moving from Lisanne O'Neill to the elusive Kylie McGillicuddy. Her image flashed into his mind: her brown eyes sparkling as she smiled up at him with twigs in her unruly hair. Rationally, he knew that a portion of her allure was the fact that she'd left without giving him any way to get in touch with her. A part of him, the cynical half that always reminded him to look at people's motives, raised the question whether she had done just that to pique his interest. Perhaps she'd known instinctively that it was getting too easy for him, that most women he met had him outfitted for his wedding tux within five minutes. He could read it in their eyes, the hope of being asked to become the first Mrs. David Gamble; the hope that then she'd be entitled to half of whatever fortune he'd amassed, beginning the second after he'd said "I do." He hadn't seen that hungry look in Kylie's eyes, though. Instead, he had seen only good humor and honest desire. Maybe that was why he was still thinking of her almost a week later.

David entered the lobby of the building through the revolving doors and was immediately assaulted by a stale air-conditioned draft. He pushed thoughts of the mysterious Kylie McGillicuddy away. He didn't have time to think about her now. He needed to concentrate on his upcoming meeting, perhaps one of the most important meetings of his entire career.

Fidgeting with the uncomfortable knot of the tie at his neck, he pushed the button for the elevator and waited for it to arrive. As the doors slid open with a quiet *whoosh*, a woman came dashing through the lobby and stuck her arm between the closing doors, as if this were going to be the last elevator for hours. Choosing not to ride up forty-three floors with the woman's dismembered arm, David hastily pushed the "open door" button so the rest of her body could accompany him on the trip upward.

She stepped in on a waft of perfume and gave him a dazzlingly white smile. David retreated back into one corner of the elevator and waited for it to take him to the forty-third floor. The small space filled with a cloying scent and David sniffed, speculating whether the other occupant had some sort of olfactory disorder that masked her ability to realize she smelled as if she'd come from an explosion at the perfume factory.

Trying not to breathe through his nose, David attempted to ignore the woman eyeing him openly. She was so young, he figured she hadn't yet learned that you were supposed to look aimlessly at the ceiling or the buttons in the panel rather than ogling your fellow passengers, but the sly smile she was giving him told him there were plenty of other things she did know. At long last, the doors slid open on the thirty-sixth floor and the woman sauntered out, her black skirt so short David wondered why she even bothered with the pretense.

Reaching the doors, the woman turned back to face him.

"Brown Modeling," she mouthed, her lips moving suggestively around the words?

She turned again with a flip of her long hair. Then, just as the doors were about to close, her arm came through them again. David wondered briefly if the woman had a secret desire to lose a limb; she was certainly not averse to risking her arm in the elevator doors.

"Suite 3604. Call me," she said, pressing a business card into his hand before finally allowing the doors to close behind her.

David shook his head, dumbfounded. He was definitely not interested in a woman who—albeit gorgeous—would no doubt be missing an appendage before long.

David knew the type of woman he was eventually going to marry. She would be financially successful. He didn't have a specific dollar figure in mind, but it wouldn't really matter as long as she was at the top of her field. She'd be classy, elegant; not the type of woman who drew attention to herself except by her exceptional talent and intelligence. She would be beautiful, too, of course. David pictured shining blond hair, the ends curled slightly; light blue, or maybe even green, eyes. Trim figure with long legs. Understated breasts, nothing that would draw anyone's attention, but not too small either.

He stepped out of the elevator on the forty-third floor and blinked as an image of Kylie McGillicuddy flashed into his mind. She wasn't blond. Her eyes were sherry brown, not blue or green. Was she successful?

David tilted his head, staring out the windows of the

reception area he'd been ushered into a moment before. He'd guess she had a creative job. Maybe an art gallery owner or an interior decorator. He was no expert on women's clothing, but he'd bet the outfit she had on the night of the party at his house had been expensive. It stood to reason, then, that she was at least moderately successful. A smile tugged the corner of his mouth. She might not be everything he imagined, but there was certainly something about the brown-eyed girl that intrigued him.

The image of Kylie vanished as a young man who David guessed wasn't a day over thirty entered the reception area. He chastised himself for letting his thoughts wander away from business again.

"David, it's great to finally meet you. I'm Mitchell Sharpe." The young man grasped David's hand warmly, and David could feel the energy emanating from him. Although he was young, Mitchell Sharpe held a position of great responsibility at Broadcast Satellite Stations, the world's largest consumer satellite provider.

"Nice to meet you, too, Mitchell. I hear you've been busy." David followed the younger man as Mitchell led the way down a carpeted hallway. Mitchell showed him into a small conference room as they discussed BSS's court battle with the cable companies over the rights to air local channels over satellite feeds.

"I hope you guys win," David said wryly after refusing Mitchell's offer of something to drink. "I can't tell you how much I hate having to watch the Los Angeles stations. No offense, but it's like watching the *National Enquirer* doing newscasts."

Taking a seat on the opposite side of the table, Mitchell grinned. "Yeah, I have to agree. I came here from Atlanta myself and have to admit I hate the perky way they inform us of the latest disaster. But you didn't come here to talk to me about our fight with cable. I've read the report you sent, but why don't you give me the pitch in your own words?"

"All right." David leaned back comfortably in his chair and watched the other man's eyes as he began his practiced spiel. "You have, what, fifteen channels devoted to music?" he asked, already knowing the answer.

"Yes."

"And what sort of revenue do they produce?" Again, he already knew the answer.

"Not much," Mitchell admitted. "The music stations are pretty much a giveaway to our subscribers."

David nodded, warming to his topic. "Well, what if I told you that you could turn those stations into huge moneymakers?" He opened his briefcase and pulled out a stack of charts. "Just look at the demographics," he continued, sliding a piece of paper across the table. "This chart shows a breakdown of consumers into key age categories. We have studies that show what percentage of disposable income each of these age groups spends each year on music. These studies tell us that fifteen- to twenty-two-year-olds spend the most money per year, followed by twenty-three- to thirty-year-olds; the purchases of music drop off steeply after the average consumer reaches thirty." David paused for a moment. "But I think these figures are misleading because they're based on the old way of doing business."

Mitchell watched him intently, and David knew he was intrigued. "Go on," Mitchell encouraged.

David leaned forward, resting his forearms on the cool top of the glass conference table. "I think the sales trend doesn't have anything to do with age, but rather with the events people are dealing with during these periods of their lives and how those events affect the traditional means of selling music."

He stood up, trying to expend some of his restless energy as Mitchell nodded in understanding. "Let me give you an example. Let's say we have a thirty-two-year-old man who listens to the radio on his way to and from work. Now, maybe this guy hears a song he likes while he's driving. He even writes down the name of the group and tells himself he's going to buy their latest CD, but then he gets to work and, unlike when he was younger and had fewer responsibilities, he doesn't get a chance to run out to the record store or surf the Net for that CD during the day. This guy has a responsible position and has more important things to tend to than adding to his music collection. So, he forgets all about it.

"Now, let's take this same guy later that night. It's late, the kids are in bed, the house is quiet. He's got a pile of work in front of him. He's got the satellite tuned to the jazz channel, because he doesn't want to listen to the commercials on the radio while he works. Our guy hears the song again, the one he'd heard that morning and vowed to buy but never got the chance. Now, without even taking his eyes off his work, he clicks the 'buy' button on his remote control."

"And we mail him the CD?" Mitchell interjected, starting to catch David's enthusiasm.

"Only if he hasn't bought our new box that enables him to download it directly off the satellite feed." David grinned. "And we know how those thirty-something-year-old males love to have all the latest technology. The latest, *expensive* technology."

"Which we'd also be happy to sell to him at a handsome profit, I suppose?" Mitchell suggested dryly.

"The thought had crossed my mind."

"I'll bet it did. So, what's in it for you? I mean, we could develop this technology without Gamble Records."

"Of course you can," David agreed, taking his seat across from Mitchell again. "But I would guess it'll take at least a year to develop the software, not to mention getting the patents on the hardware and moving that into production." David stretched his legs out in front of him and watched Mitchell Sharpe cross his arms across his chest, contemplating David's comments.

"I suppose you already have a team working on this?" Mitchell asked after a long pause.

"Yes. We've had the patents for over a year. We also have suppliers lined up for all the components and a manufacturing plant we've paid to keep an option open for a production slot in the next six months."

"You must have been confident that you'd be able to convince me, but you still haven't said what's in it for you."

"I want BSS to make the music channels a separate subsidiary, and I want a stake in the ownership." David paused. "And I want to run it," he added quietly.

"Seth, I want you to get me everything you can find out about David Gamble and Gamble Records." The soft leather of the chair creaked as Mitchell Sharpe leaned back and tapped his fingers together thoughtfully.

"Sure, Mitchell." His assistant scribbled a note on his pad before asking, "But why?"

"Because he's gonna be our boss someday," came the cryptic reply.

"I'm sorry, Kylie. I know you were hoping this last one would pan out."

Kylie held the receiver to her ear, dropped her purse on the floor, and sank down onto her couch as Kim, the recruiter she'd been working with for the past few months, gave her the bad news.

She'd forced herself to go out and run errands after her last interview to keep from dwelling on the thought that this was her last hope. She'd had six interviews this week alone, and was beginning to feel as if she'd met with every company in Seattle during the past two months.

"So, we'll just keep trying, right?" she asked despondently, absently picking up one of the floral cushions from the couch and hugging it to her chest. There was a perceptible hesitation on the other end of the line, and Kylie braced herself for the inevitable.

"I am so sorry to tell you this," the recruiter said, sounding genuinely upset, "but my boss—" Kim stopped, then started again. "I really like you, but everytime someone calls Pigeon Books for a reference, we lose them as a potential employer. My boss told me I have to give up."

Kylie sighed. "I know, Kim. I . . . I understand."

"Thanks, Kylie. Please do keep in touch. I'm really going to miss you."

Kylie's answer was noncommittal as she turned the phone off and continued to sit on the couch, staring unseeingly at the brightly colored picture on the opposite wall. Two fat, wet tears slid down her face and plopped onto her knee, soaking into her pantyhose. As if sensing her distress, Mr. Chips appeared out of his latest kitty hiding place and rubbed himself against her calves, depositing black cat hair wherever he touched. She reached down and rubbed his chin, glad to have a sympathetic ear even if it was of the feline variety.

"No one's going to hire me, Mr. Chips—not with this black mark on my résumé," she said morosely.

The cat looked up at her, his yellow-green eyes filled with an expression Kylie chose to think of as affection. It was a good thing she still had a little money in her savings account, or they'd both be eating cat food for dinner by now.

CHAPTER 3

"Disaster is my sister's middle name." Robyn Rogers leaned forward, her silky blond hair caressing the curve of her cheek as she spoke.

She looked neat and trim in a pair of navy slacks and an ivory blouse, and David told himself that here was a woman you wouldn't ever see tumbling out a window. No, Robyn Rogers had poise and dignity, unlike the mysterious Kylie McGillicuddy who seemed to have appeared out of nowhere and then disappeared again. Deborah had told him this morning she'd left three messages for Bradley Nelson, but hadn't heard back from him yet. Now, as David watched Robyn Rogers, he made a mental note to tell his assistant to call off her search for the elusive Miss McGillicuddy. Even if they found her, David decided he was not going to get in touch with her. He'd been blinded by an unexpected, and completely inexplicable, feeling of attraction. It had never happened to him before, that instant physical awareness that he had felt when she'd touched his arm, but David reminded himself his life was not ruled by impulses. Instead, he made conscious choices and followed the path he'd planned for himself, refusing to let fate or destiny make his choices for him. For one brief moment, he had given in to impulse, but it was not something he would do again, he vowed, turning his attention back to the attractive singer sitting across from him.

David studied Robyn, noting with approval the restrained way in which she spoke, her hands folded calmly in her lap. This was the type of woman he had in mind for himself. Someone calm and dignified, not to mention financially successful. He tried to push Kylie McGillicuddy out of his mind for good and focused on what Robyn was saying.

"My mother asked if there was anything I could do for my sister, and I promised her that I'd at least ask around." Robyn laid a slender hand on his forearm. "Please don't feel obligated to give her a job. I understand that you have a business to run here, and the last thing you need is to baby-sit the unemployed siblings of your artists."

David looked down at the delicate hand on his arm, willing himself to feel the same tingling sensation he'd felt with Kylie. He felt nothing. Disgusted with himself for continuing to think about his mystery woman, David leaned back in his chair.

What was wrong with him lately? He kept finding himself thinking about the woman at the oddest moments. Like now, when he should be giving his attention to the biggest star in the Gamble Records stable, he reminded himself. Well, if Robyn wanted him to give her sister a job, he was sure there were plenty of things around here she could do. He didn't mind doing Robyn a favor and, besides, hadn't he used his influence to get his own brother job after job?

"I imagine we could find something around here for her to do. We always seem to be understaffed."

David took in Robyn's look of surprised gratitude and congratulated himself on his generosity. "Ask her to come in this afternoon, and I'll have Deborah arrange an interview with Human Resources."

Robyn thanked him, and they chatted about her upcoming tour for a moment before she excused herself to leave for another appointment. David escorted her to the door of his office, then grimaced as he heard the skirmish in his outer office.

"I'm sorry, Mrs. Gamble, but you don't have an appointment. Mr. Gamble is very busy—"

His assistant's voice was cut off by a loud, jarring, and all-too-familiar voice. "I'd love to make an appointment, but every time I call, you tell me he has nothing available."

David sighed and gently steered Robyn out of his office. He didn't really have time to talk to his mother right now, but she was obviously determined to disrupt his schedule.

"I'll talk to you later," he said quietly to Robyn before raising his voice above the din. "It's all right, Deborah. I have a few minutes before my conference call."

His mother turned to glare at him, the large, brightly painted tropical fish earrings she wore bobbing against her neck. David opened the door to his office wider and gestured inside, hoping she wouldn't make any more of a scene than she already had. The bright pink spandex leggings clinging to her heavy thighs made a swishing sound as she stomped past him and into his office, a cloud of cheap cologne trailing in her wake.

David coughed, fighting back his revulsion at the familiar scent.

Pam Gamble plopped down in the chair across from his desk as David made his way more slowly to his chair. The pale morning sunlight outside pushed its way through a heavy cloud cover and into the room, and David was hit by the incongruity of the gloomy weather outside and the garish faux-tropical dress of the woman sitting across from him.

"Are you going on a cruise?" he asked hopefully.

"No, why?"

"Forget it. What do you want?"

"Now, is that any way to greet your mother, David? I haven't seen you in months, thanks to your little bodyguard out there."

David ignored the disapproval in his mother's tone and

vowed to give Deborah a raise for her efforts at keeping his mother at bay. "I'm a busy man." He shrugged, steepling his fingers together calmly.

Pam Gamble snorted. "Too busy to even call and ask how your brother's doing?" she accused, her earrings jangling.

David stiffened. "Ben's not my problem anymore."

"No, David, he's not your problem, but he is your family, like it or not, and he needs our support."

"Support?" David scoffed. "Ben doesn't want anything from me except a handout so he can buy more booze and drugs."

"That's not true. He called last night and he wants to come home, wants to check himself into an outpatient recovery program."

"Great. Then he can stay with you."

David watched as Pam shifted uncomfortably in her chair. His dark blue eyes speared her light blue ones.

"So, Mother, why can't Ben stay with you? He's your son, after all. And, apparently, he takes after you in more ways than just his looks."

"Alan won't let him," Pam muttered.

"What's that? Your *boyfriend* won't let your son come back to live with you?"

"David, you know my condo's too small for three of us—"

"That's bullshit," David interrupted, pushing himself out of his chair. "You just don't have the guts to make any decisions in your life. You're so much better at letting everyone else make your choices for you, aren't you, Mother?"

She squirmed under his gaze but ignored the question.

"Well, forget it," David continued. "Ben can't stay with me. You can tell him that I got tired of having to come home every night and take an inventory to see what he'd pawned for drug money that day."

"But you can afford it . . ." Pam's voice petered out at

the murderous look in her oldest son's eyes. "It'll be different this time," she pleaded, trying another tack. "Ben promised me he's really going to quit this time."

David looked at his mother with contempt. "Save it, Mother. I've heard that one my entire life. It loses its credibility after about the hundredth time."

"Don't blame your brother for my mistakes, David," Pam said quietly. "Besides, I haven't touched a drink for ten years."

"Yeah, well, Ben picked up where you left off. Must make you proud to know your son is following in your footsteps." David knew from her sharp intake of breath that he'd scored a direct hit, but it didn't give him any satisfaction.

His mother stood up slowly. "So you won't help him?"

David paused, ruthlessly crushing a twinge of guilt. He had nothing to feel guilty about. He'd taken care of Ben for as long as he could remember, and it was high time his little brother learned to stand on his own two feet.

"No, I won't. Not again." He turned to look out the window at the gray sky threatening to let loose with a downpour at any minute. He heard his mother's sigh as she crossed the room to let herself out, but kept his back turned as the door closed quietly behind her.

"I can't do it." Kylie shook her head as if her sister could see the gesture over the phone lines.

"What do you mean, you can't do it?" Robyn's voice crackled loudly over her cell phone. "I didn't go and ask David Gamble for a favor only to have you throw it back in my face."

"I just can't do it, that's all," Kylie reiterated firmly.

Kylie heard Robyn swear, then held the phone away from her ear as the burst of a car's horn threatened to deafen her. Her cheeks were hot with embarrassment, not from her sister's crude choice of words to the other drivers of the world, but from the memory of the night of the party.

All she could think of was how she had literally thrown herself at David Gamble and what he must think of her after her shameless behavior. Reminding herself that he had been a willing participant right up until the end didn't help either. She felt like a fool and David Gamble was the last man on earth that she wanted to see again, no matter that just the thought of him made her feel tingly all over.

She was glad that Robyn had called rather than dropping by to tell her the news, glad Robyn couldn't see her face. Her sister would undoubtedly want to know why Kylie was blushing, and Kylie knew what an awful liar she was. She'd end up blabbing the whole story to Robyn, who'd think it was hilarious and would probably share the story with their parents, just to complete her humiliation.

"Do you have another job lined up?" Robyn asked, interrupting Kylie's thoughts.

She considered fabricating a story, but knew from experience that she'd get caught in her lie sooner or later. She always did. Propping the phone against her ear with her shoulder, she began stuffing clothes into the washing machine.

"No, but I will."

"Uh-huh. When?"

She added laundry detergent, flipped the water temperature selector to hot, and started the machine, briefly considering dropping the phone in the rising water to end what was turning out to be a very unpleasant conversation. No one would have trouble believing that it was an accident, at least not once they considered the source, Kylie thought as she held the offending modern convenience over the opening of the washing machine.

Kylie stood still as Robyn's voice continued streaming out. It was no use, Robyn would just call back and Kylie had two other phones in the house that she'd have to figure out how to dispose of. It wasn't likely that anyone would believe a freak accident had destroyed all three of her telephones at once.

She put the receiver back up to her ear.

". . . and I already told Mom that you'd gotten a job at Gamble Records. She was so relieved. You know she's been worried about you and, besides, she's starting to get suspicious about why you're having so much trouble finding a job. I didn't want to have to tell her about what happened at Pigeon Books, Kylie, but if you don't get a job soon she's—hey, up yours, buddy!" Robyn shouted. Kylie heard a loud thunk, then some rattling, and she knew that Robyn had dropped her cell phone in her never-ending fight against all the other drivers in the state of Washington. Kylie could only guess what had happened, but she'd lay odds that the other driver had just received a creative hand signal from her sister.

"Anyway," Robyn continued, as if nothing had happened, "I won't lie for you, and pretty soon, Mom's going to come right out and ask me why it is that you can't seem to get a job. So, unless you want her to know the whole sordid story, I'd suggest you thank me, get dressed, and get your butt over to Gamble Records."

Kylie sat down heavily on one of her dining room chairs, wondering, not for the first time, what it must be like to always get one's way. She had no idea what it would feel like, but she was certain that Robyn did.

"Do you think . . ." Kylie hesitated, then started again. "Will I be meeting with David Gamble?"

"Of course not, Kylie. He's hardly going to take time out of his schedule to meet with you over some clerical position, even if you are my sister." Robyn laughed. "Just go and ask for the manager of Human Resources and she'll take care of you."

That was the answer Kylie told herself she wanted to hear, but for some reason it didn't make her feel any better.

"How could you let this happen?" David's question was all the more menacing for being soft-spoken.

The tall blond behind the desk fidgeted under his hard-eyed stare. "I'm so sorry, David. We just switched over to the new system, and Chanelle was the only one who understood it."

"Why did we buy a royalty program that no one could understand?"

Sandy Macgregor, Chief Financial Officer of Gamble Records, swallowed before answering. "The salesman's demo made it seem like it was the answer to our prayers. And," she added, "Chanelle said she thought it was a great system and was going to start training Brenda on it next week."

David ran a hand through his hair, making some of the strands stand on end. "But now Chanelle's gone, and nobody knows how to process the royalty checks except her, and we have contracts that guarantee payments no later than the fifteenth day after the end of the quarter."

"And today's the end of the quarter. I know," Sandy said miserably. "Maybe we can get Chanelle to come in a couple days next week . . ." Her voice trailed off as David looked at her incredulously.

Sandy's assistant, Chanelle Taylor, had gone into labor that morning, a full two months before her due date. During the day, the baby's heart rate had dropped dangerously low, and it was anyone's guess as to whether he would survive through the night, much less through next week.

David knew that he intimidated some of his employees, had a reputation for not tolerating politics or laziness, but even he would not stoop to the depths Sandy was suggesting.

"No, you're right. That was a terrible idea. I'll have to work with Brenda on this," Sandy said.

"What about hiring someone to help?"

"We've had a hard time just getting good people who have no real industry experience. I don't know how much luck we'll have trying to find someone who knows about royalties and can learn a new software program in the next two weeks. But don't worry, David, this is my problem, and I'll figure out how to solve it," Sandy said dispiritedly.

"I have confidence that you will," David said as he turned to leave. He had come in to tell Sandy about the potential satellite deal with BSS and warn her to keep quiet about it when she dropped the bomb about the royalty crisis. He didn't want any of the major record labels to get wind of his plan before the deal was etched. He knew Mitchell Sharpe would be poring over Gamble financials and evaluating David's potential as head of BSS's satellite music division. He couldn't afford to have any red flags raised at this point, and news of their failure to get royalties out on time would surely send the wrong message to BSS.

Since she had only joined the company six months ago, this was David's first chance to see how his new CFO held up under pressure. She had come highly recommended from her previous company, and David could only hope she'd be able to successfully overcome this challenge. If not, he'd be looking for a new CFO before the year was out.

"Kylie, I'd like you to meet our CFO, Sandy Macgregor. Sandy, this is Kylie Rogers."

Kylie shook hands with the older woman, then took the seat she was offered, tugging her black skirt down her thighs as she sat. One of these days, she'd have to trade her short skirts in for something more conservative, but all the business suits she tried on always seemed so . . . confining. She smoothed the fabric of her skirt with her fingers and looked at the unstylish, boxy cut of Sandy's navy blue pantsuit. Kylie stifled a grimace and decided to stick with her short skirts for a while longer.

"Kylie has a degree in accounting and worked in publishing for the last four years. Let me know when you're done with her, Sandy." With that introduction, the Human Resources manager slipped out, leaving Kylie on her own with the CFO.

Sandy's office was cluttered, with stacks of papers covering her desk and spilling onto the floor, a credenza, and a round table in the corner. In this day and age of computers, Kylie was surprised to see all the paper lying around, but knew that some people felt more secure surrounded by the physical evidence of their work.

"So, Kylie, is it?" Kylie nodded and Sandy continued, "What do you know about royalties?"

Kylie wondered at the harried look in the CFO's eyes, but kept her curiosity to herself as she answered with a slight smile, "My parents are actors, my sister is a musician, my brother is a writer, and I worked at a publisher for over four years. So, I guess you could say I know a lot about royalties."

Sandy raised her eyebrows at that, and Kylie thought that perhaps she'd said the wrong thing. Maybe the CFO was looking for someone with a blank slate of knowledge that she could fill with "the Gamble way." Kylie swallowed a sigh. Once again, it seemed she had blown it without really knowing what she'd done to mess things up.

"What about computers? How would you rank your computer skills?" Sandy asked.

"I guess I would say I'm average. I've worked a lot with spreadsheets. And, of course, I've worked with several proprietary systems. As a matter of fact," she continued proudly, "I helped my previous employer convert to a new royalty tracking and payment system."

Kylie's eyes widened with surprise when the CFO leaped out of her chair and came toward her, a wild look on her face.

"What system was it?" the CFO croaked.

Kylie wondered how long it would take the H.R. manager to find her if Sandy Macgregor stabbed her with her mechanical pencil and buried her under the mountain of paper in her office. How long before someone discovered her decaying body? Kylie's gaze locked warily on the CFO as she pondered the questions buzzing around in her brain.

"Um, it was a system designed by RoyalTech. I helped

with the customization," she offered feebly as Sandy continued to stare at her like a zealot at the messiah. Kylie closed her eyes as Sandy let out a screech and threw her arms around her shoulders. She waited to feel a stabbing pain, then opened her eyes when it didn't come.

"You're hired. Can you start on Monday? Oh, thank you, thank you," Sandy chanted, thumping Kylie's back vigorously. Kylie didn't know what she'd done to inspire such enthusiasm, but she wasn't about to ask. Perhaps she hadn't messed things up, after all.

After an uneventful weekend, Kylie arrived early for her first day of employment at Gamble Records. Butterflies the size of bats banged around in her stomach as she used the key Sandy had given her Friday afternoon after an hour-long orientation to open the glass doors of the four-story building perched on the lower south side of Queen Anne Hill.

The office officially opened at eight, but Kylie wanted to be early. Really early. She needed this job to be a success, and if that meant she'd have to come in before the birds were awake, that's exactly what she'd do. She took the elevator to the third floor and walked down the hall. Thoughts swirled around in her head as she hung the mid–thigh-length leather jacket her parents had given her last Christmas over the peg in the cubicle Sandy had assigned to her. She covered a yawn with one hand as she dropped the software manual she'd read over the weekend on the faux wood desk.

"I hate mornings," Kylie muttered, stumbling through the empty maze of cubicles in search of caffeine. She hoped to discover that Sandy was not one of those bosses who automatically equated an employee's starting time with her productivity. It seemed to be a rampant notion, Kylie had noticed, especially on the West Coast, that the earlier a body dragged herself to work, the better she was evaluated by her superiors. Never mind that the early bird employee

spent the first hour of her day completing her makeup, or
having a bit of breakfast with her morning paper rustling
noisily on her desk. And never mind that the employee
missed all of the last-minute deadlines that kept everyone
else at the office well into the night because she would have
been long gone hours before the last call of the FedEx
deliveryman.

Oh, no, Kylie thought as she viciously ripped open a
bag of coffee with her teeth, just let someone come in by
seven A.M. and her career path would be studded with gold
paving stones. She jabbed the "on" button of the industrial-
size coffeemaker and turned, the gauzy material of her
flower-flecked black skirt slapping against her thighs as she
marched back to her desk.

Sitting down, she felt her face flush with righteous indignation. Well, fine, if they wanted her to be here before
the sun rose, then by God, she would be, she thought,
searching the desk drawers for a pen. She swung around,
then stopped. The reflection of her face in the screen of the
computer monitor snapped her back to reality.

As far as she could tell, she was the only person around,
at least on the third floor, at almost seven-thirty. She had
worked herself into a frenzy for nothing.

She fluffed out the back of her hair and shook her head
ruefully, chiding herself for her unwarranted fit of pique as
she searched the computer in front of her for its power
switch.

David leaned back in his chair, enjoying the early morning
quiet he knew wouldn't last much longer.

His electronic calendar glared at him from his computer
screen, and, as he glared back at it, he wondered if his
assistant sometimes forgot that he was human. She was
incredibly, even ruthlessly, efficient, and he suspected that
one morning he'd glance at his daily planner and find she'd
arranged every minute of his day to her liking. He could
just see it now:

7:00 A.M.—review final details of contracts to be signed
    this week
7:25 A.M.—take two sips from cup of coffee
7:30 A.M.—call East Coast agents
7:45 A.M.—take two more sips from cup of coffee
7:50 A.M.—read e-mail
8:00 A.M.—greet assistant

And so on until every minute of his life was cast in glowing
black letters against the white backdrop of his calendar program. He stood up, running a hand through his hair as he
gazed out the window at the lightening sky. It wasn't Deborah's fault, he reminded himself, not her fault that he'd
felt—what?—not bored, exactly. Maybe restless? Yes, that
was it. He felt restless, and having every moment of every
day planned for him like this wasn't helping.

"The satellite deal will change that," he muttered to his
reflection in the window, staring absently out over the
nearly empty parking lot. His gaze stopped suddenly. He
leaned toward the glass, his hand touching the cold window. There were fewer than ten cars in the parking lot, so
the red Mustang convertible with the white leather interior
stood out like a white cat at a witch festival.

"It can't be her." David closed his eyes, expecting the
car to be gone when he opened them again.

The car was still there.

"There are plenty of antique Mustangs in this city. It's
a-million-to-one that it's hers," he said to himself. His Italian leather loafers made no sound as he crossed the floor
of his office and went out into the hall. Could it be Kylie?
Was she really here?

He didn't see the mop of brown curls on the fourth floor
and took the stairs two at a time down to the third.

"You're here early," he overheard Sandy Macgregor say
as he rounded the corner.

"I wanted to make a good impression on my first day."
David stopped. It was her. Even though it had been over

a week since he'd heard her voice, he recognized it as if it had been just that morning. What was she doing here? Was she a friend of Sandy's? Was that how she'd come to be at the party?

He surged forward, determined to get some answers.

Kylie's back was to him from where she sat in Sandy's office. She was pleating the material of her skirt between slender fingers, the movement drawing David's attention to the hemline creeping up her leg.

He blinked, astounded by the instant pull of attraction he felt. It wasn't as if he didn't see scantily clad women every day, not in this business. Most times, he felt lucky if they were clad at all. How was it that this woman could affect him like this?

"Oh, David, hello. I didn't see you there." Sandy's voice intruded on his thoughts.

He expected Kylie McGillicuddy to turn toward him, to hit him with that bright smile that lit up her face. Instead, she slouched down in her chair, which only succeeded in causing her skirt to creep farther up her leg. He swallowed, trying not to look at the ever-increasing patch of skin she was exposing.

"Good morning, Sandy. Who do we have here?"

Kylie leaped up out of her chair as if someone had stuck a lit match in her shoe.

Unfortunately, her foot caught on the edge of one of Sandy's notorious piles of papers.

Fortunately, she landed solidly against his chest. David reached out his hands to steady her, and was lost when she raised her gold-kissed brown eyes to his.

"Well, if it isn't my old friend, Kylie McGillicuddy," he murmured, breathing in the faint, slightly spicy scent of her. She blinked up at him, and a red-hot blush crept into her cheeks. David felt the urge to run his thumbs along her cheekbones, to trace the line of heat marching across her face.

Sandy's voice intruded on his wandering thoughts.

"McGillicuddy? I thought your last name was Rogers, like your sister's?"

It took a moment for David to re-engage his brain. "Rogers?" he echoed dumbly.

"Yes. Kylie Rogers. She's Robyn's sister and a godsend, I have to tell you," Sandy continued, oblivious to the undercurrents flooding her office.

Kylie continued looking up at him, not saying a word.

He took a step back, needing to put some distance between them so he could think.

"*You're* Robyn's sister?" he asked.

She nodded once, looking miserable.

David rubbed a distracted hand through his hair. "But you're nothing like Robyn. You're . . ." He hesitated. "And she's . . ."

"I'm what?" The voice he remembered as being full of smiles had an edge of a frown.

"Well, you're . . . you don't look anything like—"

Kylie shoved herself away from him, the gold in her eyes turning to liquid steel. "No, you're right. I'm nothing like Robyn. I'm not petite or blond. I can't sing. I can't dance. And you'll never catch me on a stage in front of thousands of people."

David stumbled as she pushed past him, trying to right himself as he, too, fell prey to the stack of papers at his feet. He landed solidly on his rump, watching the prettiest set of legs he'd ever seen stalk away from him down the hall.

"Are you all right, David?"

Sandy reached a hand down to help him up, blocking his view.

David nodded silently, wondering what in the world that had been all about.

Why did everyone insist on comparing her with Robyn?

Kylie stomped to the kitchen for a cup of coffee. Why couldn't they just accept her for who she was? Why—

Why was the carpet under her feet squishing?

Her mental tirade ended on a note of dread as she gingerly picked her way toward the kitchen. Poking her head around the corner, she watched dark brown liquid pouring from the coffee machine to where a pot was supposed to be, but wasn't. Instead, it overflowed the drip pan, running down the counter and onto the light gray linoleum before forming a river of caffeine flowing into the hall where Kylie was standing.

The doorjamb was cool against her forehead as she closed her eyes and leaned against it, despair flooding her soul like the hot coffee flooding the kitchen.

Why me? she asked the uncaring gods. *Isn't it bad enough that I'm cursed with an incredibly talented family?*

Why must I be plagued with disaster on top of all that? she wailed silently.

"Looks like you forgot the coffeepot." The deep voice behind her was tinged with amusement.

Kylie felt her bottom lip begin to tremble. Her shoulders slumped in defeat.

Her whole life was just one big disaster waiting to happen. Or, rather, one big disaster after another actually happening. There was no "waiting" about it.

She had been a fool to think someone as poised and confident as David Gamble would ever be anything but amused by a klutz like her. She couldn't even make coffee, for heaven's sake. A hot tear slid down her face, mingling with the hot liquid on the floor. It was soon joined by another.

She felt a strong hand on her shoulder. "Look, if it makes you feel any better, this isn't the first time this has happened. People wouldn't make a fresh pot of coffee after taking the last cup so we installed these new never-empty coffeemakers. They keep brewing until the sensor triggers the machine to tell it that the liquid is at the right level. That way, you can fill multiple pots just by swapping them out. Only, if you forget to put a pot under the spigot, the machine just keeps brewing. I think this is the tenth time we've had a river of Starbucks in this kitchen."

Kylie hiccupped. It didn't matter that this had happened to anyone else. It was enough to know it had happened to her. And on her first day, too.

David turned her around and put a hand under her chin. "You're not crying over this, are you?" he asked incredulously. He pushed her into the kitchen, closing the door behind them, then left her for a moment to shut off the still-brewing machine.

She should have felt comforted when he returned and put his strong arms around her, but instead, she felt like an incompetent child.

"Don't cry." David muttered the soothing words into her ear as he stroked her hair.

Kylie sniffed, wishing his assurance that this had happened before made her feel better. But it didn't. Even if the unlikely story he told was true, it didn't make her any less of a disaster magnet. She blinked back the last of her tears and looked up at him.

"I'm all right, David. Thank you for . . . well, thank you for not being angry at the mess I made. I promise I'll clean it up."

David wiped the last vestiges of moisture from under her eyes with his thumbs. The tenderness of the gesture yanked the words she'd begun to say out of her mouth.

"Why are you being so nice about this?" she asked, her voice barely above a whisper.

His thumbs were now tracing the outline of her lower lip and his dark blue eyes were clouded. She felt the unmistakable attraction start to sizzle between them, and marveled at the effect he had on her. He continued stroking her mouth and she knew he was going to kiss her again. Kylie's lips parted as David's head started toward hers.

They jumped apart guiltily as the kitchen door was flung open.

"Oh, I'm sorry, I . . ." The intruder paused for a split

second, obviously evaluating the scene in front of her. "I didn't mean to interrupt anything," she continued sweetly.

Kylie felt the heat rush into her cheeks. It was the accounting supervisor, Brenda Olson. Kylie had sensed that Brenda had taken an immediate but inexplicable dislike to her when they'd been introduced on Friday. Now, as she lowered her eyes to the floor miserably, she wondered how long it would be before word got around that she was the new office slut. It certainly hadn't taken her long to ruin this job, she thought, disgusted at herself. This was a record, even for her.

She mumbled something about going to the ladies' room, then stepped out of David's arms and slid out the door past Brenda, before she made even more of a fool of herself than she already had.

"I want all the coffeemakers in the building replaced."

Deborah looked up in surprise as her boss thundered into the outer office. She'd just finished hanging her coat on its peg when David burst in with his odd request.

"And we need to get building maintenance to clean up a wet spill in the kitchen on three. Oh, and tell Sandy Macgregor I need to speak with her right away. Hold all my calls till I'm through with her, please."

Replace the coffeemakers? Deborah silently asked herself, baffled. She wondered what the heck had gotten into her normally calm and controlled boss as she moved to her desk. She knew David valued her ability to do as he asked without plying him with unnecessary questions, but this was a situation that was going to need some answers, and she was going to get them, one way or another.

After all, wasn't that what office grapevines were for?

CHAPTER 4

Each artist's contract is different. In general, royalties on retail sales vary from seven to twelve percent with a ten percent holdback for returns. Packaging costs usually range from twenty to twenty-five percent and—

"Thanks for staying an extra shift, Kylie. That flu's got half the volunteers out sick this weekend." The hearty voice coupled with an equally hearty clap on her back pushed Kylie out of her silent recital of how royalties were calculated.

"I'm glad to help out, Ty. Besides, it's been a pretty slow day, so I'm hardly even tired," Kylie lied, flexing her sore calf muscles as she scooped a heaping spoonful of macaroni and cheese onto the tray in front of her. She was tired after her first day of work at Gamble Records, but she couldn't turn Ty down when he'd called and asked if she could help out at the shelter.

"Don't worry, it'll get busier as the weather turns colder." The tall, dark-skinned man's expression turned sad with his all-too-true prediction.

Kylie reached out and laid a comforting hand on Tyrone James's arm. Ty had started The Soup Kitchen, a nonprofit organization that provided hot meals and free counseling to the city's homeless and poor, three years ago, two years after his wife had chosen the streets over life with her husband and daughter. Kylie often wondered if Ty's efforts at The Soup Kitchen were motivated by the hope that he could help turn around someone else's life like he'd been unable to do with his own wife. No matter what his motivation, Kylie thought as she watched his sad brown eyes survey the half full dining room, Tyrone James had a kind and caring heart that was appreciated by many of the city's unfortunate.

" 'Scuse me?" a small voice hesitantly interrupted Kylie's thoughts.

Kylie glanced at the top of a blond head that barely reached to the cafeteria railing. "What can I get for you, honey?"

"Can I have more broccoli, please?"

"More broccoli? Now that's not a request I hear every day." Kylie smiled as she put two stalks of the bright green vegetable on the little girl's tray. "What about some cake? We've got chocolate or white cake with strawberries," she coaxed.

The little girl looked up at her with too-old brown eyes. "My mommy says we'll die if we don't stay healthy, and cake won't make us healthy."

Kylie blinked at the sudden pressure behind her eyes when the little girl turned, hefting the tray that weighed almost as much as she did. It was Ty's turn to lay a comforting arm across her shoulders as she sniffed.

"I know, the kids are hard. That's why we're doing this. To make it a better world for them."

His heavy arm squeezed her gently before he made his way over to where the little blond girl and her mother sat. This was the first time Kylie had seen the pair here, and she was certain Ty would get them in touch with the right resources before they left. With any luck, the little girl and her mother wouldn't be homeless for long.

"Hey, babe, I'll take some of whatever you're offering."

At the suggestively uttered comment, Kylie turned from

watching Ty talk to the girl's mother. She drew in a sharp breath as her gaze slammed into a pair of midnight blue eyes; eyes that looked almost like David Gamble's except for the telltale red lines that ringed their whites. Shaking her head, Kylie chided herself for being ridiculous. Her overactive imagination was obviously conjuring up similarities to David where none existed.

"What do you say, honey? Why don't we go to your place so I can figure out just how sweet your cake is?" The stranger leaned closer, laying his arms across the top of the glass shielding the food below.

His offensive line dispelled any lingering thoughts that he held any resemblance to David besides the piercing color of his eyes. Kylie crossed her arms across her chest and leaned back against the counter behind her. "Have you been asleep since the seventies?"

"What are you talking about, babe?"

"First of all, women in this millennium are not referred to as 'babe.' Secondly, no, I don't want to go back to my place, or any place for that matter, with some man whom I've never even set eyes on before this very minute." *At least not unless your name happens to be David Gamble,* she added silently, trying not to blush as she recalled her willingness to do just that with David the night they had met.

"Now," she said, picking up a serving spoon and eyeing the stranger expectantly, "do you want the macaroni and cheese or the lasagna?"

Kylie was surprised when the man laughed good-naturedly. She'd expected anger, not humor, after her rejection of his ridiculous come-on lines.

"Well, aren't you a feisty one? I'll take the lasagna please, *ma'am.*" He unfolded his arms from the glass casing. "And some of that salad, too, if I may."

"Certainly."

"What's your name?"

"Kylie," she answered automatically. Ty insisted the volunteers use their first names only at The Soup Kitchen. Seattle wasn't a particularly large city and he didn't want to run the risk of any of his volunteers being tracked down by some junkie needing money for a fix. Or worse. Although most of the clientele at The Soup Kitchen were harmless, there were some Kylie wouldn't want to meet in a dark alley.

"Kylie. That's a lovely name."

"Thanks, I'll tell my mother you like it." Kylie smiled, her almond-shaped eyes crinkling at the corners as she dished a heaping serving of lasagna onto the stranger's tray.

Ben Gamble watched the pretty brunette add a whole-wheat roll to his plate and wondered if she would have taken his offer more seriously if they'd met somewhere other than this dump. Resentment of his situation smacked him in the chest and he struggled to keep the anger he felt out of his voice as he flirted with the woman on the other side of the counter. His mother had told him yesterday that David refused to let him crash at his house for a while. She'd also made some lame excuse about why he couldn't stay at her condo, but Ben didn't really want to stay with her anyway.

No, David's house was better. There was always plenty of cash lying around, and plenty of action, too. He knew his brother stayed away from booze and drugs, but the people who always seemed to be hanging around his brother were some of the wildest partiers around. When Ben had stayed with David the last time, he'd been invited to countless parties just because he was the mighty David Gamble's brother. David had even let him drive the Mercedes convertible, that little black SL 600 he loved so much. Man, he'd loved living with David and it had really pissed him off when his big brother had kicked him out, telling Ben that he'd used up his last chance.

It pissed him off even more that the invitations had subsequently dried up. He'd come to think of those people as his friends and it really torqued him that they'd cast him off like some hanger-on after David threw him out. And all because Ben had needed some cash and wrote himself a check out of David's account. When David had found out, he'd acted like Ben had committed murder, not borrowed a few thousand dollars. As if the paltry amount he'd helped himself to had even made a dent in big brother's balance sheet. Ben clenched his teeth and the edges of the plastic tray bit into his hands as he thought about David's refusal to help him now.

"Here you go. There's plenty, so don't feel shy about asking for more. Ty will be happy to help you get fixed up with a place to stay for a while if you need it." Kylie handed him a full plate.

"Thanks." Ben gave the woman across the counter his most charming smile as he put a lid on the anger bubbling up inside him. He leaned toward her conspiratorially. "But I'm not really homeless, you know."

He could tell from her expression that she didn't believe him, and he pressed on with his lie. He hated for anyone to think that he was like the other people here; their dirty, disgusting poverty seeping out of their pores, smelling like yesterday's garbage.

He was Benjamin Gamble, damn it. He was the brother of one of Seattle's wealthiest citizens, not some booze-addicted crackhead who was too stupid to hold down a job. He *chose* not to get a job right now, wasn't going to let corporate America get their claws into him and corrupt his art with their lure of big money. One day, his pictures would be famous, and then they'd be crawling to him.

Of course, in order to be successful, he needed a quiet, safe place to create. Someplace where he could have a few drinks to get in the artistic mood without having to worry about some asshole stealing him blind while he slept. Ben shot a calculating look at Kylie. He'd seen the tears slip out of her eyes when she saw that little girl, and he'd just bet she was a sucker for a sob story.

She watched him, a skeptical light in her eyes, as he quickly thought up a plausible lie.

"I mean to say, I am homeless, but that's because my house burned down last month." He sighed dramatically, hoping he hadn't put too much into it. He wanted to sound heroic, after all, not pathetic.

"Oh, I'm sorry. That's awful." Ben noticed the light in her eyes had changed from skeptical to sympathetic, and knew he was on the right track.

"Yes. Well, I didn't mind that so much. I mean, after all, it was just a heap of bricks and wood. No, the worst part was what happened to my poor mama." Ben paused, closing his eyes for effect.

"What happened to her?"

"She was taking a nap when the fire started. Luckily I had decided to go home for lunch that day or . . . or she might have died." Ben watched Kylie from under thick, black lashes. He read the compassion in her expression and went in for the kill. "We had insurance on the house, of course. But she didn't have any health insurance. I've given the hospital everything we got from the insurance company, and I've emptied my savings account, but it just isn't enough." He shook his head sadly. "I can't see spending money on myself, even if it is for food or shelter, not while Mama needs everything we have."

"Don't you have any family to help you out?"

Ben shook his head, the outrage in his voice real. "I have a brother who's very well off, but the bastard won't lift a finger to help. He doesn't care if I have to live on the streets, as long as I don't inconvenience him."

"That's awful. Look, I know this might be a hard thing for you to do . . ." Kylie hesitated and Ben bit the inside of his lip to control the gleeful expression that threatened. Women had always been suckers for him, and this one was obviously no exception. ". . . but you really should talk to Ty about what help is available for you."

Ben held his face frozen as Kylie babbled on about social agencies and state aid. Was she an idiot? He didn't need any fucking welfare, he needed a place to crash where he wouldn't be continually hassled by a bunch of pandering do-gooders all the time. His lip threatened to curl up in a sneer, but Ben held back the impulse. It wouldn't gain him anything to lose his temper now, and at least he'd sown the seeds in her mind. He mumbled a thanks for the unwelcome advice and took his now-lukewarm tray of food over to a table.

Kylie might not know it, but she was going to help him, whether she wanted to or not.

"I'm sorry I didn't get a chance to show you around the rest of the building on your first day."

Kylie smiled. Day two was progressing much better than day one had, and so far she'd heard nothing about the incident with David in the kitchen yesterday. Maybe for once luck was on her side and Brenda would keep quiet about the scene she'd intruded upon.

"That's all right, Sandy. I'm glad you're able to take the time today. Robyn's always talking about recording sessions, and masters, and demo tapes, and a million and one other things that I don't understand. It will be nice to finally know what she's talking about."

"Well, I don't profess to know everything about the recording industry after only working at Gamble Records for a few months myself, but I can walk you through the basics. I guess the easiest way to explain the process is to begin at the beginning," Sandy continued as they made their way down the carpeted stairs to the first floor of the Gamble Records building. "We hear about artists in one of two ways. The first way is through people we know in the industry—agents and promoters who've heard the groups and think they have a sound that would fit in with our label. The people in our A&R department keep in close contact with others in the industry so they know what's going on at other labels and in other parts of the country."

"What does A&R stand for?" Kylie asked.

"Oh, sorry. Artist and Repertoire. They're undoubtedly the most important people in any record company. Peter Laughlin is the head of Gamble's A&R department," Sandy said, continuing her tour.

"What's the second way you hear about artists?"

Sandy laughed as she stopped in front of a door and slipped a key in the lock. "Unlike the major labels, David insists that Gamble Records listen to the unsolicited demo tapes that get sent here every day."

The door swung inward and Kylie stepped into a cavernous room filled with floor-to-ceiling steel shelving.

"Wow," Kylie said, looking at row after row of tapes.

"Yes, we get hundreds of tapes every week. The A&R department listens to every one and responds to the artist, whether they're interested or not." Sandy's voice echoed in the huge room as she reached out and touched one of the tapes sitting on the shelf nearest her. "Gamble Records' motto is that we treat the artists, even aspiring ones, with respect. That's why this whole royalty thing is such a big deal. All of our contracts have a clause that guarantees payment to the artists no later than fifteen days after the end of each quarter."

"What happens if we don't get the royalties out on time?"

"It's written into each artist's contract that Gamble will pay a percentage penalty for each day we're late."

"That's pretty aggressive, isn't it?" Kylie asked, knowing that it wasn't unusual for royalties to be delayed sometimes for as long as an entire year.

"Yes. Apparently, it's a policy that's been a thorn in the side of the major labels for years. They're always under pressure to meet the same terms as Gamble, but so far not one of them has been willing to give up the cash flow associated with delayed royalty payments."

"Why does Gamble do it?" Kylie asked as they stepped out of the room.

"It started as a way to give David a competitive advantage over the major labels, and he never phased it out. Maybe he decided he's got enough money and doesn't need to take any more away from the artists." Sandy shrugged and closed the door of the demo room behind her. The keys on her key ring jangled as she slipped them into the pocket of her shapeless slacks.

Or maybe he did it because it was the right thing to do, Kylie suggested silently to herself, wondering if anyone credited the shrewd businessman with having a conscience or caring about the people who worked so hard to create their music. Her righteous indignation on David's behalf simmered as she followed Sandy around a corner.

"Gamble has four fully equipped recording studios on the premises, which is the next step in the process after signing a new artist." Sandy stopped in front of a glass-enclosed booth, and Kylie watched a man wearing headphones fiddle with some switches on a giant board in front of him. It seemed to her there were more buttons and knobs than in the cockpit of a 747.

"Are they making an album right now?" she asked, her fascination with the process of turning notes on a sheet of paper into a salable object overcoming her silent defense of David Gamble.

"Yes. The first thing we do is come up with a budget for the recording session."

"How do you do that?"

"Well, first A&R gives us an estimate of forecasted sales. It's their job to predict how successful any given project will be, but, of course, that's not as easy as it sounds. The purpose of this is to try to make sure that the album will at least cover the production costs and have something left over to pay the artist. Recording sessions are fully recoupable against artist royalties."

"So, if we let the artist spend too much on recording, and they don't sell enough copies, they won't get paid," Kylie repeated to make sure she hadn't missed anything.

"Exactly," Sandy agreed, moving down the hall to another windowed room where a dozen people were gathered. Some sat on backless stools, playing musical instruments, while others stood around chatting. Kylie thought it was strange to see people's lips moving but not be able to hear any sound on her side of the glass. It was like being on the outside of a fishbowl looking in.

"What happens after the budget is approved?"

"Then the real work begins. First, a producer is assigned to oversee the making of the album. Then, the material for the record is chosen and several demos are made to decide the best arrangement. Often, they'll record a song with different musical instruments and at different tempos to see what sounds best."

Kylie nodded, watching the attitude of the people in the studio change as a red light went on. It was as if the teacher had just walked in on a roomful of kindergartners. Everyone sat up straighter, the idle chatter stopped, and all eyes went to the front of the room where a woman with spiky black hair tinted orange on the ends was speaking.

"Is that the producer?" Kylie asked, pointing to the spiky-haired woman.

"Yes. She's the boss in the recording sessions, especially when she's working with new artists. Once a group is established, they'll have more say in the creative process. But in the beginning, they rely heavily on the judgment of the producer. Once the producer, the A&R rep, and the artist are happy with the finished product, the master recording is sent off to be burned. Unlike the major labels, Gamble doesn't have its own pressing plant, so I don't have any firsthand knowledge of this yet. All I know is we send off the master and we get back nice, neatly packaged CDs, ready to be shipped off to the distributors or sold at Gamble.com."

"Don't they worry about the master getting lost in the mail? I mean, after all that hard work, you'd hate to have to start all over again." Kylie watched as the musicians in the room beyond the glass started to play. A thin man wearing tight leather pants strummed on a guitar, but no sound reached her. She tried to imagine what it sounded like on the other side as leather-pants man shimmied his thin hips and a long-haired drummer pounded away.

"We keep copies of the master for just that reason. They're back in the storage room, along with the demo tapes. They're kept under lock and key since they're basically the lifeblood of our business. On average, it costs over a hundred thousand dollars to produce a finished master, so it's not just hard work we're trying to save but cold, hard cash as well."

"I can see why they're locked up, then. You'd hate to lose your only copy after all that money's been spent."

"Yes. Well, that's about it for my tour."

Noticing the musicians were starting to pack up their instruments, Kylie glanced at her watch. It was already past six and she'd promised Ty she'd help out at The Soup Kitchen again tonight.

"Thank you, Sandy. I enjoyed the tour. I'll see you tomorrow." Kylie waved good-bye to her new boss and headed back down the hall to the parking lot. Tonight was her last night helping out at the shelter until after she'd finished up with the royalties. She wished she could have refused Ty's plea to help out again, but she couldn't leave him in the lurch with so many other volunteers still out sick.

The interior of the Mustang was warm from sitting out in the mild sunshine. Kylie slid onto the soft white leather and looked up at the top floor of the Gamble Records building as she started the engine. She hadn't seen David at all today, which was just as well. After the scene in the kitchen yesterday, she was glad to have avoided him. He must think she was really pathetic to keep throwing herself at him.

She put the car in reverse and backed out of her parking space, her mind on her uncharacteristic behavior with David Gamble. Why was it every time he was near, she couldn't seem to stop flinging her arms around him and kissing him as if she were some sort of sex-starved groupie? It was impetuous, and not like her at all, she thought, pulling out into the heavy traffic on Queen Anne Avenue, barely missing being sideswiped by a monster-size SUV. The larger vehicle swerved into the center lane to avoid hitting her, and several drivers laid on their horns.

At the noise, fairly uncommon in ultra-polite Seattle, Kylie glanced in her rearview mirror.

"Hmm, I wonder what that's all about," she muttered absently to herself as she continued down the road on her way to the shelter.

CHAPTER 5

He was exhausted.

David sipped his second, and final, glass of single-malt Scotch, trying to ignore the pounding from both inside and outside his head.

He hated traveling—hated the inconvenience of it, the delays, the wasted time, the strange rental cars and even stranger people he sometimes met along the way—but it seemed that was all he'd been doing for the past two weeks. And now that he was on home ground, all he wanted to do was go to his quiet house and sit in his quiet study. Instead he was stuck doing his best to act polite at a promotional party for Gamble artists, where the drink was too plentiful, the people were too beautiful, and the music was too loud.

He sighed, cursing himself for being an ungrateful son of a bitch, but unable to control the way he felt nonetheless.

"David!"

He looked up at hearing someone call his name and saw Robyn Rogers bearing down on him with a man dressed all in black in tow. Something seemed familiar about the man, and as they drew closer, David realized why. It was the cowboy Kylie had been trying to escape from the night of his party.

"Tell him what you just told me," Robyn ordered, pushing the man in front of her.

"Uh, hello, Mr. Gamble. Bradley Nelson, at your service." Bradley held out a hand.

David shook the other man's hand, surprised that someone who was so willing to be dragged and pushed around had such a firm grip. "Nice to meet you," David responded automatically.

"Yes, yes, we're all buddies. Now, tell him, Bradley." Robyn tapped one gold-shod toe impatiently.

"Well, sir, I was just telling Miss Rogers here how much I was enjoying her new release, and that seemed to have gotten her panties in a twist, as it were."

David held back a chuckle when Robyn shot Bradley a chilling glare at his vernacular. If he'd known the other man better, he might've suspected the cowboy was trying to get under Robyn's skin.

"So, he's enjoying *Moonshine*, Robyn. I'm glad to hear that—"

"No, David, he's not enjoying *Moonshine*—" Robyn interrupted.

"But I did like that one, too," Bradley cut in, earning himself another icy glare.

"He's enjoying *Sunstruck*." Robyn's tapping toe clicked rhythmically on the floor in the ballroom of the Westin Hotel.

"What do you mean?" David asked, puzzled. "*Sunstruck* won't be released until the beginning of December."

"That's what I want to know," Robyn all but shouted. "As my record label, it's your duty to keep me informed of any changes in the schedule we set. We agreed that *Sunstruck* was to be released just in time for the Christmas shopping season and I want to know on whose authority that was changed. And when I find out, I'll have his head, I promise you that."

"Now, calm down, Robyn. I can assure you no one at Gamble Records would make that decision without consulting you," David said, hoping to calm the pint-size blond singer. Dealing with temperamental artists wasn't anything new to him, but his reassurance to Robyn didn't appear to be working. She continued tapping her foot in agitation. He turned to Bradley. "Where did you get *Sunstruck*?"

"I work at Bob's Records over in the U-district. I bought a copy as soon as I saw it on the shelf."

David frowned. How could a retail record store have a copy when *Sunstruck* wasn't even scheduled to be back from the pressing plant yet? It didn't make any sense.

"My manager will be in touch with you first thing tomorrow, David." Robyn stomped away, her chin tilted haughtily upward.

"Seems she's got a burr up her knickers," Bradley drawled.

"Yeah, and unfortunately, it looks like it's going to be up to me to get it out." David considered the other man over the rim of his tumbler. Most people would have been intimidated by Robyn's fury, but not this man. As he set his empty glass on a nearby table and went off in search of Gamble's head of A&R, David wondered which category Bradley fell into: very brave or very stupid.

Peter Laughlin was easy to spot in the crowd milling about the ballroom. At well over six feet tall, his blond head stood inches above most everyone else gathered near the front of the room, listening to the band. David made his way through the throng, his progress hampered by the partygoers who stopped him every few feet to say hello. When he was within arm's length of the head of A&R, David reached out and tapped Peter's shoulder to get his attention. Peter turned and David motioned for him to follow as he waded out of the noisy crowd.

"Did you move up the release of Robyn's new album?" David asked as soon as they were far enough away that he didn't have to shout to be heard. The last thing he needed was for a rumor of this fiasco to get around. Hopefully, he'd be able to solve the problem before it got out of control.

Peter's carefree look turned to one of surprise. "No, of course not. Why do you ask?"

"I was just told that at least one record store in town has it in stock. If it didn't come from us, that leaves only one other option."

David met Peter's gaze as the seriousness of the situation settled between them. Piracy was nothing new in the music business, and something that every label, major or independent, faced regularly. This wasn't the first time Gamble Records had to deal with it either, but it was the first time it had happened right under their noses. Typically, a music pirate would copy an artist's CDs and sell them in foreign countries, where the enforcement of laws against copyright infringement wasn't so stringent.

"I don't know where they got an original to make a copy from. The pressing plant hasn't filled our order yet, as far as I know." Peter's brows drew together as he puzzled over the situation. "They must have gotten a copy of Robyn's master somehow."

David rubbed a hand over his aching neck muscles. All he wanted to do was to go home and relax. He didn't need this problem right now, not with the BSS deal pending. If Mitchell Sharpe got wind of this, it would not bode well for David's plan to take over BSS's music division. But whether he wanted it or not, the problem had been dropped in his lap and he would have to fix it. The first thing they needed to do was figure out the extent of the damage.

"How could someone get their hands on the master? Don't we keep these things locked up?"

"Sure we do. We keep them in the demo room," Peter answered.

"Who has keys to that room?"

Peter shrugged his shoulders. "You, me, Sandy. Building maintenance, I assume. That's it."

Both Peter and Sandy had been granted stock options

for their work at Gamble Records. Besides the fact that they were stockholders who would have nothing to gain by sabotaging the company, David couldn't believe either one of them would have stolen Robyn's master. Peter had been with Gamble since its inception, and Sandy's career as a CFO would be over if she were involved in something like this.

"I'll have Deborah check out maintenance. What about the pressing plant? They obviously have a copy."

"Yeah, but we've been using the same firm for over ten years and nothing like this has ever happened. Their security is even tighter than ours."

David wearily rubbed his forehead, wishing that the throbbing in his skull would stop. "I'll give their management a call anyway, just so they're aware we have a problem."

"Are you planning to contact the police?"

"Yes, but you know they don't really have the time for stuff like this."

Peter nodded glumly. "Is there anything I can do?"

"No. Thanks, though." David glanced at his watch. "I've got to go. I need to schedule a meeting with Robyn and her manager to try to smooth some ruffled feathers."

"I don't envy you that job. That one can be a real bitch when she gets riled."

"Yeah," David muttered absently. It was too bad Robyn wasn't more like Kylie that way. Kylie didn't strike him as being the bitchy type. He couldn't imagine her being pouty and manipulative. He'd thought about her often in the almost two weeks since he'd been away; had even started to dial her number several times when he was sitting in his empty hotel room at night, but had decided it would be for the best if he just kept away from her. She was a Gamble employee now, and the last thing he needed was any hint of impropriety between himself and an employee. The press loved to take those sorts of things and blow them all out of proportion, and David had no intention of being the target of some sordid scandal. He carefully controlled the type of publicity that he and Gamble Records garnered, and wasn't about to be dragged into some tawdry sexual harassment story concocted by the media.

It was something he reminded himself of every time he thought about the way he'd responded to Kylie in the kitchen that day. He should have let her go when she walked away from him in Sandy's office, but he couldn't change what had happened in the past any more than he could explain why he had so uncharacteristically given in to his impulse to follow her. He could, however, control his behavior in the future, and he intended to stay as far away from Kylie Rogers as possible.

Kylie let out the breath she'd been holding as she saw the shiny black Jaguar leave the parking lot. It was after 5:00 P.M. and the lot was more than half empty, so it was easy to spot the sleek car as it slid smoothly out into the busy traffic along Queen Anne Avenue. At least, that was what Kylie told herself as she lowered her gaze from the window. After all, it wasn't as if she'd been watching for him.

Oh, no. And she hadn't been edgy all day either, knowing that he was finally back in the office after being gone since the day she'd flooded the kitchen. No, she'd gone about her business, thinking only of the royalties that were going to go out tomorrow, right on schedule. And not even one small part of her hoped he'd find out that she'd saved the day. It didn't matter if he was proud of her for accomplishing the monumental task of learning a new software program, figuring out how royalties were calculated in the music business, and making sure Gamble Records would get their checks out on time, saving them huge penalties and loads of aggravation from their artists.

Nope, none of that mattered at all.

Kylie closed her eyes briefly, slipping instantly into the daydream where David awarded her the coveted "Employee of the Year" award in front of all four hundred Gamble employees.

"As employee of the year, Kylie, you get one wish," Dream David said in the deep, sexy voice that had haunted her thoughts for weeks. He handed her a heavy gold statue in honor of her achievement.

She smiled as she accepted the award, which, oddly enough, was shaped like the many Oscars® her parents had sitting around their home in Beverly Hills.

Standing beside her on the stage, David clasped her hand in his and looked deep into her eyes. "What can I give you, Kylie?"

Kylie sighed dreamily as she reached up on her tiptoes to whisper into his ear. "Kiss me."

David picked her up by the waist, swinging her around easily, as if she were as light as a feather. In her daydream, she didn't drop the heavy gold figure on his foot as she undoubtedly would do in real life. "Yes, I'll—"

"So, Lover Boy's gone, huh?"

Dream David dropped her and the fantasy screeched to a halt as Kylie's eyes flew open. "Pardon me?" she asked, blinking quickly as she swiveled around in her chair to face Brenda Olson.

"Is this your cue to pack it in, too, or do you two have a later appointment?" Brenda leaned indolently against the doorway of Kylie's cubicle.

"I don't have the faintest idea what you're talking about." Kylie turned her attention back to the pile of papers on her desk. "Now, if you'll excuse me, I have a lot of work to do if the royalties are going to go out tomorrow."

"Sure, I understand. It wouldn't do to let people know you're boinking the big boss, now would it? They might think that's the only reason you got this job, eh?"

Kylie felt her cheeks turn bright red at Brenda's snide comment and cursed her body for betraying the anger and embarrassment she felt. Brenda's insinuation was too close to the truth. She hadn't been hired because she was sleeping with David, but she hadn't earned it on her own merit either.

Well, she told herself angrily, that wasn't any of Brenda's business. She was going to prove to everyone that she deserved to keep this job, no matter how she'd gotten it.

"I don't care what people think," Kylie lied, calling upon the haughtiest voice in her repertoire.

Her fingers moved furiously over the computer keys as Brenda left, chuckling. As she heard the other woman's retreating footsteps, Kylie wished she'd gone with her first impulse and bashed the other woman in the nose.

Brenda's snide comments faded away as Kylie reviewed each artist's royalties line by line. Chewing the end of her pen as she watched the numbers fly by, a thought occurred to her. Right in front of her, she had a list of musicians who were about to be paid fairly large sums of money. Wouldn't it be great if she could manage to get at least a few of them to donate some of their good fortune to the EmCee foundation? Their donations would go to help feed the homeless, buy appropriate interview attire for people trying to get on their feet, fund animal shelters across the nation so former pets wouldn't have to be put to sleep, and a thousand other things.

And all she had to do was run one little report. Just two lines of data for each musician. Name and phone number. That's it.

What would it hurt? After all, she wasn't going to sell the information to spammers or anything. She'd just use it to make one innocent call to each artist at a time when they happened to have a bit of cash on hand. Nothing wrong with that. As a matter of fact, it was almost her duty to do it. She could hardly fund the EmCee foundation all by herself, and there were so many worthy causes out there that needed their help.

In a froth of righteousness, Kylie switched to her report writer and created a report, sending it directly to the printer.

As soon as she heard the telltale whirring, she walked calmly to the LaserJet, looked up and down the hall to make sure no one was watching, picked the report up off the printer, and neatly folded it before stuffing it into the bottom of her purse.

Then she went back to work, checking her calculations for the third and final time.

Seattle is not one of those cities that never sleeps, David thought as he cruised up the deserted crest of Queen Anne Hill. He continued weaving his way westward, the address he was searching for etched in his brain. The top of Seattle's most famous landmark—the eminently recognizable Space Needle—rose behind him in his rearview mirror, then disappeared when he turned left.

The Jag's engine purred as he dodged around parked cars and the concrete rounders some long-forgotten city planner had seen fit to place at each intersection to slow down traffic in this part of the city. Many neighborhood residents took it upon themselves to plant flowers in the rounders, making them beautiful as well as functional.

His meeting with Robyn and her manager this afternoon had not gone well, and had lasted over three hours besides. Afterward, he'd had dinner at Palisade, his favorite waterfront restaurant, hoping the soothing sight of the gray waters of Elliott Bay and the city beyond would calm his nerves and settle his urge for the elusive something that continued to plague him.

Unfortunately, neither the view nor the excellent crab bisque did anything to improve his mood so, on impulse, he called information to ask if they had the address of a Kylie Rogers and was given this one on the west side of Queen Anne Hill. He'd decided that it couldn't hurt to drive by her house and see where she lived. He wasn't going to go in, or even knock on the door. He just wanted to see where she lived, that was all.

All of the lights were off when he stopped his car in

front of the two-story redbrick house whose address matched the one in his memory. The small front lawn was well-tended, with neatly trimmed rhododendrons running on both sides of the front porch and flower boxes filled with late-blooming plants under the windows.

He looked at the clock on the dashboard. It wasn't even ten o'clock yet. Surely she wasn't in bed this early? But what did it matter? He hadn't intended to speak to her anyway, he reminded himself. Although a cup of coffee would be nice. Yes, that and someone to talk to. Someone who didn't want anything from him. Someone who didn't want him to fix some problem, or loan her some money, or talk about business. David took a deep breath as Kylie's house remained steadfastly dark.

The electric window slid open silently as David pressed the button to let in some cool night air. He leaned back into the welcoming leather of the driver's seat, squeezed the pack of cigarettes he kept in his jacket pocket, and made a deal with himself. If the lights stayed out after ten minutes, he'd leave, but if he saw even a glimmer, he'd walk to the door, tell her he'd just been out driving in her neighborhood at ten o'clock at night, and decided to stop by.

It sounded pretty lame, even to his own ears.

David drummed his fingers on the steering wheel.

He could see the headline now: "Gamble Stalks Employee." And the interview with Kylie: "He just sits in front of my house, waiting. I'm afraid to turn on my lights."

This was foolishness. The last thing he needed right now was the possibility of bad press.

David turned the key in the ignition and edged out of his parking space and into the deserted street, the cool air from the open window bringing him back to his senses.

Ben Gamble watched the disappearing taillights of his brother's car with speculation. He stepped out of the protective shadow at the side of Kylie's house into the pale white moonlit night.

Earlier that day, he'd overheard two of the volunteers at The Soup Kitchen gossiping about Kylie and her famous family. His ears had perked up when they'd mentioned her last name and he'd blessed his luck at finding her address listed in the phone book.

He hadn't planned on going in, had really just wanted to take a peek around the neighborhood, check out the dog situation, and see what sort of valuables she might have left lying out in the open. When he'd found the back door unlocked, though, he just couldn't resist, knew he'd be able to be long gone by the time the police arrived if she'd left the security system on.

In the end, he needn't have worried. The creaking of the back door wasn't met with the screeching of an alarm, only the growling of a large black cat who was sitting near an empty supper dish in the kitchen as Ben entered.

"I wonder if she's got any booze in here," Ben muttered as he glanced around the tidy kitchen. A cursory check of the cupboards revealed only a few bottles of wine and an unopened bottle of Scotch. Ben grabbed the latter, twisting open the cap and taking a healthy swig before continuing his unguided tour of Kylie's house.

For a rich bitch, she didn't have a lot of money lying around, at least not where he could easily find it. He'd grabbed a towel from the kitchen and used that to cover his hand whenever he touched anything. Just in case he located something worth stealing, he wasn't going to be stupid enough to leave his fingerprints all over the place for the cops to find.

He'd done a quick once-over of the downstairs and looked longingly up to where her bedroom—and jewelry, no doubt—lay. He'd had one foot on the creaky bottom stair when he'd heard the crunch of gravel from the road at the front of the house. He moved with practiced haste back to the kitchen. The cat was sitting by the back door, watching him malevolently. When it hissed at him, Ben didn't think twice before planting a well-aimed kick into the animal's soft middle. He'd never liked cats, and he damn sure wasn't going to put up with this one spitting at him.

The cat lay still on the back steps and Ben stepped over it, closing the door silently behind him. Pulling his jacket together in front, he took another swallow of whiskey as he sidled cautiously around the side of the house.

The bottle almost slipped out of his surprised fingers when Ben saw his own brother sitting in his car in front of Kylie's house. David was looking toward the second story of the house, making Ben glad he hadn't risked going upstairs.

"What the hell's he doing here?" Ben muttered, pressing himself further into the shadows. He waited for David to do something—knock on the door, let himself in, anything—but he just sat in his car, staring at the darkened house.

Ben took another thoughtful pull on the bottle, pondering the possibilities of why his brother had shown up at this house on this night. Was David following him? How did he know about Kylie? Was it all just a coincidence?

Ben waited in the shadows for a full five minutes after David left before making his way to the alley at the back of the house, stumbling a little over the steeply sloped lawn.

"Guess we'll just have to wait and see what Big Brother's up to, won't we?" Ben mumbled to himself as he concentrated on picking his way down the darkened alley to the bus stop two blocks away.

She was going blind.

The figures on the computer screen blurred. Kylie blinked, then rubbed her tired eyes.

The deadline for the royalty payments was fast approaching, and she'd spent the last—she glanced at her watch—the last fifteen hours checking and rechecking her figures. After Brenda left, taking her snide attitude with her, Kylie had worked nonstop on the royalties, trying to make sure she had everything right.

Now, at half past one in the morning, she was almost through her last review of the numbers. Sandy had even spot-checked several accounts before she'd left seven hours ago and blessed her as a godsend when everything appeared to be right. But Kylie wanted to make sure. She didn't want to be off by even a penny.

She rubbed her eyes again.

"Come on," she told herself, "only two more hours to go. You can do it."

Coffee, I need coffee, her inner voice pleaded.

Kylie picked up her cup, hoping the walk to the kitchen would perk up her tired mind.

Like virtually every office building after six P.M., the deserted third floor was spooky. Kylie knew the Internet division on the second floor was probably still peopled with the strange techies who came in at noon and worked well into the wee hours of the night. Sandy had given her a tour of that floor, warning her that it wasn't unusual to get bopped in the head by a wildly thrown Nerf ball or hit by a rogue stream of water from a Super Soaker.

But the world of the techies was quite a bit different from the rest of the business world. Kylie poured herself a cup of dark brew from the new machines that had been installed the previous week and carried it back to her desk. Propping her head up on one hand, she leaned over the steaming mug and tried to absorb the caffeine through her eyelids as she closed her eyes for "just a second."

Two minutes later, Kylie awoke suddenly when her head slipped off her hand, threatening her with a nose-first plunge into her coffee.

"Ugh. You need to wake up," she said to her reflection in the window.

Then she spotted something else and jumped up from her chair. Yes, that was it. Kylie picked up the portable

tape player sitting on the back of her desk and clipped it
to the waistband of her skirt before heading downstairs. A
little rowdy music was just the thing to pep her up. And
what better place to get it from than the mountains of free
offerings downstairs in the demo storage room?

The first floor was deserted and Kylie could hear her
own hushed footsteps across the carpeted hallway. Sandy
had given her the keys to the demo room before she left
that evening, telling Kylie she might need access to the
previous quarter's royalty reports, which were stored there.
Kylie figured she'd be able to find something down there;
something rousing and peppy to yank her brain cells out of
sleepy mode. She unlocked the door, silently thanking
Sandy for letting her borrow the keys.

Kylie figured she'd never have to buy CDs again now
that she had access to all this. She propped the door open,
letting light spill into the darkened room from the hallway.
On previous forays to the demo room, she'd been unable
to locate a light switch and assumed that the lights had to
be turned on from a panel somewhere on the first floor.

The light from the hallway would be good enough for
now, Kylie assured herself, turning her back to the door to
search the nearest shelf for something to listen to.

"Well, well, well. Here's our friend, Bradley Nelson."
Her voice echoed across the room as she plucked a tape
from the rows of choices and popped it into her player.

She listened for a few seconds.

"This is really good," she said to herself, surprised.

All of a sudden, the light from the hallway seemed to
dim. Kylie whipped around just in time to see the storage
room door swing shut.

"Oh, dang," she yelped, reaching out to feel her way
blindly along the cold steel shelving.

She came to the end of the rack and turned toward the
door, keeping one hand on the wall and putting the other
out in front of her to avoid running face-first into anything.

The doorknob rattled in her hand but refused to budge.

Kylie thought of the key stuck in the other side of the lock and groaned. She must have left it in the locked position and now she'd be trapped in the cold, dark room until someone came to find her.

Kylie let out a disgusted breath, then slumped down against the door. She closed her eyes and crossed her legs at the ankles, thankful at least that the room was carpeted. The chill air made her shiver and Kylie wished she were wearing something warmer than the thin sweater and short skirt she'd chosen so many hours ago when she'd dressed for the day in her nice, warm house with her nice, warm cat.

Kylie's eyes popped open. Mr. Chips! She'd left him a little extra food, knowing she'd be working late, but he must be starving by now, wondering why she wasn't home to feed him his dinner. Her poor baby. He was probably lonely. And hungry. She should have gone home at lunch and fed him, should have made sure he had enough to eat before she'd left. She felt awful, but there was nothing she could do but wait for someone to find her tomorrow morning.

And convince herself that there was nothing creepy in the pitch-black room with her.

And tell herself she had only imagined the shadow she thought she had seen in the hallway a split second before the door had closed.

CHAPTER 6

He was running late.

David had overslept, missed the jangling of his alarm completely because he'd fallen asleep on the couch next to the piano instead of dragging himself upstairs to bed where he belonged.

Someone had taken his usual parking space near the front door, and David cursed himself again for being tardy. One of the privileges of being the first one in in the morning was getting the best parking spot. He cruised through the lot, looking for another space.

Peter had been after him for years to assign the best spaces to top management, but David hesitated to do so. It was bad enough that they had to separate people into offices versus cubicles, but he drew the line at offering all the perks to a handful of his employees. Everyone got stock options, three weeks of vacation, and no preferential treatment for parking spaces. And Gamble Records had been listed in the Top 100 companies to work for in *Washington CEO* magazine five years running. As he dashed across the parking lot and up the stairs to his office, David figured they must be doing something right.

"Good morning, Deborah. Sorry I'm late."

David could see the question in his assistant's eyes. He'd

never been late. Not once in the entire three years she'd worked for him. He knew she was dying of curiosity and added another chunk of change to her raise when she didn't ask what had kept him.

"Good morning, David. I rescheduled your eight o'clock conference call for nine. Oh, and Sandy wanted to talk to you. She's waiting in your office."

"Thanks, Deb. You're an angel." David grinned, impressed at the efficiency with which she handled his life, and left her staring after him as he entered his office.

"Good morning, Sandy," he greeted, popping his briefcase open on his desk and unloading the papers he'd brought home last night but hadn't worked on. He'd had good intentions, but after his brief bout with insanity in front of Kylie's house, he hadn't felt like working. Instead, it was as if his piano were singing a siren's song. *Come play me*, she'd crooned. *I'm lonely and sad.*

For the first time in a very long time, David had felt the urge to put the tunes he played to paper, to add words to the notes he wrote. So he'd given in to it, had grabbed a pencil and a blank sheet of lined staff paper and tinkered with the melody that had been running through his head for weeks now, trying to get it just right. He'd fallen asleep on the couch long past midnight.

It had felt like the old days, when he'd been part of the music. He hadn't realized how much he'd missed it, how good it felt to put a tune to emotions again. So, he'd missed the alarm but had woken up feeling different . . . better. He didn't even want to put words to how he felt, he just planned to enjoy it while it lasted.

"Good morning, David," Sandy answered, jerking him away from thoughts of his music and back to his office.

He blinked. The CFO shifted in her chair, her hands clasped tightly in her lap. She was obviously nervous about something.

David braced himself for the bad news about the royalties. He knew Sandy was hopeful that Kylie was the answer to her prayers, that she'd be able to learn enough about the music business and a new computer program in less than two weeks. But he'd had his doubts, even though Sandy seemed confident it was going to work out. He guessed that she'd come to tell him she wasn't feeling quite so confident anymore.

"How are the royalties coming along?" he asked.

"Uh . . . that's what I'm here about."

"Oh?" David tried to contain his disappointment. It wouldn't devastate Gamble Records to pay late penalties to their artists, but he could do without the bad publicity that would inevitably come with their failure to get the royalties out on time. He only hoped it wouldn't make a difference in the BSS deal. Mitchell Sharpe had assured him a few days ago that everything was on track, and David didn't think this would throw a wrench in the works. After all, it was a fairly minor setback overall. The late penalties weren't large enough to—

Sandy's voice interrupted his pondering of the BSS deal. "The royalties were all finished yesterday. Kylie was going to go over them one last time when I left last night. But . . ." Sandy's voice trailed off as she fidgeted in her seat.

"But what?" David prompted.

"But Kylie's missing."

"What do you mean, 'missing'?"

"I mean, her computer's on, her purse is at her desk and so is her jacket, but she's nowhere to be found. I, uh, well, after what happened her first day, I, uh . . ." Sandy blushed and looked out the window.

"You what?" David asked.

Sandy's eyes met his, then slid away.

"You thought I might know where she is?"

"Yes."

David stood up, unconsciously tapping his dark blue Waterman pen against the edge of his desk. She hadn't been home last night and now she was missing. "Maybe she just ran an errand without telling anyone?"

Sandy was already shaking her head. "Her car was in the parking lot all night. There was dew on the windshield this morning when I got in. The coffee on her desk is cold and all the pots in the kitchen must have been from last night, because they were cold, too."

"All right. Let's start looking for her here. She wouldn't have left the building without a coat or her purse, so chances are that she probably just curled up somewhere late last night and is still asleep."

"Good idea. I'll get Brenda to help me search the third floor."

"Let's try to keep this low-key. Kylie will be embarrassed enough without having the whole building knowing about this."

Sandy left, and David shook his head. It seemed that Robyn was right. "Disaster" really was Kylie's middle name.

"Any sign of her?" David asked the small search party assembled on the second floor landing.

A trio of shaking heads answered.

"She's got to be down on the first floor, then. Sandy, you and Brenda take the recording studios. Deborah, I'll take the rooms from Production south if you'll get the rest."

"Sure thing, boss," Deborah agreed as they clattered down the stairs and headed across the hallway.

"I'm sure she's—" David stopped so abruptly in the middle of the hall that Deborah almost ran into his back.

"What's wrong?" Sandy asked.

David looked at the key sticking out of the storage room door, guessing they were about to solve the mystery of the missing employee. He turned the key and pulled open the door and should have been surprised when Kylie tumbled out at his feet, but for some reason he wasn't. Curls of brown hair fanned out on the carpet and she smiled, looking as comfortable as if she were sleeping on a down-filled mattress.

Kylie blinked, opening her eyes against the sudden light and gazing up into the face of David Gamble. She smiled, thinking this was a nice dream, and started to close her eyes again.

"Hey, there, Sleeping Beauty. It's time to get up." David crouched down beside her and pulled her into a sitting position.

Kylie's cramped leg muscles screamed in protest and her eyes flew open.

This was definitely not a dream. The strong, warm hands on her arms were very real, as was the laughter coming from behind him and the hot blush spreading like fire across her cheeks.

She had done it again—made a fool of herself once more, without even trying.

She didn't sigh, although she really wanted to. She didn't even state the obvious, that she'd somehow managed to lock herself in the demo room all night.

Instead, she smoothed her skirt, straightened her sweater, shook out her hair, and held out a hand for David to help her up.

"Good morning," she said to the small crowd.

"I was so worried," Sandy exclaimed.

"No need to worry. Just a small mishap," Kylie said, squaring her shoulders against the misery of embarrassment. "I was almost finished with my final check of the royalties when I came down to find some music to listen to. I was getting sleepy and thought it might help wake me up."

"You've already checked the numbers over twice, Kylie. I'm sure they're fine." Sandy dismissed her concern with a shrug. "It was you I was worried about. I thought you'd been kidnapped when I saw your computer on and your things here with no sign of you."

Kidnapped, Kylie thought wistfully, wishing that was what had really happened. At least then it wouldn't have been a disaster of her own doing. "Thank you for your concern, but I'm fine. Just a little tired, and sore from leaning up against the door all night."

She started down the hall with a limp, trying to put an end to this ordeal as soon as possible. "I'll just finish up my final check of the royalties. Then if you don't mind, I need to go home and feed my cat and get cleaned up . . ." She trailed off as David put a hand on her arm, stopping her progress.

"Sandy, didn't you say you'd done a review of Kylie's work last night before you left?" he asked.

"Yes, and everything looked right to me."

"Then I'd say you deserve to take the day off."

"But—" Kylie started to protest.

"Go on. Go up and get your things and be off," David ordered, shooing her up the stairs.

Kylie knew when she was beaten. It was obvious that David wanted her to go, and no wonder. She couldn't do anything without somehow screwing it up. Her shoulders sagged with misery as she shut down her computer and shrugged into her coat.

"I'll be at home if you need me," she offered to Sandy as she passed.

"See you Monday," Sandy answered with a friendly wave.

"I guess it pays to suck up to Mr. Gamble. And I mean that in the most literal sense."

Kylie halted as the comment hit between her shoulder blades. She took a deep breath, willing herself to ignore Brenda and her cattiness. David hadn't given her the day off because of—well, because of anything personal, she tried to convince herself as she trudged down the stairs. He was probably just trying to make sure she didn't mess up anything else. Tossing her purse into her chilly car, she started the engine.

After all, he hadn't so much as given her the time of day in almost two weeks, not since the day he'd realized she was Robyn's sister. Even then, he'd only felt sorry for her. Poor, pitiful Kylie Rogers, who couldn't compare with her beautiful and talented sister. She sniffed. She should tell the nasty Brenda what David thought of her. To him, she was probably just a poor substitute for her sister. One thing was certain, he wasn't attracted to Kylie, no matter what Brenda kept insinuating.

Well, so what? she asked herself. She'd never asked him to kiss her. Kylie pounded the white leather of her steering wheel with one fist. And she hadn't asked him for any favors either, hadn't begged him for a job or even asked for the day off, even though she was exhausted and it was a very nice gesture.

Her hand throbbed where she'd hit it against the car.

Dang. She'd let Brenda get to her.

Kylie unrolled the window of her car, letting in the chill October air as she shook her head with disgust.

"I'm going to go home, feed Mr. Chips, take a long hot bath, climb into bed, and forget about anyone else but myself for a while," she vowed, turning up the volume on her stereo to chase away any more thoughts of David or her obnoxious coworker as she cruised toward home.

"Mrs. Gamble, you don't have an appointment," Deborah protested as the woman pushed past her and into David's office.

David leaned back in his chair and continued to listen to his phone call as his mother entered.

She looked like a giant lime today, dressed from head to toe in clingy green spandex. The earrings were tropical again. Lemons, limes, cherries, and bananas all banging together in a gaudy fruit salad at her ears.

"Look, Clint, I've got to go. Come by the house tomorrow and we'll get this taken care of, all right?"

David held up his hand for silence as his mother opened her mouth. She could damn well wait till he was finished with this call to tell him whatever it was that was so urgent she'd seen fit to barge in on him for the second time in a month.

"Yes, seven o'clock will be fine, Clint. I'll see you tomorrow night."

Pam Gamble took the decisive click of the phone as her cue to start yammering. "David, I—"

"Shut the door please, Mother. Thanks for trying, Deborah," he added to his hovering assistant, wondering if he should add hazard pay to her salary as well.

After closing the door, Pam turned on him, a satisfied gleam in her eye. David thought about telling her he could have security get rid of her any time he wanted, that he could instruct them to refuse to let her in the building at all. But he didn't—didn't tell her or ban her for reasons he'd rather not explore at present.

"What is it?" He began their conversation in his usual manner.

She plopped down on the oatmeal-colored couch under the window, her chartreuse sandals barely touching the floor. "David, your brother is living like a homeless person and I just can't bear it." She sniffed melodramatically.

Opening his bottom desk drawer, David pulled out a box of Kleenex and tossed it across the room. She jumped as the tissues came to rest against one spandex-clad thigh. David watched her speculatively as she wiped her eyes, unable to tell if she were truly concerned about her youngest child or if she wanted something else from David and was using Ben to play on his sympathies.

"I've told you, Mother, Ben's not my problem anymore. I've done everything I can or will do to help him. He doesn't want my help, or yours either. He just wants money so he can get drunk or high."

"But he's homeless," Pam wailed.

David tried not to wince at the words. He didn't like it any more than she did that Ben chose to live on the streets, but he'd done his part to help his little brother grow up, and it hadn't worked. "That's his choice, not mine."

"But, David—"

"No. I refuse to have this conversation again. Ben knows that all he has to do is ask and I'd pay for him to go to the best treatment center in the country. I'd do whatever I could to help him, but I am not going to make it easy for him to continue his destructive behavior. Now, is there anything else?"

Pam wiped her eyes with pale green–tipped nails, and David held back a sigh at her appearance. Why couldn't she tone it down a bit?

He shook his head at the futility of his thoughts. It wasn't as if his mother was going to wake up one day and have been blessed by the good taste fairy overnight. He could remember years of his childhood when he'd wished she'd look in the mirror and realize that she wasn't like the other mothers he knew. She wore too much makeup, talked too loudly, her clothes were too bright and at least one size too small. And she'd always drunk too much.

Well, not always, David revised silently. Not before Dad had died right after Ben had been born. She'd still been too bright and too loud, but, before that, she'd always made sure they had food to eat and clean clothes to wear. Ben wouldn't remember that, of course, but David had been ten years old when his father died, and he remembered.

He remembered a lot of things, things that were pressed into his memory like the grooves of an old vinyl record.

David heard his mother talking but didn't comprehend the words at first. He pulled his thoughts away from the unpleasant past and back to the unpleasant present.

"What did you say, Mother?"

"I said Alan asked me to marry him. And I've said yes."

Her look was defiant, as if he were the parent and she the child. As if she expected him to refuse to allow her to marry again. As if he cared.

"That's . . ." David searched his mind for the appropriate word. Wonderful? No, too sappy. Great? Too enthusiastic. He liked Alan well enough, wondered what the hell the other man saw in his mother, but liked him nonetheless. "That's . . . nice. I'm sure you'll be very happy."

"Oh, I'm so glad to hear you say that, David. Listen, I was wondering if you'd give me away."

David blinked and twisted the upper half of his pen. Open. Closed. Open. "Uh, sure. Just make an appointment with Deborah on the way out, will you?" He rose, hoping she'd take the hint, then almost sat back down as she launched her significantly sized self at him. The box of tissues hit him squarely in the spine as she wrapped her arms around him in a weepy hug.

"If it weren't for this thing with your brother, I'd be the happiest woman in the world right now." She sniffled.

David hoped she wasn't using his shirt for a Kleenex as he patted her awkwardly on the back. After what seemed like an eternity, she released him and left, taking his box of tissues with her.

He surveyed the damage, noting thankfully that all he'd suffered was some wrinkling. A glance at the clock showed it wasn't even ten o'clock. The morning was dragging by.

All of a sudden, he didn't want to be cooped up in his office anymore.

He grabbed his car keys out of his desk drawer.

How long had it been since he'd played hooky?

Had he ever played hooky?

He'd been working so hard for so long that he wasn't sure he'd even know what to do in the middle of a workday besides work. No time like the present to find out, he supposed.

"I'm taking the day off, Deborah," he said, breezing by his stunned assistant, leaving her sputtering in his wake.

"Hold on, baby. Mommy's going to get you to the doctor. Everything's going to be all right," Kylie soothed frantically, laying the still body of her cat onto a fluffy towel on the passenger seat. Racing around to the other side of the car, she tried to ignore the worry clawing at her insides.

All she'd wanted to do when she got home was to kick off her shoes and take a long hot soak in the tub. Right after feeding her poor kitty, that is. Only she hadn't been able to find him. Not even the surefire method of shaking his food dish made him come out.

That was when she really started to worry. Had he gotten tangled up in a cord? Fallen down the stairs? Was he sick? Or just hiding because he was mad at her for not coming home last night?

Other people might laugh at her desperate concern for a mere animal, but he'd been Kylie's baby for over ten years and she loved him. He was her responsibility and she'd never forget how awful she'd felt when she'd heard his soft meow as she called his name; how scared she was when she saw him lying on the back stairs.

"Just hold on, Mr. Chips. We'll be there in five minutes."

Tears threatened to blind her as she shoved the car into gear and hit the accelerator.

Then hit the brakes, watching in slow motion as a tall, dark-haired man rolled over her hood with a series of loud thumps.

The face looking at her through the windshield was stunned.

"Oh, no. Oh, no. No, no, no," Kylie chanted as she flung open her door. "David? Are you all right?"

He wasn't sure, having never been hit by a moving vehicle before.

Peeling his face off the cold glass, David flexed his jaw and made a quick mental inventory. Arms okay, ribs okay, left leg definitely bruised but not broken.

"I'm okay."

"Then get in the car." She tugged his arm frantically.

Without really knowing how he'd gotten there, David found himself in the backseat of her Mustang, all buckled up as they raced through the streets of Seattle.

"Um, where are we going?" he finally thought to ask.

"Vet," came her clipped reply, as she flipped on her right turn signal.

"But I'm okay," David protested.

"Not for you. For the cat." She gestured toward a large ball of black-and-white fur lying in the passenger seat.

"Oh, yes, of course," David said, relieved that she wasn't taking him to be treated by a doctor whose usual patients were named Rover and Scamp.

The car had barely rolled to a stop in the parking lot when Kylie leaped out. In contrast to her wild movements, she picked up the bundle on the seat as if it were a vial of nitroglycerin ready to explode at the slightest movement. David closed and locked the car doors when Kylie would have left them all standing open as she hurried into the veterinarian's office.

"Hi, Kylie. What's wrong with Mr. Chips?" he heard the receptionist ask.

"I don't know, Marci. I found him like this. I don't know what happened. Please, you've got to help him," she pleaded, setting the bundle down gently on the counter.

The cat stayed motionless, his labored breathing clearly audible in the quiet waiting room.

"Come on back, I'll get the doctor."

Kylie turned to David, her face drained of color except for the faint purplish bruises of worry and fatigue under her tear-soaked eyes.

"Please, come with me?" She held out a hand to him.

David took her small, ice-cold hand in his, giving her courage and strength and receiving gratitude in return.

She watched the royalty checks spit out of the printer, doing her best to contain her elation. A clerk matched the check to the appropriate statement, neatly folded the two together, and stuffed both into an envelope.

Her smile widened as the pile of envelopes grew.

Forcing herself to walk away was difficult, but she knew she had to do it. She couldn't risk suspicion at this stage of the game, not when things were progressing so very nicely. No, the time for celebrating would be soon, but until then she needed to keep her wits about her and stay out of the limelight.

She closed the door to her office and sat down, watching as a light rain began to fall from the gray clouds outside.

CHAPTER 7

The cool air on the backs of her thighs jolted Kylie awake.

She would have tried gathering up her skirt, but with her arms pinned against David's chest, she figured the attempt would be futile. She must have fallen asleep in the car on the drive from the vet. She couldn't imagine why David had picked her up out of the passenger seat, rather than simply waking her up, but decided to enjoy it while it lasted.

After all, when was the last time someone had carried her? Probably over twenty years ago, when her father would bring her in from the car after a late night at the theater. Ignoring the draft, she snuggled closer, reveling in the sensation of being coddled. It wasn't as if she were model-thin or even petite like Robyn. She was a regular-sized person and only in her dreams did some handsome man sweep her off her feet. Of course, in those dreams there was usually something about a white horse and silk sheets and, oddly, a washing machine. But who knew what that meant, anyway?

"What are we doing here?" she murmured against David's soft blue shirt. Rather than taking her back to her house, David had driven to his house on the shore of Lake Washington. Kylie opened her eyes a crack. As always, she

was astonished by all the green around her. The abundance
of rain and year-round mild temperatures combined to produce a climate that plants appeared to love. David was
shielded from his neighbors by an interesting mixture of
trees and shrubs. In the few months she'd lived in Seattle,
Kylie had become familiar with some of their names—in
large part because the residents of the state seemed so fascinated with their plant life. There were cedars and maples
in addition to the ubiquitous pines, rhodies, and azalea
bushes, and a thousand others whose names Kylie had yet
to learn, that bloomed in the spring. Closing her eyes again,
she conceded that this was, indeed, a beautiful place to live.

"I thought you'd be able to relax better here. I left this
number with the vet, so stop worrying," David answered
her earlier question, then nudged her head back down as
she started to protest.

"I hate that I can't visit him."

"I know, but you heard what the doctor said. Cats don't
have any sense of time so if you go see him and then leave
again, he won't understand why you've left him there.
You'll be able to pick him up on Sunday."

She heard the smile in his voice and fought the urge to
wrap her arms around his sturdy chest. He had been so
sweet, holding her hand while the doctor explained that Mr.
Chips had a broken rib. He'd comforted her as she'd cried
when the vet said he needed surgery and hugged her when
the cat had pulled through just fine.

She could have coped without him, of course. But as
she inhaled the spicy scent of him, felt his strong arms
around her as he carried her into the house, she was glad
he had been there.

"Bath first?" He raised an eyebrow questioningly.

Kylie laughed. "Is that a hint?" She knew she looked a
mess. She was still wearing the clothes she'd put on yesterday morning, the ones she'd slept in last night and hadn't
changed this morning before setting off on her search for
Mr. Chips.

David thought she looked cute. Disheveled. Her curly hair tousled, pantyhose snagged from where she must have entangled herself in some shrubbery, sweater wrinkled. Although she hadn't seemed to notice, she also wasn't wearing any shoes. He hadn't seen any in her car so he assumed she'd taken them off before realizing the cat was missing and then simply forgotten all about it when she'd found her injured pet.

He hadn't seen a purse either, wondered if she even knew she'd raced off without it. He'd called Deborah earlier, when Kylie had been talking to the vet, and asked her to go by Kylie's house and make sure things were locked up, certain that she'd left at least one door wide open in her haste to get to the doctor.

Hell, knowing her, she'd probably left all the doors open with a note asking the last burglar to leave to turn off all the lights.

"You can put me down now. I'm awake."

David looked down into her sherry-brown eyes. Yes, she was awake. And he was hard, and surprised that the slightest bit of physical contact with her had the power to arouse him—and even more surprised at how much he was enjoying it.

He let her slide down onto the silky, brightly colored Oriental rug, keeping an arm across her shoulders.

"Come on, I'll show you to the bathroom. You can take a bath while I fix us some lunch. I haven't had anything to eat all day and I'll bet you haven't either."

"That sounds wonderful," Kylie agreed, vainly attempting to straighten out her rumpled clothes as David pulled her up the stairs.

Her stocking-clad feet slipped on the polished hardwood floor, and Kylie realized that she wasn't wearing any shoes. *Wonderful,* she thought, *here I am with a man who's been seen with some of the most glamorous women in the world, and I'm rumpled, wrinkled, ripped, and barefoot!* It was obvious he was just taking pity on her because she was

Robyn's sister. She wondered if she'd be here if her last name really had been McGillicuddy, if she was an ordinary person with no famous relatives.

Then she shrugged. Did it really matter? She was glad she was here, glad that she was following David up the stairs in his house, and, for once, happy that she'd been on the winning end of her family connections. It was about time something good came of them.

She followed David through an obviously masculine bedroom, getting a brief impression of a king-sized bed covered with a dark blue bedspread before he led her through another doorway into a large bathroom.

"Let me just get you some towels." David dropped his arm from around her shoulders and she instantly missed the warmth of his touch.

"I've been assured that no one can see in from outside." He gestured at the floor-to-ceiling windows affording a view of the gray waters of the lake. "But I must admit I've never tested it myself."

"I guess now's your chance," Kylie said, without thinking.

David laughed and set two huge white towels on the ledge of the whirlpool tub. "I promise to resist the temptation."

Kylie silently cursed herself. Of course he wouldn't want to try to catch her naked. What an idiot she was to even suggest such a thing. She shook her head with disgust as the door closed behind him with a decisive click.

She unbuttoned her blouse and let her skirt drop in a puddle on the floor, and was surprised to find that this room was unlike the ones downstairs. Instead of being stark, this room looked warm; the reddish-brown marble on the floor and countertop contrasted with the bright white cabinets and walls. There were several plants scattered about the room, healthy and lush from the abundance of light afforded by the windows as well as the bank of skylights overhead.

Kylie stripped off her ruined pantyhose, expecting to find the marble floor cold underfoot. Instead, the smooth stone seemed to have absorbed her body heat and felt warm under her bare feet. She tossed her bra and panties onto the growing pile of clothes on the floor. Leaning over, and turning on the faucets, she adjusted the temperature of the water flowing into the tub.

"Kylie?" The knock on the door had her scrambling for a towel.

"Yes?" She poked her head out the door, holding the towel together at her chest with one hand.

"I thought you might want some clean clothes to wear after you're done." David held out a pile of garments.

"Oh, I don't know. I'm becoming rather fond of this towel."

David laughed. "The color suits you, but you might get tired of holding it up after a while. Although, come to think of it, that could work to my advantage." He raised his eyebrows suggestively.

Reaching out for the pile of clothes, she smiled, enjoying this flirtation. David's eyes sparkled with good humor as he teased her, and Kylie thought this was as close to heaven as she might ever get.

He pulled the clothes back out of her reach, pretending to reconsider. "No, no, let me think about this for a minute."

"I refuse to eat lunch with you wearing only a towel."

David leaned against the door frame, his midnight blue eyes darkening. Kylie felt her knees go weak and her mouth go dry and wondered at what point she had become a cliché. She'd read romance novels where the heroine's legs turned to rubber at a glance from the hero, but she'd never believed it really happened that way in real life. At least, it had never happened to her. That is, not until about five seconds ago.

David reached out and pushed a lock of hair behind her ear, his warm fingers gently caressing her cheek.

"So don't wear the towel," he suggested, his voice low and husky.

Kylie's breath left her lungs. Her tongue licked suddenly dry lips as she stood in the sunlight, absolutely mesmerized by the sight of him standing so close, looking at her with desire in his dark eyes.

Rationally, she knew she couldn't be in love with him. After all, they'd hardly known each other for more than a couple of weeks. Perhaps she was just using the possibility of being in love to justify the instantaneous and irresistible rush of attraction she had felt for him from the very first second she had looked into his eyes. She'd never been one to rush into affairs, had always preferred being alone to being with someone she felt little or nothing for. But David was different. She wanted him as she'd never wanted anyone else in her life. There was something in the depths of his eyes that called to her, drew her in like a child lured into a candy store by its sweet smells. So maybe this wasn't love, but it was certainly something she'd never felt before. And obviously he felt something, too. Something more than pity. Something more than just a desire to be nice to her because she was Robyn's sister. She might not be as experienced as some people, but even she could see that the light burning in his eyes wasn't anything resembling pity.

It felt like she was about to take the biggest chance of her life.

She took a deep breath and let the towel slip out of her nerveless fingers.

David's eyes widened with surprise. He'd expected her to respond to his suggestion with something light, teasing. He should have known better; should have expected the unexpected.

She was beautiful, standing before him wearing nothing but a blush on her creamy white skin. A strange thought suddenly struck him. It had been a long time since he'd done this without candlelight and wine, without the usual props to rely on—or hide behind, depending on how you looked at it.

He swallowed. "Uh, would you like some wine?"

"No. No, thank you," Kylie stammered, starting to bend down to pick up the towel.

David's hand on her arm stopped her. "I'm sorry, I'm just a little nervous," he admitted.

She looked at him incredulously. "*You're* nervous? I'm the one who's naked here."

David pushed a hand through his hair. "Hell, yes, I'm nervous. It's not every day that a beautiful woman drops all her clothes in front of me."

"It's not every day that I do this either."

Kylie's blush was spreading rapidly from her cheeks down the smooth line of her neck, and David cursed himself for making her uncomfortable. He knew he was acting like an uninitiated teenager, as if she were the first naked woman he'd ever seen.

Get a hold of yourself, he ordered, taking a deep breath. He took a step toward her, closing the gap between her body and his.

"Let's try this again," he murmured, lowering his lips to hers.

Her mouth was soft under his, her lips parted and ready for him. No games here. No pretense of resistance. Just pure, honest passion as she pressed her body to his.

The sound of rushing water filled his ears as he raised his head from hers. Their eyes met.

"The bath," Kylie shrieked, racing to the near-to-overflowing tub to turn off the water.

David was right behind her when she turned around. He yanked his shirt over his head, tossing it onto the floor. His hands were at the snap of his jeans when Kylie's touch stopped him.

"Let me," she whispered, sliding the zipper down slowly as she followed the dark line of hair on his abdomen with her mouth.

David groaned.

Kylie delighted in the feel of him, the coarse dark hair under her lips, the hard muscles under her fingertips.

She slid his jeans down inch by inch, marveling that he was already fully aroused.

"Enough," he growled when she reached down to caress him.

Kylie laughed as he picked her up and stepped into the tub. Water splashed over the side and onto the marble floor as he lowered them both into the steamy water.

She pushed him back against the side of the tub and straddled his lap, reveling in the feel of his erection between her legs. It made her feel sexy, beautiful even, knowing that she had done this to him.

Linking her hands behind his neck, she bent down to taste his mouth, while his hands explored her body. Her breasts ached with a painful pleasure as she rubbed herself against the crisp hair on his chest. Eyes closed, her head tipped back when his fingers found the sensitive skin of her nipples.

"Mmmm," she purred as his mouth replaced his seeking fingers, her body unconsciously moving to the rhythm of his tongue. She couldn't wait, wanted to feel him inside her, to feel her body stretch to accept him.

David groaned as she impaled herself on him. He'd wanted to wait, wanted to give her pleasure first. But now, with her tightness wrapped around him, he couldn't think, couldn't stop.

She slid up his length, her tongue mating with his.

Then back down, replacing the hot water with her own heat.

David's mind shut down, sensation taking control. He reversed their positions, pushing her back against the tub; water pounded over the rim with the force of his thrusts.

He couldn't get enough of her. He slid his tongue over her neck, nipped at her ear.

"Yes, David," she moaned softly into his ear, sending him over the edge.

"I love you," he groaned, out of control with the force of his orgasm.

Kylie stiffened. What had he said?

He slumped against her, his dark hair falling forward onto her neck, his shoulders heaving with the effort to come back down to earth.

Struggling with the urge to push him away, Kylie calmed her own labored breathing.

He'd said he loved her. In the heat of passion, he'd said something that couldn't possibly be true. He undoubtedly said that to every woman he . . . he screwed, she thought, wrinkling her nose with distaste. That was all she meant to him, just another willing body to use for his own pleasure. She had fallen for his line about being nervous, about thinking she was beautiful, when all the time she was just like every other woman in his life; every other woman he probably said those words to in the heat of the moment, thinking that's what she'd want to hear.

How could she mean anything more when all she'd done was throw herself at him since the day they'd met? She was disgusted with herself. Men did not tell women they respected that they loved them before they'd even had a proper date. She'd never considered herself easy before, but his easy words of love certainly told her that's how he thought of her. She blinked back tears as David's breathing slowed against her chest. She had to get out of here, get away from him.

David stared unseeingly out the window.

He'd told her he loved her. He'd never said that to anyone. Not in the throes of passion, or even out of it. What in the world had happened to him?

He'd lost control, that's what had happened.

And, to top it all off, he'd told Kylie he loved her.

He was a miserable son of a bitch.

Wishing he didn't have to face her, knowing how awkward it was going to be, he raised his head and met her gaze remorsefully. The look in her eyes made him feel even worse.

"I'm sorry about that, Kylie. I . . . uh . . ." He didn't know what to say.

"It's fine," she interrupted. "Don't worry about it. But if you don't mind, could you go? I'd like to take a shower."

She wouldn't meet his eyes. Of course she would be disgusted with him. How was she to know he didn't always act this way? David knew he probably couldn't be considered the world's greatest lover, but he also wasn't the worst. None of the women he'd been with had ever complained, except when he insisted they leave after it was over.

David sighed, rolling off her.

I'll make it up to you, he promised silently as he grabbed a towel and wrapped it around his waist. He paused at the door, wanting nothing more than to get back on even footing. Being around Kylie made him feel slightly off balance, as if the world had tipped a few degrees off its axis.

"Come down to the kitchen when you're done and I'll make you something to eat," he said, hoping she'd accept his peace offering.

Without waiting for a response he left, leaving Kylie alone with her misery.

The second-to-last stair creaked loudly when Kylie put her foot on it. She froze, waiting to see if David noticed the sound.

When no one emerged from the kitchen, she continued to creep down the stairs and into the hallway that had led her to his office the night of his party. She'd have left through the front door, but it was in full sight of the kitchen and she wasn't going to risk getting caught. All she wanted to do was get away without having to confront David again.

She'd managed to stop crying during the hasty shower she'd taken, had even maintained her composure when she'd slipped on the borrowed shirt that smelled so much like him that all she wanted to do was curl up into a ball and hug it to her chest. Instead she'd put it on, along with the navy blue sweat pants that were threatening to fall down around her ankles at any moment and the thick white socks that had been neatly folded on top of the pile. Then she'd crept down the stairs, intent on escape.

His office looked the same as it had before. She longed to linger this time, to look at the framed photos hanging on the wall, to see what books held the favored place on his bookshelves. But what did it matter? She'd botched her one chance to be anything more to him than just an employee, had acted like some cheap—

Oh, what was the use? She interrupted her self-pitying rant. *Every time you act impulsively you end up regretting it*, she admonished herself.

"Get used to it already," she muttered crossly, shoving the ottoman under the window.

The afternoon had warmed up considerably and the air that hit her when she slid open the window was pleasantly warm against her face. Popping out the screen, Kylie put her hands on the sill and prepared to haul herself up and out of the house.

"I can see I'm going to have to put padlocks on all my windows."

Kylie whirled around, catching a split-second glance of David leaning casually against the doorjamb before she lost her balance.

He was across the room in two quick strides, catching her before she crashed into his bookcase.

"I do have a front door, you know." He set her feet down on the soft carpet, but didn't let her go.

"I know that," she muttered to his chest.

David tightened his hold on her and smiled at the mutinous expression on Kylie's face. Having had some time to reassess the situation, he had decided he was acting like a first-rate jerk. Reaching up with one hand, he captured a soft brown curl between his fingers.

Kylie would surely think he told every woman he slept with that he loved them. She'd never know she was the only one, so he didn't need to worry on that score. As for not giving her the same pleasure she'd given him, well, that was something he could fix, given the right opportunity. He vowed to rectify the situation at the earliest opportunity, but that opportunity wouldn't come if he let her sneak out the window as she obviously intended.

He wasn't going to let her go. At least, not yet. He'd already decided the press wouldn't be a problem. Even if they did find out about them, it wasn't as if she were an underpaid clerk and he the all-powerful boss. She came from a wealthy family and no one would ever be able to say she'd had to accept his advances or starve on the streets. With that obstacle out of the way, he'd decided they could at least spend some time together. He enjoyed Kylie's company. She made him feel relaxed, at peace, and he didn't want her to go.

He rested his chin on the top of her head for a moment, wondering how to convince her to stay. Her hair smelled like a spring breeze, fresh and clean.

Lifting her chin with his hand, he met her gaze with a wry smile and tried for a lighthearted approach.

"What, then? Was I boring you like that Bradley fellow, but you didn't want to tell me?"

"No, I . . . uh . . ." She was trapped. She couldn't tell him how she really felt, that she was disappointed with him for pulling the old wham-bam-thank-you-ma'am routine on her, but couldn't think of a plausible lie either.

David laughed, enjoying the fact that he had her off balance, enjoying being a bit off balance himself for once. "Forget it. Come on, the least I can do is feed you. How about grilled cheese? Or turkey? I have turkey."

Pushing her in front of him, David reeled off the culinary possibilities, resisting the urge to stop in the middle of the hallway and take her in his arms again.

He wanted her again, but wasn't ready to test his self-control so soon.

CHAPTER 8

"It was a beautiful weekend, Mr. Chips." Kylie stroked the soft black fur as she arranged a towel in the cat's bed. The vet had cautioned against stair-climbing for a day or two, so Kylie had brought the cat's fleece-covered bed down into the kitchen for him.

The cat stepped gingerly into the padded nest and lay down, watching her with steady yellow-green eyes as she readied the coffeepot for the next morning.

"We went sailing yesterday. David made us a picnic lunch and the sun even came out for a while. Except for that little incident with the boom, it was a perfect day." She smiled at the memory.

"Now I guess we know why they call it a boom." The remembered sight of David, wet and sputtering, had her chuckling all over again.

He hadn't been paying attention, had claimed he had spotted an eagle flying overhead, but she'd suspected from the gleam in his eye that perhaps he wasn't telling the absolute truth about what had distracted him. She had just stripped off his borrowed sweats, hoping to get some color on her legs. Although she didn't want to be accused of imagining things, she could have sworn he was staring at her when she bent over to loosen the lines on the jib as they tacked. That was when it had happened, the heavy metal pole catching him at chest level and shoving him into the light blue water of Lake Washington.

Kylie had scrambled to loosen the lines so the boat would stop, then stood giggling as David swam up, muttering something about lavender-colored panties. She should have suspected something when he ordered her to give him a hand, should have known he could get himself back into the boat without any help from her. But, like a fool, she'd stuck both arms out to help him in and a split second after she'd realized that she'd made a grave tactical error, she was in the lake with him, and they'd spent the next half hour laughing and splashing like children.

She'd spent the entire weekend at his house, which was ridiculous since she only lived twenty minutes away. But it had been so easy to accept his offer of staying in a guest room, and David had behaved like a perfect gentleman, flirting with her, kissing her at every opportunity, but never taking it any further than that. If someone had asked her why she stayed, she wouldn't have known how to answer. All she knew was that she enjoyed David's company, and every once in a while, she'd turn and catch him looking at her with an intensity that made her skin tingle. He asked her questions and really listened to her answers. She supposed it all boiled down to one thing: He made her feel special.

So she'd puttered through his house, looked at the photos on his wall—taken years ago by his brother, he'd told her with a frown that hinted of a sadness he wasn't ready to share—and his books, an interesting mix of autobiographies, legal thrillers, and every book ever written about Bill Gates. She'd discovered he was more of a night person, even though he forced himself to be one of the first people into the office in the morning.

She had also been surprised to discover it had been his love for music that had inspired him to start a record company.

"I just assumed you'd seen it as an opportunity to make money," she had said.

He was playing a lovely tune on the piano, something she didn't recognize, but had stopped playing to stare at her strangely.

Kylie sat on the floor a few feet away, her legs crossed at the ankles as she sipped a glass of Columbia Chardonnay and watched the lights of the city come on across the lake as twilight deepened. If she hadn't known better, she might have thought she'd hurt him.

He resumed playing. "It wasn't always about the money."

Ah, so she *had* hurt him. She stood up and walked over to the piano, then sat down on the bench next to him.

"Tell me about the beginning. When you first started Gamble Records." She laid a hand on his knee by way of apology.

David didn't say anything for a while and Kylie was beginning to think there was something painful in the telling, when a slow smile spread across his face.

"Once upon a time there was a callow youth named David Gamble who thought he could change the world with his music."

Kylie's eyes widened. He was a wonderful piano player, but she would never have guessed he'd chosen music as his first career. Law, perhaps. Finance, definitely. But the thought of the ever-practical David Gamble as a career musician just didn't seem right.

"That surprises you." David looked at her through his thick, dark lashes and tapped her on the nose, kissed her soundly on the mouth, then continued to play his tune on the piano. "We capitalists have dreams, too, my dear."

Kylie laughed. "Of course you do. Please, go on."

"Back in high school, I was in a band. A rock-and-roll band to be exact. We were good, not great, but of course we didn't know that. We thought we were going to be the Rolling Stones of the eighties. Problem was, we couldn't get anyone to take us seriously. We were teenagers and barely had two bucks to rub together between the five of us."

"What was your band's name? Please tell me it wasn't the Dee Gees."

"Stop giggling." David kissed her again, his lips lingering this time, teasing her tongue with his. His fingers stilled on the keys.

Kylie scooted closer on the bench, all thoughts of amusement gone at the touch of his lips. She felt her pulse start to race, then sat back in disappointment when David raised his head and ended the kiss.

"Now, where was I?" he asked, his voice husky and his blue eyes darker than usual. "Oh, yes, the band's name. Let's see, if I recall correctly, it was 'Gamble'."

"Clever. And without the ego that most artists have." Kylie masked her growing sexual frustration with humor.

"Well, the band was my idea, and I was the lead singer," David protested with a grin and a shrug.

"Wow, a singer, too. You're just full of surprises."

"Now you know why we never went anywhere. I've since learned that I should confine my singing to the shower, but when you're a teenager, nobody can tell you anything," David said wryly.

"So you started Gamble Records to encourage young bands?"

"No. Most high school bands don't have what it takes to succeed in the music business. They don't usually last more than a few months. Gamble broke up after about a year. I got a musical scholarship to the University of Washington, and that's where I got involved in college radio. Since we didn't have the monetary pressures of a commercial radio station, we played a lot of unknowns, mostly demo tapes sent to us by aspiring musicians. I heard so many great artists in that job, acts that couldn't get record deals. By then, I was in a new band and we were in the same position.

"This time, I was really convinced we had something that would sell, but the record companies wouldn't take a chance on us. That's when I decided to start my own label. I borrowed money from everyone I knew and bartered whatever I could to get that first record produced." David laughed. "I think I promised to play the piano at the wedding of every man, woman, and child in the recording industry."

"So did your first record become a hit?"

At this, David laughed so hard Kylie could have sworn he had tears in his eyes.

"What's so funny?" she asked.

David wiped his eyes. "We pressed five thousand records, spent every penny we had between the four of us, and called in every favor anyone owed us."

"And how many did you sell?"

"At last count, I believe we were up to eighteen."

"Eighteen?"

"Yep. We gave away more than we sold. I had boxes of records everywhere. For the next ten years, I used them for tables, chairs, bookshelves." He shrugged. "The only good news was that I didn't have to buy any furniture for a decade."

"But you turned it around."

"Yes. I learned a lot from that first experience, mostly about my own arrogance. I picked a different band to promote the next time, and the second record sold much better. I even managed to make a small profit. And with each one after that I did even better."

"Whatever happened to that band, the one from college?"

"I'm not sure what happened to our bass player. After college, he ended up working for me. Problem was, he acquired a bit of a drug habit, one that got so expensive he couldn't pay for it out of his regular salary. He'd been granted stock options, but those couldn't be cashed until a year after we went public. So, Rory stole from Gamble Records instead."

"That's awful. What did you do?"

"I fired him and rescinded the stock grant, but I didn't press charges. The last thing we needed right before our IPO was bad publicity and accusations of lax accounting. It was a real disappointment to me. I had considered Rory a friend, and would have gladly done what I could to help him with his problem if he had come to me. I guess the drugs just became more important to him than anything else. I have no idea what he's up to now."

"What about the other band members?"

"The other two went on to successful careers in music. Have you met Peter Laughlin, the head of A&R?"

"Yes."

"He was our drummer. And have you ever heard of a guy named Clint Walsh?"

"The singer? Yes, of course I've heard of him."

"Clint was our backup guitarist and lead singer. He went on to bigger and better things musically. We still keep in touch." David paused, then muttered to himself, "As a matter of fact, Clint was supposed to have come by tonight. It completely slipped my mind. Will you excuse me for a minute?" he had said.

She stroked under the cat's ear, recalling that David had seemed a bit distracted when he'd returned, but he hadn't said anything to her about it at the time.

"I hope nothing was wrong, Mr. Chips," she said now.

The jangling of the phone pulled her from her memories of the weekend, and Kylie followed the ringing out of the kitchen and into the darkened living room. Pulling open a drawer in her coffee table, she wondered briefly how in the world the phone had ended up in that particular spot. It was as if the thing had a life all its own, like some animated character in a Disney movie.

"Hello," she greeted after picking up the receiver and punching the "on" button.

"Hi, baby. How's my favorite girl doing?" a hearty voice on the other end boomed.

Kylie's grin spread from ear to ear. "Daddy! How are you? Mom says filming's going terrible."

"No, no, it's fine. You know how your mother exaggerates. We're just having a small problem with one of the leads. Actors these days are such prima donnas, they want stand-ins for everything. And the unions . . . don't even get me started on the unions."

Kylie laughed. Same old Dad. He'd been complaining good-naturedly about the same things for as long as she could remember.

"Enough about me, though. I hear you've got yourself a new job."

"Actually, Robyn got the job for me, but I'm working hard for them."

"I'm sure you are, baby. You've always been a hard worker, and one of the most loyal employees anyone could ever ask for."

Kylie's smile faded as she plopped down on the couch and tucked her feet under her. "Pigeon Books didn't think so," she said glumly.

"That's not true, honey. You know they never believed you'd taken that money. There just wasn't much else they could do but let you go. The Board of Directors was insistent."

Closing her eyes to shut out the humiliation brought on by that failure, Kylie responded, "I know, Dad. I don't blame them. It was my own fault. It was just like they said in their report. I showed a 'marked lack of judgment' for someone in my position. Please tell me nobody's told Mom about it. She'd be so disappointed . . ."

"Of course your mother doesn't know. If we told her, you know she'd march down there and cause a ruckus. She'd probably kill someone and it'd be in the tabloids before I could bury the evidence."

"That's just what I need. To have my mommy fight my battles for me."

"How did we get on this subject anyway?" George Rogers asked gruffly. "I refuse to let you judge yourself on the results of one unfortunate incident, Kylie. You're a sweet girl with a big heart, and you know I couldn't love you any more than I do, don't you?"

She couldn't stop the tears that welled up in her eyes. "Dad, stop it. You're making me cry," she protested with a sniffle, blinking quickly.

"Good, then you know I'm telling you the truth. Even I'm not that good an actor."

He cleared his throat and Kylie knew he was as big a sentimental fool as she. She could picture him standing on the back patio wearing his favorite baggy corduroy pants, a glass of Scotch in one hand as he leaned against the railing. She was his first daughter and she'd always felt that, somehow, that made her special in his eyes.

"Now, tell me that you're planning a trip home soon. Rocky's damn near driving me nuts asking about you."

"Daddy, please tell me you didn't call him that to his face," Kylie said, laughing. Her parents' latest cook was a dead ringer for Sylvester Stallone, something that both the cook himself and Kylie's mother seemed completely oblivious to. The last time Kylie had visited her parents, her father kept humming the theme song of the *Rocky* movies whenever the cook was around, or imitating Sly's famous line: "Yo, Adrian." Her father's antics had sent Kylie into a fit of uncontrollable giggling, while her mother looked at her as if she'd lost her mind.

Ending the conversation with the promise to fly down to L.A. soon, Kylie hugged the phone to her chest, wishing she were hugging her father instead. He was such a wonderful man, the one person in her life who loved her just the way she was, and always had.

Absently, she set the phone down in the potted Christmas cactus on the coffee table, wondering if her father would like David.

Of course he would. What's not to like? she asked herself. David was strong and honest. He wasn't even a tiny bit like that rat, Marcus, who had been the closest thing she'd had to a boyfriend in years. Her father had detested Marcus on sight, and, as it had turned out, quite rightfully so.

"I should have listened to him," Kylie muttered as she got up to wander around the room.

It had been a while since she'd thought about Marcus, the lying, thieving creep. Shaking her head, she admonished herself for rehashing a past she couldn't alter.

"The secret to success is in acknowledging your mistakes, learning from them, and moving on," she repeated the advice her father had given her when the whole fiasco had erupted over a year ago. She didn't want to think about it again; didn't want to rehash the awful nightmare her life had become during those last weeks at Pigeon Books. She had moved to Seattle for a new start, and, with her job at Gamble Records, she had vowed to put the past behind her and let herself move forward with her life.

The sterling picture frame on the mantel was cold to the touch as Kylie picked it up and brought it closer. She smiled back at the handsome man in the photograph before putting it back in its place of honor.

"I love you, Dad," she whispered.

"Come on, man, let me in. I can see your girlfriend's car is gone now so I won't be interrupting your sex life."

David heard the mocking tone in his brother's voice and leaned his head against the cool plaster wall. Ben's words were slurred into the intercom at the locked front gate, and David wondered how he'd gotten there. His house across the lake from Seattle was easily a mile from the nearest bus stop, and David figured Ben was in no condition to have walked that far. But he knew his brother could be extremely charming when he wanted to be. He'd probably conned someone into dropping him off at David's front gate. No matter how many horror stories were told about the dangers of picking up hitchhikers, there always seemed to be someone stupid enough to take the chance.

He pushed the intercom button. "Ben, I am not letting you in. I told you you're not welcome here until you get treatment. If you want to check into a detox center, go there and have them call me. I'll send them whatever they charge to get you clean. Until then, stay away from me."

"Fuck you, man!" Ben yelled. "Just because you're rich you think you can tell me what to do with my life. Well, I got news for you, big brother, you can't—"

David turned off the volume to his speaker, effectively ending Ben's rant session. Watching his brother wave his arms wildly through the security camera he'd had installed after his last bout with Ben, David put a call in to the local police.

Closing his eyes, David rubbed his throbbing temples. Ben would get charged on a D&D; would spend the night in a cold, sterile cell. David turned away from the scene outside, not wanting to watch his brother's arrest when the police arrived, and went into his favorite room at the back of the house, facing the lake.

D&D. Drunk & Disorderly.

He stared out at the inky black waters of the lake.

The Double D. That was how they'd jokingly referred to the charge when they'd been growing up. Whenever their mother stumbled home in the early afternoon reeking of spent booze and vomit, tracks of long-since-dried mascara drawing black lines down her face, he and Ben had made a secret sign, pinkies up, fingers interlocking in two circles.

He couldn't understand why Ben had chosen the same path. Unconsciously, David's fingers flew over the piano keys, filling the room with a sadness that seeped into the paint and pushed through the hairline cracks between the floorboards.

Maybe it was because Ben had never known a different kind of life. He'd been born two months after their father had been killed in an automobile accident. David was ten at the time and he remembered life before Dad died. Pam Gamble had always been loud—David remembered her shrieking voice even from his early years—but back then there had been kindness and laughter, too.

The change in her hadn't happened overnight. David had memories of curling up in his mother's lap after his father's death; of soft, comforting hands holding him close while they both poured out their grief.

But then the savings account had run out, and the life insurance was barely enough to cover funeral expenses, and Ben was born prematurely, and the bills started adding up.

Pam couldn't afford to go back to work and pay a sitter, but Social Security wasn't enough to pay all their bills either. She sold their little two-bedroom house and they moved into an even smaller one-bedroom apartment. David had been happy to take the couch, thankful that he didn't have to share a room with the squalling baby who woke up every two hours wanting to be fed. He had enough to do just trying to take care of himself.

Things were okay for a little while. His mom cried a lot, and she didn't seem to like Ben much, but then, neither did David. It was hard to like something that didn't do much more than cry and poop and throw up all the time.

Then one night, a night David recalled as if it were yesterday, everything had changed.

He'd been trying to sleep on the couch, but his too-small pajamas were bugging him. The legs kept riding up and twisting the wrong way and he couldn't sleep, angry at his mother for not buying him a new pair like she said she would last week. He yanked the pajama leg down again, and the thin orange blanket he slept with slipped off onto the floor.

"Damn it," he cursed, then looked around guiltily. His dad had said real men didn't need to cuss, but David had heard him let loose a zinger every now and then. He felt his dad would agree the situation warranted it.

Shivering, he pulled the blanket up over his bony shoulders. His mom said he was tall for his age, had said it real proud, as if he'd done something good. But, of course, it was God and your parents that made you look like you did, so David figured maybe she was proud of herself for it, and not him. In any event, he didn't feel proud about it right now, not with his damn pajama pants riding up every five seconds and making it so he couldn't sleep.

Restlessly, he turned his face into the back of the couch. That's when Ben had started to cry.

And cry.

And cry.

Ben must have hollered for a full five minutes, but his mother didn't get up like she usually did. David stared at the purple Kool-Aid stain on the faded brown couch, his body still, listening to Ben wail.

Maybe she was dead. Maybe she'd had an accident like Dad. Then he'd be an orphan. They'd stick him in one of those awful places like his teacher had told them about in one of the stories she liked to read on Friday afternoons, where the kids only got oatmeal to eat and they got hit all the time.

What would happen to his little brother then? It wasn't like he really cared about him or anything, but David remembered his dad telling him he was going to have a little brother or sister and that it was going to be David's job to look out for him, to make sure the bullies didn't pick on him, because he was the big brother and that's what he was supposed to do.

He was older, and strong, too. He'd be okay, even if they did stick him in some dark place like an orphanage where they beat him up.

"Just let 'em try. I can beat them," he railed, raising a fist into the air, then letting it drop to his side again.

But Ben was different. He was just a baby. There was no way he could take care of himself.

David sighed.

He threw off the covers and stood up. He didn't have a choice. Ben was his responsibility, his dad had said so. So whatever needed to be done, David would do it. Straightening his shoulders, he padded into his mother's bedroom on bare feet, the thin carpet gritty under his toes.

"I'll make you a deal, kid. You stop crying and I'll take care of you, okay?" David whispered desperately. Pushing down the gate on the side of the crib, he picked up the crying baby. David looked into his baby brother's big blue eyes, eyes that were almost identical to his own.

The wailing stopped immediately.

The deal was struck.

Of course, it hadn't been that easy, David reflected now as his fingers stilled on the keys. He hadn't known how to raise a baby, but he'd done his best to keep his brother fed and clean, had learned how to buy groceries and clothes, had learned what day of the month the Social Security check came and made sure to get what they needed before his mother had a chance to drink it all away.

She had slipped further and further away, staying out later and later at night, sometimes not coming home at all. For the most part, she was just a sloppy, weepy drunk. She'd stagger around the apartment, bumping into walls and furniture, start to cry and want to hug them. Then she'd pass out and David and Ben would go on about the business of living. But sometimes she'd get angry, would yell at them to shut the TV off, would blame them for making her life harder, as if it had been their choice to pick her as a mother.

During those times, David tossed her car keys out into the living room and barricaded himself and Ben into the tiny puke-green-and-white tiled bathroom. She'd pound on the door for a little while, but eventually she'd leave them alone. Those were the nights she usually didn't come home, but it wasn't until David was thirteen that he spied the police report with her name on it and the charge "Drunk & Disorderly" written on top.

From then on, whenever he and Ben locked themselves into the bathroom and sat in the cold tub with the dingy white shower curtain pulled close around them, they made the sign. The Double D.

David slammed his hands down on the piano keys.

The harsh sound echoed into the empty room.

"Why didn't I let them take us? Why didn't I ask for help?" he yelled into the now-silent room, torturing himself with a familiar guilt. He laid his arms down on the piano and cradled his aching head in his hands.

"I'm sorry, Ben. I should have let them take us." The words stuck like tiny nails into every surface of the darkened room.

CHAPTER 9

"Good morning, boss. Did you have a nice weekend?" Deborah called cheerfully from the outer office.

She'd been accosted as soon as she'd arrived that morning with people wanting the scoop on her boss's relationship with Robyn Rogers's sister. The rumor had started Friday and was spreading through the building faster than baby rabbits on a warm spring day.

She, of course, had claimed no firsthand knowledge of anything. After all, all she really knew was that David had asked Sandy to have a talk with Brenda Olson after the infamous coffee incident and that he had been acting a bit strange lately. Of course, she'd also figured out the Kylie McGillicuddy David had had her search for after the party was the very same Kylie Rogers who now worked in accounting, had even gone so far as to research Kylie's family to find that McGillicuddy was Kylie's mother's maiden name. If nothing else, she wanted to make sure her hunch was correct. But none of that meant anything. Not even the ludicrously veiled requests for updates on Kylie's progress that David had posed when he had been out of town or his request to check on her unlocked house last Friday meant anything.

Deborah hid a smile as she hung up her coat. All it

meant was that her boss was definitely smitten.

As far as she was concerned, it was about time, but David wasn't looking too happy when she poked her head into his office.

"My weekend was fine, thanks," David answered distractedly. "I have an appointment with Bob Buchanan of Bob's Records in the U-district at one, and I have something I need to do before that, so can you take care of rearranging my schedule for the afternoon?"

"Sure thing, boss. Consider it done."

Deborah watched as he paced to the window, seemingly fascinated by the parking lot below. Her hope for a blossoming love affair fizzled to the ground like a balloon losing all of its helium. A man in love couldn't possibly look so gloomy. For once, her instincts must have been wrong.

She closed the door softly behind her, leaving David alone with his thoughts.

Tapping her toe in time with the music, Kylie watched the studio engineer adjust one of the countless knobs on the panel in front of him. She'd read somewhere that a studio engineer had to know more about electronics than a pilot, and looking at the complicated array of buttons, knobs, and levers before her, she wasn't surprised. It looked more difficult than flying a plane, and, as far as she could tell, there was no autopilot button the engineer could press when he wanted to take a break.

"This is so interesting, Sandy. Thank you for letting me watch." Kylie leaned closer to her boss as the song ended and a flurry of conversations began.

"I thought you'd like to see your sister at work, and you deserve a breather now that the royalties are done."

"I can't believe the things they all seem to hear that I can't. Like now, Robyn's saying she missed a note at the end. I didn't hear anything wrong."

Sandy laughed. "I suppose that's why they're the musicians and we're the accountants."

"I guess you're right," Kylie agreed. She'd been listening for over half an hour as Robyn recorded and re-recorded the same song. Each time, after the song was over, the producer, Robyn, Robyn's manager, and a handful of others would immediately start talking, suggesting something or another they wanted to fix in the next go-around.

Kylie was proud of her sister, knew she had a reputation for being a real professional, and now she could see why. Robyn performed the same song over and over again, even encouraged another take when she wasn't satisfied.

"I hate this song, Alicia," Kylie heard Robyn say now to her manager. The recording studio was divided into two parts, the room where the musicians performed and the engineering booth where the nonperformers sat during a take. They were separated by soundproof glass, with speakers coming into the engineer's booth. Remembering her first tour of Gamble Records, when she'd stood outside in the hall unable to hear what was going on inside, Kylie decided it was much more interesting to be on this side of the fish-bowl. She tuned back in to the conversation going on in the other half of the recording studio.

"I know you do, Robyn. But I think it's going to be one of the best on this album."

"Wanna make a bet on that? I'll bet you a percentage point off your usual commission that this song doesn't make the charts."

Alicia O'Donnell laughed. "No way, Robyn. I'm already underpaid for all that I do for you." Kylie watched as the other woman threw an arm around her sister's small shoulders.

"All right then, let's get on with it so I can finish this stupid song and prove you wrong, even if you aren't prepared to put your money where your mouth is."

Kylie sat quietly on a stool in the corner of the engineer's booth as they set up to record the song again. It really was fascinating to watch how much effort went into recording a single song on an album. Now she knew why the record company put up such huge amounts for their recording budgets. It could take anywhere from two weeks to six months to produce a finished master to send to the pressing company to be made into CDs, which would then be shipped to the distributors who'd take the product to the stores. During all that time, there would be expenses to be paid: producers, engineers, musicians, studio time, tape, equipment, food, drinks, transportation. The list went on and on.

Kylie was most surprised by the amount of cigarettes and alcohol being consumed, especially this early in the morning. It seemed that it was an accepted practice to drink on the job if you were a musician, which was a strange reality for her accountant's mind to accept.

She'd noticed that Robyn wasn't drinking, but she had lit up a cigarette, and Kylie watched the wisps of gray smoke rise from a nearby ashtray as Robyn sang. Kylie was surprised—she had never seen her sister smoke before.

This time when the song finished, the air filled with applause.

The producer patted Robyn on the back. "That was great, Robyn. You ready to call it a wrap?"

Robyn agreed, and Kylie went into the other room to congratulate her sister.

"Good job, Robyn. That was—" Kylie broke off sharply as a sharp, almost acrid smell hit her nostrils. Her eyes widened with horror as her sister took a deep pull on her cigarette.

"Please tell me that's not marijuana," she whispered.

Robyn closed her eyes, then slowly exhaled. "Okay, sis. It's not marijuana."

"That's not true. I can smell it."

"How do you know that's what pot smells like?" Robyn grinned, her catlike green eyes mocking.

"I went to college. I know what it smells like. If Mom and Dad find out you smoke pot, they'll kill you."

"So who's going to tell them?"

"I will. If you don't put that thing out right now, I'll tell them," Kylie said. She wasn't going to just stand by and let her baby sister turn into a drug addict without trying to do something to stop her.

Robyn shrugged. Kylie would be gone in a few minutes and there was plenty more pot around. "Fine, here you go, sis. It's all yours."

Kylie wrinkled her nose distastefully as Robyn held out the offending cigarette. Grabbing it between her thumb and forefinger, she tossed it into a seemingly empty wastepaper basket before turning back to her sister.

"That's better," she said, resisting the urge to wipe her hands on her skirt.

Robyn rolled her eyes heavenward. One thing about Kylie, things were always black or white with her. Right or wrong, love or hate. No shades of gray around to clutter up her big sister's life. It was almost enough to make Robyn jealous. Almost.

She turned and set her headphones down on a stool. "So, I tried calling you this weekend, but never got you. What were you up to?"

There was a full five-second beat of silence before she turned to look at her sister. Kylie's face had turned the same shade of red as her car, and Robyn immediately knew something was afoot. She put one hand on her hip and tapped her foot on the thin carpet.

"All right, give."

Kylie swallowed visibly. "What?"

"If your face gets any redder, it's going to burst into flames, that's what. Now, tell me where you were all weekend."

Robyn watched Kylie open her mouth, then close it again. Suddenly, it came to her—the rumor she'd heard earlier about her sister must be true. "It's David Gamble, isn't it? Someone mentioned to me this morning that he's been seen hovering around your cubicle lately, but I didn't believe it. Why didn't you tell me?"

She hadn't thought it possible, but her sister's face turned a new shade of red, and Robyn knew she'd hit upon the truth. Well, good for Kylie. It was about time her sister got laid.

"You and David Gamble. Who would have guessed?"

Kylie blinked, the silence in the room around them penetrating her haze-filled brain. Her eyes darted left, then right, mortified to find everyone staring at her and Robyn. If there was one thing she had learned this weekend, it was that David Gamble was a man who liked his privacy, a man who liked to control what people knew or didn't know about him.

He was not going to like this.

"*Nobody* would have known if you hadn't just announced it to the entire band," Kylie said, resisting the urge to bury her head in her hands. She closed her eyes briefly as the silence continued, then turned and grabbed her purse from the engineering booth.

"I'm going to lunch, Sandy. I'll be back later." She squeezed past her boss and out of the studio, ignoring the buzz that started even before she had closed the door. Walking quickly down the hall, Kylie let out a deep breath, then burst out the front doors at a half run.

"This is worse than humiliating," she said, yanking her car door open and shoving the key into the ignition. She gunned the engine and slammed the car into reverse, not knowing or caring where she would go after she left the parking lot. She just wanted to get away from her sister and all the wagging tongues that had followed her out of the recording studio.

At five minutes before noon, the parking lot at Gamble Records was a crush of activity with everyone trying to leave all at once. Looking down at the scene, David wondered if some sort of famine had hit that he hadn't heard about. As far as he knew, there was still plenty of food at the grocery stores in Seattle, but he supposed that lunchtime on the Monday after a payday was bound to be a special event.

"I'm going to lunch now, David. Your schedule is all clear until your meeting with Peter at three," Deborah said, poking her head inside his office.

"Thanks. I'll be at the hospital and then at Bob's Records by one." David turned to see her off when he heard the sickening sound of steel tearing into metal. His startled gaze turned back to the window and Deborah raced over to stand next to him.

They both noticed the culprit at the same time and groaned in unison, "Kylie."

David wasn't surprised to find Kylie in the middle of the mess, but he was surprised by her unsuspecting victim. It was his new convertible, the sleek black luxury model he'd splurged on after Ben had wrecked his twelve-year-old Mercedes.

The back end of her Mustang was planted firmly in the driver's-side door of his brand-new Jaguar.

His teeth clenched. He tried counting to ten. Then to twenty. Forward first. Then backward.

It didn't work.

"Kylie!" he roared, dashing out of his office and down the stairs.

Kylie sat in her car, head buried in her arms.

She was upset and hadn't been paying attention to where she was going. As usual, she had nobody to blame for this fiasco but herself. The good news was that it looked like she might not have to worry about any more disasters after this one. From the way David was glaring at her from the other side of her car window, she figured he was going to kill her. Soon.

She rolled down the window half an inch. Then another. Enough for a bit of fresh air to enter the suddenly stifling atmosphere inside the car, but not enough for the lethal-looking fingers that David kept clenching and unclenching at his sides to make their way through the glass and around her throat.

"Oops," she said contritely, looking at him from under her lashes.

"Oops!" David repeated incredulously. "Oops!"

In retrospect, Kylie thought perhaps she could have phrased that better. Taking a deep breath for courage, she pushed open the door and prepared to face the wrath of David Gamble. A crowd of employees had gathered around to ensure her humiliation would be complete and well documented in the company's lore: Chapter Four—Kylie Demolishes David's Jag and Lives to Tell About It.

At least, she hoped she'd live to tell about it.

"I'm really sorry, David. I must have misjudged the distance."

"Obviously," he said dryly.

"There's no need to get nasty. I said I was sorry."

David glared at her before moving over to inspect the damage. The entire driver's side of his car was crushed in. She doubted that he could even open the door, and figured he'd guessed as much when he turned to look back at her car. Kylie's glance followed his to her fender.

There wasn't a scratch on her car. Just a scrape of black paint on her shiny chrome bumper.

"You do have insurance, don't you?"

"Of course I do."

David nodded and turned back to do a further survey of his car.

"But, I'd appreciate it if you wouldn't report it to my insurance company. I'll pay for the damages myself."

David continued to check out the damage.

Kylie continued, "My insurance agent told me they'd give me another chance, but one more claim and they'd have to cancel me. I guess I can't really blame them after the lawnmower incident, but I'd hate to see them lose my premiums after everything they've done for me."

David tried to contain his curiosity. He was mad at her,

he reminded himself. She had wrecked his brand-new car, which he'd now have to get hauled into the shop. If anything he'd heard about Jaguar mechanics was right, he'd probably never see his baby again. Yes, he was definitely mad at her.

In his head, he could hear the ticking seconds of silence as if someone had implanted a tiny timepiece in his brain. He'd always had an inquiring mind, and had considered it an asset before today. The curiosity continued to peck at his brain like a sparrow with a saltine cracker.

"All right," he shouted finally. "What lawnmower incident?"

The crowd around Kylie's car let out a collective breath. David was not going to commit murder right here in the parking lot. They could save the chalk for another purpose besides outlining her slain body on the sun-warmed concrete.

"Oh . . . are you sure you want to hear about that?" Kylie refused to meet his eyes, her gaze shifting from the pavement to the pale blue sky and back again.

David sighed. "Yes, I'm sure."

"Well, I was mowing my front lawn just after I first moved in. And you know that Queen Anne Hill is pretty steep, right?"

David nodded, wondering at the seemingly unrelated question. Then, folding his arms against his chest, he leaned back against Kylie's Mustang, settling in for what was probably going to be a very long story. The thought struck him that he hadn't seen her at all since he'd ridden back to her house yesterday afternoon to get his car. Certainly not long, especially by his standards, and yet he found himself studying her as if it had been weeks. She gestured wildly as she talked, as if the only way she could adequately tell her tale was to draw it out in the air around her. Her mad cap of curls bounced in unison with her hands and David felt a sudden urge to bury his fingers in their lively softness. An even stronger urge to bury his mouth against her soft lips had him shifting uncomfortably against the cold steel of her car.

He forced himself to concentrate on her story.

"So, I have a very steep lawn, being on a hill and all. And, like I said, I was mowing the grass, and it was hot out. I guess my hands were..." Kylie paused, taking a deep breath. "Well, to put it indelicately, they must have been rather sweaty. Anyway, the lawnmower just sort of ... slipped."

David watched as she spread her arms wide. A light wind played with the flowery skirt she wore, ruffling the edge against her legs. David pushed his hands into his pockets and shifted his position against her car again.

"Slipped?"

"Uh-huh. Slipped ... and ran out into the road. It hit my neighbor's car first and just kept going, like it was possessed or something. Caused a three-car pileup before it died. If you ask me, those other two cars must have been following way too close, but they pinned the blame for the whole thing on my lawnmower. Luckily, no one was hurt, but the paperwork was awful. I mean, who would've thought my poor old lawnmower could cause over thirty thousand dollars' worth of damage?" Kylie sighed. "I invited everyone in and we all had some lemonade while I passed out my insurance information. Actually, everyone was very pleasant about the whole thing. Matter of fact, I got a birthday card from that nice old Mr. Chesterson last month. Said his car was running just fine. Thanked me for the lemonade, too."

David put his head in his hands, his shoulders shaking with silent laughter. Kylie was the only person he'd ever known who could ever be charged with assault with a deadly lawnmower.

Deborah, who had probably come down to protect Kylie from his murderous temper, looked at him as if he might have finally lost his hold on his sanity.

David saw Kylie look over at Deborah and shrug as if

agreeing with his assistant in her assessment of David's mental state. Then she reached out and patted him on the back, offering comfort. "I happen to know a good body shop if you need one," she said.

He watched as her eyebrows drew together thoughtfully. "As a matter of fact, they sent me a birthday card, too, though I could never figure out why."

CHAPTER 10

"I really am sorry about your car, David. You don't have to worry about the damage. Just have your mechanic send the bills to me."

David muttered something appropriate, knowing that he'd just take care of it himself, surprised to find that after the initial shock, he really wasn't all that upset. He'd expected to be angry with her for a long time; after all, he knew how hard he'd worked to be able to afford things like luxury cars and nice houses in the best neighborhoods.

He'd surprised himself by almost saying, "It's just a car." But how could he say that? He didn't believe that. Expensive possessions were proof of his success. They proved that he was better than his upbringing; better than his gaudy drunk of a mother; better than some no-account musician who didn't make enough money to take care of himself; better than his homeless brother.

David stared hard at the buildings passing outside the passenger-side window of Kylie's car and wondered where that last thought had come from. He wasn't in competition with Ben, had never felt any of the sibling rivalry that so many others laid claim to.

So what was it? Why was he so angry at his brother? That his brother had stolen from him was inexcusable, but

David wasn't really angry with Ben over that. Disappointed, yes, but not angry. So, where did the anger come from? Could it be because Ben wasn't financially successful?

David recalled a fight he and Ben had had almost ten years ago, when Ben was a senior in high school. Their mother had finally started to pull herself together, and Ben had hopes of going to college. Gamble Records was seeing its first blush of success, and David hoped he'd be able to pull some money together to help Ben pay his tuition. Then David made the mistake asking his little brother what he planned to major in, and Ben made the mistake of being honest. Ben had always loved to take pictures. Even when he was ten or eleven, he'd slung a camera around his neck wherever he went. So when David asked what Ben was going to major in, Ben told him about a liberal arts school that offered a major in photography.

David had just laughed at him. After all, practical people didn't go to college to major in *photography*, they majored in computer science, or business, or marketing, or finance. A major in photography wasn't going to get Ben a job anywhere and David refused to help fund such a ridiculous endeavor. After all, David had figured, he wasn't working his ass off seven days a week so his brother could waste his hard-earned money on four years of a useless education. Hadn't David himself realized the folly of an impractical education? He'd changed his own major from music to finance in the middle of his junior year.

So, instead, Ben had gone to the University of Washington for two quarters before dropping out. Now, at twenty-six, his little brother had held a series of meaningless jobs and drank himself into a stupor more days than not. David shook his head and stared unseeingly out the window.

Would Ben be this way if David had supported his brother's dream, despite its impracticality?

"David, we're here." Kylie looked at him strangely as they sat in her car in the parking lot of Seattle Memorial Hospital on First Hill, more commonly referred to as Pill

Hill because of the plethora of medical establishments located there. David shook himself back to the present, guessing they'd been sitting there for some time. He'd asked Kylie to give him a ride to the hospital so he could take care of seeing his friend Clint before his meeting with Bob Buchanan of Bob's Records. He wasn't looking forward to this visit.

"Why don't you come in and sit in the waiting room? I won't be more than fifteen or twenty minutes." David started to get out of the car.

Kylie's cheeks brightened. "No, thanks, I'll just wait here."

David looked at her suspiciously.

She sighed. "I can't. I used to volunteer here and, well, there was a little accident involving a food cart and the nursery."

"And?"

"And let's just say they asked me not to come back. They were very nice about it, of course," she added.

"Of course."

Kylie shot him an annoyed glare at his patronizing tone.

David leaned over and pressed a warm kiss on her lips. His arm slid behind her neck as her mouth opened under his. Her tongue touched his and David groaned, feeling himself go hard.

He had vowed after last Friday's disaster in the tub that he was going to slow down their physical relationship, so even though she'd stayed at his house all weekend, he'd kept his hands to himself. Even when they'd gone sailing and she'd taken off his sweatpants and gone running around in nothing but his T-shirt and that tantalizing scrap of lavender lace he'd spotted when she leaned over to change the lines—well, okay, he'd admit that he was on his way to the front of the boat with distinctly ungentlemanly thoughts in his mind when the boom had knocked him into the lake. Luckily, the water had been cold, and his good intentions and well-honed sense of control had been saved.

She applied a gentle sucking pressure to his tongue, and David felt an answering pull in his groin.

She was doing it again. He was ready to strip her naked and go for it like a teenager on prom night. He had to get her out of his system before they did something they could both be arrested for. But what if he lost control again?

It won't happen again, he promised himself. *This time I'll be in control. I won't let it happen again,* he vowed. He had to do something to slake this constant state of arousal or he'd go crazy. He pulled back, his breathing heavy.

"I'll be back in a few minutes. Try to stay out of trouble, okay?" He kissed her lightly on the nose, staying well away from those dangerous lips of hers, before walking into the hospital.

The unmistakable smell of ammonia, urine, and cafeteria food had the instant effect of calming his libido. He knew popular TV shows often portrayed doctors and nurses as borderline sex maniacs, but David wondered how anyone could even think about sex after seeing broken-down, wrinkled, sick bodies all day. Not to mention the fact that the smell of illness must cling to their hair and clothes. It certainly didn't strike him as an atmosphere ripe for sex as he took the elevator up to the ninth floor oncology unit.

He tapped lightly on the door to Room 916 before poking his head inside. Clint was expecting him, but he didn't want to intrude on his friend's privacy.

He paused just inside the door, taking in the sight before him. His best friend for the past two decades was sprawled across an uncomfortable-looking metal chair, his head leaning against the cold steel bars of the bed next to him. A little girl lay sleeping on a green fake-leather couch, her arms and legs pulled into a ball like a newborn kitten. She had white-blond hair, the same color her mother used to have, before the chemo had made it all fall out in clumps.

Amy Greenberg had been beautiful once, not so very long ago. She'd be beautiful now, too, David thought, ex-

cept for the purple bruises under her eyes and the tubes
sticking out from every conceivable appendage.

Clint Walsh stirred and opened his eyes. After living
with someone with cancer for the past year, he seemed to
have gained the ability to sense the smallest changes around
him, even when he was asleep. Seeing David, he gestured
toward the hallway and gently extricated himself from
Amy's grasp. He paused for a moment to make sure mother
and daughter were still sleeping soundly before joining David in the hall.

David did not consider himself a hugger. Although he
was finding it easier than usual to be physically affectionate
with Kylie, he was not a physical person by nature.

Clint would not have considered David a physical person
either, and so was more than a little astonished to find himself on the receiving end of a very genuine hug from a man
he'd known for almost twenty years. He thought it would
be awkward, knew it should be awkward to be embraced
like this. Instead, he felt overwhelmed with emotion. For
the past twelve months, he had been watching the woman
he loved being taken away, killed bit by bit by a disease
that modern medicine didn't know how to cure.

They'd been living together for a year when she'd found
out about the cancer. Clint had tried to insist they get married but she wouldn't relent, didn't want the bill collectors
to be able to come after him when all her accounts were
drained trying to pay the doctors to keep her alive.

But at least she'd given him Lexi. The father of Amy's
daughter was happy enough to sign over his rights, hadn't
wanted Amy to have the kid in the first place, he'd said.
Clint would have been angry at the bastard, but since he'd
never have to see him again, he figured he'd just be glad
the asshole didn't want the job of raising his own child.

That little girl was the only thing that had kept him sane
these past few months. That and knowing that whenever he
needed to borrow some strength, he could always call
David.

"She worse today?" David asked gruffly as he pulled away from his friend.

" 'Bout the same. Doctors can't do much but they're letting her administer her own doses of morphine, which helps a lot."

David didn't know what to say in the face of his friend's pain. He patted the pack of cigarettes in his jacket pocket awkwardly.

Clint had given up smoking when Amy got sick, had to promise to quit before she'd agree to let him have custody of Lexi. Watching David fondle the familiar rectangular pack, Clint shot his friend a weak grin. "Why the hell are you still carrying those things around? You haven't smoked since college."

David dragged his hand away but didn't answer the question. Instead, he asked, "Do you need anything? Money . . . ?" He shrugged, hating the feeling of helplessness that came over him. What could he offer that could possibly make this any better?

"Sorry, man, all the money in the world isn't going to help. I already tried that." Clint's laugh was hollow. "I think that's the worst part. You work hard all your life, thinking that if only you have some magic amount of money in your bank account, your life is going to be great. Then something like this happens and you can afford to pay anyone—doctors, hospitals, drug companies, acupuncturists, herbalists; shit, anybody who holds out their hand—but it doesn't make any difference because no amount of your money can cure cancer." Clint shoved his hands in his pockets. "God, I want a smoke."

David uncomfortably shuffled his feet in the quiet hallway. There was no way he'd let Clint have a cigarette, even if he thought his friend was serious. He felt helpless, useless, and he wasn't accustomed to feeling that way. In business, there had never been a problem he couldn't solve, but he was at a loss to know what to do here. He'd offered his friend everything he had, including the use of his house and his car, but Clint didn't want to be that far from the hospital. Instead, he and Lexi were staying at a hotel a block away. David didn't know what else to do, so he just leaned against the pale yellow wall next to his friend, breathing the smell of sickness in companionable silence.

The fire department was just leaving when the phone on Deborah's desk rang.

She raised her weary head from the hand it had been resting on. It had been quite an afternoon already and it wasn't even one-thirty yet.

"David Gamble's office," she answered, striving for her best Executive Assistant voice.

"Where the hell is he? I've left three messages already, damn it. You get him on this phone right now," the voice on the other end of the line shrilled.

Deborah had forwarded all of David's calls into voice mail while she'd been dealing with the fire down on the first floor. She recognized the angry voice on the other end of the line as Robyn Rogers's manager, Alicia O'Donnell.

"I'm sorry, Alicia, but David's not here. He had an appointment in the U-district at one, and I expect him back no later than two-thirty. I'd be happy to give him your message—"

"No, goddamn it, I need to speak with him now. I just got Robyn's royalty check. Is this supposed to be some kind of a joke? I tell you, I am *not* laughing."

"Did you try his cell phone?" Deborah asked, pushing her long, chestnut brown hair out of her face with one hand. She'd tried her boss's phone earlier herself, soon after the sprinkler system on the first floor had deployed, ruining millions of dollars' worth of electronic equipment in the recording studios. She was glad she'd been there to supervise, having ended up canceling her lunch to deal with getting David's car to the service station and arranging for a loaner. Fortunately, no one had been hurt in the fire, but Deborah had wanted to prepare David for the disaster before he returned to the burned-out shell. But there had been no answer on his cell phone when she'd called, so she hoped he was ready for another surprise today in addition to his bashed-in car.

"Of course I tried his cell phone," Alicia said tersely. "No one answered and he always takes my calls. You'd better tell him that if he's avoiding me, he's going to be sorry."

"I'm sure that's not it. I promise to give him the message first thing when he comes in."

Relieved to have finally placated Robyn's manager, Deborah hung up the phone and laid her head back in her hands. For a day that had started out with so much promise, it was not turning out well.

The fire captain had told her it would be weeks, maybe even months, before they could determine the exact cause of the fire. She hadn't been too concerned about that; after all, they had enough insurance to take care of the damage, even if they did have a fairly high deductible.

Then one of the studio engineers had pulled her aside. He told her he'd been working on the Robyn Rogers recording session that morning and that he'd noticed Robyn's sister tossing a lighted cigarette into the trash and had thought at the time that it might cause a fire. When Robyn's sister stormed out, he'd forgotten all about it. He wasn't trying to get anyone in trouble; he thought Robyn's sister was a real nice person and all. He just felt bad that he hadn't gone with his instinct and made sure the cigarette was out before he'd gone to lunch.

Deborah had thanked him, but inside she felt sick. She liked Kylie, too; it was hard not to like someone who always had a smile or a kind word to say. But the string of mishaps that had occurred since Kylie started working at Gamble Records was becoming a little too eerie.

Her phone rang again and Deborah reached out to answer it, praying David would return soon.

*   *   *

"What do you mean you don't know where you got the CDs?" David speared the tall, thin owner of Bob's Records with a steely blue gaze.

Bob Buchanan tapped the ash off the end of his cigarette into the overflowing trash at the side of his desk before answering. "Look, Mr. Gamble, I'm just telling you like it is. Do you know how many distributors I get product from?" He spread his arms wide and started ticking off the list. "There's the big six, of course, those are easy. But I get shit from every independent record label from here to fuckin' Timbuktu. Sometimes they leave invoices and sometimes they don't, and they leave their product with any Larry, Moe, or Curly who happens to be workin' the front.

"Might help if I got a computer, I know, but frankly, between you and me, the way I got it set up now, the fuckin' IRS maybe doesn't get half my business like they might if everything was a little better documented, you know?" He took a deep drag, then let the smoke out in a cloud. "Besides that, with the handful of numskulls I got workin' for me, I doubt the brainpower of all of 'em combined could figure out how to change a lightbulb, much less run a computer system. That said, I'd be happy to look through my desk for the invoice if you've got a couple hours."

Another pile of ash drifted into the wastepaper basket as David studied the man in front of him. Even if there was a clear paper trail to who had supplied Bob's Records with the pirated copies of Robyn's CDs, they'd probably never find it in the mountain of paper on Bob Buchanan's desk. He'd wondered how Sandy could work with all her piles of paper, but at least her stacks were fairly neat and orderly. This guy's filing system seemed to be nonexistent, with a huge mound of paper piled on his desk as if a filing cabinet had exploded and Bob had simply left everything where it fell.

David absently toyed with the thick blue pen he'd taken out of his shirt pocket and contemplated the problem of

Robyn's pirated CD. He hadn't wanted to get the authorities involved—didn't want the publicity, especially now, with the pending deal with BSS—but Robyn and her manager would not be satisfied if he refused to act on this.

He couldn't really blame them. Robyn wouldn't get paid royalties for any of the pirated copies of her CD that sold, and Gamble Records wouldn't see any money to help defray their costs of production, either. The only one who would benefit from the deal would be the thief who'd pirated Robyn's master.

David declined Bob's offer to search his desk and asked him to call if he thought of anything that might help. He doubted if Buchanan would be of any assistance in this matter, and allowed the man to usher him out of the dingy back office and into the busy front of the store.

He spotted Kylie talking to the guy who had started this whole mess last week: Bradley Nelson, the guy who had told Robyn he was enjoying a CD that wasn't supposed to have been released yet. The same guy that Kylie had leaped out a window to escape the night of his last party. She certainly didn't seem to be avoiding the other man's attention now, David noticed sourly as he approached them.

"Bradley," David acknowledged, holding out a hand in greeting.

"Nice to see you again." Bradley grabbed the hand he proffered.

After a moment, David extricated himself from Bradley's enthusiastic grip and turned to Kylie. "You ready to go?" he asked.

"Sure. I picked up some new CDs that Bradley recommended." Kylie rattled her shopping bag. "You know, you really ought to hear Bradley's demo tape. I was listening to it the other night when I got locked in the demo room, and it's really very good."

David saw the light of undying devotion in Bradley's eyes and fought back his growing irritation. "Peter makes all the decisions about any new artists we sign. I'm sure he's given it all due consideration."

"Of course, David, I didn't mean to imply—" Kylie stopped as David began not-so-subtly pushing her toward the door.

"Nice to see you again, Bradley." David waved nonchalantly as he shoved Kylie out the door. He felt irritated, edgy after seeing Clint and getting nowhere with Bob Buchanan. Why did life have to be so damn difficult? Events were starting to spin out of control, and David didn't like it. His unpredictable feelings for Kylie and the unexpected jealousy that had just stabbed him when he saw her cooing over Bradley Nelson brought his simmering temper to the boiling point. He hadn't been able to control his physical responses to her, but his emotions were another matter. He could, he would, control them. She might think, after a weekend together, that she had some kind of hold on him but she'd be wrong. David shoved his pen into his shirt pocket, next to the pack of cigarettes he kept there.

Stunned to find herself out on the busy sidewalk, Kylie turned to the man behind her. "That was rude," she protested.

A couple walking past them turned their heads.

"Lower your voice, Kylie. You're causing a scene." David clamped a hand on her arm and began dragging her toward her car.

"What are you doing? Let go of me."

"Fine." David abruptly released her as he continued stalking down the sidewalk.

Kylie trotted to keep up, her bag of new CDs thumping at her thigh. "David, what's gotten into you? Why are you acting so strange?"

He stopped so abruptly that Kylie barreled into his back, then took a hasty step backward when he turned on her. "Couldn't you tell that Bradley was just using you to get to me? The only thing that cowboy wants is a record deal, and you just did everything but offer him a final contract to sign."

"No, I didn't. I was just being encouraging and honest. I *did* like his demo tape. What's the harm in telling him that?"

"What's the harm in it? I'll tell you what the harm is. Bradley Nelson saw us together, and I'm sure he thought that he could use you to get Gamble Records interested in him. Obviously, his plot backfired because he doesn't know your opinion about his music won't influence me. I make up my own mind about who we sign or don't sign, and if that idiot thinks he can use you to get to me, he's dead wrong."

If David had been searching for the one thing to say that would cause her the most pain, Kylie was willing to concede he had found it. The little bubble of hope in her heart, the one that had started to grow over the weekend, turned into a bitter stone as she looked at the angry man standing before her. Like so many other people she'd met in her life, David saw her as nothing more than a conduit to the talented, successful people she knew. He didn't think Bradley might appreciate her opinion for anything except how it might influence his own career.

Why did people continue to look at her as if she had no valuable opinions of her own? As if who she was and what she thought was of no consequence except for what she might pass on to those around her?

She opened her mouth.

Then closed it.

What could she say? In all likelihood, he was telling the truth about Bradley, just as it had been true about so many others in her life. She'd had plenty of so-called friends who were only friends until they found out that Kylie's parents weren't going to help them break into Hollywood, her brother wasn't going to get them the publishing deal they'd hoped for, and her sister wasn't going to help them set the recording industry on fire. From the day she'd been born, she'd been prey to people like that. But it wasn't her nature to believe the worst about people, so rather than withdrawing from the world, she'd simply learned to deal with the consequences. She hadn't expected David's contempt to be one of those consequences but, like every other disappointment or disaster life had thrown at her, she tried to handle it without losing herself.

Calmly, Kylie opened her purse and withdrew a twenty-dollar bill. Pressing the money into David's hand, she walked the few remaining steps to her car and unlocked her door.

David stared at the bill in his hand, his uncharacteristic spurt of anger starting to fade. "What's this for?" he asked, walking to the passenger side of the Mustang.

Kylie turned the key in the ignition, glad to hear the familiar loud hum of the motor. She put the car in gear, then met David's gaze squarely through the window of the still-locked passenger door.

"Cab fare," she mouthed clearly, stepping on the accelerator and leaving David standing in the street, staring after her as he got smaller and smaller in her rearview mirror.

CHAPTER 11

At one minute after five P.M., Kylie shut off her computer and grabbed her purse, eager to end what had turned out to be an awful day.

Since she'd returned from playing David's chauffeur, she'd sensed something odd with the people at the office. Whenever she walked into a room, conversation came to a halt. And people kept looking at her strangely. She'd gone to the ladies' room three times to make sure she hadn't borrowed a scene from her worst nightmare and had somehow lost a vital piece of clothing or had her skirt tucked up into her pantyhose.

She'd heard about the fire on the first floor, but that didn't explain the strange looks that kept coming her way. She didn't have anything to do with that.

In the end, she decided they were probably all talking about her conversation with Robyn. It was always big news when the boss had a fling with someone new.

Well, pretty soon they'd have somebody new to gossip about. After his behavior this afternoon, it was obvious that David's fling with her was flung. His criticism hurt, had hit her where she was the most vulnerable. She pulled on her coat, rubbing a cheek against the soft leather. Obviously, her hope that David could accept her for herself was nothing more than a silly dream.

" 'Bye, Sandy." Kylie smiled weakly as she passed the door to her boss's office on her way out.

"Just a second, Kylie. David called and asked me to come up and bring the third-quarter royalty report. Do you remember where you put it?"

"It's in your in-box." She pointed to the overflowing black plastic tray on the corner of Sandy's desk. "Is there something wrong? Anything I can help with?"

"No thanks, Kylie. I'll see you tomorrow." Sandy absently waved her off and pawed through the mess of papers in her in-box.

Kylie heard the phone ring in the office next to Sandy's and waited to hear the occupant pick up the receiver. She didn't feel up to facing Brenda Olson and her rude insinuations right now. All she wanted to do was go home and nurse her aching heart, but she had promised Ty she'd work a shift at The Soup Kitchen first.

She swept past Brenda's office a split second after hearing the other woman answer her phone, thanking fate for sending a distraction her way. Slowly, she made her way down the stairs and out the front door of the Gamble Records building, trying not to think about David and his hurtful comments this afternoon.

Sighing, she unlocked the door to her Mustang and slipped into the warm interior. Hadn't she thought much the same thing herself when she'd first met Bradley—that he was only talking to her to get to Robyn? So why had she let David's observation to the same effect get to her?

"Because I want David to believe that Bradley could simply like me for myself. Even if it isn't true," she answered her own silent question, the words sounding hollow and sad in the interior of the car. Staring unseeingly out the windshield, Kylie touched the ring on her finger. The prongs holding the stone in place pressed into her fingertips as she spun it around and around.

What did it matter anyway? David would probably never want to see her again after she'd abandoned him this afternoon, and she could hardly blame him. After all, all he'd done was state the obvious, that Bradley was probably using her.

It certainly wouldn't be the first time in her life that had happened.

David thumbed two Tums out of the roll he kept in his top desk drawer and chewed them absently. The cab ride back to the office from the U-district had not improved his mood, or his digestion.

He wondered how it was possible for so many things to go wrong all in one day. The phone was quiet for the first time since he'd been back and he used the time to make a list of all the problems he had to solve.

First, there was the piracy of Robyn's latest CD. He'd called the pressing plant and was assured by the owner of the plant himself that all masters waiting to be processed were kept locked in the company vault. Only the owner and his wife knew the combination, and they checked their inventory every night at six and every morning at eight. Even if a thief had stolen Robyn's master, they'd have had less than fourteen hours to get it duplicated and put back in the vault. Based on the quality of the copy David had bought this afternoon from Bob's Records, that feat would have been virtually impossible.

On top of that, the owner said they'd installed a security camera to watch the vault. He offered to send David copies of the last month's tapes, but assured David he reviewed them himself every morning to make sure nothing amiss had happened during the night.

David had asked why they took so many precautions and was told the plant had had a crooked employee about five years back who had duped tapes from the master recordings in the vault. The employee made a fortune and skipped town, and the record companies had filed suit against the pressing plant. The owner had almost been forced out of business, and he'd vowed never to let the same thing happen again.

So that meant the master used to produce the pirated CDs had most likely been "borrowed" from the demo room of Gamble Records. And the only ones with keys were people he knew and trusted.

David doodled on the pad in front of him, geometric shapes drawn aimlessly in the margins of the yellow legal pad.

Suddenly, his head snapped up, his eyes unfocused.

What had Kylie said this afternoon? She'd been listening to Bradley's tape the night she got locked in the demo room. The demo room, where the master recordings were kept. The night she'd been locked in the storage room, she'd mentioned that Sandy had loaned her the key. David had assumed that night was the first time Kylie had access to the demo room, but what if Sandy had loaned Kylie her key two weeks ago, when Kylie had first started working at Gamble Records?

If she hadn't had access to the room before last Thursday, when she'd been locked in, there was no way it could have been her. But if Sandy had loaned her the key on her first day, it was possible Kylie could have taken Robyn's master and had duplicates made.

The ink in David's pen spread out in a blotchy blue circle from where he pressed the tip into the pad of paper. He lifted it up off the page, then made a note to ask Sandy when she had first loaned Kylie the key and checked off the first item on his list of the day's disasters. He moved to the next item.

Second, of course, was the damage to his car. Deborah had arranged for a temporary loaner car, which had been delivered this afternoon. She'd mumbled something about being happy it was only temporary as she'd tossed him the keys and David wasn't looking forward to seeing what she'd meant by that. He supposed he could rent a car—hell, he could buy a new one without even making a dent in his bank account—but he hated wasting the money. It had been a hard climb to having enough cash always at his disposal, and the memory of never having enough had not yet loosened its grip. Besides, he asked himself now, how bad could the loaner car possibly be?

He checked off the second item on his list and moved on to the third.

The fire. They were going to have to take a fourth quarter hit to earnings to pay their deductible, something David wouldn't normally have worried much about. But he wanted their stock to look its best while the BSS deal was being investigated and he didn't want even a small dip in their earnings at this point. Unfortunately, there was nothing he could do about that. It certainly wasn't possible to hide the fact they'd had a fire and needed to start rebuilding the studios as soon as possible. Farming out their recording to other studios was expensive and inconvenient, so the claim would need to be reported and settled as quickly as possible.

He moved on to the last item on his list. At least, he hoped this was the last disaster that was going to befall him before the day was out.

Yes, the last item, the royalty problem. His phone had been ringing off the hook all afternoon with complaints of miscalculated royalty checks. The very same checks that Kylie had been working on for two weeks and had assured him were in perfect order before they were mailed out last Friday.

He looked down at the paper where he'd been making the list. Next to each point, he'd written Kylie's name. Each one of the disasters had involved the curly-haired woman who had abandoned him on a busy street in the middle of the U-district this afternoon.

David leaned back in his chair, looking out at the gathering rain clouds as he pondered the questions rolling around in his brain. Why was Kylie seemingly at the heart of these problems?

And what was it about her that kept him intrigued?

She was attractive, certainly. Her smile could light up a room. But he'd known plenty of women who were more glamorous and beautiful than Kylie Rogers, and none of them constantly intruded on his thoughts like she did. When she'd left his house on Sunday afternoon, the place had felt dead and empty, as if she'd packed all the energy with her into the cherry red Mustang when she'd gone. Even before Ben had shown up, he'd felt moody and restless. And this afternoon, he had been uncharacteristically irritable after watching Bradley Nelson mooning over her. Still, even knowing that she threatened to disrupt his carefully controlled world, David wished she were here with him.

His head jerked up at the knock on the door.

"Come in." He stood up, surreptitiously turning the notepad facedown on his desk.

"Hello, David."

Sandy poked her head into his office, and David swallowed the disappointment in his throat, telling himself it was for the best that it wasn't Kylie. She was linked to the string of problems besetting his life, and he needed to figure out how she was involved in all this before he saw her again.

"Did you bring the royalty report?" he asked, pulling his thoughts away from the impetuous brown-eyed girl who tracked trouble behind her like footprints in the virgin snow.

"Yes, I have it right here." The CFO laid a stack of paper on his desk.

"Have you reviewed this?"

"No. I spot-checked about twenty percent of the statements Kylie had prepared last Thursday before I went home. I picked some of the most difficult accounts to review and there wasn't one mistake in any of them."

"Did Kylie process the checks after your review?"

Sandy shook her head. "No. She was so concerned about doing them right that she wanted to go over her calculations a third time. That's why she was staying late the night she got locked in the demo room."

"Did you check her figures again on Friday before the checks were processed?"

"Of course not. She told me she hadn't changed any of the calculations I'd already reviewed and I was confident that her figures were accurate." Sandy leaned forward in her chair. "What's going on, David?"

David leaned back, lacing his fingers together on his desk. "I've received no less than fifty calls today from irate artists and their managers asking what the hell's wrong with their royalties."

"What do you mean?"

David pulled the report closer and flipped through it, searching for a specific record. "Here. Here's a summary of Robyn's check." He turned the report around for Sandy to see.

"Publishing royalties, three dollars and twenty-six cents. Royalties from *Moonshine*, eight dollars and ninety-nine cents," Sandy read, her voice rising incredulously as her eyes followed David's finger. She looked up and met David's gaze. "I thought Gamble recouped Robyn's advance on *Moonshine* a year ago. Last quarter's royalties on that album alone were almost eight hundred thousand dollars."

"I know. So you can imagine how Robyn's manager felt when she got a check for twelve dollars and twenty-five cents in the mail this afternoon."

"David, I have no idea how this happened. I take full responsibility, of course, but Robyn's was one of the statements I checked on Thursday. I would have noticed if Kylie's calculation was this far off."

David watched his CFO with a sick feeling in the pit of his stomach. Had Kylie changed the numbers that night, hoping that Sandy wouldn't check again before the statements went out? And why would she do such a thing? David wondered absently as he flipped through the report. What did she have to gain by—

His flipping stopped on page thirty-eight. There, about two-thirds of the way down the page, was the motive he was looking for. A check for over ten million dollars had been sent to Kylie Rogers at a P.O. box in Seattle.

David stared out the window at the darkening October sky. Somehow, he must have ended the conversation with Sandy because he was alone in the office, but he couldn't recall exactly what had been said.

He went down his list again in his mind, the chain of events beginning to take shape in his mind. He knew Kylie came from a wealthy family, so he doubted money was driving her. But what was it, then? What would make her take money from her sister and the other artists, money she didn't really need?

As he watched a light rain begin to fall, another thought struck him. Every one of Kylie's immediate relatives were household names. Her parents, her sister, her brother—they were well known to virtually everyone in the United States, if not the world—but not Kylie. She was totally unknown, and uniquely untalented compared to the rest of her family.

What did it feel like to be a nobody in a family of some-bodies? All her life, Kylie had been outshone by each and every one of her family members. If it were him, he would be jealous, resentful that he hadn't been given an equally special talent. Was that how Kylie felt? Did she hate her sister because Robyn was a blockbuster musician? Was that why she'd stolen the royalties and Robyn's master, to take away some of the physical evidence of her sister's incred-ible success? And where did his car and the studio fire fit into all this?

David stood up, pacing in front of the windows as his mind tried to find the answers.

Was she mad at him for helping to make Robyn's sing-ing career a success? He was willing to accept that the accident with his car was truly an accident, but he began to wonder if the fire was something she had deliberately set. After all, she had been trying to leave the parking lot in an awful hurry when she'd rammed into his car. Had she been trying to flee the scene of her crime?

His eyes narrowed as his thoughts took a sinister twist. David had heard about Kylie's argument with Robyn that morning. Perhaps Kylie had lost her temper and set the fire, hoping that Robyn would still be there when it sprouted to full flame.

He took a deep breath, willing that suspicion away. Surely she hadn't meant to hurt anyone. He couldn't imagine that a woman who would jump out a window to spare the feelings of a stranger would intentionally harm anyone, even a sibling she'd resented all her life. She'd probably just wanted to destroy the recording Robyn had made that morning; to make her sister have to work harder for her success.

And what about the royalties? Kylie had diverted money from more artists than just her sister. Had she moved from resenting her own family to being jealous of anyone who was talented and successful? She must have known they'd find out about her misappropriation almost immediately. Was she planning to leave town, even leave the country with her ill-gotten gains?

David recalled Robyn mentioning the trust funds her parents had established for their children. Perhaps they had rescinded the money for Kylie, bestowing their favor on the two talented siblings instead. Perhaps they didn't feel that Kylie was worthy of their money, and this *was* about cash after all.

David clenched his fists as his own family situation reared its ugly head. Wasn't that what he'd done to his own brother—withheld money from him because Ben's dreams didn't live up to David's expectations?

"One catastrophe at a time," he muttered into the empty room, forcing himself to unclench his fists and focus on Kylie's situation rather than his own.

Was it only her sister Kylie resented? Had she targeted her brother as well? Daniel Rogers was a successful writer of commercial fiction, and David recalled Kylie mentioning she had worked at a publishing house in L.A. before moving up to Seattle. Had she sabotaged her brother first and then moved on to her sister?

David laid his forehead against the cool window of his office and watched the lights on the cars speeding by as the city of Seattle went about its nighttime business. He wanted to be wrong about Kylie. Even though he'd been irritated with her earlier, he didn't want to believe she was capable of these things. But what other explanation could there be? There was too much coincidence, too many things that pointed to Kylie as the most likely suspect.

The phone was cold in his hand as he picked it up and dialed Robyn's number. Her answering machine picked up on the fourth ring.

"Robyn, this is David Gamble. We need to talk. Right away. Can we meet first thing tomorrow morning?"

After leaving his message, David gathered his briefcase and keys, locked his office, and headed out of the building. His loaner car was easy to spot in the parking lot. David groaned as his earlier conversation with Deborah came back to him.

"Are you sure you don't want to spring for a rental car?" she had asked. "I'm sure we can get you a nice Mercedes or another Jaguar," she'd suggested.

But he'd been adamant. He hated spending money unnecessarily and the loaner car was free.

"Okay," she had said skeptically, "but just remember it's only temporary."

Standing in the parking lot now, looking at the lone vehicle parked near the building, David wished he'd paid a bit more attention to the tone of Deborah's voice. The white lettering on the side of the purple, egg-shaped car shone in the light from the overhead streetlight. "European Imports— Your Luxury Vehicle Headquarters," it read in bold script. And underneath, in very small print, were the words he read with dread. "Complimentary Loaner Car for Our Valued Customers."

Ugh. This is what they gave him to drive in lieu of his sleek, powerful Jag? David shook his head with disgust as he turned the key in the lock. He slipped into the driver's seat, and wrinkled his nose as the smell of cheap vinyl assaulted his nostrils. Instead of the smooth mechanical slide he was used to, the seat clunked into place as he pushed it all the way back to accommodate the length of his legs.

"Now I know what a sardine feels like," David muttered as he closed the door, wincing at the tin can sound it made as it slammed shut. The engine sputtered to life, and David backed the purple car out of its parking space. Pulling up to the exit, he looked left, then right as indecision hit him.

Should he confront Kylie about his suspicions? Shouldn't he give her the chance to explain things for herself before drawing his own conclusions? Certainly, there was a mounting body of evidence pointing directly at her, but didn't she at least deserve a hearing before he condemned her?

David flicked on his turn signal, put his foot down on the accelerator, and grimaced as the car puttered out into the traffic on Queen Anne Avenue.

CHAPTER 12

None of the lights were on at Kylie's house when David drove up. He eased the small purple car into an empty space across the street. The Grapemobile, as he'd un-fondly termed it on the drive up Queen Anne Hill, shook as if it were going to fall apart when the speedometer inched anywhere near forty miles an hour. As he turned off the ignition, the engine shuddered with an ominous rattle before it died.

Unfolding himself from the small car, David conceded that perhaps his value system may have gotten a little bit out of whack over the past decade. Perhaps he had become too caught up in the pursuit of wealth and the luxuries that money afforded. But that didn't mean he wouldn't hesitate to trade the tin can back for his heavy, solid car. Soon.

Vaulting up the steps leading to Kylie's front door, David pressed the doorbell and waited. When there was no answer, he leaned out over the stoop to peer in the window, balancing himself against the wall as he hovered out over the bushes. She hadn't closed the curtains all the way, but all he could see were vague shapes in the darkened living room. David realized it was his first glimpse into her home, and he was disappointed to see that the place looked like a cluttered mess.

"Why should it surprise me that her house is as big a disaster as the rest of her life?" he said to himself, jiggling the front door handle.

It was locked, so he decided to go around and try the back door. The yard sloped steeply and David shook his head as he recalled Kylie's ridiculous out-of-control lawn-mower story. His favorite Cole Haan loafers sank into her waterlogged lawn as he walked through the grass at the side of her house. They'd had a bit of rain in the past few weeks, but the ground seemed soggier than the recent rain-fall warranted. He grimaced as mud sucked at the expensive leather of his shoes.

Turning the corner at the back of the house, David re-alized why the ground was so wet. A garden hose lay across the back porch, pouring water onto her lawn.

Rolling his eyes, David cranked the spigot into the "off" position.

"Leave it to Kylie to wander off and leave the water running all evening," he muttered, glad that he wasn't re-sponsible for paying her water bill.

The back door was closed, at least, but it wasn't locked. Hoping that he wasn't going to have to explain his presence to the police, David pushed open the door. No alarms went off. He prayed she wasn't using a silent alarm that wouldn't let him know he was busted until the cops showed up with guns drawn. The last thing he needed right now, on top of everything else, was to be accused of breaking and entering. After Kylie had left him standing on a busy street corner this afternoon, he wasn't sure she'd agree not to press charges. Of course, if his hunch about her was correct, they might end up sharing a jail cell if she did.

"Hello," he called into the darkness. "Anybody home?"

There was no answer. He took a step into the house, and something crunched beneath his feet.

Blindly searching for a switch, David exhaled a horrified breath as light filled the filthy kitchen. There was food everywhere: an open loaf of bread on the counter, coffee

grounds strewn over the tile, cans of Sprite and Barq's Root
Beer scattered on the floor, a half gallon of milk slowly
dripping its contents down the cabinets. David looked
down. The crunching under his feet was from an opened
bag of potato chips that looked as if it had been tossed to
the counter, then left where it fell when it missed its mark.

David's top lip curled with distaste as he wandered to
the living room. Things weren't much better there, but at
least it didn't turn his stomach like the mess in the kitchen.

"What does she do, just leave things right where she
hurls them?" he asked the empty room. This was awful.

Magazines and books were lying about the room even
though David noticed a perfectly good set of bookcases on
either side of the fireplace. There wasn't a lot of furniture,
which was good, since it was cluttered enough with all the
other junk that was thrown about.

It was like watching a car wreck, David supposed, as he
slowly climbed the stairs to where he guessed her bedroom
might be located. He didn't really want to see it, but something kept pressing him on.

There were three bedrooms on the second floor, one of
which David guessed she must use as a home office based
on the papers that littered the floor. It took some effort to
push open the door to the second room and once he got it
open, David could see why the door was stuck.

There were clothes piled all over the place; on chairs,
on the floor, lying across the bed like an orgy without bodies. The inexorable force drew him on, the ghoulish sensation that he couldn't leave without seeing it all.

Wading through the sea of fabric, he pushed through the
jumble of clothes and on toward the bathroom.

All of the lights in her house were on when Kylie drove
up the back alley to her carport.

She knew that she had turned them all off after she'd
come home from work to change into the jeans and sweat-
shirt she had on now before running back out to do a shift

at The Soup Kitchen. Cursing herself for not remembering to set the security alarm, Kylie turned off her headlights and the engine of her car, letting it coast to a stop in the alley. She was certain someone had come into her house the night that Mr. Chips had been injured. The vet had told her the cat's injuries were most probably the result of being kicked, and there was no way someone could have gotten to her cat if he or she hadn't come into the house. Quietly setting the parking brake, Kylie clenched her teeth with fury.

If someone was in her house again, she wasn't going to alert them that she was home. No way. If the person who had hurt Mr. Chips was back, she was going to go in and defend her home and family.

Looking around for something in the car with which to defend herself, Kylie was disappointed to come up empty-handed. She kept her car pretty neat as a rule, and she didn't think the owner's manual and registration in the glove compartment could in any way be construed as lethal weapons.

The gravel crunched under her Keds as she cautiously stepped out of the car and crept toward the back door. She wished she'd remembered to bring her cell phone so she could call the police, but she hadn't been able to find it earlier. And, of course, she'd been running late and hadn't thought it important enough to spend much time searching for it. She vowed from now on to leave the darn thing in her purse, not just drop it anywhere that seemed convenient at the time.

"Hold on, baby. Mommy's coming," she whispered quietly now, hoping Mr. Chips was safely hiding under a bed somewhere. If the intruder had dared to so much as touch a whisker of her cat, she'd . . . well, she didn't know what she'd do, but it wouldn't be nice.

As she neared the steps, Kylie spied the small trowel she'd used to plant flowers in her window boxes. Picking up the garden implement, she held the metal blade out in front of her like a knife and slid open the unlocked back door.

The trowel almost fell out of her stunned grasp when she saw the chaos that had become of her tidy little kitchen. The entire contents of her refrigerator were sitting out on the counter; a dozen eggs sitting in an open carton, at least half of them broken and oozing yellow goo over the gray cardboard; milk dripping down the cupboards; sticks of butter ripped from their neat packaging; frozen chicken breasts thawing in a soggy mess.

Clenching her teeth, Kylie renewed her grip on the garden tool. If somebody had hurt her cat again, she was going to split open his skull. She picked her way as silently as possible through the crunchy mess on the floor.

As she peered out into the living room, she heard the creaking of floorboards overhead and tried to pinpoint the location of the noise.

Someone was in her bathroom upstairs.

She tiptoed over to the staircase and peered up but didn't see anyone. Plastering herself against the wall, she crept quietly up the stairs. With one hand on the worn banister and the other gripping the trowel, she stepped over the squeaky fourth step and poked her head up to the second-floor level.

She couldn't see anyone in her room, but was certain she would have heard if the intruder had moved out of her bathroom. Trying to make herself invisible, she sprinted up the last few steps and pressed her back against the wall.

"Stay calm, stay calm," she chanted silently, trying to force a breath past her racing heart. The trowel in her hands shook, scattering little bits of dirt over the light-colored carpet.

Hoping to best the intruder using the element of surprise, Kylie slithered along the wall to her bedroom door.

"You can do it," she breathed, preparing herself for the coming confrontation.

A man suddenly stepped out of the doorway.

Kylie did two things simultaneously. She dropped the trowel . . . and ran.

Perhaps his instincts were a little better honed than hers. Or maybe he just wasn't frightened for his life. In any event, David caught her by the arm before she managed to hurtle herself headfirst down the stairs.

"Kylie, stop. It's me, David." He shook her in an attempt to get her to stop struggling.

She turned huge, frightened eyes to him and David let go of her arms.

She threw herself at him, wrapping her arms around his waist and laying her head on his chest.

"Thank God it's you. I thought you were an intruder."

"If you thought a stranger was in your house, why didn't you go to a neighbor's and call the police?"

Hearing the censure in his voice, Kylie dropped her arms and took a small step back. "I don't know. I guess I just didn't think. I was afraid somebody might hurt Mr. Chips again, and I came in to rescue him."

"With that?" David's gaze shifted to the small garden spade. "What were you going to do? Plant me?" he asked, his dark blue eyes spearing hers.

There was nothing she could say to that, no defense she could offer against his criticism. Of course, he was right. Any sane person would have gone to the safety of a neighbor's and called the police. But not her. As usual, her impulsiveness had ruled the day.

Her shoulders slumped.

"Have you seen my cat?" she asked dispiritedly.

"No, but I don't know how you could find anything in this mess."

Kylie blinked against the harshness in his voice. Was he blaming her for someone breaking into her house? Wearily, she pushed a lock of unruly hair behind an ear. She was not going to fight with him and didn't want to hear any more of his low opinions of her. She didn't know what had happened to make him angry with her; perhaps he was taking the accident with his car much more seriously than she'd thought. Whatever it was that was bothering him, though, he didn't need to take it out on her.

"I'm sorry that my criminals don't do double duty as housekeepers, David."

"What do you mean?"

The pale moonlight filtered in from the skylight overhead, making a golden part down David's dark hair. Kylie was tired and leaned a shoulder against the wall as she answered, "I mean, this is the second time this month that my house has been broken into. Now, if you'll excuse me, I'd like to call the police and start getting this mess cleaned up."

"Why didn't you tell me someone had broken in? And why didn't you set your alarm?" David took a menacing step toward her, and Kylie resisted the urge to step back. If she hadn't been so weary, she might have seen the humor in the fact that he'd just gone from casting aspersions on her intelligence to being overprotective all in one minute. But, with his earlier criticisms still ringing in her ears, she was having a hard time appreciating his caveman routine right now.

"Go away, David. I can take care of this myself."

"I'm not leaving until I'm sure whoever has done this is gone. You find a phone and call the police, and I'll search the rest of the house," he ordered, pushing her toward the bedroom. Kylie had to resist rolling her eyes at his highhandedness, but did as she was told.

She found the phone—on its cradle, oddly enough—and dialed the number for the police department. After explaining to an officer what had happened, she hung up and surveyed the damage in her bedroom.

It didn't appear that anything was broken, just strewn about as if a tornado had passed through. Getting down on her hands and knees, Kylie peered under the bed. The steady yellowish-green gaze that greeted her filled her heart with gratitude. Lying down on the floor, she stuck an arm under the bed and stroked the cat's soft fur.

"How's my baby?" she crooned, closing her eyes with relief as the cat began to purr. Kylie wished she could squeeze herself under the bed and curl up in a ball next to Mr. Chips.

She was lying on the floor in the same position when she heard David's footsteps on the second-floor landing.

"It looks like whoever did this is gone."

Kylie pushed herself into a sitting position and nodded. She hadn't expected the burglar to still be here, but then again, what did she know about criminal behavior? "Thanks for checking."

David stuffed his hands into his front pockets and stared at her with a strange expression on his face. It looked as if he wanted to say something, but wasn't quite sure how to phrase it.

Looking up at him, Kylie waited expectantly for him to speak.

"Listen, Kylie, I—"

Whatever it was David was about to say was lost forever when the doorbell rang. They stared at each other for the space of a heartbeat.

"That'll be the police," Kylie said after a moment.

David nodded, then held out his hand to help her up. Once she was standing, he let her go immediately, and Kylie almost wished he hadn't, no matter what he thought of her housekeeping abilities. Instead, she told herself she was glad he didn't offer her any more comfort than was absolutely necessary as she headed down the stairs with him following a few steps behind.

He stood off to the side of the living room while she went to open the door. She shoved a pile of papers out of the way and showed the officer in, introducing him to David as she explained the events of the evening.

"Let's take a look at the rest of the house," the officer

suggested, taking notes in a small yellow notebook as they talked.

"I'll just stay here," David said absently.

Kylie looked over at him, noticing he looked a bit distracted, but dismissed the thought as she led the policeman into the ransacked kitchen.

The officer continued taking notes as they toured the downstairs, then started back toward the living room.

"Is it all right if I go now?" David intercepted their progress and directed his question at the officer.

"Yes, of course, Mr. Gamble. We have your contact information just in case we have any more questions."

David nodded, then turned his attention to Kylie. She noticed he still had a strange expression on his face, but she didn't have the energy to delve into his troubles at this point. She was going to be up all night cleaning up this mess, and the lingering fright from knowing someone had broken into her house—not once, but twice now—was threatening to make her teeth start chattering.

"We need to talk tomorrow," David said quietly. "I'll have Deborah make an appointment for nine."

"Fine," Kylie agreed, too tired to think about what David might want to talk to her about first thing in the morning.

CHAPTER 13

David sat outside in the little purple car, staring at the papers in his hand.

While Kylie had been talking to the officer, he had idly looked around at the scattered mess on the living room floor. His gaze had scanned over paperback novels, CDs, and videotapes; then something familiar had leaped out at him, something odd.

As Kylie went to the kitchen with the policeman, David had leaned down and picked up a half folded report lying on the floor. What had caught his eye was the letterhead—the Gamble Records letterhead. He flipped through the pages filled with names and phone numbers of Gamble artists. Next to many of the names were handwritten notations. Dollar amounts and dates. Paper-clipped to the report were several checks written to Kylie from a handful of his artists.

He sat in the car now, clutching the report, a sick feeling in his stomach. What was going on here? Were these the amounts she had changed the royalties to in the company's computer? What were the checks for? Was Kylie blackmailing Gamble artists?

He hit his palm against the steering wheel in frustration. God, none of this made sense.

Whatever the reason might be, it certainly put a more

personal note on the string of recent events. Maybe he had
been wrong. Maybe Kylie's target in all this hadn't been
her sister but Gamble Records itself.

"But why?" he wondered aloud, setting the report down
on the passenger seat before starting the car. The engine
groaned to life and he pulled out on the darkened street.
Why would Kylie try to sabotage his company?

David pondered the unanswered questions floating
around in his head as the Grapemobile rattled through the
night.

"We've rescheduled your recording sessions to a studio at
First and Lenora," David said, opening the conversation
with Kylie's sister the next morning, unsure how to best
broach the real reason he'd asked for a meeting with Robyn. He could hardly blurt out his suspicions of Kylie's in-
volvement in this latest string of disasters at Gamble Records, but he hoped Robyn could provide him with some
clues about her sister's strange behavior.

He watched as Robyn took a sip of coffee, her elegantly
manicured nails curled around the white porcelain cup.
There was no familial resemblance between this green-eyed
pixie and her sister, David realized as he studied Robyn
dispassionately. Robyn was reserved and contained, not impulsive like Kylie. When Robyn brought attention to herself, it was because of her beauty and talent, not because
she'd caused some mishap to occur.

So why, he wondered, glancing down at his lap, *why
can't I get you excited about someone like* her *instead?*

Realizing that it was ridiculous to be having a conversation with his penis, David shook his head ruefully. He'd
never let that part of his anatomy rule his life before, and
he wasn't going to let it start now. He needed to get some
answers, needed to find out why Kylie was in the eye of
this storm swirling around him so he could figure out what
to do to clean up the mess she'd left in her wake. Perhaps
once he knew what was motivating her, he'd be able to—

"David? You haven't been listening to a word I've said." Robyn's petulant voice interrupted his musings.

"I'm sorry," he said, then decided to jump in with both feet. "Why did Kylie leave L.A.?"

Dark liquid sloshed over the rim of Robyn's cup as her hand jerked in surprise. "Uh, I don't really . . . Why don't you ask her?"

David was surprised to see Robyn so flustered. She was clearly trying to evade the question so he tried another tack. "Do you know why she might have had a list of Gamble artists in her house? Or checks from our musicians?"

Shifting uncomfortably in her seat, Robyn set her cup back in its saucer on the table beside her. The silence lengthened uncomfortably before she answered, "Um, no. I have no idea."

It was obvious that Robyn was lying, but he couldn't very well force her to tell him the truth. He tried yet another line of questioning. "Where did your sister get the money to buy her house? Queen Anne is an expensive place to live. She'd never be able to afford a house there on an accountant's salary."

"She had a trust fund and she used some of the money from that to pay the mortgage."

"What do you mean 'had'? Did the house use up all the funds?"

Robyn twisted the coffee cup around on the saucer, refusing to meet his eyes. "Well, not exactly. The money's gone, but I . . . I'm really not at liberty to discuss my sister's finances."

So, money *was* an issue. But what had Kylie spent her trust fund on? Every answer just seemed to bring up more questions. Sighing with frustration, David asked, "Why did Kylie move to Seattle?"

Robyn hesitated and David watched a heated flush creep up her pale white neck. Obviously, there was one trait the sisters shared—their penchant for blushing. She leaned forward and lowered her voice. "Well, I suppose it won't hurt for me to tell you the truth. Kylie got in some trouble at her last job, and my father encouraged her to move. He thought it would be easier for her to start over in a new town, one where nobody knew her."

"But why Seattle?"

"She wanted to stay on the West Coast, and I think Dad hoped I could help keep her out of trouble if she moved here."

David was beginning to think there was no one alive who could keep Kylie out of trouble, but he didn't bother pointing that out. Instead, he focused on something else Robyn had said.

"What kind of trouble was she in at her last job?"

"It's a long story." Robyn shook her head ruefully before picking up her coffee cup and taking a sip.

David leaned back in his chair and glanced at the clock on his desk. "I have half an hour until my next meeting. Shoot."

"I suppose I should have told you about this before you hired her, but you never asked."

"I'm asking now."

Robyn sighed and pasted a martyred look on her face. David wondered why she was acting all put out; after all, it was Kylie who was probably about to be crucified. He pushed aside the uncharitable thought and turned his attention to Robyn's story.

"Kylie's last job was at a publishing house in Los Angeles called Pigeon Books. She'd worked there for about four years before she got fired."

"Was your brother one of Pigeon's authors?" David asked when Robyn paused.

"Yes. He helped her get the job there."

Perhaps Kylie had already done something to her brother, and was now working on her sister. But where did he fit into all this? What about the report and the checks from Gamble artists he'd found in her house? What did they mean?

David kept his questions to himself and nodded encouragingly to Robyn. "Go on."

"Well, Kylie had been working at Pigeon for about three years when they hired a new editor named Marcus Cambrio. He and Kylie were friendly. They went out to lunch together and had a few drinks after work, but according to her there wasn't anything romantic going on. Marcus was married, you see."

Air hissed through his teeth at David's intake of breath. He felt as if he'd been punched in the gut. Had Kylie been having an affair with a married man? He couldn't believe it. The Kylie he thought he knew would be too loyal to do such a thing, she'd be too worried about hurting the man's wife to go through with it. That was the Kylie he wanted to believe existed. Had she played him for a fool? David gritted his teeth and tried to concentrate as Robyn continued.

"Anyway, one day, Marcus told Kylie that his wife had kicked him out and he had nowhere to go. He said he had to pay his wife almost his entire salary for alimony and child support and didn't have any family he could go to for help."

"What did she do?" David asked.

"You know Kylie—she's a sucker for a sob story. She let him move in. Rent-free, of course. It was a sweet deal for him and I think . . ." Robyn hesitated. "Well, I think Kylie liked having someone to take care of besides that cat of hers."

David got up, ostensibly to pour himself a cup of coffee. He was finding it difficult to sit still and listen to details of Kylie's relationship with another man.

"She insisted there wasn't anything romantic between them, but I find that hard to believe. Whether there was or not, though, the rumors around the office had them pegged as a couple and, in the end, that was enough."

"Enough for what?" David tried to contain his impatience and set his coffee cup down with a clatter.

"This is where it gets a bit convoluted." Robyn shrugged, taking another sip of her own drink.

As if he expected anything involving Kylie to be anything but convoluted. David forced himself to remain still when all he wanted to do was stalk around the office.

"An author who had submitted her manuscript to Pigeon came across her book at the bookstore and called the senior editor to threaten a lawsuit."

David raised a dark brow in question, "Come again?"

"I told you it was convoluted. You see, this author—I think her name was Lila something-or-other—anyway, this Lila had sent her manuscript to Pigeon Books, specifically to Marcus Cambrio, after he'd requested a full submission. After a few months, Marcus sent Lila's manuscript back with a rather scathing rejection letter. From what I heard, the author was pretty upset, so she filed her book away and went to work on something new. You can imagine her surprise, then, at seeing a book with an identical story line to the one Marcus had rejected hitting the bestseller lists a year later. She apparently ran down to the nearest bookstore and bought the book, only to find it matched her manuscript word for word."

"What does this have to do with Kylie?"

"The author's name on the bestseller was Kylie McGillicuddy. McGillicuddy is our mother's maiden name," Robyn explained. "And it didn't take long for the editor-in-chief to put two and two together. She questioned Kylie, who claimed to have no idea what the editor was talking about. So the editor called Kylie's boss and found out that they were sending royalty payments for Lila's book to a Kylie McGillicuddy at a post office box in Los Angeles. They asked Kylie to bring in copies of her bank statements and there were two deposits in the exact amounts of the royalty checks the publisher had sent. Apparently, the bank saw our mother's maiden name in Kylie's records and didn't have a problem cashing checks made out to her in that name."

"No." David groaned and stood up, giving in to the urge to pace.

"Yes." Robyn shrugged. "Kylie said she didn't know anything about it, and the money was withdrawn from her account a few days after it was deposited in both instances. She said she never even noticed these two rather large deposits and corresponding withdrawals being made to her account. The way she is with her money, I can certainly believe that." Robyn shook her head with affectionate disgust at her sister's lack of business acumen.

David leaned back against the credenza, his knuckles turning white as he clenched them against the urge to hit something. Why he felt this need to defend Kylie against her sister's undoubtedly well-deserved criticism was beyond him. Knowing Kylie, she almost certainly guarded her money like she guarded all her other possessions—which was to say, not at all.

"So, how did it all end?" he asked, keeping his clenched fists at his sides and hoping the worst was over.

"Marcus must have suspected the trail was eventually going to lead back to him because he left town within hours after Pigeon asked Kylie for her bank records. In the meantime, Kylie went to the bank and got copies of the deposit slips and canceled checks. In the end, it became clear that virtually all the documentation was in Marcus's handwriting. But by then, Marcus was long gone. Kylie agreed to reimburse Lila for the stolen royalties. She even wrote an apology to Lila and paid to have it run in *Publishers Weekly*. Then Pigeon went through their records to see if there were any other books that Marcus planned to release under Kylie's name."

"Were there others?"

"Yes. Apparently Marcus had been a very busy man. Apparently, he thought he could use Kylie's name as a front and her bank account to launder the money. Fortunately, though, nothing else had been published by the time his scheme was uncovered. Marcus obviously hadn't counted on any of the books becoming bestsellers and I guess he figured he'd pick up some easy money, maybe a couple small advances for a year or so, and no one would be the wiser. But when the big checks started rolling in, he wasn't about to just walk away. He must have known he'd get caught, though, because the police discovered he'd bought a one-way ticket to Argentina right after he'd deposited the first check into Kylie's account."

David's eyebrows pulled together in a frown. "So why did Kylie get fired if none of this was really her fault?"

"Pigeon's board of directors was pretty adamant about it. They said that someone with a fiscal responsibility to Pigeon's authors should have shown better judgment."

The intercom on David's desk buzzed, interrupting his next question.

"David, Kylie's here for her appointment," Deborah announced.

He let out the breath he hadn't realized he'd been holding. He hadn't yet figured out how this latest story fit into the picture he'd begun to form in his mind. Kylie's actions at Pigeon Books hadn't hurt her brother, except perhaps his reputation for recommending that she be hired in the first place. She hadn't gained financially, had even paid back everything this Marcus had taken from the original author. So where did that leave him?

Wearily, David ran a hand through his hair. It seemed the fiasco at Pigeon Books was unrelated to the present situation. Maybe Kylie *had* been totally innocent of wrongdoing at the publishing company, but perhaps that had given her the idea about diverting royalties from Gamble Records when her own trust fund had run out.

Hell, he didn't know. There were too many strange things going on right now for him to be able to make any sense of it all. One thing was certain: Kylie was involved in this mess up to her ears.

He thanked Robyn for her time and walked her to the door.

CHAPTER 14

Kylie blinked with surprise to see her sister coming out of David's office. Robyn mumbled a greeting but refused to meet her eyes.

"Robyn, what are you doing here?" Kylie asked.

"Just chatting with David. Nothing important. Hey, we should do lunch sometime," she suggested.

"Maybe tomorrow," Kylie started to say, when David grabbed her arm firmly and started pulling her into his office. She waved a surprised good-bye to her sister as David ushered her in, closed the door, and twisted the wand of the Venetian blinds to shut out the sight of the outer office.

"Sit," David ordered.

Kylie did, noticing that he seemed uneasy as he paced the floor. For all that was wrong between them, he looked like he needed a hug. Maybe something had worsened with his friend at the hospital. She longed to stand up and wrap her arms around him and ask what was wrong.

So she did.

"David, I know something's been bothering you since yesterday afternoon. Is it your friend? Do you want to talk about it? You can't keep your feelings all bottled up inside like this. It'll make you sick."

David stopped pacing as Kylie pressed her body to his.

Her head rested on his shoulder comfortingly as her hands caressed the taut muscles of his back.

Without realizing quite how it had happened, she found that David's arms had somehow managed to wrap themselves around her. She felt so good, so right against him. Chances were he'd never see her again after the next hour, not after what he was going to have to do. He knew he was going to regret it, but seemed unable to stop himself as he put a hand under her chin and lifted her mouth to his.

She tasted of toothpaste and coffee, and the clean scent of her filled his nostrils. Her tongue touched his and David felt himself get instantly, frustratingly hard.

What was it about her that made him react this way? David groaned when she pushed her hips against him. Her hands kneaded his buttocks, encouraging him to press closer.

He tangled his hands in her hair, letting the silky curls slip through his fingers as he angled his head for better access to her luscious mouth. Her fingers slid under his shirt and David felt a cool draft on his back as her hands slid around to tickle the hair on his chest.

"Kylie," he groaned as she stroked her way down his stomach and caressed his erection through the fabric of his slacks.

"Mmm," she purred, rubbing against him like a cat.

He made quick work of the buttons on her blouse and unhooked the front latch of her creamy white bra. Her full breasts were heavy in his hands, her nipples already puckered with desire.

David backed up, pulling Kylie with him until he felt the sturdiness of his desk against the backs of his thighs. Resting against the wood, he leaned forward and teased one of her already distended nipples with his tongue.

It was her turn to groan, and David let slip a smile of smug satisfaction. His hands reached up under her loose skirt and slowly slid her stockings down her legs. She kicked off one high-heeled shoe, then the other as he pulled the pantyhose from her feet and tossed them to the floor. He ran his hands up her legs, reveling in the silky, smooth feel of her soft skin under his fingertips.

Her breath came faster as his hands met at the juncture of her thighs. He slid a thumb under the elastic of her peach-colored lace panties, and she whimpered as he stroked her.

God, she was wet. He held back his own groan. She obviously wanted this as much as he did. He moved his other hand up to the back of her head, bringing her mouth down on his. He devoured her, hungrily swallowing her moans as their tongues mated. She pulled back for an instant and freed his erection as her hands busily stroked him.

"Kylie," he ground out in protest, knowing he couldn't take much more.

"Mmm." She licked the sensitive skin just under his ear and David felt his hips thrust upward in response.

He wanted to be inside her, to feel her surrounding him with her heat. The last time . . . God, the last time had felt so good. He had to have her again, one last time before she was out of his life forever.

He murmured incoherent words into her ear while divesting her of her panties, then pushed her thighs apart and pulled her onto his lap. The desk was cool under him, but he could feel her heat, her slick wetness against him.

Her whimpering, panting breaths in his ear were driving him mad. He couldn't seem to get close enough. Reaching down between their heated bodies, he guided himself into her. With her knees on the desk on either side of him, Kylie lifted herself, teasing him with the promise of her.

He kneaded her smooth, white buttocks as she tortured him, slipping down an inch, then two, then rising again as she stretched to accommodate his length.

Beads of sweat broke out on his upper lip with the effort of restraining himself. He wanted to bury himself in her softness, to slam into her, to lose control.

He couldn't take it anymore.

"Enough," he growled and pressed upward, bringing her down fully on his erection. He groaned as her legs tightened around him, taking him even farther into her. Her head tipped back and her eyes closed as she moaned his name.

He thrust into her, feeling his orgasm build like a river sent out of control by too much rain. He didn't want to come without her, but he couldn't stop himself as he pounded into her.

"Don't stop," she panted, and David drove harder, gasping out her name with every thrust.

Her legs clenched around him and she moaned, low and deep in her throat. David felt the contractions of her body milking his erection, then everything went dark as he pressed into her one last time.

If he let her go now, she'd slide to the floor in a boneless heap.

Kylie knew she'd ache later from the unusual workout her body had just been through, but it had been worth every minute. Her fingers toyed with the silky dark hair at the nape of David's neck.

She'd never had sex on a desk before.

Kylie opened her eyes and tried not to giggle. She had always thought that it was just something romance writers made up to add some variety to their love scenes, hadn't thought anyone really ever made love this way.

Obviously, she'd been wrong and, although she wouldn't want to do it like this every time, it had been a pretty exciting experience.

"Uh, are you all right?" David, on the other hand, seemed a bit uncomfortable about the entire situation. Kylie watched a faint flush color his cheeks as he let her feet slide back down to the floor.

Her skirt wafted back down to its proper position, and Kylie felt a draft on her bare bottom.

So much for cuddling, she thought crossly, looking

around for her panties. David would hardly even meet her eyes.

Spotting the scrap of peachy fabric, Kylie grabbed her underwear and yanked them back into place.

"Yes, David, I'm fine. Why wouldn't I be?"

"I thought I might have been a little rough."

Stepping in front of him, Kylie waited for him to finish zipping up his pants.

"If you were being too rough, I would have told you to stop." He finally raised his eyes to hers and Kylie felt like he'd punched her when she saw the regret in his gaze.

"Kylie, we have to talk," he said quietly. "Do you want to get straightened up first? There's a bathroom through there." He waved to a door in the corner.

What the heck was going on here? "No, if you have something to say, just say it."

David ran an agitated hand through his hair as Kylie had noticed he frequently did when he was upset about something. He took a seat behind his desk and Kylie sat down opposite him, thinking it felt like she was about to receive a reprimand from the principal for setting all the frogs loose from biology class again.

"It's, uh, it's come to my attention that ever since you came to work at Gamble Records some strange things have happened."

"I already apologized about the coffee overflow. And your car. I expect you to send me a bill for the damages, although I may have to pay you back in stages. Money's a little tight for me right now."

David raised his eyebrows. "It's not just the flood and my car. What do you know about piracy in the recording industry?"

What in the world was he talking about? They'd just gone from cars and coffee to pirates?

"Pirates? Like yo-ho-ho and a bottle of rum?"

"No. Piracy, like stealing a master recording, pressing

your own CDs, and selling them behind the record label's back?"

"Why would anyone do that?"

"Because the record label incurs the significant costs to produce the master and the thief can sell the recordings without having to use his profits to pay those costs or the artist who made the tape."

Kylie fiddled with the bottom button of her blouse. It sounded just like what that louse Marcus had done to those poor authors back at Pigeon Books.

"That's awful," she muttered. David's eyes pinned her to her chair, and Kylie awkwardly rearranged her bare feet on the carpeted floor. She didn't want him to know about what had happened at Pigeon, about how gullible she had been. "Why do you want to know?"

David watched a guilty flush steal up Kylie's cheeks, and he fought the urge to pound his fists on his desk, to make her deny that she had anything to do with the theft of Robyn's master. Instead, he kept watching her, looking for proof of her innocence. He was surprised by how much he wanted to believe she had some logical explanation for all these mishaps, some story that would tie up all these loose ends and prove to him she was not guilty of sabotage and theft. He watched her closely as he continued, "Someone 'borrowed' your sister's tape from the demo closet and made unauthorized copies to sell around town. That's why I had you take me to Bob's Records yesterday. I found out from your friend Bradley that Bob's has some copies of Robyn's latest recording. We weren't planning to release it until the Christmas season, so I know they didn't get it from us."

Her look of surprise seemed genuine, but David wasn't convinced. Leaning forward, he said softly, "Tell me about the royalties, Kylie. What did you do with the ten million dollars?"

Kylie leaped to her feet, her mouth dropping open. "What are you talking about?"

"I'm talking about the royalty payments that went out last Friday. They were all wrong. And I found the payment you mailed to yourself. Why didn't you come to me if you had money problems? Robyn told me you don't have any money left in your trust fund."

"I don't have money problems," Kylie protested with a sick feeling in her stomach. Her trust fund was empty at the moment because she had donated the last of her yearly stipend to fund an emergency rescue team for pets trapped in flooding in Missouri. On January first, though, the fund would be refreshed with the interest earned off the principal of a very large sum being held for her. And while it was true that she'd probably donate the vast majority of the fund to the EmCee Foundation (named in honor of her beloved Mr. Chips), nobody could accuse her of having money problems.

The springs in his chair protested as David leaned back. "I just want to know why. Why would you take money like that from Gamble's artists? Those people work for months, sometimes years, just to earn a decent living doing what they love. Who were you trying to hurt? Is it Robyn? I can imagine how it would be hard for you not to be jealous of all the success your sister has enjoyed, especially since the rest of your family is so talented as well."

Kylie fell back into her chair, numbly watching the words drop out of David's mouth as her insides froze up.

"Or is it me that you're after? I have the report you ran listing all of Gamble's artists. It was on your living room floor last night."

Kylie continued to stare at David in openmouthed horror. She couldn't believe it was happening again and, even worse, that David was so quick to believe these things about her. His words continued to wash over her, but she barely heard him. It was as if she were lying on her back in her parents' swimming pool, her ears just under the water—everything he said came out muted and garbled.

She stared at him, shocked, barely able to comprehend

all the charges that he was leveling at her. Apparently, he thought she was a pirate, a thief, a liar, and stupid to boot. How could she have ever thought there might be a chance for them to have a meaningful relationship? How could he believe these things about her? Even worse, how could she have just had the best, most mind-numbing sex with a man who thought so little of her? Despair washed over her in waves as she tried to put it all together in her head.

"How could you just have had sex with me if you believe these things about me?" she asked dispassionately, her voice dulled with shock.

David had the grace to look embarrassed. "I'm sorry, Kylie. I didn't mean for that to happen. I just can't seem to control myself around you, but that doesn't change the fact that you're in real trouble here."

Kylie's eyes narrowed in anger. The nightmare just kept getting worse, but she was determined to keep what was left of her dignity. She tried to remain calm as her world started collapsing around her once again. "I am not a thief," she said quietly.

"Prove it to me." David's eyes locked on hers, and she thought she saw hope in the deep blue depths.

"How?" she asked.

"Call your bank. Ask them to give you your account balance," David suggested, turning the black phone on his desk around to face her.

Of course! It would be easy enough to prove her innocence. Why hadn't she thought of calling her bank? Rummaging through her purse, she pulled out her checkbook and dialed the phone number that was printed on her checks, then punched in her account number, followed by her PIN.

David reached over and pressed a red button and the voice of the automated phone system filled his office.

"For checking account balance, press one; for—"
Kylie pressed one.

"Just a moment please, while we access your account."

Kylie sat back, crossing her arms across her chest. David was going to feel like a fool when he heard she had less than five hundred dollars in her account. Although she wasn't going to let him off the hook that easily. He'd—

"The balance in your account is ten million, three thousand, six hundred and fifty-seven dollars and one cent," the mechanical voice intoned.

Kylie's ears started ringing. She did not have over ten million dollars in her account. She couldn't. This could not be happening to her again.

David pressed a button and ended the call, his dark gaze spearing her to the chair like an insect pierced through the heart with a sharp pin. Kylie blinked at him unseeingly. She pressed an errant lock of hair behind her ear with one shaking hand.

"No. This is . . . I don't . . ."

"I can't tell you how disappointed I am in you, Kylie. I hoped you had some explanation, something that would have made this all make sense. I can't tell you how much I wanted to believe it wasn't true."

He got up and walked to the windows, then turned again to face her, his body framed by the angry gray clouds outside. He was quiet for a long time, a time in which Kylie just stared dumbly at the carpet in his office. When his voice came, it was cold and controlled, devoid of any emotion. "You're fired. I'd like to keep this as quiet as possible, as I'm sure you would, too. I expect a certified check made out to Gamble Records on my desk by the end of the day."

Kylie shook her head, trying to refute the words that came out of David's mouth, but unable to say anything as he walked over and gathered her pantyhose and shoes, then dropped them in her lap. She stuffed her stockings into her purse and slipped her feet into her shoes, watching as David pointedly opened the door to his office. Still in shock, she followed his unspoken order out the door and into his assistant's office.

She didn't turn as David's office door closed behind her with a cold, controlled click.

Her fury came too late to be of much good against David's attack.

Kylie drove through the pouring rain, her wipers angrily scraping dirty water off the car's windshield. She didn't know who deserved her ire more, David or herself.

In a moment of passion, he had said he loved her, and she had wanted it to be true so much that deep down she'd let herself believe it. But he couldn't love her. He couldn't even know her at all if he really believed the awful things he had accused her of doing. Even worse, she hadn't fought back, hadn't stood up for herself, out of some stupid sense of false pride. Now, she'd lost everything: her job, any hope of a relationship with David, and her self-respect.

This time, though, she wasn't going to take it lying down.

She glanced over at the cashier's check sitting on the passenger seat of her car. She didn't know how the money had ended up in her account, but she knew from past experience it wasn't particularly difficult for someone to make false deposits into a bank account. After all, how many people would complain at finding an extra ten million dollars to their name?

Her stomach grumbled, reminding her she had missed lunch in her haste to get the stolen royalty money back to Gamble Records.

Someone was obviously setting her up again, undoubtedly the same person who had broken into her house last night. The officer had been very helpful, but since nothing appeared to be missing, all he had done was advise her to get her locks changed and remind her to set her alarm whenever she left home.

But that wasn't enough for her.

She was not going to sit back and let this person, whoever it was, ruin her life. She had tried that with the Pigeon

Books disaster, had let Marcus tar her with a guilt that wasn't hers. She'd lost a job she liked and friends she'd worked with because they were uncomfortable around her after she'd been fired. She had been willing to shoulder some of the blame for being too trusting. Perhaps it had been wrong to offer help so easily to someone she thought was a friend, but in retrospect, she wondered if she had given in to Pigeon's board of directors too easily. After all, they had trusted Marcus, too. They'd hired him and put him in a position of responsibility, and she'd taken the blame when he abused their trust.

Kylie pounded a fist on her steering wheel as she stopped behind a green Mazda at a red light. She was not going to just lie down and let them bury her alive this time. She was going to prove to David that she was not someone to be pitied. She was not the spineless crook he believed she was. She'd make him eat his words if it was the last thing she did.

Before she was through, David Gamble was going to be begging for her forgiveness.

She'd make him walk through crushed glass. On his knees. Carrying her. Wearing a pink dress. Him, not her.

Oh, this was getting good.

Lost in her elaborate revenge fantasies, Kylie automatically stepped on the accelerator as the light turned green. She sped down Queen Anne Avenue toward the Gamble Records office, her car splashing through puddles of water as the rain continued to pour down.

CHAPTER 15

The Grapemobile sputtered a gasping death rattle two blocks from the office.

It had been so long since he'd had car trouble that David simply sat in the driver's seat, staring at the dashboard without a clue what to do next. There were no red indicator lights flashing, no signs as to what might be the problem. The heavy noontime rain splattered on the windshield, blurring his view of the outside world as he sat unmoving in the creaky vinyl interior of the car.

The rude noise of a horn behind him snapped David out of his stupor. He hit the emergency flashers and looked around for his cell phone to call for assistance.

Where was the damn phone?

David frowned, trying to recall the last place he'd seen it. He usually left it in his car. Yes, of course. He'd left it in his car, which was in the shop, which was why he was driving around in this purple piece of crap in the first place. Laying his head on the steering wheel, David ignored the irritated glares of the other drivers as they made their way past him.

After his run-in with Kylie that morning, he'd wanted to get away from the office for a while. Knowing Clint would appreciate the company, he'd gone to the hospital to have lunch with his friend. The sadness in Clint's eyes almost made David glad he'd found out the truth about Kylie. It reminded him that you left yourself open to pain and anguish when you started caring about someone else. In the end, it was better to depend only on yourself for happiness, he decided, raising his head. He'd learned early that you couldn't control the behavior of other people. All you could do was take charge of your own actions and make sure you protected yourself from hurt and humiliation. From what he knew of Kylie, the word "control" wasn't even in her vocabulary. "Impetuous," "trouble," "disaster": yes, those were words she'd know quite well, but not "restraint" or "control."

Shaking his head, David looked up and down the busy road, searching for a convenient place he could push the car so it would be out of the way of traffic. He spied a parking lot a few feet away. Grabbing the keys from the ignition, David pushed open the door and stepped out into the rain. His hair was immediately plastered to his head by the downpour and David cursed the uncommonly heavy shower. Why couldn't it just drizzle like it usually did? Day after day of dripping gray skies was the norm in Seattle, not this deluge. Some people said they could go a full year without moving their windshield wipers off the intermittent setting, but a day like this would ruin that claim.

It only took a moment to push the tiny car into the parking lot and out of traffic. He vowed to have it towed before the day was out, then started toward the office. He tried to ignore the cold trickle of water down his spine. Seeing the office ahead, he picked up his pace. After his—what would he call it? Discussion? Episode? Debacle?—well, whatever it was, he'd needed to clear his mind of the sight and scent of Kylie Rogers. It was probably only his imagination, but his office had seemed to reek with the smell of hot sex, even after Kylie had left.

That smell, coupled with an alien feeling he couldn't define, had driven him out into the rain and across town to visit Clint. But now, he needed to get back, needed to develop a strategy for how to deal with the Kylie situation. He should probably call Mitchell Sharpe at BSS just to let him know what was going on. David didn't need any surprises getting in the way of the satellite deal he'd worked so hard on over the past year.

He stopped at the final intersection before the office, waiting for the "Don't Walk" sign to change. Idly, he wondered why the walk signs flashed white instead of green like the traffic signals.

The light changed, and David took a step toward the crosswalk.

Lost in thought, his head snapped up as a wave of cold water splashed waist-high, splattering mud halfway up his chest.

"Damn it, look where you're—" He broke off mid-yell as he watched the taillights of a red Mustang speed off and turn into the parking lot of Gamble Records.

"Kylie!" he shouted after the disappearing vehicle.

Kylie thought she heard someone calling her name as she turned off her wipers and pulled into one of the coveted visitor spots near the front entrance of Gamble Records. Then she figured no one would be walking around out in this mess. She had to be imagining things.

"You fired me, so I guess I'm a visitor now," she muttered, as she gathered her purse and the cashier's check from the passenger seat.

She slammed her car door a little harder than was necessary and sprinted to the heavy glass doors of the office building and up the stairs to the fourth floor. The elevator would probably have been faster, but the pounding of her heels made a satisfactory clomping sound on the carpeted stairs. She imagined she was stomping on David's head instead of the solid concrete stairs. The thought made her feel better.

The door to David's outer office swung open easily when Kylie shoved on it.

"Where is he?" she asked a startled Deborah, who looked to be enjoying a cup of soup at her desk.

"Hi, Kylie. He's not here right now. Can I give him a message?"

"Sure, how's your right hook?"

"Pardon me?"

"Never mind," Kylie said. "I need to give him this check. Can I borrow a piece of paper? I'd like to leave a note."

"Sure." Deborah ripped a yellow sheet off the pad in front of her. Kylie bent over and started to pen a note to David as Deborah continued, "Listen, Kylie, I was really sorry to hear about . . ." Her voice floundered, then finished, "Well, about everything."

"Thanks, Deborah. I'm going to—" Kylie began, then squealed when the door swung open, smacking her rear end and sending her sprawling over Deborah's desk. Chicken noodle soup went flying, ending up all over the front of Deborah's pale yellow dress.

Deborah leaped to her feet. "Oh, no. This is my favorite dress!"

"I'm so sorry," Kylie sputtered, pushing herself up from her ignominious sprawl on top of the desk. She turned to see who had pushed open the door forcefully enough to send her flying, then glared at the culprit.

"David, this is all your fault. You can't just go around shoving doors open in other people's, er, faces," she scolded, her hands on her hips. "Look what you made me do. Don't worry, Deborah, David will pick up the dry-cleaning tab."

David stood in the doorway, dripping rain and mud onto the formerly champagne-colored carpet. He tried to summon up the righteous anger he'd felt only moments before, before he'd opened the door to see Kylie's firm, bare legs topped by her curvy, tight bottom bent over his assistant's desk. He'd wanted her all over again, wanted to run his hands up the outside of her thighs, pull her panties down around her ankles and slip inside her, right there, right then, and to hell with the audience.

What was happening to him? Where was the control that he worked so hard to maintain? He knew Kylie was a walking disaster, but still, he wanted her. What was wrong with him?

Kylie glared at him, her sherry-brown eyes bright with anger as she stood there, her hands on her hips like an outraged schoolmarm. At that moment, he didn't care what she had or hadn't done to him or Robyn or anyone else.

He wanted to bury his hands in her curls and kiss her until the rest of the world just melted away.

She said something and held out a piece of paper. He grasped it and looked at it dumbly, trying to rein in his errant thoughts and get the blood that was pooling around his groin back to his brain where it belonged.

Watching her leave, David wondered why the room seemed darker after she was gone. The wind pelted rain against the windows, as if trying to penetrate the glass and finish up the job Kylie had begun. He shook his head, sprinkling water across the papers on Deborah's desk. He obviously needed a vacation, some time in the sun to relax and forget all about Kylie Rogers.

"What happened to you?" Deborah asked, mopping at her dress with some paper napkins and eyeing him curiously as he continued to stand in the doorway, dripping onto the floor.

David looked down at himself, at his mud-spattered clothes and sopping leather shoes, then looked back at Deborah as she stood dripping noodles and chunks of chicken onto the carpet.

"Same thing that happened to you."

Deborah grinned. "Hurricane Kylie?"

"Hurricane Kylie," he confirmed with resignation.

* * *

The alarms that flanked the entrance emitted a loud squawk as Kylie pushed open the heavy glass door. As usual, the employees of Bob's Records in the U-district ignored the summons. Bob had a penchant for staffing his establishment with a mix of pseudo-intellectual professional students and unemployed musicians, both groups holding to the belief that actually serving paying customers would be beneath their intellectual or creative dignity.

Fortunately for Kylie, she spied what, or rather who, she had come for immediately and made a beeline directly for the back of the store. His back was to her and she could see wires hanging down from his ears.

"Bradley." She tapped his shoulder to get his attention.

He whipped around, startled, pulling the headphones down around his neck. Kylie noticed he was wearing a different uniform today of blue jeans and heavy metal T-shirt, but hadn't forgone the ever-present snakeskin cowboy boots. He wasn't wearing his hat and she saw that, like Garth Brooks, his sandy brown hair was getting a little thin on top.

"Hey, Kylie," Bradley greeted, sounding genuinely delighted to see her. "What brings you here?"

"Actually, I'm here to ask a favor."

"Sure thing. What can I do for you?"

He seemed so eager, so pleasant, that Kylie found herself feeling a small twinge of guilt for being so willing to dismiss him before. She silently promised that she would push his demo to Robyn when this was all over, see if there was anything she could do to get someone to pay some attention to his music.

Opening her purse, she pulled out the pirated copy of Robyn's CD that she'd bought yesterday and handed it to Bradley. "Do you remember David Gamble asking about these?" she asked.

"Sure. It was only yesterday."

Surprised by the subtle amusement in his voice, Kylie looked at him suspiciously. Perhaps Bradley wasn't quite as simple as he tried to let on. She wasn't sure if that was a good thing or not, but had no choice but to continue.

"David thinks I had something to do with stealing Robyn's master and producing these." Kylie looked around the crowded store. No one appeared to be watching them, but she couldn't be too careful. She moved to a deserted corner in the back of the store, motioning for Bradley to follow. Lowering her voice, she leaned toward him and continued. "He fired me, and I'm going to find out who did this and bring them down," she whispered fiercely.

Bradley's eyes opened even wider than usual. "No shit," he exclaimed, then blushed furiously. "Oh, pardon me," he stammered out, obviously remembering that he was a gentleman.

"Somebody stole Robyn's master and is cloning it, and I'm going to find out who. Gamble Records didn't have the release scheduled until the start of the Christmas season, but whoever did this sent advance copies to one of the local radio stations and the CDs are already selling like crazy. David mentioned he's put on the pressure to move up the production schedule, but in the meantime, the only one who's making any money off it is the thief."

"That really stinks." Bradley shook his head in disgust. "Most artists work for years in dingy bars, barely making enough money to cover travel expenses, while trying to get a deal with a record company so they can make enough just to pay the rent or buy a decent car that won't break down every thousand miles. Then some jerk comes in and steals their work, and the artist who's worked his butt off doesn't even get a dime. Wish I could find the bast—" Bradley stopped himself just in time, then continued, "—the jerk who did that to Robyn."

"Me, too," Kylie agreed. She had her own motivations, though, namely proving to David Gamble that he was wrong about her. She gritted her teeth, then forced herself to relax. In order to get Bradley to agree to help her, she needed to play on his sympathy for the artists. She worked on blinking her eyes innocently as she put her plan into action.

"Hey," she said, as if the idea had just occurred to her, "do you think we could take a look at Bob's inventory records and maybe see if we can find a clue there?"

Kylie saw the hesitation in Bradley's eyes and knew she had no choice—she looked up at him, her eyes wide and hopeful, giving her best damsel-in-distress impression. She felt ridiculous, but only until she saw Bradley beginning to waver. Having seen her mother use the same tactic on her father a million times, she fluttered her lashes just a bit, hoping to sway him.

"Well, okay. I'll see what I can do. Bob doesn't usually come in till after two." Bradley glanced at his watch. It was just after one o'clock now. "Be outside the back door in ten minutes. I'll tell the manager I need a break." He rubbed his chin thoughtfully. "I'm going to have to find some way to get the keys to Bob's office."

Kylie couldn't believe her silly, helpless female act had worked. She'd never tried it before, believing that it would only work for people like Robyn or her mother. She made a silent note-to-self to remember this particular act for future reference.

Out loud, she whispered, "What are you going to do?"

"I don't know yet. I'll figure something out," Bradley answered, obviously lost in his own thoughts. "I'll see you in ten minutes," he said absently, ushering her through the store and out the front door.

CHAPTER 16

Trying to look as if she made a habit of hanging out in alleys, Kylie leaned nonchalantly against the chilly cement wall behind the record store. The distinctive smell of Asian cooking wafted through the air, and Kylie's stomach rumbled, reminding her it was past lunchtime and she hadn't had anything to eat all day.

Trying to ignore the emptiness in her belly, she looked at her watch for the fifteenth time in as many minutes and wondered what was taking Bradley so long. Tapping her fingers on the old wall, she watched cars speed by the opening of the alleyway, students rushing to their afternoon classes at the nearby University of Washington, and businesspeople racing back to work after their lunch appointments. The rain had slowed to the usual Seattle drizzle, and Kylie stood back from the overhang to avoid the occasional droplets of water the gutter sent her way.

Watching the rain, Kylie recalled the scene earlier in Deborah's office. She hoped Deborah would be able to get the chicken soup out of her dress and idly wondered why David had been so wet when he'd stomped in. Her first thought was to hope he wouldn't catch a cold, but she squelched it. She hoped he *did* get a cold, a bad one that would make his nose drip and his throat ache for at least a week. It would serve him right for being such a disloyal jerk. She gnashed her teeth and shivered a bit, wishing Bradley would hurry up.

The door beside her creaked open with a loud groan. A man's arm snaked out to grab her by the arm and yank her inside the dark hallway.

"Hasn't your boss ever heard of WD-40?" Kylie whispered.

"Shh." Bradley pressed a finger to his lips and tugged her down the corridor. He stopped in a doorway and pulled a ring of keys out of his jeans pocket. Fumbling a bit, he finally found the key that fit the lock. The office door slid soundlessly open. Bradley flipped the light switch beside the door and Kylie gasped. It looked like someone had taken five years' worth of filing and dumped every piece of paper willy-nilly around the room. The pile on the desk was at least two feet thick.

"Do you think someone got here before us?" she asked, shocked at the disarray.

Bradley looked puzzled. "Why do you ask?"

She waved her arms around the room. "Just look at this mess."

Bradley looked around and shrugged. "Bob's office always looks like this."

Kylie stared at him in disbelief. "How in the world could anyone work with this clutter?"

Bradley shrugged again. Kylie looked at the mountain of paper and wondered if she should try her luck at another record store. The problem was, she didn't have a contact at another store, and she doubted she'd be allowed to riffle through other people's files. Besides, the trail to the counterfeiter was growing colder by the minute.

"Is there any method to this at all?" she asked, hoping that Bradley might be able to give her a place to start.

"Near as I can tell, everything must be chronological."

Kylie groaned. "That's a big help." She tentatively began picking up papers on the nearest corner of the desk and studying them. "I guess we'll just have to start at the top and work our way down."

"All right, boss, whatever you say," Bradley said good-naturedly before picking a piece of paper off the top and digging in.

Three-quarters of an hour later and two inches down, Bradley finally found something.

"Hey, look at this." He held the yellow sheet of paper under Kylie's nose.

Grabbing the paper, Kylie had only a second to see the name Robyn Rogers before hearing footsteps in the hall. Bradley noticed the noise at the same time.

"Bob's back," they said in dismayed unison.

Kylie hurriedly glanced around the small office. There were no windows. The only door was the one they themselves had entered through. She saw the knob turn just before she heard Bradley murmur, "Okay, just follow my lead," then her line of vision was blocked as Bradley grabbed the paper from her nerveless fingers, stuffed it into his shirt pocket, wrapped his arms around her, and pressed his lips to hers.

Kylie had just enough time to silently congratulate Bradley for staging the perfect distraction maneuver when she heard a voice—a cold, unmistakable voice—say, "Excuse me, are we interrupting something?"

Kylie saw Bradley's eyes fly open wide, but she had to give him credit, he didn't give away their plan.

"Kylie and I were just, uh, talking," he stammered, after removing his lips from hers. "We had something personal to discuss so we borrowed Bob's office." Bradley nodded a greeting to David Gamble and Bob Buchanan.

Kylie peeked her head around Bradley's arm. What in the heck was David doing here? And why didn't he seem surprised to see her? She saw a spark of something in his eyes and wished she could believe it was jealousy, but it was probably only irritation at having to see her again. Then she cursed herself for wishing that Bradley's kiss

would give David something to be jealous about. She
shouldn't care. It was obvious that David didn't care anything about her except for the physical sport she had so
willingly offered him. A physical sport that she had enjoyed
immensely, she recalled, feeling her pulse start to race at
the memory.

Damn. Why couldn't Bradley's kiss have made her feel
that way? Looking at the coldness in David's eyes, Kylie
straightened her shoulders. Well, so what if Bradley's
kisses didn't do anything to stir her blood, didn't so much
as raise her pulse even one beat per minute? At least Bradley trusted her. At least he was willing to help her find the
real counterfeiter instead of trying to pin the blame on her.

Kylie matched David's glare with one of her own.

Standing beside her, Bradley watched the sparks fly
from David to Kylie and back again. The tension in the air
was as thick as Grandma's split-pea soup—or at least as
thick as he thought it would be if she were ever to actually
make split-pea soup. But his grandma was an artist who
lived in New York City and bought takeout from the deli
seven days a week, so what did he know about Grandma's
cooking? He shrugged and waited for the bomb to explode.

Kylie was the first to break the silence. "What are you
doing here?" she asked belligerently.

"I'd ask you the same question, but it's fairly obvious
what you and Bradley are up to," David answered.

Kylie's fists curled as her mind echoed with the injus-
tices of the past twelve hours. Her house had been ransacked, she'd been accused of stealing millions of dollars,
David had charged her with pirating her sister's CD, and
the bastard had had casual sex with her before firing her
from her job. All in all, she'd had all she was going to take
from him. Without thinking, her hand shot out and touched
a ceramic pencil holder that, amazingly enough, wasn't buried under all the paper.

Pencils clattered to the floor as the cup hit him squarely
in the chest.

David grunted with surprise as the projectile fell to the ground and broke in two.

Kylie would have been pleased, except she'd been aiming for his head.

Oh, well, she thought philosophically, *you can't win 'em all.* Her nonchalant attitude slipped slightly, however, when David took a step toward her, a murderous light in his eyes.

"Come on, Bradley, we're finished here," she said haughtily, stepping behind Bradley's back. It was a cowardly move, she knew, but one had to do what one had to do.

Grabbing the back of Bradley's T-shirt, she pushed him past David and Bob and out of the stuffy little office. "Nice to meet you, Mr. Buchanan. Thank you for the use of your office," she mumbled as she and her human shield scooted past. It was difficult to resist the urge to stick her tongue out at David but she managed to restrain herself.

"What was that all about?" she heard Bob Buchanan ask as the door closed behind them.

David shrugged his shoulders and moved a pile of papers from a chair onto the floor and sat down. He was not prepared to discuss what had just happened after seeing Kylie in a clinch with Bradley Nelson. He wanted to think their little act had been staged for his benefit, but he wasn't absolutely certain. Kylie's eyes had been wide open, not closed with pleasure as they were when he kissed her, and her creamy white skin wasn't flushed like it had been this morning.

He clenched his fists. What the hell had they been doing in here? And for how long had they been doing it? Goddamn Bradley Nelson for touching her. He couldn't get the image of Bradley's lips on Kylie's out of his head.

David cursed silently, unconsciously squeezing the pack of cigarettes in his shirt pocket. He had to control his train of thought, get his mind back to the original reason he'd come. Taking a deep breath, he managed to focus on the problem he'd come to solve.

After having had some time to reflect on the conclusions he'd drawn about her, he was plagued with the hint of a doubt that Kylie might not be involved in at least some of the problems they were facing. Her distress over the misappropriated royalties had seemed to be genuine, and if she'd gone to all the trouble to steal them, why had she so quickly and willingly given them back? On top of that, she'd worked at Gamble Records for less than a month and, even if she'd taken Robyn's master on her very first day, the timing was pretty tight for the pirated CDs to have been produced and distributed to the record stores. He wanted more evidence of her innocence, though, and Bob's Records seemed the best place to find it, even though Bob's filing system appeared to be nonexistent.

"How can you ever find anything in this mess?" David asked, leaning forward in his chair.

"You get used to it after a while," Bob answered cheerfully as he sat down across from David. "Now, what are we looking for?"

"I need anything you can find relating to Robyn Rogers's latest release."

Bob steepled his fingers over the paper pile and pursed his lips in thought. "You know, after you came in yesterday, I racked my brain about that release. I remember thinking something was weird when the distribution guy came by," he said after a moment.

"Like what?" David asked.

"Well, for starters, I didn't recognize him as one of yours. I thought maybe he was a new employee. But Robyn's new release was all he brought, even though I'd ordered more stock from your label. When I asked the guy about the rest of my order, he said you'd sent him on a special run to stock us up on Robyn's records because she was getting a lot of advance hype. I thought that was strange, but I heard one of her new songs on the radio the next day, so I just let it go."

"That's understandable. Do you have a copy of the delivery record or invoice?" David asked, hoping that would give them a clue.

"I must have something in here." Bob placed his hands on top of the pile on his desk and closed his eyes, as if trying to divine the whereabouts of the documents in question through some sort of spiritual contact with the paper. A moment later, he began sorting through the stack on the far left corner of the desk.

He shuffled some papers, then stopped. "It should have been right here." He sorted the stack again.

"Maybe you're thinking of the wrong day," David suggested.

Bob shook his head. "No, no. I remember it clearly now. I know it's hard to believe, but I'm really very organized."

David resisted the urge to raise his eyebrows in disbelief, hoping they weren't going to have to search Bob's entire office. "All right, let's start on this pile. Maybe it just got misfiled. I'll work backward and you work forward."

"Okay," Bob said, confusion knitting his brow. "But I never misfile things."

Bradley sat in Kylie's kitchen, Mr. Chips lying in his lap, purring contentedly as Bradley scratched under his chin. The clouds has dispersed and pale afternoon sun shone in through the windows as a light breeze lazily wafted its way through the house, bringing with it the scent of drying rain. The invoice they'd discovered half an hour ago sat in the middle of the kitchen table, barely moving as the wind touched its corners.

Kylie had told Bradley about last night's break-in, but all evidence of the mess she'd described was gone. Sitting across the table from her, Bradley noticed her eyes were beginning to droop as the sunshine warmed her back.

"It looks just like one of ours. Theirs," Kylie corrected, rubbing her eyes sleepily. "I can see how someone would be fooled by it."

"Yeah, with computers, it's easy to duplicate invoices and stuff like this."

Stifling a yawn, Kylie got up and looked out the kitchen window into her sloping backyard. The pansies she'd planted near the back steps were still blooming, and she was glad to see that the extra watering the night before hadn't killed them. She'd been up most of the night talking to the police and trying to restore order to the chaos in her home, and the lack of sleep was catching up with her. Bradley must have noticed her sleepiness earlier, because he'd offered to drive her home. He'd been very sweet, offering to do whatever he could to help her find the counterfeiters.

Why couldn't I pick someone like Bradley to fall in love with? she asked herself, continuing to stare out the window. Someone kind and caring, someone who wanted to protect her and was willing to fight for her? She sighed, knowing that she couldn't just turn off her feelings for David like turning off the water from a spigot.

Bradley, who'd been studying the invoice while Kylie sadly lamented the demise of her love life, suddenly shot out of his chair. A startled Mr. Chips raced into the living room to hide under the couch. "The phone number!" he yelled, grabbing the paper up from its resting place.

Catching his excitement, Kylie rushed over to look at the invoice, half expecting some answer to come leaping off the paper like a giant bullfrog. She stared at it intently, waiting for inspiration to strike.

"What about the phone number?" she asked after a moment of studying.

"It's not right. I should know, I call Gamble Records at least twice a week to check up on my demo," Bradley said dryly.

At that moment, Kylie began to wonder if there was a totally different man hiding somewhere behind that façade of a slow-witted backwoods country boy. She started to catch Bradley's enthusiasm as she looked at the number again.

"Oh my gosh, you're right," she said excitedly. "Let's call them."

"Now hold on there, Kylie," Bradley drawled. "What do you think they're gonna say—'Hello, you've reached con-artist counterfeiters, to report us to the authorities, press one'?" he asked, mimicking a phone-answering service.

"Dang, I suppose you're right," Kylie said, pacing the length of the kitchen. "So, what do we do?"

"We need more evidence. We can't go to the police on the basis of a wrong number." Bradley started to pace, too.

"Hey, I know. I've read those alphabet mysteries by Sue Grafton; you know, *A is for Alibi*, *B is for Burglar*, and so on?" Bradley nodded and Kylie continued, "Well, when-ever Kinsey Millhone has a phone number but needs the address, she goes to the library and looks at some kind of cross-reference directory."

"Good thinking, but if you have Internet access, we could do it from here," Bradley suggested.

Kylie looked at him incredulously. It seemed there really *was* a brain hiding behind that cowboy hat, a fairly sharp one, too. For the first time that day, she started to feel some hope that this whole mess could be cleared up. Leading the way up the stairs to her computer, she allowed herself a hint of a smile as Bradley's cowboy boots echoed off the hardwood floors. Maybe she'd be able to prove David wrong after all.

They eyed the ordinary-looking building from the parking lot across the street. The lettering in the window spelled out "Bert's Appliance" in bold white script.

"Let's go check out the back," Kylie suggested, shading her eyes from the late afternoon sun. For a day that had started out gray and gloomy, the weather at least had done a complete, 180-degree turnaround. Kylie could only hope everything else would go in the same direction.

Nodding his agreement, Bradley followed her across the busy street and into the alley. They picked their way over discarded fast-food wrappers and broken glass and stopped under a small window placed about ten feet off the ground.

Kylie glanced up at the window, then back at him. "Let me get on your shoulders and have a look."

Bradley obligingly crouched down for Kylie to climb on, grunting as he pulled himself upright. Kylie was glad she'd changed into a pair of jeans for this mission. She could just imagine how this would look if she were wearing one of her favorite short skirts instead.

"I still can't see," she whispered loudly, one hand clutching the windowsill and the other clutching the top of Bradley's head. He seemed to be doing his best to steady his legs while Kylie wiggled around, trying to peer into the dusty window.

"Try to pull yourself up," Bradley said.

"Hold still," she ordered as Bradley corrected his position under her shifting weight.

"I'm trying," Bradley muttered, placing his hands against the wall for support as Kylie used the windowsill to yank herself into a standing position.

"Ugh, this window is filthy." She wrinkled her nose distastefully. Using her shirtsleeve, she gingerly wiped at a corner of the window, then nearly lurched off his shoulders when her cleaning revealed two figures in what appeared to be a cramped office. Bradley clutched at the wall to steady himself under her erratic movements.

"There are people in there," she hissed, pulling at the windowsill to get a closer look. A woman was seated behind a desk, her back to Kylie. Dishwater blond hair strayed down her back. As Kylie watched, the woman pushed a strand behind her ear with her right hand. Something about the woman seemed vaguely familiar but Kylie couldn't think what it was right offhand. She switched her attention to the man facing her. He was dressed in a light tan uniform, stood about six feet tall, and had curly red hair. He smiled at something the woman said.

As Kylie watched, the woman got up out of the chair

and went to the man, her back still to Kylie. They embraced, the man's hands moving to the woman's hips to pull her to him.

Not wanting to add voyeurism to her list of crimes, Kylie lowered her eyes. She wondered briefly if she and Bradley were even looking into the right warehouse when her lowered eyes noticed something on the desk that had been hidden from view when the woman had been seated.

In her excitement, Kylie jerked forward. Unfortunately, Bradley had relaxed his grip on the wall after Kylie seemed to have found her balance. Her sudden movement took him off guard.

He swayed to the right.

She swayed to the left.

She seemed suspended in midair for timeless seconds before she came crashing down. An empty cardboard box helped cushion her fall, as did the stray cat that had picked that unfortunate spot to take a midday siesta. Startled from its hiding place, the cat bolted down the alley, noisily scattering trash as it went.

Kylie fleetingly hoped the animal wasn't hurt before Bradley yanked her up and dragged her in a run behind him.

"C'mon, they might have heard us," he urged.

They flew out of the alley and headed across the street. Bradley pulled her down behind a brown Chevrolet, panting after the adrenaline rush. Kylie peeked out around the car's rear tire in time to see the red-haired man peer down the alley where she and Bradley had just been. Apparently noticing nothing amiss, he glanced up and down the street. Kylie held her breath as he looked straight at the parking lot, not daring to breathe again until, seemingly satisfied, he went back into the building.

"Whew, that was close." Bradley sat back on his heels and closed his eyes.

"You can say that again," Kylie agreed, then nearly

screamed as a huge black man in a police uniform rounded the trunk of the car.

"Can I help you?" he asked in a booming voice, rattling the keys in his hands.

"Oh, no. Thank you, officer. I . . . uh, I dropped an earring and my friend here was just helping me find it." She scrunched her left ear to her shoulder so the officer couldn't see that she wasn't really missing an earring.

Taking her cue, Bradley picked something up off the ground and grinned widely at the policeman. "Yes, here it is. I found it. We can go now."

Kylie stood up, yanking Bradley to his feet. She kept her ear pressed to her shoulder and nodded to the cop. "There we are, then. We'll just be off. You have a nice day, officer." She grinned widely and nervously backed away, hoping the policeman would let them go, assuming she was just stupid and not dangerous.

CHAPTER 17

"Do you really think this is necessary?" Bradley asked as Kylie dipped her index finger into the small pot of black goo. The faint beginnings of a glowing sunset turned the clouds outside the kitchen window to golden wisps against the watery blue sky.

"Of course it is," she answered, smearing shoe polish over his cheeks. "Didn't you ever see *The Dirty Dozen*?"

"Actually, no, I don't think I ever have," he mumbled as she continued to cover his face.

"Well, you'll just have to trust me, then, won't you?" Stepping back, Kylie surveyed her handiwork with satisfaction.

Bradley looked at his blackened face in the handheld mirror, still wondering how exactly he had been roped into agreeing that a warehouse break-in was the only way to go about catching the counterfeiters.

"Are you sure you saw Robyn's CDs in that warehouse?" he asked, wishing she'd waver just a bit in her stance so he could convince her to try another tack. Unfortunately, he'd already learned, even in his short acquaintance with the woman standing before him slathering inky paint on her face, that once Kylie Rogers made up her mind that she was doing the right thing, there was no changing it.

"As I told you before," Kylie began, in the same tone of voice a parent might use when discussing bedtimes with a recalcitrant child, "I couldn't be absolutely certain they were Robyn's CDs since the window was so dirty, but there were at least twenty CDs on the desk and the artwork looked very much like Robyn's. If you hadn't toppled over, I might have been able to get a closer look. But you did your best under the circumstances." She patted his arm comfortingly, and Bradley found himself astounded at how she had managed to both pin the blame on him and make him feel quite happy to accept it at the same time.

Shaking his head with bemusement, he touched a particularly large clump of polish, smearing the stuff across his throat. Oddly enough, even though he knew this was probably going to end in disaster, he found himself agreeing with Kylie's assessment. "I suppose it does seem a bit suspicious for what's supposed to be an appliance warehouse to have two dozen CDs lying around," he conceded, smoothing another patch of polish over his cheek and checking the result in the mirror.

He turned his face one way, then another. The shiny black polish caught the light, setting off his firm jawline. It was actually a rather good look for him. He'd have to remember to try to work it in somehow if he ever filmed a music video.

"Come on, stop admiring yourself. We have to get going. Don't forget your flashlight." Kylie applied the finishing touches to her own face, pulled down the hem of her black turtleneck, and headed resolutely to the front door with Bradley trailing a safe distance behind. Her mind made up, she was determined to follow through on her plan, full speed ahead.

Yanking open the door, Kylie charged outside and headlong into the blond woman who was standing poised on the stoop. The blonde took a hasty step backward in surprise, missed her footing, and took a slow-motion dive backward into the dense evergreen shrubs flanking the porch.

Kylie rushed down the steps and bent over the inert form lying in the rhododendrons. "Robyn, are you okay?"

A pair of arresting green eyes focused on Kylie.

"Yes, I think so." Robyn winced as she checked on various muscles.

"Here, let me help you up." Kylie dropped the flashlight she'd been clutching and offered a hand to her sister. Accepting Kylie's offer of assistance, Robyn managed to get both feet on the ground.

A deep voice halted her in the act of dusting herself off. "Are you sure you're all right? Nothing broken?"

"Yes, I'm fine," Robyn snapped, brushing twigs from her jeans-clad derriere. "What are you doing here, Bradley? And what the hell are you two doing dressed like that?"

"I believe we're going on what you might call a reconnaissance mission," he drawled.

"A what? Have you lost your minds?"

"What are you doing here?" Kylie's voice intruded on Robyn's line of questioning.

"Mom called me this afternoon and told me David had fired you over this royalty business. Why didn't you call me right away?"

Kylie shrugged. "Your career with Gamble is going so well, I didn't want my problems to interfere. Besides, this is between me and David."

"What do you mean, it's between you and David?" Robyn's voice rose to her usual cursing-at-others level. "You're my sister, Kylie. What David Gamble does to you he does to me, too."

Remembering what had happened in David's office that morning, Kylie attempted to contain her blush and hoped her sister's last statement wasn't true.

"He can't fire you," Robyn continued to rant. "I mean, really, who does he think he is, anyway?"

"The owner of the company, for starters," Kylie said, trying to inject some reason into the conversation.

"Well, I'll talk to David myself and we'll get it all straightened out." She patted Kylie's hand comfortingly. "I didn't understand why David wanted to know about what happened at Pigeon Books when we met this morning, but if I'd known he was going to blame you for his accounting messes, I wouldn't have told him anything."

"You told him about Marcus?" Kylie asked with a sinking feeling.

Robyn shifted her weight from one expensively shod foot to another and refused to meet Kylie's eyes. "Yes, but I didn't think it would get you in trouble. I'm sure this doesn't help, but I'm really sorry. I know how hard you worked at Gamble Records and that you have feelings for David. I know you wouldn't have spent the weekend with him if you didn't care for him very much."

Kylie knew her mouth had dropped open but she didn't think she could close it, even if a bug threatened to fly in. Her sister, Robyn Rogers, was apologizing? It was an unprecedented event and Kylie wasn't sure how to respond.

She cleared her throat against an unaccustomed tightness. "Thanks, Robyn, but there's nothing you can do to change David's mind. He thinks I stole the royalty money and he also accused me of pirating your CD."

"That's ridiculous. He should know you better than that."

Kylie shrugged helplessly. Robyn was right. David *should* have known better than to think she'd do those things, but it was obvious that he didn't. "I agree. That's why I'm going to find the real culprits and prove to David that I'm innocent."

"Good. I'll help."

Kylie immediately shook her head. "No, Robyn, this is my problem and I'll deal with it myself. It will only make it worse if you get involved."

"I'm coming." Robyn crossed her arms across her chest and stood her ground.

Kylie locked gazes with her sister, seeing in Robyn's eyes that as far as she was concerned, the argument was over. Her eyes moved from the petite blonde's well-coiffed hair to her impractical, high-heeled, sandal-clad toes. *I could take her*, she thought. It wouldn't take much to lock Robyn in the basement, then she and Bradley could be on their way.

Robyn's eyes widened as Kylie's narrowed. Kylie guessed she'd make a lousy poker player when her sister raised her hands in supplication. Were her intentions *that* obvious?

"Now, look here, Kylie, I have a stake in this, too. Besides, I want to help. David might not believe you, but I know you didn't have anything to do with this mess."

Kylie blinked back sudden tears at her sister's show of support. Robyn reached out and squeezed her arm, and Kylie knew she'd lost. She couldn't fight those family ties and, besides, there didn't seem to be anything she could do to stop Robyn.

"So, where are we going?" Robyn asked again, knowing the battle was won.

"We think we've found the warehouse where the counterfeit CDs are being stored. We're going back there tonight to investigate," Bradley answered, joining the conversation.

"I thought we should darken our faces just in case there's a night watchman," Kylie added.

"Okay then, you'll need to do me, too."

"I don't think that's such a good idea," Kylie protested, not wanting to drag her sister into the fray any further than was necessary. "Why don't you just stand guard for us outside the warehouse?"

"No, I want to come in," Robyn said stubbornly.

"I agree with Kylie. We wouldn't want you to break a nail," Bradley drawled, leaning against one of the columns on the front porch.

"Why don't you mind your own business?" Robyn snapped.

"Robyn!" Kylie looked at her sister, aghast.

"Sorry," Robyn mumbled an apology in Bradley's general direction before continuing, "Look, Kylie, my albums are the ones being counterfeited, right?"

"That's true," she admitted.

"So, I think I have as much right as you to try to catch the crooks who are taking royalties out of my pocket, don't you?"

"Well, when you put it that way..." Kylie's voice trailed off. Her sister did have a point there.

Knowing she'd won again, Robyn trotted up the stairs, brushed past Bradley, and entered the house. She picked up the small tub of shoe polish from the kitchen table and handed it to Kylie, who had followed her in.

"Come on then, let's get moving," Robyn ordered.

By seven o'clock that night, David had gained a new respect for anyone whose job required filing. He was sick of looking at paper. His hands were dry and cracked and he had no fewer than fifty tiny cuts on his fingers. Never again would he make jokes about people filing workers' compensation claims for paper cuts. The damn things hurt like hell.

And to make matters worse, they hadn't turned up anything.

Bob riffled through the last pile of papers in the far corner of the room. "I don't understand this. I was sure I remembered receiving some paperwork from that delivery guy."

"Maybe it's just mixed up in here somewhere," David suggested wearily.

Bob shook his head. "We've been through it three times already. I guess I must have been mistaken."

Suddenly, something tripped in the back of David's mind. All along, he had been assuming it was coincidence that brought Kylie here this afternoon. But what if she, too, were trying to find the pirates? If she wasn't involved with the criminals, it was very possible that she had taken his accusations personally and was taking it upon herself to try to find the real culprits.

Or, the devil's advocate in him argued, perhaps she was trying to cover her tracks and had enlisted Bradley's help to remove any evidence she might have left behind. In either event, David was convinced that Kylie held the key to the missing invoice.

David muttered an absent, "Thanks, anyway" to Bob, then grabbed his car keys and dashed out into the unseasonably warm Seattle evening. He grimaced at the all-too-familiar sight of the little purple car.

"Just a loose distributor cap. It won't happen again," the dealership had assured him when they'd fobbed the Grapemobile off on him again. He'd tried to protest, but they'd insisted this was the only loaner they had available at the time. He could see why. Who else would put up with this little rattletrap? The engine putt-putted to life, like a wind-up child's toy, and David headed out of the busy U-district toward Woodland Park Zoo.

Deborah had suggested again that he could spring for a luxury rental car, but the expense seemed awfully wasteful. Besides, the mechanic had assured him his Jag would be ready by next Monday. As the little car powered up the hill, David hoped the mechanic was right. He missed his car: the purring of the big motor, the powerful leaps it made when he pressed on the accelerator, the dashboard fashioned from a rare hardwood found only in Tennessee.

After a brief brush with death trying to get up enough speed to merge with the traffic on Highway 99, David made his way to Queen Anne Hill, and Kylie's house.

As he turned left onto her street, he noticed that the unmistakable red Mustang was parked in front of her house, rather than in the carport at the back. He slammed on the brakes as the front door opened, then watched in disbelief as three black-clad figures came out and piled into the red car.

"What's she up to now?" he muttered to the acrylic dashboard of the Grapemobile as the Mustang shot off down the street. David put the car in gear and followed at a safe distance.

The wind rattled the windows as the small purple car trailed its red prey through the sparsely trafficked streets of Seattle. Although technically considered a big city, Seattle was like a small town in many ways. Traffic in the city itself, though busy during the day, slowed to a trickle after six P.M. Chicago, New York, L.A.—now those were big cities with traffic twenty-four hours a day and people wandering around downtown at all hours. The only people wandering the streets of Seattle at seven-thirty on this mid-October evening were the multitude of homeless who took over the city once all the businesspeople had gone back to their cozy homes in the suburbs for the night.

David kept his distance as the Mustang sped through the city, knowing he'd be easy to spot on the semi-deserted streets. He followed as Kylie turned right on James Street, heading toward the waterfront. At First Avenue, the Mustang paused while a lone pedestrian meandered through the crosswalk against the light. David cursed Seattle's polite treatment of its pedestrians and slowly eased his car to the side of the road behind a large white truck. In New York, the person crossing against the light would have hurried out of the way of the approaching vehicle, knowing that he could be plowed down at any time. But here, he felt free to stop traffic, knowing that no Seattlite would run him down, much less even honk, as he strolled at a leisurely pace across the road.

David pulled back out into the street just as Kylie's car turned left onto First Avenue.

They raced on, past the former site of the ill-fated King-dome and the old Sears building, which had been taken over as the corporate headquarters of Starbucks, and into the heart of the industrial section of town. David shot past Kylie's car as she suddenly turned into an alley.

Wondering if perhaps he'd been spotted, David pulled a hasty U-turn. As he drove past the alley, he saw that Kylie had stopped about halfway through. Spying a parking lot across the street, David hurriedly slipped into a space, leaped out of the car, crammed a handful of bills in the appropriate slot at the box just in case the lot was being monitored, and sprinted back across the street.

Poking his head around the corner, David felt as if he'd suddenly, strangely, been transported into some sort of a spy movie.

Kylie was standing on Bradley's shoulders, fumbling with something. They were both dressed all in black and they had some sort of black paste slathered on their faces. A third person—someone he didn't immediately recognize, but could tell was obviously female wearing black leggings and a sweater with her hair tucked up under a black beret—stood behind Bradley. Shaking his head, David wondered briefly if Kylie had no end of kooky friends to recruit for her crazy schemes.

It looked as if Bradley was having a hard time keeping steady under Kylie's shifting weight. David had almost finished debating whether he should interrupt when the top half of her body disappeared into the building, as if she were being swallowed by a giant concrete monster.

Bradley held on to the disembodied legs for a brief moment before letting go. Then they, too, disappeared into the building, completing the creature's meal.

David crept silently forward, hiding behind a Dumpster as the remaining two figures faced each other. From his new vantage point, he could just make out what they were saying.

"Okay, darlin', your turn," Bradley drawled.

"Don't call me 'darling,' " the woman snapped, turning to face the wall. Bradley crouched down, stuck his head between her legs, then strained into an upright position.

Their intent was unmistakable. David closed his eyes
and rested his head on the cold metal Dumpster. Whatever
had possessed Kylie to break into this place? It must have
something to do with the evidence she'd found in Bob's
office earlier that day, but why was she taking matters into
her own hands? Didn't she know it could be dangerous?
And what if she and her accomplices were caught? Had she
even thought of that possibility?

When he opened his eyes again, David saw the woman
reach up and grab the windowsill, struggling to get enough
leverage to stand up.

"Now, darlin', this is what you might call a compro-
mising situation." David watched as Bradley slid his hands
up the woman's slender legs, ostensibly to help her stand.

"Would you just shut up?" she said peevishly.

David heard a deep, masculine laugh as the woman disappeared through the window after Kylie.

Seconds later, a heavy office chair appeared at the window. Bradley grabbed a leg to help ease the chair down,
then stood up on it and pulled himself up and through the
window. David waited a full two minutes before removing
himself from his hiding place. Climbing up on the chair
Bradley had just used, he peered into the building.

It took his eyes a moment to adjust to the darkness, but
when they did, David found himself looking into a small,
glassed-in office. He could make out the shape of a desk
with a computer sitting on it directly in front of him. The
office opened onto a cavernous, dark space. David could
hear Kylie and her band of merry nuts huddled together
just outside the office door.

"Lights?" He heard her loud whisper even perched as he
was outside the building.

There was some rustling before three pinpoints of light
appeared.

"Should we split up?" Bradley asked.

"Yes, I think so. It'll go faster that way," Kylie answered.

The lights dispersed, weaving like fireflies in the night. David watched for several minutes, waiting for an alarm to go off and for police cars to come and surround the building. When that didn't happen, he came face-to-face with the inevitable. He'd have to go in after her.

"I can't believe I'm doing this," David mumbled to himself as he heaved his left leg up over the windowsill. He landed with a soft thud on the thin carpet, trying not to think what the newspapers would have to say if he got caught at this.

Keeping an eye on the beam he believed to be Kylie's, David moved silently out of the office, down a short flight of stairs, and into the main part of the building. He followed the light down an aisle of boxes stacked to a height just over his head. Kylie had stopped at the end of the aisle where two smaller boxes were stacked. She slipped something out of her pocket as David crept closer. He saw that she had a small pocketknife in her hand and was struggling to get one of the utensils to pop out.

He wouldn't have been surprised if she'd opened a spoon and sat down on the boxes to have a bowl of ice cream. Suddenly, he understood how Alice felt after she fell down the rabbit hole. What would have seemed ludicrous to him two weeks ago now seemed normal. Breaking into a deserted warehouse almost felt like a routine event.

Resigned to the fact that he'd somehow been dragged right into the middle of this mess, David watched as a silver blade flashed out of Kylie's pocketknife. Holding the flashlight under her chin, she sliced open the packaging tape holding one of the boxes on the floor closed. Coming up behind her, David saw her shake her head as she pawed through the contents of the container.

Suddenly, she turned, taking a step forward and almost colliding with him. Reflexively, knowing what was going to happen next, David reached out to clamp a hand over her mouth milliseconds before her scream would have shattered the silence. Instinctively, she started to struggle

against the unknown force holding her, dropping her flashlight in the process. It skittered across the bare concrete
floor, turning to shine on their entangled feet.

"It's me, David," he whispered.

She stopped struggling, raising her eyes to his warily.

Unable to see him in the darkness, Kylie could tell it
was David by the scent that filled her nostrils and the familiar tingle of her skin as his hot breath tickled her ear.
She cursed him for having this immediate effect on her,
even now, when she was furious with him.

He pressed closer to her, his hand still over her mouth.
"Are you going to scream?"

She shook her head and David slowly removed his hand.

"Why are you here?" she asked.

"I followed you. Why are you here? And where the hell
are we?"

"I think this is the warehouse where the counterfeiters
are storing their stolen CDs. Bradley and I found it this
afternoon, but the counterfeiters were here so we couldn't
investigate. We decided to come back tonight for a better
look."

"Did you find some of the pirated CDs?"

Kylie hesitated. "No," she answered finally, with a sigh.
"These boxes all seem to be empty. I was so sure we'd find
something."

"You mean you broke into this place without any evidence at all?" David asked incredulously.

Kylie narrowed her eyes and looked up at David in the
darkness. "Yes, we had evidence. We found an invoice with
a telephone number and traced the address here. When we
were here this afternoon, there were CDs all over the desk
in the office. That seemed mighty suspicious, so we decided
to come back tonight and investigate. Now, if you'll excuse
me, I need to go find Robyn."

"Robyn?" David's question echoed off the walls of the
deserted warehouse. "You involved your sister in this mess,
too?"

"Shh," Kylie hissed, grabbing David's arm. "Do you want us to get caught?"

"No, Kylie, I don't want us to get caught. It's bad enough that you and Bradley are involved in this mess, but now you've dragged your sister and me into it with you. I have a major proposal pending with a satellite company, and if they get wind of this, I'm sure they'll kill the deal. I wouldn't blame them. How could they trust me to lead an entire music division if I can't control one crazy female?"

Kylie straightened to her full five feet five inches. "Listen, David, I didn't ask you to get involved in this. You followed me, remember?" She poked his chest with a cherry red–tipped fingernail. "You made it perfectly clear this morning what you think of me. I don't know why you felt it necessary to have one last—" She hesitated, knowing exactly the right word, the only word that described perfectly what had happened this morning in David's office, but she couldn't seem to force the vulgarity out between her clenched teeth. "Well, I don't know why you needed to use me like that. I'm sure there are plenty of other women who would have been happy to oblige you. But what's done is done and I would appreciate it if you would just go away." She gave another jab to his chest. It felt good, so she did it again.

David grabbed her index finger, stopping her from poking him again. "I'm just trying to straighten out this mess—"

"So am I," Kylie interrupted, attempting to yank her finger out of David's grasp. "And I don't need your help."

"What's all the racket over here?" Robyn poked her head around the pile of boxes.

Abruptly, David released Kylie's hand as she bent down to pick up the heavy flashlight, then crossed her arms across her chest. "David followed us here," she told her sister.

"Good, then I won't have to make an appointment to tell you what an asshole you're being." Robyn stalked up to him and poked him in the exact same spot her sister had already abused.

"What is it with the poking?" David asked, taking a step backward.

"Don't bother, Robyn. It doesn't matter," Kylie said, the fight leaching out of her as they stood in the darkened warehouse. They hadn't found any evidence that the pirated CDs had ever been stored here, nothing that would help clear her of the charges David had leveled against her. Besides that, she didn't need her baby sister to stick up for her. "Let's find Bradley and get out of here," she said, looping her arm in her sister's.

"I'm sorry we didn't find anything," Robyn said quietly, sounding genuinely distressed.

"Me, too. I suppose it was too much to hope for, that we'd find boxes of CDs just lying around."

They rounded the corner and Kylie stopped abruptly. An eerie bluish light pulsed out from the warehouse office. She pushed Robyn behind her.

"What's wrong?" David whispered the question in her ear and Kylie crushed the tingly feeling running down her arms.

"Someone's in the office," she whispered back.

"Stay here, I'll go find out who it is," David ordered before creeping into the shadows.

Kylie snorted. "He thinks he can tell me to 'stay,' like I'm some kind of dog?" she muttered, then turned to Robyn. "Stay here. I'm going to follow David," she said, before doing just that.

It was Robyn's turn to snort, only no one was left to hear it.

Bradley used the "Start" button on the computer to open the "Find Files or Folders" feature. He clicked on the "Advanced" tab, then entered the parameters to find files that had been used within the last week.

As the program slogged its way through gigabytes of

data, Bradley searched the desk drawers for a spare diskette. This computer was old, relatively speaking, and didn't have a writable CD-ROM drive like most of the newer computers. He'd have to make do with the antiquated method of saving files to diskette, although he supposed if he had the time he could always configure an e-mail account and send whatever files he found to himself or Kylie.

After finding a box of disks in one of the drawers, he looked back at the results of his search. He sorted the files by type, eliminating the system files that were routinely accessed, and selected the files he wanted to copy. They were small enough that they could easily fit on a couple of disks, so he decided not to bother with setting up his own e-mail account. This way would leave less of a trail anyway. Leaning back in the remaining office chair, Bradley propped his boots up on the desk and waited for the copy process to complete.

"Oh, it's only you."

The comment startled him and he jerked in response. The wheeled office chair skidded back and Bradley's boots hit the concrete floor with a loud "thunk." He looked to the doorway to find David Gamble leaning against the frame.

Bradley grinned sheepishly. "Howdy."

"How in the world did Kylie convince you to join her in this harebrained scheme?"

Before Bradley could answer, David let out a yelp and whirled around.

"My scheme was not 'harebrained,' and I think you should apologize," Bradley heard Kylie say.

"What would you call it, then? And stop poking me."

"I'd call it a calculated risk, that's what. And I'll stop poking you when you stop insulting me. If we'd found the pirated CDs, you wouldn't be so rude."

"But you didn't find them, did you? All you found was a bunch of empty boxes."

"Yes, but how were we going to find out they were empty if we hadn't come in and looked? We could hardly

have shown up at the front door and asked for the counterfeiters to let us in, could we?"

David sighed. He wasn't going to win this argument and,
frankly, he was tired of fighting. Raising his hands in supplication, he gave up. "Fine, you win. I'm just happy we've
escaped this episode unscathed. God only knows what the
press would do if they found out about this. Let's get out
of here. Robyn, why don't you go first?"

CHAPTER 18

"Here they come." The young man standing behind the Dumpster danced from foot to foot excitedly.

"The tip said there's four of 'em, Shawn. Wait until the last one is out before you do anything," the older man said. He'd been in the news business a long time, and didn't want the youngster to ruin this story by being overeager.

It wasn't every day a reporter got an anonymous tip that one of the city's richest men and America's newest singing sweetheart were in the process of committing B&E in the industrial part of town. He could almost see the picture on the front page, and the byline would be his. He was already tinkering with the headline. Maybe "Billionaire Busted for Breaking & Entering," or how about, "Rogers & Gamble: The Next Bonnie & Clyde?" Hmm. He liked the billionaire one best. It had a nice ring to it.

"Look, Henry, the last one's just coming out."

"I can see him. I've got eyes haven't I?" These youngsters were annoying. Henry leaned back on his heels, watching as two expensive leather shoes and their attached legs slid out the window. "Get ready," he warned, elbowing the kid in the gut.

David hopped down out of the window, wincing as his heels slapped the pavement loudly in the quiet night. "Let's meet back at—"

"David, can you tell us why you and Robyn Rogers were breaking into this warehouse?" The question and a flash of light directly in his eyes interrupted David's command.

Shit, reporters! That was just what they needed. He should have known that involving himself in Kylie's crazy plot would land him in a pile of trouble. Wondering if he would be permanently blinded, David took a step backward and ran into the cold wall of the warehouse behind him.

"Robyn, is there any truth to the rumor that you and David are lovers?" The reporter shouted another question as David struggled to recover his night vision.

"No," David heard Kylie shriek before he could stop her from saying anything.

"No comment." David held up a hand to ward off further questions. His worst nightmare was unfolding right here in this darkened alley.

"Can we get the names of you two for the record?" The reporter turned toward Kylie and Bradley as the photographer continued to snap pictures. From what little vision had been restored, David saw Kylie's mouth open and he hastily clapped his hand over the opening before she could spill her guts. In five minutes, she'd probably tell them everything except her bra size. Matter of fact, she'd probably tell them that, too, if they asked.

He clamped his hand tighter over her mouth as she tried to bite him.

Having decided he'd rather face running headlong into unseen objects than face down reporters, David quickly herded Kylie, Robyn, and Bradley out of the alley, the reporters at their heels. "Don't say anything to them," he whispered in Kylie's ear as they emerged onto the sidewalk. She nodded in agreement and he cautiously removed his hand.

"But David, we could tell them about the counterfeiters,

get them on our side. I'm sure they'd understand why we had to do what we did," she protested as he pushed her along in front of him across the empty street.

"No, don't say a word. We're in enough trouble as it is." David knew whatever they said would be twisted in such a way as to make them all look as foolish as possible—which wouldn't be too difficult considering the situation. David tried not to groan as he thought about how this fiasco was probably going to end.

The reporters continued trotting along after them, shouting inane questions that he had no intention of answering. They weren't the police, couldn't arrest them, and really, all they had were pictures of the four of them standing in an alley outside the warehouse. Since nothing had been taken from the warehouse, he doubted the police would even bother checking to see if their fingerprints were inside the building. At least, that was what he told himself, trying to convince himself that this disaster could possibly have a happy ending.

"Meet me back at your house," David ordered as Kylie, Robyn, and Bradley piled back into her Mustang. Kylie nodded wearily, and David waited until her car pulled away before pushing past the two reporters and getting into his own car. He wasn't about to let her have time alone with the reporters. There was no telling what she might say, and she'd only make matters worse.

David clenched his teeth as he started his car. The older reporter kept shouting questions at him as he yanked on his seatbelt and pulled out of the parking spot, leaving them with some great pictures but not much of a story.

Unfortunately, David knew that wouldn't make much difference. In the absence of information, they'd make something up.

He slammed a hand on the steering wheel as he followed the red car back the way they'd come, his anger growing with each traffic light they passed.

How could Kylie be so foolish? She'd endangered her-

self, not to mention the rest of them, all to prove some
stupid point. Would she ever stop being so impetuous, start
having some control over the impulses that seemed to run
her life? Didn't she realize what this bad publicity would
mean to him? To her own sister?

His teeth snapped together as he imagined the ridicule
he'd be subjected to when the story came out in the newspaper. He'd be made to look like a fool, standing with a
shoe-polish-smeared Kylie outside the warehouse with a
stunned look on his face. What would people think?

Hell, he knew what they'd think. They'd think he was
an idiot, that he had no control over himself. Even worse,
if they found out that Kylie had spent the weekend with
him, as they surely would, they'd think he'd been so
swayed by his libido that he'd lost his own free will.
They'd think he'd do whatever she wanted whenever she
crooked a little finger at him, but they would be wrong.
She meant nothing to him.

Nothing.

And if Kylie thought any differently, it was high time
he disabused her of that notion.

By the time he pulled up in front of Kylie's house and
watched them all pile out of her Mustang like some circus
car full of black-garbed clowns, David's head felt as if it
were about to explode. He heard Kylie's voice as she
stepped out onto the sidewalk. The tinkle of her laughter
set off a sharp pain in the pit of his gut. He could feel the
pulse pounding in his forehead as he pushed open the door
of his car.

Catching up with her in four quick strides, David
grabbed Kylie's arm and spun her around to face him. The
black smudges on her cheeks were shiny in the glow of her
porch light.

"What the hell did you think your little stunt was going
to accomplish?" he yelled.

Kylie seemed surprised by his outburst. "What are you
so upset about? Everything has turned out all right."

"All right? You call having our names trashed in the headlines 'all right'?" David asked incredulously. "We're going to look like morons. You could have called me or the police with your suspicions and let someone else handle it. Instead, you broke in like some ridiculous cat burglar, endangering yourself and everyone else in the process. And for what? You didn't find anything, not even a crumb of evidence that would help our case. Instead, we're all going to have our pictures in the paper tomorrow as if we're a bunch of criminals. This is the type of publicity I've worked my whole life to avoid." He gave her arm a shake with each of his points, as if it would help to emphasize the stupidity of her stunt.

"David, stop yelling. No one got hurt. We're all fine, and whatever those reporters say will blow over in no time. Now, why don't we go inside and I'll make you some hot cocoa and we can talk about this rationally? It's been a long day and I'm tired of arguing with you." She turned around and tried to pull him toward the front stairs.

He refused to budge. The pounding at his temples was getting stronger. Whatever control he had once had on his temper snapped.

"You may not take this seriously, Kylie, but I do. Unlike you, I don't like being made to look like an idiot. If you would think before you act, just one time, I'll bet that your life would stop being the screwed-up mess it is right now."

Kylie stared at him, her eyes wide.

David felt a strong hand on his arm, wrenching him around, and had no time to react before a fist slammed into his jaw. The force of the blow knocked him back against Kylie's car. It took him a moment to right himself. Leaning back against the engine-warmed hood, he looked up at his assailant with stunned surprise.

"How dare you talk to my daughter that way?" The man shoving his face belligerently into David's bore a strong resemblance to Kylie. David rubbed his injured jaw as he tried to think of an appropriate response. He was saved from responding when Kylie stepped in front of the other man.

"Daddy, leave David alone. I can fight my own battles," she said, sounding tired. She tugged her father's arm as he continued to glare at David, and he finally gave in, allowing himself to be pulled away.

Kylie started to follow her father, then stopped, turning back to face David where he stood, unmoving, on the sidewalk next to her car.

"You're right, David. I am impetuous . . . and probably even foolish sometimes. But I don't let what other people think of me control my life. I like who I am, and I'm not going to change—for you, or for anyone else," she said quietly, her words wafting to his ears on a light October wind.

Her shoulders were straight and her head high as she turned back toward the house, stopping at the top step to look at him one last time. For an instant, her face was framed by the porch light above, and David could see the hurt in her eyes.

The pain in his jaw was nothing compared to the jab in the vicinity of his heart he got now, looking at her. It was a two-second look into Kylie's soul; the disappointment, the longing for something that could never be. He wanted to run to her and crush her to his chest, but he didn't do it. All his life he had struggled for control, and when he was around her events kept spinning out of his grasp. He was right, he knew it. She had to stop leaping without looking, had to start thinking things through before acting. She had to take control of her life.

He stayed where he was.

She turned away, closing the door quietly behind her as she took her wounded heart inside.

CHAPTER 19

Chaos reigned inside the house. Besides her father, who was in the kitchen regaling her mother with the tale of how he'd defended Kylie's honor, her house had been invaded by her mother, three shih tzus, and a cook who strongly resembled Sylvester Stallone.

"Is that . . . ?" Bradley whispered in Kylie's ear, trying not to point.

"No, he's my parents' cook, Tony Pellgrini. If my father calls him Rocky, don't laugh," Kylie warned as she surveyed the scene in her kitchen and tried to ignore her aching heart.

Tony was stirring something in a huge pot that smelled heavenly, and Kylie walked over and gave him a hug. He'd been the Rogerses' cook for the past five years and was one of the sweetest men Kylie knew. When she'd lived in L.A., he used to drop homemade lunches by her office, including freshly made cookies for the whole accounting department.

"How are you? I looked through your cupboards when we arrived and I'll tell you just like I told your mother, you are not eating right," he scolded, landing a hearty smack on her back.

Kylie supposed his assessment must be correct when his

thwack threatened to topple her over. Perhaps she did need
to bulk up a bit. She smiled up at him. She missed his
mothering almost as much as his oatmeal-butterscotch
cookies. "You're a sweetheart, Tony. But I'm hardly on the
verge of starvation."

"Well, don't you worry. I went to the grocery store and
got you all stocked up." He opened her now-packed freezer
and gestured like Vanna White, showing off his treasures.
"We've got your T-bone steaks, your porterhouse steaks,
your filet mignon . . ."

It would take her five years to eat all that meat, but Kylie
appreciated the sentiment behind the stockpile. She gave
the cook a heartfelt hug. "Thank you, Tony. I've missed
you, too."

Tony patted her gruffly on the back, then released her
before the moment could turn too mushy. Kylie blinked
back a sudden hint of tears, then picked up one of the pom-
pom dogs lying like miniature mops on the kitchen floor.
Nuzzling the dog's fluffy fur, she walked over to the table
where her mother was seated, holding ice to George Rogers's bruised knuckles. The familiar scene of her loved ones
eased the pain in Kylie's heart a notch. She was fortunate
to have such a wonderful family, even if they were a bit
overwhelming at times.

"Hi, Mom." She kissed the top of her mother's perfectly
coiffed blond head, glad she had stopped to wash the oily
shoe polish off her face before venturing into the kitchen.

"Hello, dear. How are you?"

Kylie twirled her fingers in the soft topknot of black-
and-white hair on the dog's head and considered her
mother's question. How was she? Her beloved cat had been
harmed, her house trashed, her hopes of a new career
crushed. And, even worse, she'd been—to put it bluntly—
fucked and fired by the first man who had made her feel
special in a long time. Now, as a final insult, she'd been
invaded by a family who loved her but didn't trust her
ability to solve her own problems.

How was she? She was miserable.

She took a deep breath. It wouldn't do her any good to tell her mother that. Elizabeth Rogers would simply pat her daughter on the head and tell her everything would turn out all right, like she always did. Instead, Kylie changed the subject.

"I see you brought the kids with you."

"Yes, I just couldn't bear to leave them at home without us. They get so lonely when we're gone."

Kylie met her father's amused gaze, his expression telling her he thought the dogs didn't much care who was home as long as they got fed on time.

"Which one is this?" she asked, nodding to the mop in her arms.

"That's Robyn. You can tell from the black hair on her ears. That one there with the brown tail is Daniel, and this little baby with the white fur around her eyes is Kylie," her mother cooed at the sleeping dogs.

Kylie wondered what in the world had possessed her mother to name the three dogs after her children. Her father had suggested perhaps she was going through some sort of delayed empty-nest syndrome, and Kylie figured he ought to know; but still, it was strange to think her mother had named these hairy beasts after her own children.

"So, why are you guys here, anyway?"

"We came to help get this whole mess straightened out," her father answered. "I'm not going to just stand by and let someone steal Robyn's CDs and pin the blame on you, dear. We've got to develop a plan of action and fight back."

"Hear, hear, George. That was a wonderful speech," Elizabeth encouraged.

"Mom, Dad, you have to promise to keep out of this. I'm in enough trouble as it is, and I don't need the entire Rogers family in this mess with me. It was bad enough when Robyn got involved, but the rest of you need to stay out of it."

Kylie held up a hand as her mother started to protest.

"No, Mom, I mean it. This is my problem and I'll find a way to handle it."

George stood up, placing an arm around his daughter. "All right, dear. If you want us to stay out of it, we will. Now, where is that sister of yours?"

"Thank you, Daddy. I knew you'd understand." Kylie gave her father a squeeze. "Robyn's upstairs with Bradley. I'll go see what they're up to. Why don't you and Mom stay here and relax?"

Kylie left the warm, fragrant kitchen, still carrying the dog, and missed her father's impish wink at her retreating back.

"Click there." Robyn leaned over Bradley's shoulder and pointed to a spot on the glowing computer screen.

Bradley enjoyed the feel of her small breasts pressed against his back. "Where, darlin'? Right here?" He purposely opened the wrong file and grinned when Robyn leaned even closer.

"No, you idiot. That one. Here, let me have the mouse."

Bradley picked up the light gray piece of equipment by its cord and handed it to her, knowing full well that it was useless like that. He didn't have a degree in computer science for nothing, but Little Miss Snooty Singer didn't need to know that.

"Ugh. Move." Robyn pushed against him and Bradley graciously got out of the chair. It sure was easy to aggravate her.

"What are you guys doing?" Kylie poked her head into the bedroom-turned-home-office and set down the little dog she'd carried upstairs with her.

"Hey, Kylie. Hey, pooch." Bradley chucked the hairy creature under its chin. The only way to tell which end was up on the thing was by the two bright black button eyes that stared out of the eating end. "We're going over some of the files I copied from the warehouse. So far, we haven't found anything that might help, but now that Robyn has taken control, we might just get somewhere."

Bradley ignored Robyn's curled lip. Yes, sir, this was one shrew he was going to enjoy taming.

"Come here, Robyn." Kylie whistled and snapped her fingers.

Waiting for the inevitable blowup that would surely result from Kylie's order, Bradley was amazed when Robyn ignored her sister. Wow, he'd have to try that one himself. The thought was immediately followed by an image of himself sitting naked on a bed of silky sheets, crooking a finger at the blonde wearing nothing but a black collar around her neck. He swallowed, hard, and played the scene again in his mind, appreciating it even more as a rerun.

"Why in the world did Mom have to name those mutts after us? It's embarrassing," Robyn muttered, continuing to stare at the computer screen, oblivious to the direction Bradley's thoughts had taken.

"They're hardly mutts, more like purebred lion dogs from Tibet," Kylie protested, snuggling the bundle of fur in her arms.

"Ah, yes, the mighty shih tzu of the Ottoman Empire," Robyn said dryly.

"Well, they're more like the furballs of the ottoman of Mom's favorite chair." Kylie laughed. "But they're nice little dogs. Of course, Mr. Chips hates them and won't come out from under the bed till they're gone."

"What's new? Your cat hates everybody except you."

"No, he doesn't. He's just not particularly social. He likes Bradley."

"Hmph," Robyn snorted.

Kylie turned her attention back to Bradley, who was standing next to Robyn with an odd, faraway look in his eyes. "What made you think to poke around in that computer? It was a great idea."

She watched as Bradley blinked, a faint flush creeping up his neck as he returned from his mental vacation. "I don't know. I just thought I might find something interesting."

"Damn, I can't open this file," Robyn interrupted.

Bradley looked at the screen, then scooted Robyn out of the chair. "Here, let me give it a try. We'll just open it as a text file and see what's in it," he muttered.

Kylie met her sister's eyes over Bradley's head and raised a questioning eyebrow. Who would have thought Bradley would turn out to be such a handy fellow?

Robyn shrugged, obviously just as perplexed as Kylie by Bradley's hidden talents.

"Well, would you look at this," Bradley drawled, leaning back in the chair.

Setting the warm little dog back on the floor, Kylie moved closer to the computer. The screen was filled with incoherent symbols interspersed with letters and numbers, hardly anything to warrant Bradley's excitement. "What? All I see is a bunch of gobbledygook."

"No, look. You have to ignore the codes that tell the program how to behave. If we get rid of those"—Bradley tapped a few keys and the symbols were gone—"look at what's left."

Kylie leaned in closer and read some of the names off the screen. "Lisanne O'Neill, Lunar Eclipse, Robyn Rogers. It's a list of Gamble Records' artists. What are all the numbers, though?"

"It looks like a database of some sort," Bradley suggested.

Unconsciously, Kylie nudged Bradley out of his seat with her hip. Something seemed familiar about this, she thought, staring at the glowing monitor. But what? What was it?

Suddenly, it was as if she were looking at one of those Magic Eye pictures, the ones that at first appeared to be nothing more than a repeating pattern of jumbled colors and shapes but turned into a crystal clear, three-dimensional picture if you stared at it long enough to become almost cross-eyed.

"Oh, my gosh. It's the royalties," she squealed, clutching Bradley's sleeve excitedly. "The ones I was working on the night I got locked in the demo room."

"So what?" Robyn asked. "Those royalty checks went out last Friday and were all messed up."

"No, no, don't you see? These are the right figures. Here, look at this." She touched the computer screen. "This is the royalty amount for you."

"That's certainly a lot more than the twelve dollars and twenty-five cents I got on Monday."

"I know. I tried to tell David that I wouldn't have made such stupid mistakes, but he wouldn't listen. Here's proof that I did the calculations correctly." Kylie leaped up out of the chair. "Thank you, Bradley." Throwing her arms around him, Kylie stood on her tiptoes and planted an enthusiastic kiss on his cheek.

"Anytime, darlin'." Bradley wrapped his arms around her and waggled his eyebrows lecherously.

Kylie laughed and pushed at his chest. Besides being smarter than she had originally given him credit for, he was also becoming an outrageous flirt.

"Should I leave you two alone?"

Surprised at the cross note in her sister's voice, Kylie pulled out of Bradley's embrace. Was it possible that Robyn was jealous? Of her? Now, there was an interesting thought to ponder.

"Time for dinner." The shouted announcement echoed up the stairs, wafting up on air scented with onions, roasted garlic, and hot buttered bread. Pushing aside thoughts of her sister for the demands of her stomach, Kylie followed Robyn and Bradley down the stairs and into the noisy kitchen.

It was just past four-thirty on Thursday afternoon when Deborah slipped the newspaper under his nose.

David looked up from his phone call and grimaced at the picture on the front page. Of the four faces staring back at him, only his was clear of black warpaint. Unconsciously, his finger reached out to touch the image of the woman standing next to him in the picture. The photographer must have shot it right after David had hopped out of the window, because none of them were wearing the stunned looks they'd all had once the fracas had broken out.

Instead, Kylie was looking up at him, a smile playing about her mouth. He traced the line of her lips with a fingertip. Her curly hair was flying loose in the breeze, and her left hand was raised, as if she were in the process of moving an errant lock out of her eyes.

David noticed the ring she wore, the one she'd said her father had given to her when she was a teenager. He couldn't imagine someone giving a young girl such an expensive piece of jewelry, but obviously Kylie had taken good care of it. He remembered the way her eyes had softened when she'd mentioned her father. Rubbing his still-sore jaw, David wished she'd also mentioned her father had a strong right cross.

Damn. He missed her bright smile, the way her eyes sparkled when she laughed. He missed the way she found so much to be amused about in the ordinary things around her. He'd met some beautiful women in his life, but never had he seen one who could light up a room like Kylie did.

So why did she have to be so wrong for him?

Sighing, David shook his head as his gaze moved from the picture to the article itself.

His eyes widened in shock as he read the headline.

CHAPTER 20

Billionaire Bad Boy and Rising Rock Star Don Duds for Kids.

"Your publicist called. She said she had no idea about this." David's head jerked up. He hadn't realized Deborah was still there in his office. He felt a flush creep up his cheeks and tried to control his embarrassment at being caught caressing a newspaper while he read the story accompanying the strange headline.

Local billionaire David Gamble and popular rock star Robyn Rogers donned dark clothing and pretended to be burglars in a publicity stunt designed to aid The Soup Kitchen, a Seattle organization that provides food, shelter, and aid to the area's homeless. The event was arranged by Ms. Rogers's sister, Kylie, and the shelter's founder, Tyrone James. According to Mr. James, an anonymous donor agreed to fund the addition of a childcare facility if the shelter was successful in convincing at least two local celebrities to go along with the stunt. Kylie, a regular volunteer at the shelter, took on the project and, as evidenced here, was indeed able to enlist the aid of her sister and Mr. Gamble in pulling it off. Pictured here are (left to right) David Gamble, Kylie Rogers, Robyn Rogers, and Bradley Nelson, an aspiring country music singer and personal friend of the Rogerses. In addition to arranging the publicity for the event, Kylie also donated an undisclosed amount to ensure that the new daycare center is successful. Said Mr. James, "Kylie has been a great supporter of The Soup Kitchen since she moved to Seattle. I could only wish that more Seattle residents were as kind and generous as she."

David read the article over three times, then continued to stare blankly at the newspaper.

"That was mighty generous of you, David. I know how much you value your time and your privacy," Deborah said, an unmistakable glint of amusement in her eyes.

David knew then that his assistant didn't buy a word of it. He added another chunk of change to the amount of her ever-increasing raise when she refrained from calling him on the lie.

The newspaper rustled as he folded it and stuffed it in his briefcase. He cleared his throat. "Well, uh, I like to do what I can for a worthy cause."

"Uh-huh."

David thought vaguely that he should be offended by Deborah's sarcasm, but instead, he just felt a strange kind of numbness as he watched her leave his office. Swinging his chair around to face the windows, he leaned back and laced his fingers together, staring out at the pale October sky.

He hadn't seen Kylie since the night before last, after she'd left him standing in front of her house. Apparently, while he'd been busy hoping the story would be stopped for lack of facts and planning a strategy for damage control in case it wasn't, Kylie had spun this straw into gold.

David rested his head wearily against the back of his chair. He missed her, disasters and all. He missed how she always looked at things in her own funny, cockeyed way that made situations seem good instead of bad. But he was a realist. Kylie couldn't always cover her tracks as well as she had with the warehouse break-in, and he had worked too hard during the past twenty years to make sure his public image was exactly how he wanted it to give it up now. He'd had enough years of being laughed at, of having people snicker at him behind his back because of things that were beyond his control.

A vision sprang to his mind, one he wished he could delete from his memory like a corrupted file on his computer. It hadn't been long after his dad died. David had been in the fifth grade, Mrs. Weinand's class. He remembered the teacher's short red hair and how much her son, Eddie, who was in the same class, looked like her. In a larger city, Eddie wouldn't have been allowed to be placed in his mother's class, but in the small town where David grew up, there weren't any other options. Maybe that was why Eddie had invited the entire fifth grade class to his birthday party in late May, so his mother could honestly say there was no favoritism in her class.

Whatever the reason, even though David and Eddie weren't friends, David got invited to Eddie's party. He probably wouldn't have gone, but the invitation had said they should bring their swimsuits. It was then that David realized Eddie's family must have a swimming pool, a rarity in Washington State and the envy of every eleven-year-old around. The invitation also asked each person to bring something: hot dogs, potato chips, soda. David's invitation said to bring cupcakes for the twenty-five kids in the class.

A week before the party, David started reminding his mother that they needed to make the cupcakes. Every day on his way home from school, he prayed that he'd open the door to the sweet smell of chocolate cake, that he'd see a platter full of little brown goodies topped with multicolored sprinkles like she used to make before Dad had died. But by Thursday night, the night before the party, there was nothing—no sweet smells and no moist, chocolaty treats.

The next morning, David's anger erupted. He'd spent the entire night awake, gnawing on the worry about what the other kids would think of him if he showed up without the cupcakes. He could hear Mrs. Weinand say, "I'm sorry, everyone, there won't be any dessert. David Gamble didn't bring the cupcakes like he was supposed to." And everyone would hate him, they'd tell him to get out of the pool, to leave the party, and he'd have to walk home, even though it was miles and miles and he wasn't even sure he knew the way.

Refusing to give in to certain humiliation without a fight, and wanting to go to the party and swim in a real swimming pool—not a lake where the muddy bottom squished through your toes and you always wondered if you were stepping in someone's poop, or a public swimming pool that was so crowded you were always bumping into some-one; but a real, honest-to-goodness swimming pool that was sparkling clean and full of floating toys—yes, he was going to do everything he could to go to that party.

"Mom, wake up." He shook her lifeless form. "You gotta get up."

She snorted and rolled over, but didn't open her eyes. David felt helpless tears gather in his eyes but refused to give up. Ben started crying, but David knew that wouldn't make her get up either. But what would? A sudden thought occurred to him. She always seemed to perk up when she started drinking her special orange juice. She liked it so much she had even forbidden David to drink it or put any in Ben's bottles.

David ran to their small kitchen and pushed a chair against the cabinets. It made a loud noise as it scooted across the linoleum, but David didn't care since Ben was already awake. He climbed up on the chair and got a large plastic cup out of the cupboard, then stepped up onto the counter. Leaning over the top of the refrigerator, he opened another cabinet door and pulled out a bottle of clear liquid. The top of the fridge was nice and warm and David almost wished he could climb all the way up there, curl into a ball, and stay there forever. Instead, he let the heat seep through the shirt he'd picked out to wear that day for just a minute longer.

Setting both the bottle and the cup on the counter, David hopped off the chair, got the pitcher of juice from the fridge, and filled the cup half with juice and half with vodka like he'd seen his mother do countless times in the last few months. Then he put the pitcher back inside the refrigerator to keep it cold like Mom wanted and pulled the party invitation out from under the magnet he'd used to stick it in a prominent place on the fridge door in the hopes it would help remind his mother about the event.

Doing his best not to spill, David walked carefully back to his mother's room. "Wake up, Mom. I brought you some juice." He set the cup down on her nightstand and gave her shoulder a shake.

"Hmm?"

"I brought you some juice."

She opened her pale blue eyes. "Oh, thank you, honey."

David watched as she struggled to sit up, then waited until she'd gulped a few swallows before getting to the point. Walking over to the crib, he picked up Ben to make him stop crying. He wanted some peace and quiet for his conversation with his mother. Ben was soaked and he continued to cry even after being picked up, so David set his brother on the floor, grabbed a clean diaper and the box of wipes, and sat down on the floor beside his brother.

"Mom, you have to make cupcakes for Eddie's party today." He nodded toward the invitation that he'd pulled off the refrigerator as he neatly pinned one side of the white cloth he'd wrapped his brother in.

"Oh, is that today?"

David sighed with the irritated frustration that only a disappointed eleven-year-old could manage. As he fastened the other side of Ben's clean diaper, one of his brother's fists clamped around David's finger and he marveled at how strong the little guy was. "Yes, Mom. It's today. I could have brought them to school if you'd made them yesterday like I reminded you, but now you'll have to bring them to the party."

His mother took another drink of the juice. "All right. What time do I need to be there?"

He let out a relieved breath. She was not going to let him down after all. After filling her in on all the details and putting Ben into his playpen in the living room, David ran to the bus stop, cursing himself for being such a worrywart.

The party started out like one of his best dreams. The day was sunny and warm and all the kids in his class were in a good mood, even the usually grouchy Beth Morrison who was always chasing David on the playground at recess. They had played some games and Beth had even gone so far as to congratulate him when he'd won the three-legged race with his best friend Alex Martinez.

David lay back on the inflatable raft, cradled his head on his hands, and listened to the other kids splashing around in the shallow end as he drifted lazily around the pool on a soft breeze. They were going to have hot dogs and potato salad, then Eddie's father was going to organize everyone into two teams for a baseball game.

David loved baseball.

He was dreaming that he'd just hit the winning home run and all the kids were chanting his name when an all-too-familiar voice had him bolting upright. The sudden movement flipped the raft and he was unceremoniously dumped into the pool. The water felt cold on his sun-warmed skin and David shivered as he kicked over to the side.

Pushing his wet hair out of his eyes with one hand, he clung to the rough concrete with the other as he searched out the cause of the disruption with a growing sense of dread.

"David, honey, where are you? I brought your cup-cakes." His mother's voice was more high-pitched than usual, her words slurring as she tottered toward the pool on shiny red high heels. She had a platter of sloppy-looking brown cupcakes balanced on one arm and held Ben in the other. Her once-white T-shirt was smeared with streaks of flour and chocolate. It was also about four sizes too small and was riding up dangerously close to her boobs, David noticed as an ever-increasing band of her white flesh became exposed.

Some of the kids started to laugh and David wished he could disappear. Taking a giant gulp of air, he slid underwater, hoping she would magically be gone by the time he ran out of air and had to resurface.

Instead, she must have thought he was drowning because she picked up her pace toward him. Unfortunately, just as she reached the side of the pool, her bright red stiletto heel stuck in one of the cracks of the concrete patio. As David surfaced, he watched his mother, his baby brother, and two dozen chocolate cupcakes fly into the pool as if propelled by a giant slingshot.

The laughter behind him was unbearable and David would have hauled himself out of the water and run until he dropped from exhaustion if he hadn't seen Ben start to sink to the bottom of the pool as if his diaper were full of lead. His mother was flailing around, screeching and splashing, but she seemed oblivious to anyone except herself.

David dove under the water, keeping his eyes open even though the chlorine stung. He saw Ben and swam frantically toward him, kicking with all his might to reach his brother. The water fought his efforts, trying to force him to the surface, but David wouldn't give up. Grabbing the back of Ben's small shirt, David kicked upward. They shot out of the water and he set his brother on the warm concrete before pulling himself out of the pool.

He didn't know what to do next, but fortunately, nature took it from there. Ben coughed up a little water and started crying. The sun beat down on David's naked back as he picked up his little brother.

The whole thing had probably taken less than fifteen seconds. The other kids from the class were still laughing, their attention focused on the brown globs floating in the pool like so many turds.

His mother stood at the edge of the pool, looking dazed. Her blond hair was plastered to her head and twin rivers of black mascara trailed down her cheeks. Her sopping wet T-shirt was completely see-through, giving anyone who bothered to look an up-close and personal view of her bra-less breasts. Her red leggings clung to her legs, outlining her panties underneath, and she was missing one of her shoes.

Eddie's parents had come running out of the house at the uproar and Mrs. Weinand elbowed her husband, whose attention was focused on Pam Gamble's one-woman wet-T-shirt contest.

"Ed, get the skimmer and get those cupcakes out of the pool before they clog the filter."

Holding his brother, David looked up at his teacher and saw the disgust in her eyes as she looked at his mother.

As quickly as he could with a squirming baby in his arms, David grabbed his clothes and the hand-held radio he'd won in the three-legged race. Handing his mother her shoe, which had been stuck in the concrete deck by the side of the pool, David muttered a hurried "thank you" to Mrs. Weinand as he led the way out to the car and away from the ruined party.

It wasn't the last time his mother would embarrass him, but from that point on in his life, he had always done what he could to avoid being the butt of other people's laughter. Even in college, when the other kids were getting drunk and doing stupid things like running naked across campus or wrapping each other in tinfoil, David was the one in control. If he sometimes felt like an outsider, just an ob-server of life, he could always comfort himself with the thought that at least he knew people weren't laughing at him.

In the end, besides teaching him that life was something to be taken seriously, the day his mother fell into Eddie's pool brought him another benefit, too. The Monday after the party, David dreaded going back to school, but he knew he'd have to go back sooner or later.

He'd taken the bus as usual, but had waited until the last minute to go into the building, hoping he could just slip into his seat unnoticed. He spied Beth Morrison waiting in the hall and groaned, expecting her to say something rude.

Instead, she had seemed uncomfortable, too.

"I saw how you saved your brother when he fell into the pool," she blurted.

David shuffled his feet. "Yeah?"

"Well, I just wanted you to know I thought that was really cool. I have a little sister and I don't know if I'd save her if she was going to drown. She's always crying and she barfs a lot."

"Yeah, they do that." David paused, wondering if he should test their brief truce. "Do you ever have to change your sister's diaper?"

Beth looped her arm in his. "Yes, and it's just dis-gus-ting."

David had grinned as they made their way side by side into the classroom. He remembered thinking at that moment maybe Beth wasn't so bad after all.

He blinked as a dark rain cloud skidded across the blue Seattle sky, then shifted in his familiar leather chair. It had been a long time ago. He and Beth were still friends, and David still cringed at the thought of being made a laughingstock. Which brought him back to his original thought, like a hamster running around and around on one of those wheels, never going anywhere: If he pursued this relationship with Kylie, no matter how much he enjoyed her company, he'd be exposing himself to the results of her impetuous actions—actions that landed her in trouble more often than not.

Shoving his hands in his pockets, David stood up and wandered aimlessly across the room. He couldn't go through it again, couldn't let himself get caught up in the unpredictable, often laughable, events surrounding Kylie's life. No matter how much he wanted her now, it wouldn't be long before he started to resent the chaos she would undoubtedly bring to his world.

As the first drops of rain started to fall, he made his resolution. It would be best for them both if he never saw Kylie again.

The thought didn't improve his mood, and David found himself turning to the liquor cabinet in the corner of his office. He glanced at his watch. It was past five o'clock, besides, one drink wasn't going to turn him into his mother. Pouring a healthy measure of Scotch into the glass, David added a handful of ice cubes from the small freezer and sat back down at his desk. He stared at the papers in front of him unseeingly. None of it interested him right now.

He took a sip of the amber liquid, telling himself he didn't notice how the gold color reminded him of Kylie's eyes in the sunlight. God, he wanted a cigarette. He patted the pocket of his French-blue oxford shirt.

They weren't there.

David coughed. Had he forgotten to put them in his pocket this morning?

It wasn't possible. He never forgot them, not once in over ten years.

He turned as the door to his office was flung open.

The overpowering scent of perfume preceded his mother through the door. David took another healthy swallow of his drink.

"Hi, honey. I just came from getting my hair done. Do you like it?"

David coughed, stalling for time. They'd dyed it a blond so pale it was almost white and had dried and sprayed it so it looked like one of those beehive hairdos from the sixties. "Uh, it suits you," he said at last, having finally thought of something that was truthful yet not openly insulting.

"Thank you, dear. I've had so much fun today." Obviously not noticing her oldest son's dark mood, Pam plopped down on the couch by the window, chattering the whole time. "I got my hair done, then splurged for a manicure and pedicure. After that, I talked to the caterer again about the cake. I never knew how many options you could have. She told me that green cakes were in fashion this year. Green! Can you imagine?"

David tried not to grimace. "I don't suppose you ordered a plain white cake?"

"Heavens, no." Pam raised a blue nail polish–tipped hand to her ample breast. "I seriously considered the green one, but thought it might clash with the rest of my colors. So I got a purple one instead. They make it with blueberries, but it comes out purple, not blue."

David supposed that was better than a cake made with spinach or kiwi or whatever it was that would make it turn green.

"And I got the most fabulous dress, David. You should see it," she twittered. "Well, I guess you will see it tomorrow afternoon. I'm so excited. I can't wait. It's going to be such a beautiful ceremony, especially with the lake in the background."

"If it doesn't rain." David eyed the dark clouds outside his window. In Seattle, it was impossible to plan an outdoor event in advance, even in the summer. In late October, it was more than risky; it was an almost absolute certainty it would rain. But Pam would not be diverted in her insistence to have the wedding in his backyard.

"Oh, pooh. It will be fine." She paused, a small frown coming over her brightly painted lips. "I tried to get in touch with your brother, but none of his friends have seen him lately."

David looked down at his hands, fighting his feelings of guilt. He hadn't seen or heard from Ben since he'd had his brother arrested. "I haven't heard from him either."

"I wish I knew where he was. I'd like to invite him to

the wedding. I put an announcement in the paper and told all his friends to let him know if they talk to him before tomorrow."

"That's all you can do," David muttered.

"Excuse me for interrupting." Deborah poked her head in just as he was wishing for a way to end the conversation. Whether or not her timely interruption was intentional, David tacked another percentage point onto the raise he was tallying in his head. "Clint Walsh is on the phone. He said it was urgent."

"Thanks, Deborah. Mom, I have to take this call. I'll see you tomorrow afternoon."

He waited until his mother had gathered up her packages and the giant purse she toted everywhere, kissed him on the cheek, and closed the outer door behind her before waving to Deborah to put the call through.

An urgent call from Clint could not be good news. David took a final drink of his Scotch before picking up the buzzing phone.

CHAPTER 21

"We're so excited to have you help out at The Soup Kitchen, sir." Tyrone James beamed at Kylie's father as he handed an elderly homeless woman a tray.

"Please, call me George. No sense in standing on formality." Kylie's father smiled at the woman next to Ty as he heaped a spoonful of green beans onto her tray.

"All right, George, then. It's always nice for people to see a fresh face around here, especially a famous one."

"Tyrone, stop flattering him. He's hard enough to live with as it is," Elizabeth Rogers said, tying an apron around her slim waist.

Wiping a wet dishrag over the top of a table, Kylie watched her parents charm Tyrone and put everyone around them at ease. When she'd mentioned that she was volunteering at The Soup Kitchen tonight, they'd asked to come along and help. Her father had even stopped at the movie theater a block from the shelter and bought gift certificates that he was now busily dishing out with helpings of beans.

"Everybody needs a little entertainment in their lives now and then," he'd said. Kylie smiled now as he handed a certificate to a little boy who grinned from ear to ear because of the gift. George Rogers had just given him two hours of freedom from worry, two hours where he could become anything he wanted. And, who knew, those two hours might change the boy's life forever. Even if it didn't, Kylie thought as she watched him fold the slip of paper and carefully stow it in the pocket of his too-small jeans, at least it gave him something to look forward to for a while.

Kylie sent up a silent prayer of gratitude for her family. A lack of talent was nothing when compared with the lack of hope she saw every time she volunteered here. She knew that was Ty's mission, to try to give hope to the hopeless, and he was even fairly successful at it. When she looked around at the sad faces, especially the little ones, she couldn't help but stop feeling sorry for herself.

"Hey, Kylie."

She spun around, startled. "Ben, you scared me. How are you doing? I haven't seen you around for a while."

The chair scraped loudly across the hardwood floor as he pulled it out and sat down. Kylie noticed his bloodshot eyes and recalled the obviously untruthful story he'd told her the first night he'd come to The Soup Kitchen. His clothes were wrinkled like he'd slept in them, which he undoubtedly had, and his hair had the dull look of infrequent washings. The man in front of her was not an otherwise successful man made homeless by a disastrous fire. There were too many places someone like that could go for help. She wished she could talk to him about the wonderful treatment centers for drug and alcohol abuse that existed in the city, but knew Ty was right when he told the volunteers that people who came to the shelter would ask for help when they were ready and that the volunteers shouldn't try to force it on them. Still, it was hard to watch someone throw his life away and not attempt to offer assistance.

"Can I get you something to eat? We've got roast beef tonight," she offered.

"What I really need is something to drink."

"Well, we have milk or orange juice or—"

"Fuck that. I mean a real drink," Ben interrupted. "I just

found out my mother's getting married tomorrow and my asshole of a brother is probably paying for everything, even after all the rotten crap she pulled on us when we were kids."

Kylie ignored Ben's foul language and addressed the other thing he had said. "Maybe your brother has chosen to forgive your mother and get on with his life."

"Ha. 'Forgive' isn't in his vocabulary. He's still punishing me for crap that happened a year ago. That's why I'm here, because he's still mad and refuses to help me out."

Kylie chose not to point out that Ben seemed perfectly capable of taking care of his own problems. He didn't need her to pass judgment on him, but she couldn't help but feel a pang of sympathy for Ben's brother. As with Ty and his wife, she guessed Ben's brother suffered guilt at turning away a family member in need. It was hard to let them go, to force them to choose between the addictive behaviors that were destroying them and their own families.

Kylie sighed, wishing again that she could push Ben toward the help he so obviously needed. She gave the table in front of him one last swipe with the clean cloth, then jumped when he reached out and grabbed her hand.

"That's a beautiful ring. How come I never noticed it before?"

Kylie pulled her arm back, uncomfortable with him touching her. "I'm usually behind the counter where we have to wear rubber gloves. It's nothing anyway, just a little joke between my dad and I."

Yeah, right, Ben thought, releasing her hand and watching her walk away. Just a little two-carat joke between Daddy Warbucks and his little girl. She must have been wearing it Monday night when he'd gone over and searched her place after getting out of jail. He'd turned the place inside out looking for where she stashed her jewelry and cash, but hadn't found a damn thing. After two hours of looking, he'd given up. He hadn't even seen a safe, and figured she must have a safe-deposit box down at the bank or something. That rock on her finger must be worth a fortune. It was huge and, since it had been a gift from her movie-star father, he'd bet it was top-quality ice.

How could he get it, though? Most chicks he knew wore their jewelry all the time except when they went to bed or when they washed their hands.

He had to find some way to get that ring. He needed cash. It was obvious after David had him arrested that his brother wasn't going to help, so wouldn't it be fitting that he take something from David's girlfriend after David himself had turned Ben away?

Ben watched Kylie walk through the swinging doors into the kitchen with an armful of dirty trays. Glancing over at the food line, he saw that everyone's attention was focused on her famous parents, who were busy doing some kind of skit. Unable to believe his luck, he got up from his seat, quietly walked to the double doors leading to the kitchen, and peered inside.

Kylie was standing over a large stainless steel sink with a big silver sprayer in her hands. She had put on a pair of bright yellow rubber gloves and Ben glanced around the sink to see if he could spot her gold band. He thought he saw something on a ledge to her left and figured he had nothing to lose.

Pushing open the heavy door, Ben sauntered into the kitchen as if he had every right to be there. Kylie turned toward him and frowned.

"You're not supposed to be in here."

"I know." Ben casually leaned a hip against the counter where she'd stacked the dirty trays. "But your parents have stolen everyone's attention and I wanted someone to talk to."

"All right, but if you're going to stay, you can help me. Put these trays in the dishwasher after I rinse them." Up to her elbows in suds, she nodded her head toward the dishwasher on her right. A stray curl landed across her eyes and she blew it away, but it came right back.

Thinking fast, Ben stepped forward, lifted his right hand and brushed the errant lock of hair behind Kylie's ear. With his body blocking her view for a split second, his heart pounded wildly as his left hand grabbed the shiny trinket. Walking to the other side of the sink, Ben tried to slow his heart rate as he waited to see if she'd noticed his pilfering. He could hear the blood roaring in his ears as he stood there, waiting for her to start screaming for help.

Instead, she sprayed water onto one of the trays, getting herself just as wet as the dish. "I hate dish duty," she said, handing him the tray.

Ben surreptitiously slipped the ring into his pocket at the same time he loaded the tray into the dishwasher.

"So, what did you want to talk about?" she asked.

"Huh?" Ben searched his mind for something to say. "Oh, how's your cat?"

She shot him a strange look. "My cat? How did you know I have a cat?"

Shit! Why had he said that? "I . . . you must have mentioned it."

From the suspicious glance she shot him, Ben figured his luck had just run out. He wasn't about to stick around and make sure his hunch was correct. "I gotta be going, Kylie. See you around," he said, before bolting out the nearest exit.

Kylie watched as the door slowly slid back into place, wondering at Ben's hasty departure.

"Weird," she muttered, then shrugged her shoulders and went back to her spraying.

Kylie sat on the back stoop of her house, leaning against her father.

"I know you're upset that it's gone, honey." George Rogers put his arm around his daughter's shoulders.

Kylie continued rubbing the bare spot on her left hand where her ring should be. She'd discovered it was gone after finishing up her shift at The Soup Kitchen. They'd searched the entire place, but it was nowhere to be found. Kylie had a hunch where it might be, and she didn't think it had fallen into the plumbing at the shelter either.

"It meant a lot to me, Dad. You gave that ring to me almost twenty years ago."

"I know. I still remember the day I gave it to you. Do you?"

Kylie smiled. "Of course. I was fourteen, had braces, and felt like the ugliest, gangliest girl in my class. I also had my first serious crush on Randy Harwell, the only boy in the eighth grade taller than me."

"He certainly seemed like a nice boy at first."

"He was nice. He just couldn't seem to keep his eyes off my little sister. I don't think he set out to break my heart. But, let's face it, if you put Robyn and me side by side in a roomful of men, I'm going to end up in a corner by myself except for the one guy who's intimidated by her and wants to spend the entire evening asking me what it's like to have grown up with a goddess."

"You've always been such a good sport about it, though. I admired that you had the courage to not settle for someone who thinks of you as second-best. That's what the ring was for, to remind you that all that glitters—"

"—isn't gold," Kylie finished.

"And cubic zirconia shines just as bright as diamonds but you don't have to treat it with kid gloves and worry about it all the time."

"It's not as susceptible to being stolen right out from under your nose either. Except when the thief thinks he's getting the high-maintenance stuff, that is." Kylie shook her head with disgust. It was obvious that Ben had taken her ring since he'd been the only one in the kitchen with her before she'd discovered it was missing. Ty warned all the volunteers not to wear jewelry, but Kylie had figured her faux-diamond ring was safe. Apparently, she'd been wrong.

"I can just imagine his surprise when he tries to pawn it and is told that it's worthless."

"Worthless to anyone but me." Kylie laid her head on her father's shoulder. "Oh, Daddy, I know I'm right not to settle for anything less than the love that you and Mom have, but sometimes I wonder if I'm ever going to get that. I mean, maybe that kind of love doesn't exist for someone like me."

"Baloney. You seem to have some strong feelings for this David Gamble fellow."

"*My* feelings aren't the issue, Dad. It's him. One minute he's hauling me close and the next he's tossing me away. I feel like that animal in that Dr. Dolittle book you used to read to us."

"The pushmi-pullyu?"

"Exactly. With David, I'm never sure if I'm coming or going." She shivered a little in the cold night air and watched the red lights of the planes heading into Sea-Tac mingle with the stars overhead.

"Then why don't you just walk away, refuse to see him again, like you did with that Harwell boy?"

Kylie studied the pale band on her finger, the empty strip of skin where her ring should be, as she pondered her father's question. David may have already made that choice for her. She hadn't heard from him in two days and she wasn't sure she ever would again. She'd been busy calling every Gamble artist, trying to straighten out the royalty mess she was convinced had not been her fault. But even after that hurdle was surmounted, would he want to see her again? And did she really want to take another chance with him? Could her heart withstand it?

She worried the skin at the base of her finger. His presence in her life was like the ring she'd worn for almost twenty years. For a few magical weeks, he had made her feel special, just like the silly trinket her father had given her. The thought that she might never see him again made her feel dead inside, as if some part of her would never be the same if he pushed her away for good. As with Randy Harwell, though, if David didn't want her for herself, just the way she was, she had to be able to walk away with her self-esteem intact. The problem was, she wasn't sure she could do it, wasn't sure her feelings for David would just go away because she wanted them to.

"Kylie," Robyn's voice sounded through the screen door, "David Gamble's on the phone for you."

George Rogers watched the emotions flicker across his daughter's face in the twilight: hope chased by fear, then longing and pain. This was no eighth-grade schoolgirl crush, not for her to feel it this deeply. It was the real thing this time.

He squeezed his daughter's shoulders. "You should take this call, honey."

Kylie looked up at him, her eyes filling with tears. "I can't, Dad. What if he breaks my heart?"

"Sometimes you have to take a risk in order to get what you want. You just have to ask yourself if the prize is worth it. Is David worth it to you?"

"He shouldn't be." Kylie blinked and twin tears trickled down her face. "Unfortunately, I can't seem to get my heart to agree with my head."

"You know, Kylie, one of the things that I've always loved best about you is that you live your life according to what your heart tells you. It's what makes you so special. Other people analyze all the angles, trying to figure out what would be best for themselves, but not you. You believe wholeheartedly in everything you do. It makes you passionate about your life and the people you love. You might want to ask yourself what it is your heart is telling you to do now."

Kylie paused, before slowly standing up and turning back to him. She smiled at him then, this daughter whom he loved so much, and George found himself blinking back his own tears. If David Gamble hurt his baby again, he'd make the bastard regret it.

"I love you, Dad," she said, before disappearing into the house with a bang of the screen door.

* * *

"Thanks for coming over, Kylie."

David stood in the doorway, his dark hair in disarray. His face looked thinner than usual, his skin pale under his tan. But it was his eyes, the midnight blue gaze that usually flashed fire at her, that told her the depth of his distress. They looked dull, tired, as if he didn't have enough emotion left to light them to their usual brilliance. She felt herself leaning forward, ready to offer him comfort. Then she stopped.

Every time she impulsively offered him consolation, she was the one who got hurt. So, rather than going with her first instinct, which was to throw her arms around him, she held back.

"What can I do to help?" she asked instead, still standing on the stoop.

David put out a hand, reaching for her. When she hesitated, he took a step toward her, then gathered her fiercely in his arms. Too stunned by his gesture to do anything but hug him back, Kylie laid her head on his shoulder.

She had never seen him this vulnerable before and it scared her. As much as she wanted to remind herself that she was still angry at him, she didn't have the heart for it. He had reached out to her, had invited her into his pain, and that was enough for now. She only hoped she had the emotional strength to give David what he needed, and then be able to walk away.

Inhaling the clean scent of Kylie's hair, David wanted nothing more than to lay his head down on top of her soft curls and stay there forever. His best friend of twenty years had just lost the woman he loved, and the raw pain was too much for David to handle alone. He didn't know what to do to comfort his friend, and had even less knowledge of how to console a three-year-old who had just lost her mother to an awful disease. His vow to never see Kylie again had crumbled in the face of this tragedy. He couldn't handle it alone, and before he'd had a chance to think, he'd found himself dialing her number.

God, he needed her.

He held her tight, taking all that she offered.

They stood in the doorway, wrapped in each other's arms for what felt like an eternity.

Finally, David stepped back. Grabbing Kylie's hand again as if he could continue to draw on her energy so long as they had a physical connection, he led her back to the music room.

Clint Walsh sat on the couch, his eyes red from crying over the loss of his soulmate. Lexi was asleep beside him, her golden head resting against her adopted father's thigh.

David felt bereft when Kylie released him. He watched as she sat down next to Clint and took his hand in hers without saying a word. David saw his friend's shoulders beginning to shake and blinked back tears of his own.

For the first time in his life, he began to wonder if this was how his mother had felt when his father had died. Was this the kind of pain she had endured, this awful, gut-wrenching sorrow? Was it this terrible feeling of sadness and hopelessness that had made her want to bury herself in a liquor-induced haze?

He didn't want to forgive her, didn't want to excuse her inexcusable behavior, but watching Clint wrestle with this almost unendurable pain made him reexamine some of his own feelings. Even more, Clint was nursing a bottle of Scotch, trying to drown the anguish. But David wasn't going to let his friend slide down that path. He'd give him tonight to deaden his sorrow, but after that, he wouldn't let up, wouldn't watch his friend ruin his life and put Amy's little girl through what David and his brother had gone through. David wasn't going to let it happen to Clint, wasn't going to just stand by and let history repeat itself. Perhaps that was the difference, that Pam Gamble hadn't had anyone to hold her up when she was in danger of falling.

"Why don't I take Lexi upstairs and put her to bed?" Kylie suggested quietly.

Clint brushed a hand over the little girl's blond curls, then nodded and allowed Kylie to take her away.

David sat down facing Clint and watched his friend pour himself another drink. Ice clinked against the side of the glass as Clint raised it to his lips. They sat in silence, letting the sorrow fill the room to the point of saturation. David didn't know what to do, what to say, so he simply sat there, feeling more inadequate than he had felt in the past twenty-five years.

"I told myself I wouldn't be bitter," Clint said finally, swirling the amber liquor in his tumbler.

David looked at his friend questioningly.

"We talked about it, before she died. Amy wanted me to promise her that I wouldn't let the anger about her disease ruin my life." Clint laughed without amusement. "I didn't understand what she meant before now. You know, I sat in the hospital after she died and I couldn't help looking at the doctors, the nurses, the other patients, and wishing they were all dead instead of Amy. Someone came up to me and said, 'God always takes the good ones first,' and you know what I wanted to do?"

David shook his head, noticing the way Clint's hands had tightened on his glass.

"It was this sweet old lady who was just trying to be comforting, but I wanted to grab her and shake her, to scream that she didn't know what the hell she was talking about. If Lexi hadn't been there, David, I think I would have done it."

What could he say? He could tell Clint that anger was a normal reaction to the death of a loved one, but that would be just as ridiculously inadequate as the other comments his friend had heard.

"I didn't know your girlfriend, but I'm sure she'd have been glad to know you didn't beat up somebody's grandma in front of her daughter," Kylie said from the doorway.

To David's surprise, Clint started to laugh. "To tell the truth, I think she would have been amazed at my restraint. She was always saying my temper was too quick to ignite."

David watched as Kylie curled up in the corner of the couch after casually pulling off and tossing aside a pair of white Keds. She looked comfortable in her jeans and a bright red shirt, with very little makeup on her face. He guessed she had not even paused when he'd called and asked her for help, since she'd arrived at his house in record time. He'd bet that if he'd called any other woman, it would have taken at least an hour before the proper makeup, hair, and clothing routine was complete. But not Kylie. She'd obviously dashed out without taking the time to—

"Did you lock your doors?" he asked suddenly.

Kylie looked at him curiously, her eyebrows drawn together. "No. My parents are staying at my house so they'll lock up when they go to bed," she answered before turning her attention back to Clint. "Did Amy have a bad temper?"

Clint smiled and his whole face softened. "She didn't get angry very often, but when she did, man, all you could do was get out of the way."

Leaning back in his chair, David watched Kylie and listened as Clint talked about Amy. He had done the right thing by calling her. She was doing a hell of a lot better job than he of comforting his friend. Hell, he had thought Clint wouldn't want to discuss Amy. He thought it would just make the pain harder to bear, but instead it seemed to be calming his friend down. He'd stopped drinking, anyway, for which David was grateful.

It didn't take long for Clint's eyelids to start drooping and he didn't protest when David suggested he call it a night. He left the room after dropping a grateful kiss on Kylie's cheek.

An uncomfortable silence filled the void after Clint's departure. Kylie shifted positions on the couch, suddenly noticing her left foot was starting to fall asleep.

"I guess I'll be going now," she said, slipping her feet

back into her tennis shoes, not bothering with the laces.

David stood up just as she did and took a step toward her. She breathed in the smell of him, the faint whisper of cologne combined with the unique scent of man. The fire was back in his eyes, and Kylie wished she could take a step back before she got burned again. But it was no use, she was just as trapped by him emotionally as she was physically, so she lifted her gaze to his and welcomed the inevitable.

He was so close she could count the individual lashes surrounding his eyes. He lifted a hand and traced her bottom lip with the pad of his thumb. Her lips parted and her tongue reached out to touch his fingertip. He tasted salty.

"Thank you for coming over. I think it helped Clint to talk about Amy. We need to talk—"

Kylie didn't want to talk about Clint right now, didn't want to think about anything except the way David's husky voice was sending shivers down her arms. "Glad I could help," she interrupted, then sucked his thumb into her mouth, sliding her tongue around it.

David groaned. "And thank you for taking care of those reporters. I'd be happy to chip in on a donation to The Soup Kitchen."

Reaching up on her tiptoes, she pressed her lips to his. His lips parted under hers and Kylie felt his instantaneous response pressing into her stomach. She was the first to pull back.

"I don't want to talk anymore, David."

"Mmm. What do you want, then?"

"This." She started to pull him down to the couch.

"No, wait. I want to do it right this time. Slowly. In bed. Let's go upstairs."

Kylie's eyes crinkled with amusement as she let him lead her upstairs. If they'd done it wrong before, she couldn't wait to see what doing it right was like.

CHAPTER 22

Doing it right was awful.

Kylie sniffed and wiped a fat tear from her cheek as she sped across the 520 bridge that spanned Lake Washington, connecting Seattle to the suburbs to the east. Mt. Rainier rose out of the clouds to the south, looking as if it were part of the sky instead of the earth.

She'd been able to handle the wild, passionate sex they'd had before last night. That kind of sex didn't rip at your heart, didn't make you ache with tenderness and hope. She hadn't known what to expect when David said he wanted to do it right, but if she'd known how she'd feel this morning in the cold, predawn light, she'd have jumped in her car and sped away as fast as she could.

The wind skimming the surface of the lake whipped across the bridge, threatening to push her car into the other lane. Kylie gripped the steering wheel even tighter, allowing the tears to flow down her face unchecked.

Why hadn't she guessed he could be such a tender and generous lover? She felt as if his touch had branded her from the tips of her toes to the top of her head. Even now, her skin felt flushed from his caresses. He had undressed her slowly, taking his time to follow the path of each garment with his lips. She'd never known it could be like that, slow and tender, but with all the passion of their previous hurried couplings. Having sex on his desk had been just that—sex. But last night, they had made love, and Kylie knew she'd left a chunk of her heart back there in David's bed, a piece of herself that she'd never be able to get back, even after David eventually pushed her away for good.

She sobbed, her eyes blurring with hot tears. How could she survive when he pushed her away again, as he inevitably would?

David cared for her, Kylie knew that much. He would never have called her last night and let her into such a personal part of his life if he didn't. But she wasn't foolish enough to believe that his feelings for her wouldn't die, little by little, with each fiasco or impetuous decision that haunted her life. It was inevitable that she'd find herself in the middle of some sort of disaster again. Probably soon. That was just the way her life was, but David's was not. His life was calm and orderly. He was in control of the events that happened to him, not the other way around. And trying to get her to change was like asking a leopard to put on a beak and fly south for the winter. It was simply not something she could do, nor was it something she wanted to do. She had vowed long ago to be herself without trying to contort her personality to suit anyone else.

Damn David and his uptight code of conduct that she could never live up to, she cursed, pounding the steering wheel with the palms of her hands. Why couldn't he love her enough to just accept her as she was?

But Kylie knew David well enough by now to know he would never be able to do that; not when the next disaster befell her, dragging him down with her.

Kylie clenched her teeth, her jaw aching with tension.

No, it would be better to end it now, before the inevitable catastrophe did it for her. The light that burned in David's eyes now would go out by degrees and she'd be left with nothing of herself, because each time he made love to her like he had last night, she'd lose another part of herself to him.

Tears rolled unchecked down her cheeks as she merged onto the freeway.

She hadn't said the words out loud before, not even to herself, but now she knew it was true.

"Damn it, why did I have to fall in love with him?" she asked, her voice echoing hoarsely in the quiet interior of the car.

David rolled over and reached out an arm, trying to locate Kylie and pull her warmth into him. Last night had been incredible, he thought sleepily. He had never felt so sated and relaxed after sex.

He frowned when his fingers touched nothing but cold sheets. His eyes jerked open and he abruptly sat up in bed, the comforter sliding to his waist. If she'd escaped again, he'd . . . he'd . . . well, he'd go find her and bring her back, that's what he'd do. In the meantime, the thought of attaching a bell around her pretty neck was beginning to sound appealing.

Slipping out of bed, David tugged on his jeans and padded down the stairs on bare feet.

The ogre in his kitchen was barely recognizable as his best friend. Clint's eyes were red-rimmed and bloodshot and his light brown hair stuck up in every direction.

"I'd forgotten how bad you look in the morning." David reached around his friend for the coffeepot, ignoring Clint's suggestion that he perform a physical impossibility on himself.

"How's Lexi?"

"Still sleeping. How's Kylie?"

David frowned, stirring cream into his coffee. "Gone."

"Why? You still enforcing the 'no sleeping over' rule?"

"No . . . I . . . Kylie's slept over before," David answered uncomfortably. That was the problem with old friends, he thought, watching white liquid swirl into brown. They knew too many of your secrets.

He waited for Clint to hit him with some smart-ass comment, then raised his head at the continued silence. Clint met his eyes straight-on.

"She's different," Clint said. It was not a question.

"Yeah." David pulled out one of the stools around the granite-topped island and sat down. "She's definitely different."

"What're you gonna do about it?" Clint speared him with the question.

"Nothing. I don't know." David shook his head and focused his attention outside, on the wispy gray clouds scudding across the sky and the whitecaps frothing the surface of the lake. The leaves of the maple trees in his back yard had just begun to turn to gold. It would be at least another month before they fell, creating a carpet of yellow and red over the lush lawn. "Kylie's very impetuous. I can't control the things that happen when she's around."

Clint snorted. "You and your precious control. David, when are you going to learn that you can't control life? If you could, don't you think I would have been able to change what happened to Amy?"

David hated the pain he saw in his friend's face. "This isn't the same thing at all."

"No, it's not the same. You're involved with a wonderful woman who seems to care a great deal for you, but you won't do anything about it because she's not afraid of taking chances like you are."

"I'm not afraid of taking chances." David carefully set his coffee cup back on the countertop and the ceramic made a hollow *thunk* on the granite.

"Bullshit. You could have been a great songwriter, but you were too afraid to put down on paper the pain you kept inside of you; too afraid that exposing your emotions would make you vulnerable like the rest of us. Instead, you've kept it all bottled up. So, rather than being able to put the pain in the past, you have to live with it, day in and day out, never letting any of it go."

David felt a hot flash of anger. "What would you have me do, Clint? Walk away from the company I've been building for the past twenty years to sit around all day and tinker with the piano? And for what? To prove that I feel pain just like everyone else?"

Clint stepped closer. David hadn't realized that he'd stood up, too, until Clint stepped in front of him. They stood toe-to-toe and David watched as the anger drained out of his friend's eyes.

"No, David. I just want you to be happy. I've known you for almost two decades, and I've never seen you let go and enjoy the moment. You're always too busy thinking about how to maintain your carefully crafted image, about how to make sure the world approves of the David Gamble you've created for public display."

"But look at you, you're not happy," David said quietly.

"No, right now I am not happy. I hurt like hell, but I wouldn't have given up even one second of my life with Amy, even knowing how it would turn out." Clint sat down on one of the bar stools, as if he no longer had the strength to stand.

David looked at his friend and shook his head in disbelief. "How could you feel that way? Wouldn't it have been better not to have known her at all than to live through this?"

"Man, didn't you ever listen to any of the songs we used to play?" Clint laughed without any of his usual humor. "I couldn't control my feelings for Amy any more than you can control yours for Kylie. They just are. Besides that, without Amy, I wouldn't have Lexi. My life would be empty." He paused, then continued quietly, "You can't expect work to fulfill you forever, David. At some point, the challenge of making your next million will start to seem irrelevant. I hope, for your sake, you learn that before it's too late and Kylie's gone. Women like her, and like Amy, are a once-in-a-lifetime thing. Don't let your own stupidity ruin your one chance for happiness."

"Daddy." Both David and Clint whipped around at the soft voice in the doorway.

"Hey, good morning, Sweet Pea." Clint swooped the little girl up and balanced her on one arm. She laid her head on his shoulder and he felt a tingling of peace nibbling away at his sadness, like a tiny mouse hoarding a cracker for the long winter months ahead. "Want some juice?"

She nodded, her soft hair tickling under his chin. "Where's Kylie?"

"She had to go home."

"Oh." Lexi looked disappointed. "She's nice. Last night she told me a story about a dragon and a princess."

"She did? That was nice of her." Clint looked pointedly at his friend. If his three-year-old could figure out what a treasure Kylie was, why couldn't David? "Was there a prince in the story, too?" he asked idly, searching David's cupboards for a plastic cup appropriate for serving orange juice to a toddler.

"Yeah, and he was handsome and had dark hair just like Uncle David."

Clint laughed, with genuine amusement this time. He noticed David was listening intently to their conversation. "Oh, and did the prince kill the dragon and save the princess?" Clint asked Lexi, then turned to David. "Don't you have anything besides Waterford around here, man?"

Lexi shook her head vigorously, her eyes open wide as saucers. "No, Daddy. The princess captured the dragon and they made friends, and then they saved the prince from a fate worst than death."

"Worst than death, huh?" Clint smiled at the three-year-old's interpretation of the saying, then took the plastic cup David handed him and poured a healthy measure of juice for his daughter.

"The prince was locked in a castle, all by himself, with no friends, and the princess and the dragon came and

brought him a birthday cake, even though it wasn't his
birthday, because they wanted him to not be lonely anymore. So, then they all liked each other, and they had birthday parties every day, and they lived happily ever after.
Even the dragon."

Clint met David's gaze over the top of Lexi's head. He
hoped his eyes accurately conveyed his thoughts.

David would be a fool to let Kylie go.

"That's the last of them." Kylie turned off the phone and
marked through the last name on her list of Gamble artists.

"They all agreed to waive the penalties?" Robyn crossed
her legs at the ankles and bit into a Red Delicious apple.

"Yep. Most everyone I talked to told me how well David
had treated them over the years, how he's always made sure
they got paid on time and how he got rid of the onerous
clauses in his contracts that hurt artists." Kylie pushed a
stray curl behind her ear and leaned back on the green-and-
white–striped couch in her living room. "As a matter of
fact, the only people I had trouble with were Lisanne
O'Neill and you."

"Lisanne O'Neill is a bitch," Robyn said without heat.

Kylie silently agreed but, since her feelings about the
other woman were based solely on the jealousy she felt
about Lisanne's rumored relationship with David, she decided to keep her opinion to herself. Robyn's own initial
refusal to waive the late penalties, however, was still an
issue.

Robyn studied the apple in her hand as if deciding on
the perfect place to take her next bite. Kylie suspected her
sister was simply trying to avoid her accusing gaze.

"I *did* agree to ignore the penalties," Robyn said defen-
sively.

Kylie snorted. "Sure, after Dad pointed out how unrea-
sonable you were being."

"Well, all's well that ends well, I always say."

"Hmph."

Robyn munched her apple in the ensuing silence. Kylie finally gave up trying to make her sister feel guilty. It was no use anyway. She loved Robyn, but was realistic enough to see her sister as she really was. As the beautiful, talented baby of the family, Robyn had been doted on since the day she was born. Because of the attention she'd received her entire life, Robyn's view of the world had become more than a little self-centered. Fortunately, she could be convinced to do things that weren't in her own self-interest, but not without some effort on the part of the people she cared about.

"Did you finish your calls?" Bradley sauntered in from the kitchen where Tony was undoubtedly cooking up something delicious for breakfast. Her parents had decided to stay through the weekend and Kylie worried that she'd gain ten pounds by the time they left. She had heard them upstairs earlier, her mother taking her father through his lines for the upcoming scenes in the movie he was currently filming. She'd fought back a smile, remembering how many times she'd come home from school and interrupted a fight scene or a love scene, how normal it had seemed for them to drop out of character to say hello, then pop back into the scene like throwing on a light switch.

Kylie realized Bradley was still waiting for an answer while her mind had been meandering down memory lane. Yanking herself back to the present, she glanced down at the printout on her coffee table. One by one all the names had been crossed off. "Yes. I got them all."

"Good, let's take the disk to David then."

Kylie felt the blood drain from her face. She couldn't see David again, not after last night. It would be better to end it now, while her heart was only broken in two pieces, rather than prolonging the agony and having it chipped into a million splintered fragments.

"I . . . I can't, Bradley. Why don't you and Robyn take the disk to him?"

"I can't go, I have a recording session in an hour." Rob-

yn finished the last bite of her apple and tossed the core in
the wastebasket.

"And you know I can't get past his assistant," Bradley
said ruefully. "I've certainly tried it often enough."

"You could just leave it with Deborah. She'll make sure
he gets it," Kylie suggested hopefully.

Bradley shifted his weight to his left foot, looking uncomfortable. "Well, Kylie, I was kind of hoping you could
get David to listen to my demo tape. I'm not getting anywhere through regular channels and I was hoping you could
give me a little help. Going with me to drop this off would
give us the perfect opportunity to capitalize on David's
gratitude."

Watching his eager face, Kylie knew he had her. As
much as she wanted to avoid seeing David again, she had
to help Bradley. He had stuck with her during this latest
crisis and she had no choice but to do what she could to
return the favor. She was sure David would suspect Bradley's motives for helping, but she didn't—not after all he
had done to help her these last few days.

Besides, she knew she needed to end the relationship in
person. She had taken the coward's way out, sneaking out
the door before the first morning light. She needed to tell
David, to his face, that he didn't have to worry about any
more of her disasters because she was bowing out of his
life. Her heart just wasn't strong enough to take any more.

"All right," she said morosely as Bradley waited expectantly for her answer. "I'll do it. Let me just go and get
another cup of coffee first."

Bradley watched Kylie drag herself into the kitchen as
if heading to the gallows. As soon as she was out of earshot
he turned to Robyn.

"Fast thinking about the recording session," he com-
mended.

"You, too, about the demo tape." Robyn returned the
compliment.

"I had to think of something that would make it necessary for her to come with me."

Robyn uncrossed her legs and leaned closer, lowering her voice. "I know. We have to get her to see David again. Dad said he heard her crying in her room this morning when he got up. Whatever went wrong between them won't get resolved if they don't see each other. One thing about Kylie, she can be as stubborn as a mule once she's made up her mind about something."

"Must be a family trait."

Robyn peered at him balefully. "Very funny. I'm not stubborn. I'm determined."

Bradley sat down on the couch next to Robyn and ran a hand up her bare arm. He felt her slight shiver. "So am I, darlin'. So am I." His breath caressed her ear.

Robyn turned to him, prepared to protest. Bradley stopped her the best way he knew how, his lips pressing against hers. It only took a split second for her mouth to soften under his. He kept the kiss light, teasing, even when she would have deepened it. He was the one in control here and he had no intention of letting her get what she wanted so easily. He suspected she'd gotten her way her entire life and figured he'd make her work a little more for him than she was used to.

When he drew back, her green eyes were as dark as emeralds. He noticed with satisfaction that her breath was shallower than usual.

"Are you ready to go, Bradley?" Kylie called from the kitchen.

"We'll continue this later, darlin'," he promised, kissing the tip of Robyn's nose lightly and enjoying the bemused look on her face as he walked away.

"Yes, Mother, I'll be home in an hour." David watched the gathering clouds as his mother's chattering continued.

"No, I'm not sure the weather will hold." He held the receiver away from his ear as the volume increased, then rubbed the pounding spot at his temples. "Fine, then, if your wedding planner doesn't think it's going to rain, set the cake up outside, Mom. I'm the president of a record company, not a damn weatherman."

Deborah waved at him through the window beside his office door and tapped the glass to get his attention.

"Look, Mom, I have to go. I'll be home as soon as I finish this last appointment." Despite his hint, the talking on the other end of the line continued. "Good-bye, Mom." David hung up, wondering how long she'd continue yammering after the phone went dead.

Deborah popped her head into his office. "Sandy's here for the conference call. I'll get Mitchell Sharpe on the line."

"Thanks, Deborah, send her in. Did you have any luck getting Kylie on the phone?"

"No. Her line's been busy all morning. I'll keep trying."

David gritted his teeth. He should have gone straight to Kylie's house this morning instead of coming into the office first. He'd only wanted to get his laptop and be on his way, but the minute he'd stepped into the building, people had started clamoring for his attention. To top it off, he'd received a voice mail from Mitchell Sharpe at BSS asking for a conference call with David and his financial people this morning.

What he really wanted to do, however, was get up right now and drive to Kylie's house to ask why in the hell she'd felt it necessary to sneak out of his house in the wee hours of the morning as if she were ashamed of making love with him. David clenched his teeth and the ache in his jaw increased.

He wished he could believe that Kylie had crept out under cover of darkness to avoid being seen by Clint, but he was honest enough with himself to know better. After all, he had taken much more from her last night than he had given, turning to her for the comfort she alone seemed to be able to provide to him. He hadn't offered anything besides sex. At least, that's probably how Kylie saw it, since he hadn't actually put any of his feelings into words.

He pulled the pack of cigarettes out of his shirt pocket and forced himself not to crush it in his hand as the pounding in his head continued. For once, he really was carrying them just in case a wedding guest had a sudden fit of nicotine withdrawal, not to prove anything to himself. Hell, he'd figured out days ago that it didn't prove much to resist something you weren't even tempted by. Maybe he should take up carrying Kylie around and trying to keep his hands off her. Now, that would be proving something.

David pushed away that ridiculous thought as he glanced at his watch. He wouldn't have time to see Kylie before his mother's wedding, not with the conference call and all the other things he had to get done before he could go.

It was just as well, he supposed, that he didn't have time to talk to her. He wanted to see her, but even now he wasn't sure what he wanted to say. Despite his conversation with Clint this morning, he wasn't ready to make a lifelong commitment to Kylie. She *was* special to him, there was no denying that. But her penchant for disaster left him too open, too vulnerable to ridicule.

David closed his eyes, trying to shut out the vision of Kylie's smiling face. If this was how he felt, even after their incredible night of lovemaking, then it would appear that nothing really had changed.

Why, then, did it feel like he was on the brink of . . . something. Not an abyss, but frightening just the same. It was as if he were grasping for something unknown, something niggling on the outskirts of his brain, just out of his reach.

"Good morning, David."

Sandy's greeting yanked David back from the edge of whatever revelation he'd been chasing. Frustrated, he muttered something appropriate and shoved the cigarettes back in his pocket before lifting his gaze to his CFO.

He marveled at how thin Sandy looked as she walked into his office. David had never liked skinny women. He preferred them shapelier, women like Kylie with lush curves in all the right places. He thought of the perfectly rounded breasts he'd stroked last night, the shapely behind he'd caressed. His hands started to tingle.

"David?" Sandy prodded as the phone buzzed a second time.

"Sorry." David shifted in his chair. He had to concentrate, had to stop thinking about Kylie and the spell she had cast over his usually well-controlled libido. He had thought their leisurely lovemaking would at least diminish the hold she had on him, but it seemed that the opposite was true. He couldn't get her out of his thoughts.

David cleared his throat and tried to concentrate on business. He picked up the phone and hit the button to put it on speaker.

"Hello, Mitchell? This is David Gamble. I've got our CFO, Sandy Macgregor, here with me."

"Yes, David. Good morning," Mitchell greeted, then introduced his own financial staff attending the call before coming right to the point. "I have some good news, David. I had the opportunity to pitch your idea to our board of directors last night, and they're very interested in the proposed joint venture with Gamble Records."

David waited for the expected feeling of elation at this latest triumph, at knowing the problems of the past week had been successfully overcome. He should be thrilled at this coup; a joint venture with a major corporation like BSS was going to add significantly to the value of his stock, not to mention the added challenge of being the front-runner on a hot new wave of music distribution. So why wasn't he more excited? Why did he feel as if it really didn't matter?

His best friend's words from that morning came back to him and, at last, the revelation he'd been grasping at minutes before smacked him right between the eyes.

"At some point, the challenge of making your next million will start to seem irrelevant," Clint had said, as if predicting exactly the way David would feel at this moment. This victory, no matter how grand, seemed pointless when the rest of his life was so empty. His personal life was suddenly—astoundingly—more important to him at this moment than a few more millions in his bank account.

Mitchell continued, obviously unaware of the turmoil roiling about in David's mind. "We'd like to begin our financial evaluation next week, David. Our CFO can e-mail you a list of the records we'll need to review, but I see this as a mere formality. This is going to be a fabulous opportunity for both our companies."

David opened his mouth to say something appropriate as Mitchell finished, then shut it again. The silence lengthened.

He didn't care. Not about the silence, or about the job. He was thirty-six years old, had more money than he could ever even begin to spend, and was suddenly, absolutely certain that he did not want to do this anymore. He was tired of being stuck in an office, smothering his creativity with percentage points, statistics, and legally binding contracts. He missed the music, missed working with artists to create something lasting like a song that haunted you day and night. He wanted that again. And he wanted Kylie. How it had happened, he wasn't sure, but just as surely as he knew he didn't want to head up the new music division at BSS, he knew he wanted Kylie in his life, disasters and all.

His voice, when it came, was strong and sure. "I've been impressed with what you've accomplished so far at BSS, Mitchell. What would you say if I recommended you to head up the joint venture?"

There was a short, stunned silence, before Mitchell and Sandy simultaneously burst out with an incredulous, "What?"

"I'm not going to be in charge. I think you'd make a great candidate for it, Mitchell, but if you're not interested, I'm sure you'll be able to find someone else."

The door to his office popped open before Sandy or Mitchell could respond to the bombshell he'd just dropped into the conversation.

"Sorry to interrupt, David, but Kylie's here, and she said she has some new information about the royalties. Should I let her in?"

"Yes, thank you, Deborah. I think this conversation is over. I'll be glad to share my thoughts with you on Monday, but I have some important business I need to attend to. If you'll excuse me?"

David could tell Mitchell was too stunned at the sudden change of events to do anything more than agree. As he hung up the phone, David felt as if an anvil had been lifted from his shoulders. All of a sudden, the problems of the last few weeks didn't seem quite so important anymore. Instead, what mattered was that Kylie was here.

She breezed in wearing another of her short, flowery skirts and a heavy orange sweater over a fitted white T-shirt. The room seemed to brighten and David had to force himself not to leap up and crush her to him, to grab her, pull her close, and never let her go.

Damn, she made him feel good.

Standing up, he leaned his hip against his desk and crossed his arms over his chest. "I'm surprised you have the courage to come up here," he commented, trying not to let his desire for her show.

"Hello, Sandy," Kylie greeted the other woman before turning her attention to him. He noticed she seemed nervous and edgy, her usually active hands clenched at her sides. "Why's that, David?"

"There aren't any windows to sneak out of up here," he answered, raising his eyebrows.

Kylie looked into David's eyes and almost backed down, probably would have if Bradley hadn't been standing right behind her. It looked as if David was angry with her. Again. As usual. But she had to stand her ground. This was her chance to clear her name. She hadn't tampered with the royalties, and now she had proof. Besides, she'd promised Bradley she'd try to help him and she owed him as much for all the help he'd given her. So she refused to back down, no matter how mad David might be. She'd clear up the royalty problem, ask David to reconsider Bradley's demo tape, then get David alone to tell him good-bye.

Lifting her chin, she met David's gaze head-on and realized how hard this was going to be. All she wanted was to lose herself in his deep blue eyes, but somehow, she had to find the courage to stick to business, then walk away from him forever. Reminding herself that it would just be worse if she tried to hold on to him, Kylie tried to find the strength within herself to go on. She couldn't cling. If she did, there would be nothing of herself left to pick up and put back together in the end. It would be better this way. It couldn't possibly be worse.

Kylie blinked rapidly to clear her eyes of the suspicious moisture that gathered there. She straightened her shoulders. She had to get through this and get out of here before she fell apart.

Unsnapping the small orange purse she'd tossed over her shoulder, Kylie pulled out a computer disk. "You remember how Bradley was fiddling around with that computer in the warehouse the other night?" she asked, holding the disk out to David and doing her best to keep her voice calm and professional.

"Yes. Believe me, it will be a while before I forget any of the events of that night," David answered, fingering his jaw.

She thought she read amusement and a tinge of regret in David's eyes, but told herself she was being ridiculous. He would be nothing but angry at her and her father for that episode. The David Gamble she knew would not be amused at getting punched by an overprotective father.

Kylie turned her attention back to the disk in her hand. "Bradley copied several files from the computer that night, and we had a chance to look at them. One of the files appears to be the original quarterly royalties, the one I was working on when I got locked in the storage room."

"Are you sure?" David asked.

Catching a slight movement to her left, Kylie turned her head slightly and saw Sandy push a strand of hair behind her ear. Kylie frowned. There was something familiar about that gesture, something in the back of her mind that was tickling to get out, like a spider trapped in the bathtub drain.

"We reviewed every record," Bradley said.

Bradley's comment drowned the tickle in Kylie's memory, and she turned back to David. "If you look, you'll see that there's no phony entry for me, just legitimate Gamble artists."

David looked from her to Bradley and back again, as if trying to decide if their story made sense. Suddenly, he leaned forward and pressed his intercom button.

"Yes?" Deborah answered.

"Can you come here for a minute?"

"Sure." The door opened almost immediately.

"Could you make a copy of this disk, then take one copy down to the second floor and get someone to load it into the royalty program?"

"What should I do with the original?"

"Lock it in your desk."

"No problem." Deborah took the disk and disappeared.

"Sandy, if you'll go over those figures once the data is loaded, we may be able to get checks out tonight and minimize the late fees."

"You don't have to worry about the penalties," Bradley interrupted.

"Pardon me?" Sandy asked incredulously.

"Kylie called every one of your artists and got their agreement to waive the penalties."

"When did she do all that?" David's question was aimed at Bradley but his midnight blue eyes were locked on Kylie's.

"She's been on the phone all morning."

"I see," David said quietly. So even after the fiasco at the warehouse, after he had chastised her in front of her family for being a walking catastrophe, she had been working to fix a problem that she'd been telling him all along was not her fault.

David shook his head in disbelief. Would anyone but Kylie do something like this? He doubted it. Impulsive, big-hearted Kylie, in charge of righting all the wrongs she could find, able to leap out of tall buildings in a single bound, as long as the windows were on the ground floor.

What was he going to do with her?

Even more importantly, what would he do without her?

His pondering was interrupted when a message popped up on his computer screen, the insistent flashing catching his attention. He groaned inwardly as he rechecked the time. An idea started forming in his head.

He turned to Kylie and said, "I have to go. My mother's getting married this afternoon at my house, and I promised I'd pick up the flowers on my way home." He stood up and walked around the edge of his desk, stopping in front of her, ignoring everyone else in the room. She looked up at him, her almond-shaped brown eyes opened wide with surprise. Unable to resist, he picked up one of her soft hands and began toying with her fingers. He felt the same familiar tug of attraction, only this time it was tempered with a tenderness he'd never felt before. "We need to talk, Kylie. Why don't you come to my mother's wedding this afternoon at two o'clock? Afterward, we can slip away. There are some things we need to take care of, once and for all."

He sensed her hesitation and tried to sweeten the pot. "Bring your folks along, too. There's plenty of food and drink and my mother hired a band for the reception. I'll bet your parents love to dance."

"That sounds like fun. I'm sure they'd love it," Bradley interjected, startling them both. David smiled as Kylie jumped, looking at Bradley as if she, too, had forgotten that she and David weren't alone.

Kylie paused a long moment. A part of her wanted to avoid the pain that would result from the inevitable outcome of their "talk." She'd never see David again once they both agreed it was over, but not talking about it would just prolong the agony. Besides, she needed to try to get him to give Bradley another chance. She braced herself for David's anger.

"All right, David. I'll come on one condition." She pulled a cassette out of her small orange bag with her free hand. "I promised Bradley I'd ask you to listen to this. It's his demo tape, and it's very good."

David kept toying with her fingers, rubbing the soft pads of her fingertips between his. "Okay. I'll listen to it in the car on my way to the florist."

"We wouldn't have found the royalty file without Bradley's help. If you listen to this, and promise to be objective, I'll come," Kylie said, as if she hadn't heard David's agreement.

"Kylie, I said I'd listen to it." David almost laughed at the shocked expressions mirrored on Kylie's and Bradley's faces. He leaned forward to accept the tape and placed a kiss squarely on Kylie's lips, unmindful of their audience. "Bradley, why don't you come to the wedding with Kylie and her family, and I'll let you know what I think of it then?"

"Uh, sure. I'd love to come," Bradley answered, while Kylie stared at David as if he were speaking Swahili.

"Good, I'll see you both at two o'clock, then." David straightened from Kylie's inviting lips, grinning. "I guarantee it will be an event you won't soon forget."

CHAPTER 23

David's good mood had deteriorated somewhat by the time the wedding ceremony began. The clouds overhead threatened to let loose a downpour, but his mother's wedding consultant—who he'd learned an hour ago was also her hairdresser—insisted that they'd be rain-free for hours yet. David wasn't so sure and, from the glances the guests kept throwing at the sky, he guessed he wasn't the only one who was nervous. He had been able to convince the caterer to erect a small tent over the food, so at least that was one less thing to worry about.

The wind started to pick up, whipping up the bright pink and purple balloons his mother had insisted be tied to people's chairs.

"They're festive," she'd said.

David pointed out that they were also a nuisance, but she refused to relent. Now, as the wind gusted, they thrashed about, striking people randomly on the back of the head or right in the face.

Standing at the front of the small crowd, David shook his head and continued to survey the scene out of the corner of his eye. The vases of fresh flowers near the lake where the ceremony was taking place had already tipped over twice and David had surreptitiously had them removed

while his mother was saying her vows. The musicians'
sheet music kept flying out of their stands and over the
lawn, causing odd breaks in the music that grated on his
ears.

All of this kept David so busy, he barely had time to
greet Kylie and her family before being forced to take care
of yet another pending disaster.

He prayed it would all be over soon, then sent up a silent
thanks as the reverend said the magic words: "I now pro-
nounce you man and wife. You may kiss the bride."

Alan grabbed David's mother in a passionate embrace,
which David was saved from watching as Pam's neon pink
hat flew off her head and came sailing his way. He started
after it, then drew up short when a tennis shoe–clad foot
stomped down on the brim.

Straightening, David came face-to-face with another pair
of blue eyes, lighter than his own but similar enough to
allude to a familial connection.

"Ben, what are you doing here?"

"I was invited, so don't even think about calling the
cops," his brother answered belligerently.

David took a step backward at the stench of stale liquor
on Ben's breath. Of course, he should have known Ben
would show up drunk. What else could possibly go—

A clap of thunder interrupted David's thought. The
downpour started almost immediately.

"Everybody under the tent," he shouted before bending
down to pick up his mother's hat. Ben stumbled a bit as
he shifted his feet.

"Come on, let's get out of the rain," he suggested, starting toward the tent.

"Stop ordering me around, David."

David stopped, closing his eyes at the petulant tone in
his brother's voice. If Ben wanted to come to their mother's
wedding, that was fine, but David didn't want to be dragged
into a fight with him. Not today. He wanted this whole
thing over with so he could be alone with Kylie and tell

her how he felt; tell her how much she meant to him. He did *not* want to stand here, arguing with his brother about the same things they'd argued over a million times in the past ten years.

"Fine then, stand out here in the rain. Don't let me stop you," he said, before turning and walking away, leaving Ben standing out in the chilly October rain.

The undersized tent was bursting at the seams with people as David stepped under cover. Fortunately, a cool breeze wafted in from the open side so it wasn't stifling. There was plenty of food set out on the tables that flanked the closed sides, and a bar had been set up in the corner. It might not have worked out as perfectly as David would have wanted, but he was surprised to see that people were generally laughing good-naturedly about the situation.

Of course, free booze always helped people's attitudes, David thought dryly as he watched the wine begin to flow. He saw Alan and his mother huddled close together in one corner, and let his gaze run over the crowd, searching for Kylie.

He found her surrounded by people, holding Lexi in her arms. She appeared to be listening earnestly to something the little girl was saying, a slight smile on her lips. David stepped back against the side of the tent, a sudden tightness in his chest. The sounds of the partygoers washed over him as he stood there, watching. He realized that what he had thought was just an illusion wasn't. Kylie didn't appear to brighten a room; she *did* brighten a room, just as she brightened his life.

He'd been an idiot to ever push her away. She made his life fun and unpredictable, and was kind and compassionate besides. He didn't know at what point she had insinuated herself into his heart but now he realized he wanted to hold onto her . . . forever.

He loved her. It was as simple as that. He'd made a mess of things so far, but there was time to fix that. After this whole wedding fiasco was over, he'd have plenty of time to tell her how he felt. Smiling, David leaned back against a cold metal tent pole.

Still holding Lexi in her arms, Kylie turned to Bradley, who held a small brown-and-white lump of wiggling fur. David had seen Kylie's mother earlier with her little dogs and assumed Bradley had been given charge of one of them.

"See, she's a nice doggie," he heard Kylie encourage as she reached out and patted the dog.

Lexi put out a tentative hand, drawing back with a squeal as a pink tongue snaked out toward her fingers. Kylie laughed. "Here, she was just going to lick you." Kylie held out her own hand and Lexi giggled as Robyn—or was it Daniel?—gave her fingers a bath.

Suddenly, Kylie spotted a familiar figure in line at the bar and frowned.

What was Ben from the homeless shelter doing here? Had Tyrone sent him to look for her? Was there some sort of emergency? And how would Tyrone have known that she'd be here at David's house? Whatever the reason, she was going to give him a piece of her mind for stealing the ring her father had given her. Homeless or not, he had no right to take something of hers, and she wasn't going to let it slip by, as if nothing had happened.

"Bradley, can you watch Lexi for a minute?" She handed the little girl over with a promise to bring her back some cake, then made her way through the crowded room.

"What are you doing here, Ben? And what did you do with my ring?" she asked, tapping him on the shoulder.

Droplets of water splattered as he turned around. Kylie was startled by the venom in his eyes. What in the world was he so mad at her about? After all, he was the one who had stolen something from her, not the other way around.

He answered the first question first. "I'm the son of the bride—or the son of a bitch, depending on who you ask."

Kylie's mouth dropped open. He was David's brother? Kylie studied the other man for a moment. Ben looked so much more used-up than David, with lines of dissipation and unhappiness etched at the sides of his mouth. His lips were thinner than David's, his eyes a lighter blue, but there was definitely a resemblance between the two; one she thought she'd only imagined when she'd first seen Ben at The Soup Kitchen.

He spoke again before she could say anything. "I guess I have as much right to be here as David's newest piece of ass."

Kylie took a step back from the snide tone in his voice. "That was uncalled for, Ben. I've never done anything to you to deserve such disrespect."

"Bullshit. You lied to me about that piece of crap ring you were wearing. Precious jewels from Daddy, huh? Goddamn piece of glass, that's all it was."

"I never said it was worth anything to anyone except me, and besides that, you stole it from me. What did you want, a certificate of authenticity?" She was angry now, too.

"What the hell's going on here?" David appeared suddenly at her side.

Kylie didn't even see Ben's fist until it connected with David's chin. It must have surprised David, too, because it connected squarely with his face and knocked him off balance.

"Why, you . . . you jerk," Kylie sputtered.

"Shut up." Ben shoved her. Hard.

Kylie fell backward, tripping over something that yelped in protest. Her hip hit one of the tables laden with food, and Kylie watched in horror as the top of Pam and Alan's three-tiered wedding cake swayed toward her. In an attempt to stop the inevitable, Kylie reached out to grab the pink-and-purple frosted cake, which she could have saved if only she'd had both feet on the ground. Trying to regain her balance, she put down her right foot only to jerk it back when it came down on something soft. There was another yelp. Her left foot slipped and she fell, trying to avoid squashing one of her mother's dogs as she landed in the grass, the garishly frosted confection sliding down on top of her.

She opened her eyes when a warm, pink tongue caressed her cheek.

Concerned faces tinged with amusement surrounded her, and Kylie sighed. Assuring everyone she was fine, she sat up, wiping purplish blueberry cake from her blouse as she battled her misery.

Why did this sort of thing have to happen to her whenever David was around? It was no wonder he couldn't wait to get rid of her. She was a publicity nightmare.

She blinked when a photographer, there to cover the wedding of the mother of one of the wealthiest men in Seattle, snapped a picture as she sat on the lawn, globs of cake being nibbled off her skirt by three hungry dogs. For want of a better term, she knew this would be the icing on the cake for David. He hated bad publicity; she'd discovered that after the episode with the reporters outside the counterfeiter's warehouse. This was even worse. There was no way she could slant this story, no fake publicity stunt she could chalk it up to. Instead, she knew the paper would find some way to make the story even more sensational, and David's name would be right in the middle of it. He would be humiliated. If nothing before had convinced her that she and David had no chance of staying together, this episode proved it without a crumb of doubt.

A pink frosting rose dropped from the top of her head onto her skirt. The photographer's flashbulb went off again and he snickered as he backed away.

At that moment, Kylie knew any lingering hopes that remained of a relationship with David had disappeared like the bright spots in front of her eyeballs. Tears gathered in her eyes and she lowered her head miserably.

A pair of Italian leather shoes stopped in front of her.

Kylie sniffed.

"You okay?" David crouched down on the ground and wiped a smear of frosting off her forehead.

Kylie nodded morosely. He looked perfect, as always. Even being knocked down by his brother hadn't seemed to have affected the tidiness of his appearance. It was as if his clothing wouldn't *dare* get out of place, no matter what forces worked upon them. She looked into the deep blue eyes that had become so dear to her and, not wanting to give him the opportunity to tell her what she already knew—that there was no hope for a future with him—she changed the subject. "Where's Ben?" she asked.

"Out cold. He had no right to treat you like that." David shrugged, and Kylie had to resist the urge to reach out and touch his strong arms, to pull them around her own shoulders and hug him tight. She missed him already.

"Go away, Robyn." She shooed the little dog who was licking her skirt, then caught David's raised eyebrow. "The dogs. My mother named the dogs after her children. Don't ask." She shook her head, anticipating his next question, which had to be, "Why?"

Kylie watched as a grin spread across David's face. It was like watching the sun emerge from the gloomy October clouds, and she wondered how he could smile when she felt like crying.

"Come on, sweetheart. Let's get you cleaned up." David stood up, offering her his hand. Kylie grabbed his strong fingers in hers as if reaching for a life preserver. She closed her eyes briefly in misery as he helped her to her feet.

The party continued around them as they made their way across the tent toward the house. Kylie wished she could leave right now, before David had a chance to tell her he never wanted to see her again, but she knew they might as well get it over with, even if fleeing seemed awfully tempting right about now . . .

"You're not plotting your escape, are you?" David asked, narrowing his eyes at her.

"Of course not." Kylie blushed as David led her through the crowd. Since when had he become a mind reader?

He stopped and turned her to face him. "You were. You

were thinking about escaping again," he said incredulously
before rolling his eyes heavenward and shaking his head.
"I can see I'm going to have to board up the entire first
floor to keep you around."

Kylie felt a sudden glimmer of hope in her heart. He
wanted to keep her around? Even after she'd embarrassed
him in front of everyone again?

"David—" she began, trying not to sound too patheti-
cally hopeful.

"Where do you two think you're going?" Ben's sullen
voice interrupted.

"Go away, Ben. Kylie and I need to talk and you've
already caused enough trouble here." David guided Kylie
out into the light rain and away from his brother.

Ben followed them. "I told you to stop bossing me
around, David. You've told me what to do my entire life
and I'm sick of it!" he shouted.

"Can you wait a minute?" David asked her.

Kylie nodded. The way she looked now, a little rain
wouldn't make a difference. They stopped near the concrete
breakwater separating David's lawn from the gray waters
of Lake Washington. The lake was fairly deep on the other
side of the wall, built that way so the homeowners' boats
could come right up to the edge of the lawn to load and
offload their passengers.

"It's obvious you need someone to tell you what to do,
Ben. Look at you—you're homeless, you're drunk, and
you're throwing away your talent because you don't have
the backbone to live your life without help from me. I'll
admit I should have been easier on you about college. I
shouldn't have tried to force you to major in something that
didn't interest you. Does that help? I wanted what was the
best for you, and obviously I was wrong to try to force my
own will on you. But you're twenty-six years old now.
There's nothing stopping you from accomplishing anything
you want. You're not some kid who has to rely on his
parents for money or approval. You want to go back to

school and major in photography? Then do it." David's voice was calm, reasonable, as he strode over to stand in front of his brother.

"Yeah, that's easy for you to say. You, with all your money, you don't have to worry about paying rent or school loans."

Out of the corner of her eye, Kylie absently watched a twenty-something-foot Bayliner approach, the buzzing motor getting louder as it came closer to the concrete wall. *Must be one of the wedding guests arriving late*, she thought, listening to David as he contradicted Ben's weak argument.

"You have no idea what kinds of things I have to worry about, Ben. Things like meeting payroll, staying ahead of the major record labels, and making sure I'll be in business forty years from now so I can guarantee my employees a secure future. When I was your age, I didn't have a dime to my name either. You can't tell me you've forgotten the dump of an apartment I lived in? How many nights did you come over to help me package up CDs for shipping? A thousand? Don't you remember that all we ever ate was macaroni and cheese? Did you think that's because I liked it? Shit, I hated that stuff. But it was cheap and I was broke. So that's what I ate, breakfast, lunch, and dinner."

David and Ben were so engrossed in their argument, they didn't even turn their heads as the boat's engine slipped into neutral when it came alongside the seawall. Kylie was surprised to see that Sandy Macgregor was a passenger. The driver of the boat had his back to her and Kylie could see red curls poking out of the bottom of a dark green baseball cap.

"Hi, Sandy. What are you doing here?" Kylie automatically caught the line Sandy threw and looped it loosely around a cleat.

"I have some business to discuss with David," Sandy said smoothly, hopping easily off the boat and onto the lawn next to Kylie. Her hands were buried in the pockets of an oversized windbreaker and Kylie wondered how she'd managed to keep her balance. She knew if it was her, she'd probably have ended up face-first in the water, but that seemed to be her own particular brand of luck. Nobody else seemed as cursed as she was.

Kylie started to tell Sandy that today was perhaps not a good day to bother David with business when the driver of the boat turned toward her. Kylie gasped. It was the man she'd seen in the warehouse when she and Bradley had gone to look around the first time.

"Get in the boat," Sandy hissed, drawing a gun out of her pocket and pointing it at Kylie's chest.

Suddenly, realization smacked her in the face. Sandy had been the woman who'd had her back to the window at the warehouse the day Kylie peeked inside. That was why her gesture this morning seemed familiar. Why hadn't she realized it earlier?

"Why are you doing this?" Kylie asked.

"Shut up. If you don't get in the boat, Rory will shoot your little boyfriend."

David could hardly be considered little, but Kylie didn't think it prudent to argue the semantics with the red-headed man's gun pointing at the back of David's head.

"All right, I'm going." Kylie put one foot on the seawall and tried to balance the other on the rocking boat.

"Get in!" Sandy pushed her from behind and Kylie screeched as she landed in a heap at the bottom of the boat. Sandy tossed the rope on top of her as Kylie struggled to sit up.

Sandy's shout was loud enough to interrupt David and Ben's argument, and David turned to look at the boat. "Kylie? Sandy? What's going on? Rory, is that you?" David raised his voice against the rising wind as Sandy hauled Kylie up and stood behind her, holding the gun to her head.

"Let's get the brother, too. It'll be nice to have insurance," Sandy said, then pointed with her free hand to Ben. "Get in here or she dies."

Kylie shivered at the empty sound of the other woman's voice as the cold metal barrel of the gun dug into her temple. She had never suspected that Sandy was one note short of a full sonata, but it was obvious something was very wrong here.

"Just wait a minute, Sandy. Let's talk about—" David began.

The sharp retort of a gunshot echoed in the quiet neighborhood, cutting off David's plea. Ben screamed, grabbing his left hand. "Get in now or Rory will kill you," Sandy ordered, her eyes locked on Ben's.

Without hesitating, Ben pushed past David and leaped into the boat, leaving a trail of blood from the wound on his hand on the white fiberglass.

David stepped forward, his hands reached out in supplication. "No, don't do this. Kylie . . ."

"Rory, pull away so he can't reach us," Sandy interrupted. The driver, who Kylie assumed to be Rory although they hadn't been formally introduced, gave the engine some gasoline and the boat pulled away from the shore.

"Yes, Kylie. She ruined our plan, David, and we're going to make her pay," Sandy yelled above the hum of the engine.

"What are you talking about?" David sounded as confused as Kylie felt.

"You'll find out soon enough. Hit it, Rory."

Kylie stumbled as the boat lurched forward but Sandy held her tightly. For such a thin woman, she was certainly strong, Kylie observed, trying to use the rocking motion of the boat to her advantage. But Sandy's sea legs were better than Kylie's and none of her attempts to catch the thinner woman off balance worked.

"Sit down." Sandy waved the gun in the direction of a seat.

Kylie plotted her escape as she weaved her way to the back of the boat. Her first thought was to jump overboard when Sandy's back was turned.

Sandy turned to Rory at that exact moment and Kylie took her opportunity, diving over the side. The water was cold, but she tried to ignore the shock as she kicked off her shoes and started paddling toward shore.

It took only seconds before the Bayliner started circling.

"That was a stupid thing to do, Kylie. Get back in the boat." Sandy pointed the gun at her.

"No." Kylie's teeth started to chatter.

"Do it or I kill him." Sandy switched tactics, pointing the gun at Ben's head.

Kylie hesitated. Ben had stolen her ring but, even so, she couldn't let Sandy shoot him. She swam to the side of the boat.

"Get her in here," Sandy ordered, waving the gun at Ben.

Ben yanked her unceremoniously back into the boat. Kylie smoothed her skirt down over her rear end and went back to her seat, shivering as the cold air hit her chilled skin. Rory punched the accelerator again.

Sandy sat on a stool at the front of the boat. Swiveling around to face them, she said tersely, "Don't try that again."

"I won't," Kylie muttered through chattering teeth. She hugged herself, noticing that Ben was watching her with an odd look on his face. She tried to ignore him as the boat banged up and down against the whitecaps frothing at the surface of the lake, tried to formulate some sort of plan to get them out of this mess.

"Thank you," Ben said finally.

"For what?"

"For not letting her shoot me. I might not have done the same thing in your position."

Kylie paused, feeling the light drizzle pelt her cheeks as the boat sped across the lake toward the University of Washington. "I know."

"You two shut up back there," Sandy warned.

Kylie ignored her in an attempt to find out what in the world was going on. "What's this all about, Sandy? You said I've ruined your plans but I don't have a clue what you mean."

Sandy eyed her silently for a moment, and Kylie thought she wasn't going to answer. Her answer, when it came, was so strange Kylie wasn't sure she'd heard correctly. "Rory and I had a plan to ruin David Gamble."

"But why?"

"Because he's a bastard, that's why," the red-haired man said angrily.

"Tell me something I don't know," Ben muttered. Kylie shot him an irritated glance.

"Rory was in a band with David in college, the same band as Peter Laughlin and Clint Walsh."

Kylie remembered David talking about his college band and how all the members had gone on to successful careers except one. Obviously, Rory was that one. What had David said about him? That he'd given the man a job, but he'd embezzled money to buy drugs? It seemed to her that David had been more than generous by not having the man arrested for his crime.

"David took care of everyone else in the band except Rory." Sandy confirmed Kylie's hunch. "He helped promote Clint Walsh, gave Peter Laughlin a high-powered job as head of A&R, but left Rory to fend for himself."

"That was over fifteen years ago," Ben protested.

Kylie looked at David's brother in surprise. Couldn't he see his own grudge was just as ridiculous? From what she could tell, David had done plenty of things to help Ben, too, but all he did was throw David's assistance back in his face.

"Yes, and for decades David, Peter, and Clint have been living the good life while poor Rory has been forced to take menial jobs just to pay the rent. He's been reduced to being a goddamn janitor for the parks department!"

"I don't understand, Sandy. David's going to make you wealthy from stock options, too."

"No, I'm going to have to cash them all in as soon as I

vest just to support us. If I could hold onto the options longer, they would be worth something, but as it is, they probably won't be worth much more than a few dollars a share."

Kylie resisted the urge to tell Sandy that that was her own fault for supporting the drug habit of an obvious addict, but decided that wouldn't help her cause much.

"What do Ben and I have to do with this?" she asked instead, watching Rory barely slow the boat as they raced through the Montlake Cut, which connected Lake Washington to Lake Union. Rory passed an unfortunate couple paddling a canoe at the mouth of the Cut. The wake from the Bayliner slammed the canoe against the concrete sides of the canal and it tipped over.

"Jerk," the woman in the water shouted, grabbing the side of the capsized boat with one hand and shaking her fist at them with the other.

Ignoring the disturbance, Sandy answered Kylie's question. "David's brother doesn't have anything to do with it. You, on the other hand, do. Your meddling ruined our plans to get ten million in royalties, make money from pirating Gamble artists, and garner a whole lot of bad publicity for David Gamble."

"How did I do all that?" Inside, Kylie was glad she'd been able to spoil Sandy and Rory's plan. She only wished she knew how she'd managed to accomplish it all without having any idea what she was doing.

"After we deposited the royalty check in your account, we were going to get it right back the next day. But we didn't count on you finding out about it so soon. By the time we were ready to get it back out of your account, you'd already given the money back to David."

"Well, technically, that's not my fault. David is the one who found the missing money," Kylie pointed out reasonably, then another thought struck her. "How did you know my account number, anyway?"

"We broke into your house, found a box of new checks,

and took a check and deposit slip from it. By the way, has anyone ever told you you're a terrible housekeeper?"

Kylie sat up straighter on the seat in the back of the boat. It really shouldn't matter what this insane woman thought of her, but she still felt the need to protest. "I am not," she said, then opened her eyes wide. If Sandy and Rory hadn't been the ones who messed up her house, then who had it been? Good grief, was her house the target of every crook in the city? Did she have neon signs on her roof, flashing "Get Your Free Lunch Here"?

Sandy shrugged, obviously not inclined to believe her. "In any event, it made our job easier since everything was lying on the floor. We found what we needed, and then, when the royalty check was mailed to you, we pulled it out of your mailbox, endorsed it for deposit only, and put it into your account. After it cleared, we were going to write a check to Rory from you in the amount of ten million dollars."

"And you didn't think I'd notice?" Kylie asked, her eyebrows peaking together on her forehead. Did they think she was so stupid she wouldn't notice that amount of money going into and out of her account?

"You didn't notice it when you worked at Pigeon Books," Sandy said, leaning back on the stool in the front of the boat. Strands of dishwater blond hair whipped across her face, and she pushed them back with one hand, holding the gun on them with the other. "I called your old boss for a reference after you came in that first day and she told me the whole story. She didn't blame you for it, but she thought it would be best if I knew. That's actually where I got the idea. I figured the money wouldn't be in your account more than a day or two, and once you got a statement, you'd just figure it was a bank error. By that time, Rory and I planned to be long gone."

Kylie shook her head with disgust. She was sick and tired of being the dupe in other people's rotten schemes. It looked as if she were going to have to open a secret, coded account in Switzerland just to keep other people's hands off of her financial affairs.

Sandy continued, "We had barely gotten your sister's pirated CDs out to a couple of stores when you found our warehouse. After a policeman came nosing around, we knew we had to clear out of there, fast."

Remembering the large policeman who had scared her and Bradley that afternoon, Kylie smiled. Maybe it had been their presence in the parking lot that had made him suspicious enough to hang around. In any event, Kylie was glad Seattle's finest had been on the scene.

"It was bad enough that you screwed that up for us, but then you found the corrected royalty data. And this morning, when I found out that you'd called all the artists and they agreed to waive the penalties, I knew it was time to move on to Plan B."

"Which is?" Kylie asked when Sandy seemed inclined to stop talking.

Sandy met her gaze, and for the first time Kylie began to realize the seriousness of the situation. Even with all the gun-waving before, she hadn't really been frightened. It had felt as if she'd been a kid again and had walked in on her parents' rehearsals, as if it were just some bizarre play that would soon end. The overly bright look in Sandy's eyes changed her thinking. It told Kylie that Sandy's intent was very serious, indeed.

"We have a check that you're going to sign that will severely diminish your trust account, then you and Little Brother here are going to disappear."

Kylie didn't think now was the best time to mention there was no money in her trust account. She figured it would be better to let Sandy think she was going to get away with millions—maybe then they'd let her and Ben go.

"What are you going to do with us?" Ben asked as the boat began to slow. Kylie looked over at David's brother and noticed that he wouldn't meet her eyes. She thought

about how Ben had stolen her ring, thinking it was valuable, and wondered if he had been the one to break into
her house, ransacking it when he didn't find anything of
value. She didn't so much care about the mess, but if she
found out he had been the one to hurt Mr. Chips, she'd kill
him with her bare hands.

Kylie noticed they were approaching Gas Works Park,
a rusting refinery the city of Seattle had converted into an
open-air park.

"We're going kill you, of course," Sandy answered
Ben's question in an oddly matter-of-fact tone, as if she
were ordering lunch rather than stating an intent to murder
two people. "What better way to hurt David Gamble than
to kill two of the people he cares most about in the world?"

"David doesn't care about me," Ben and Kylie said in
unison.

Rory turned to look at Ben as the boat bumped into the
cement wall lining the park, and spoke for the first time.
"Ha. All David ever talked about in college was his little
brother. He drove us all nuts with stories about everything
you did. We heard about your grades, what classes you
liked, who your best friends were. On and on till I just
wanted to tell him that nobody cared that his little brother's
favorite ice cream flavor was chocolate chip mint or that
his first girlfriend had a heart-shaped tattoo on her ass."

Ben's mouth dropped open in shock. "I never realized
David paid so much attention to the stuff I told him back
then," he muttered.

Rory snorted, then turned and cut the engine.

"And you." Sandy nearly spat the words at Kylie. "He
moons over you like a lovesick calf. I thought I was going
to puke this morning when he was all but pawing you in
his office."

"Now get out, both of you." The silver barrel of the gun
pointed the way off the boat.

CHAPTER 24

"Did you see which way they went?" David asked frantically as he sped across the freeway to the Mercer Street exit. They'd been able to watch the boat's progress as the little purple car chugged across the 520 bridge, but they'd lost sight of them once they hit the Montlake Cut.

David pushed the Grapemobile's accelerator to the floor, cursing when there was no noticeable difference in their speed. His Jaguar would have had no trouble keeping up, but in this car, he barely had enough power to pass even the slowest-moving vehicles.

"I think they went north, toward the locks," Robyn said from the backseat.

"Good, if they're at the locks, they'll get delayed for sure." David got in the left lane at the red light, planning to head for the Hiram Chittenden locks that allowed boats to pass from Lake Union out to Puget Sound and back.

"Wait a minute, David. I see a powerboat moving over near Gas Works Park. That could be them, too." Bradley leaned into the dashboard, squinting.

"Can I get to the locks around that side of the lake, too?"

"Yes," Bradley said, frantically waving at the red car to their right to stay put. The light turned green and David floored it, pulling out in front of the other cars and making a highly illegal right turn across three lanes of traffic. Hardly anyone honked as David waved his apology to the other drivers.

David watched in his rearview mirror as George Rogers followed in Kylie's Mustang, with Elizabeth riding shotgun and Tony, the cook, buckled up in the backseat with the three dogs. He turned his attention back to the road as he turned onto Eastlake Drive, which ran along the east side of Lake Union.

"They'll be all right."

David hadn't realized he'd spoken his prayer aloud until Robyn answered, "Yes, they will. Kylie can take care of herself." For some reason, her comment made him angry.

"She's not as tough as you seem to think," he said irritably, weaving between cars while trying to keep his eyes glued to the lake on his left.

"I know; I'm just scared," Robyn said quietly.

David met Robyn's eyes in the rearview mirror, saw that she was trying to blink back tears. "They'll be all right," he repeated as the purple car chugged through a red light. He'd pay a million traffic tickets if only he could reach Kylie before it was too late.

"They're at Gas Works Park, David. Look, they've tied their boat up over there." Bradley gestured to the apparently empty watercraft bouncing in the water.

Hooking a sharp left on Northlake Way, David left half the rubber of the tires on Eastlake Avenue.

"Hurry, David. Hurry," Robyn urged, and David barely slowed down as he turned into the entrance of the park. They all leaped out before the engine sputtered a death rattle, followed closely by Elizabeth, Tony, George, and the three dogs.

As one, they started toward the field of grass with its ugly, rusted machinery topping the hill above Lake Union. David had never been particularly fond of Gas Works Park, thinking it was more of an eyesore than somewhere people might go to relax, and today's events cemented his negative feelings of the place.

The sound of a gunshot punctured the air around them.

Everyone stopped, as if waiting to see which one of them had been hit. David was the first to recover; he continued toward the abandoned machinery at a run.

"I'm sick of you telling me what to do, Sandy. Shut up or I'll shoot you again."

Kylie watched the thin woman's eyes widen with shock as she slumped down on a rusted iron step, blood pouring from the wound on her shoulder.

"You shot me." She looked at Rory accusingly.

"And I'll do it again if you open your mouth one more time. I don't need you anymore now that I have this." He waved Kylie's check triumphantly in front of Sandy's nose.

Kylie surreptitiously kicked Ben's ankle. She didn't know this park well, but the way she saw it, this might be their only chance to escape. They were standing on a landing at a Y in the staircase wrapping around one of the old, rusted gas towers. Kylie had no idea where the stairs ended, but anything was better than just waiting for Rory to kill them.

Ben nodded almost imperceptibly and Kylie shifted her weight to the balls of her stocking-clad feet with a sudden movement. The rusty metal scraped her heels and she wished she hadn't kicked her shoes off in the water when she'd tried to escape from the boat. Ben reached out and shoved Rory's arm, then twisted to dash up the right side of the staircase. He tottered a bit, still under the effect of the Scotch he'd had for lunch, but the cold boat ride and the fear for his life had obviously done a lot to help sober him up. Kylie took the left side of the Y, grabbing the handrail to keep from slipping on the metal steps.

"Kylie!" She heard a familiar voice call her name.

Without pausing, she yelled back, "David, be careful. They have guns."

She almost collided with Ben as the stairs converged on the other side of the tower and led to a walkway. "Come on." She pulled Ben behind her across the catwalk.

A shot ricocheted off the railing, and Kylie kept running, knowing Rory wasn't far behind.

They reached the landing on the other side of the walkway and another shot exploded on the tower in front of her. She looked back to see that Rory had started across the catwalk after them. They had a chance, Kylie thought, starting down another set of stairs, if only they could run fast enough.

The metal stairs were cold under her almost bare feet. As she stepped on the second stair, Ben stumbled, knocking against her from behind. She tried to grip the slick metal with her toes, but she couldn't gain purchase on the wet iron. She screamed as her feet slipped out from under her.

Kylie felt herself pitching forward and instinctively covered her head as she tumbled down.

David heard a gunshot ring out right before Kylie's scream came to an abrupt halt. He redoubled his efforts to pull himself up the scaffolding on the side of the decrepit tower where he'd last seen Kylie and Ben. His arm muscles strained as he pulled his body up onto a flat platform jutting out of the side of the tower. Quietly, David pushed himself against the tower itself and looked up. He could see Rory on the level above him, pointing a gun at Ben, who had stopped halfway down a curving staircase. Kylie was nowhere to be seen and David had to force himself to stay calm when all he wanted to do was race up to Rory and tear the man apart. He plotted his next move while searching for some sight of Kylie.

Please, God, let her be all right, he prayed, closing his eyes against the image of her lying at the foot of the stairs, a bullet marking the end of her life and, effectively, of his. The fates couldn't be so cruel as to take her away just when he'd realized he couldn't live without her. No, he refused to let her go, even in his mind. She'd be all right. He'd make sure of it.

Another circular staircase ran around the tower, with the bottom of it just above David's head. Grabbing one of the supports, David swung himself up, trying to get a toehold without attracting Rory's attention.

The heels of his prized Italian loafers made a loud "clunk" as they connected with the metal grate, and Rory turned in the direction of the sound.

David didn't waste precious seconds waiting to see if Rory had pinpointed the source of the noise. Instead, he crouched down, then started inching around the tower toward his brother.

He was sweating by the time he'd reached the other side, a cold sweat that chilled rather than heated. Poking his head around the curve of the tower, David felt his heart clench with despair. Kylie was lying motionless at the foot of the stairs, a trickle of blood running across her forehead.

What mattered to him now? If Kylie was dead, his life would stretch out before him in an endless array of empty days and nights. Nothing, no merger or acquisition, no joint venture or divestiture, would ever make him feel as alive as he had with Kylie. Giving up all pretense of staying hidden, David walked toward her lifeless form like a man in a coma.

As he came closer, he saw that her chest was moving up and down. A glimmer of hope awoke in his chest.

"Kylie?" He knelt beside her, stroking her hair. "Sweetheart, can you move?"

Her eyelids fluttered open. "David, is that you?"

"Yes, it's me."

She closed her eyes again and grimaced. "I think I sprained my ankle. And my head aches something awful."

"I've got to get you out of here." David looked around, seeing no other option but to carry her. It was going to hurt her like hell but there wasn't much else he could do. He bent down to pick her up, and the pack of cigarettes in his shirt pocket fell out, hitting Kylie in the chest. She grabbed them in one hand as he stood, staggering to get his balance.

"What about Ben?" Kylie groaned as another wave of pain hit.

David saw his brother standing at the curve of the stairs. For a brief instant, David wanted to take Kylie and go, to leave Ben to his own devices. But he couldn't do it.

"Ben," he whispered loudly, trying to get his brother's attention.

Ben turned, his eyes widening with surprise when he saw his brother at the foot of the stairs.

"Behind you!" Ben shouted, his voice filled with warning.

David spun around in one smooth movement and Kylie got a split-second image of Sandy, arms raised, gun outstretched. Without thinking, she threw the pack of cigarettes in the other woman's face.

Sandy flinched, her arms jerking as the gun discharged. The bullet went wild, ricocheting off the rusted metal and hitting her instead. She screamed and dropped the gun, her eyes widening with shock as a red spot appeared on her previously uninjured shoulder. Her face went from ruddy to pale white as the spot widened into a pool, soaking her shirt. David stepped forward awkwardly, still holding Kylie, as Sandy swayed. But it was too late. Kylie's free hand grabbed at empty air just as Sandy tumbled off the catwalk to the ground below.

It had seemed to take hours, but in reality only seconds had passed. Whatever spell had caused Rory to pause was broken at the sound of Sandy's gunshot. Ben spun to his left as another shot rang out and suddenly there was activity everywhere.

"Kylie, Robyn, Daniel, sic him!" David heard Elizabeth Rogers's high-pitched voice shout. Bradley and Robyn topped the staircase below him, meeting from opposite sides of the Y at breakneck speed. Their collision knocked them both off balance, but Bradley managed to steady them both before they met the same fate as Sandy. Ben stumbled down the stairs, a red stain spreading down the front of his shirt, his own face getting paler by the second.

"Take that, you bastard." George Rogers's voice mingled with the growling of three small but very angry dogs and the unmistakable sound of a fist connecting with someone's flesh.

The clattering of footsteps was soon masked by the sound of sirens.

"Bradley, Robyn, go get help up here fast," David ordered, taking charge of the chaos around him.

Ben slumped on the step next to them. "Always bossing people around," he muttered, then closed his eyes.

"Damn right I am." David gently laid Kylie back down on the steps, then sat down between them. Bunching Ben's shirt up around his wound, David pushed hard against the hole in his brother's shoulder. "Now just sit back. Help will be here soon."

Keeping one hand on his brother's chest, he gently lifted Kylie's head onto his lap.

They would be all right, by God; if he had to stand over them twenty-four hours a day, they'd both be all right.

Who said he couldn't control what happened when Kylie was around?

CHAPTER 25

Kylie sat on the edge of the hospital bed and let the sounds of conversation wash over her. Tony had finally taken the dogs home after her mother's little darlings had pranced around for an hour's worth of photos for the local papers. Her mother's prized shih tzus were being hailed as hound heroes, and Elizabeth couldn't have been prouder if they'd been her own children. The hospital staff, who normally wouldn't have allowed a dog within ten feet of their sterile rooms, seemed delighted to have the visiting heroes clicking about the pristine halls on well-manicured toes. Of course, it didn't hurt that the children in the hospital were delighted by the brown, white, and black fluff balls, or that her parents had promised to visit some of the sicker patients in exchange for letting the animals stay, but Kylie was used to George and Elizabeth being allowed to do pretty much anything they wished. Nothing they got away with surprised her anymore, not after a lifetime of watching the pair charm their way into people's hearts.

She sighed, resting her head on her hand as she looked over at Bradley and Robyn, who were having a hushed conversation on the couch in her private room, yet another privelege granted on the basis of her parents' fame. Kylie watched with amusement as Bradley ran his hand up Robyn's arm and her sister slapped his hand away. She would have taken this to mean that Bradley's advances were unwanted, except for Robyn's blush and the way her sister scooted closer to him on the couch. It appeared that Robyn was having better luck in the romance department than Kylie was. She hadn't seen David since he bundled her into the ambulance, saying he had to ride with Ben, but he'd see her later.

She hadn't heard yet how Ben was faring, but her father had told her earlier that Rory had been taken to jail after being treated for minor injuries. Sandy wasn't quite so lucky. Her hospital stay would be longer, but eventually she'd end up in jail with her lover. Kylie knew Ben's wound was serious and hoped he'd be all right. If he hadn't warned David about Sandy, she probably would have managed to kill them all.

Kylie shuddered at the thought of how close they'd come to death. She wanted to grab David and never let him go at the thought, but he wasn't there for her to hold. She assumed he was with Ben but, although rationally she knew that was where he should be, some part of her still wished he were by her side.

She sighed again, then tried in vain to scratch part of her leg that was now covered by a thick bandage.

"Didn't the doctor say he'd be back to release me half an hour ago?" The pain in her leg, coupled with the itch she couldn't scratch and an urgent need to see David, was making her irritable.

Robyn looked up from flirting with Bradley and glanced at her watch. "Yes, he did, but you'll just have to be patient. Here, I'll turn on the radio. Maybe the music will help you relax."

Kylie hardly thought a few tunes were going to make her feel any better, but Robyn had already flipped on the radio at her bedside and was fiddling with the dials.

"Hey, it's five o'clock on a Friday and we're heading into prime drive time. This is KXRM, 88.1 on your dial,

and we have a special announcement for one of our listen-
ers out there."

Kylie scooted up to rest her head on the pillows of the
bed and closed her eyes tiredly, barely listening to the dee-
jay.

"Kylie Rogers, this is David Gamble."

Kylie's eyes popped open and she stared at the radio
incredulously. The pain medication she'd taken must be
making her hallucinate. The David Gamble she knew would
not be sending messages over one of Seattle's most popular
radio stations during a prime-time broadcast. No, the David
Gamble she knew would be horrified at such a public display. He liked his world ordered and predictable, and would
never open himself up to humiliation by talking to her on
the radio.

Vowing to ask the doctor to lower the dosage of her
pain medication—if he ever showed up, that is—Kylie
shook her head to clear it, then reached out to turn off the
radio.

"Turn that back on," Robyn protested, springing back
up off the couch.

"Don't you want to hear what he has to say?" Bradley
asked.

Kylie slowly sat up. "You mean I'm not hearing things?"

"No!" they shouted in stereo.

Kylie sat straight up in bed, flipped the radio back on,
and turned the volume up full blast, unable to believe what
she was hearing.

"And I'm going to repeat this message every hour on
the top ten radio stations in Seattle until you agree to marry
me. So please say yes, quickly, before the citizens of our
fair city are driven crazy by this song."

The humor in his voice turned to tenderness as he finished. "I love you, Kylie."

David's voice faded as Joe Cocker started his rendition
of "You Are So Beautiful."

Kylie's eyes filled with tears as she swung her legs over

the side of the bed. "Hand me my crutches, please."

Robyn gave them to her without a word. Struggling with the awkward pieces of aluminum, Kylie hobbled out into the hall. She looked up and down the hallway, then realized she had no idea where David would be, didn't even know if he was in the hospital at all. She had thought he was with Ben up in ICU, but obviously he'd left at some point to record his message to her.

Spying the nurses' station, Kylie thought perhaps they'd have a way to find out if David was in the building. Her crutches thumped alternately with her one good leg across the linoleum floor.

"Excuse me," she said to the petite, dark-haired nurse behind the desk.

The woman turned and Kylie saw the gleam of tears in her eyes. Belatedly, she heard the tail end of Joe Cocker's song from the radio behind the counter.

"I'm Kylie Rogers. Is there some way to tell if David Gamble is still upstairs with his brother, Ben?"

"You're Kylie Rogers?"

"Yes. Yes, I am."

"What are you going to tell him?" the nurse asked eagerly, wiping the wetness from her cheeks.

"I'm going to tell him yes, of course."

The nurse's answering smile was impish as she pulled a microphone from under the counter. "If you push this blue button, anyone in the hospital can hear you. If anybody asks, I was checking on a patient down the hall and you thought of this all by yourself." She winked.

Kylie grinned, then took a deep breath before pressing the blue button on the mike.

"Um, yes, hello. Hello. This is Kylie Rogers. David Gamble, if you're in the building, I just wanted to tell you, my answer is yes. Definitely, yes."

She let up on the blue button, and heard her answer to David echoing off the linoleum floor and bouncing against the white-painted walls. It seemed to linger in the hushed hallway. Expectant. Waiting.

The seconds ticked by as Kylie waited for David to appear. And waited.

And waited.

"He must not be in the building," the nurse offered finally.

Kylie sighed. Just her luck. She'd made a fool of herself over the loudspeaker and David hadn't even been there to hear it.

The sound of the elevator bell announcing its arrival on the third floor made her jump after the silence of a moment before. Kylie turned as the elevator doors behind her whooshed open, then smiled when David stepped out.

He looked tired, and unsure of himself for what Kylie guessed must be the first time in his life.

His footsteps echoed in the quiet hallway as he walked toward her. He didn't say a word until he stopped a few feet in front of her, gazing intently into her eyes.

"Are you sure?" he asked, ignoring the curious stares of the hospital patients and staff who had stopped to watch the unfolding drama.

Kylie laughed, then threw her arms up, letting the crutches fall to the floor. She hopped the two steps to him and buried her head against his chest.

"Am I sure? David, I love you. I've loved you since the moment we met. Of course I'm sure. Are you sure? You haven't known me for long, after all. And, you do know the disasters probably aren't going to stop, don't you? I mean, I try, I *really* try, to lead a normal life, but . . ."

David's strong fingers cupped her face as he gently raised her eyes to his. Kylie was astounded at the emotions she saw in his deep blue eyes.

"I've never been more sure of anything in my whole life, Kylie. I wouldn't want you to change a thing about yourself, even if you could. I love you, disasters and all. And as for not knowing you for long . . . well, I guess we can tell our grandchildren that I fell in love with you in record time." He smiled down at her, then dug a hand into his left front pocket and took out a light blue box.

"Will you marry me?" he asked softly, wanting to say the words to her; wanting her to hear them from his heart, just the way he meant them. He popped open the box to reveal a brilliantly sparkling square-cut emerald flanked by two triangular-shaped diamonds.

David heard Kylie's sharp intake of breath before she lifted her gaze to meet his. "Is it real?" she whispered.

"Yes, it's real. It's genuine and special—something to be cherished. Just like you."

The smile started in Kylie's eyes and spread across the rest of her face like a field of spring flowers blooming for the first time. "Yes, David, I'll marry you."

People around them cheered and clapped as David lifted her up and carried her to the elevator. David pushed the call button, then frowned when the doors opened to a car filled with people and medical equipment.

"Never mind," he muttered, looking around for a quiet place where he and Kylie could officially seal their engagement. He spied what appeared to be a closet and headed across the hall, his progress followed by the stares of curious onlookers.

"It should be quiet in here," he said, awkwardly pulling open the door as he balanced Kylie in his arms.

The couple making out up against the neatly stacked towels hastily broke apart as the door flew open and light from the hall spilled in.

"I was just getting some towels," the man lied, grabbing a stack of clean white terrycloth before dashing out into the hall, not stopping to button up his shirt.

The woman was too busy tucking her own shirt back in to formulate a story. Instead, she finished pulling herself together and picked up a clipboard, apparently resuming the inventory job that had been interrupted by the arrival of towel-man.

Ah, yes. The old *inventorious interruptus*, Kylie thought with a chuckle.

David shook his head and backed away from the closet. "What room were you in?" he asked.

"Three twenty-four, but . . ."

David just looked at her, his frustration clearly evidenced by the vein pulsating in his throat.

Kylie noted this physical response for future reference, certain the knowledge would come in handy at some point, then continued, "But I think Robyn and Bradley are still in there, and unless I'm mistaken, we might just get a repeat of that last scene if we go barging in."

His sigh was long and heartfelt, and Kylie almost started to feel sorry for him.

"Forget it. We'll do it right here. I don't care who's watching," David growled, setting Kylie gently on her feet. He backed her up against the wall and placed one hand on either side of her head, trapping her as effectively as he knew how.

Then, paying no heed to the claps and cheers from the crowd gathered in the hall, David proceeded to demonstrate to Kylie exactly how much he loved her.

WELCOME TO TEMPTATION

Jennifer Crusie

Sophie Dempsey is content living a quiet life filming wedding videos until an assignment brings her to Temptation, Ohio. From the moment she drives into town, she gets a bad feeling; Sophie is from the wrong side of the tracks and everything in Temptation is a little too right. And when she has a run-in with the town's unnervingly sexy mayor, Phineas Tucker, making a little movie turns out to be more than a little dangerous.

As events spiral out of control, Sophie and Phin find themselves falling deeper and deeper in trouble . . . and in love.

GOT YOUR NUMBER

A Novel by
STEPHANIE BOND
author of *Our Husband*

Roxann Beadleman just received an ominous message that resurrects old secrets, and her debutante cousin Angora Ryder was just jilted at the altar. A roadtrip to accomplish things on a life list they made in college leads them back to their alma mater for Homecoming, and to the professor they were both in love with...But Angora doesn't know that Roxann is wanted for questioning in a police matter, or that a dangerous criminal could be following them. Detective Joe Capistrano is on their heels, too, determined to charm information out of Roxann and to protect her, whether she wants it or not...Roxann and Angora soon find themselves thrust into a chilling lesson of murder, and if either of them gets out of this mess alive, could true love be at the end of their chase?

AVAILABLE WHEREVER BOOKS ARE SOLD
FROM ST. MARTIN'S PAPERBACKS